"YOU KNOW, I THINK I'VE GOT JUST THE GIRL FOR YOU."

"Blond," the man said, "with the prettiest eyes, man, the most *gorgeous* eyes you've ever seen. Big and brown. She needs someone like you. A knight in shining armor to fight for her honor. Sort of a"—he chuckled—"big brother." The stranger's blond hair fluttered as he walked beside Jeff through the nearly empty mall. Jeff stopped and faced the man, suddenly filled with an icy mixture of fear and anger.

"I knew you'd be interested," the stranger said, his smile creasing the pale skin around his golden eyes. "I can arrange it. A real dream come true"—he winked—"if you know what I mean."

Jeff felt sick, confused, and afraid. "Stay away from me," he said quietly.

"My name is Mace."

"I don't care who you are, just leave me—"

"You shouldn't say that until you know what I can do for you."

"There's nothing you can do for me, whoever you are, so just—"

"Maybe not today," replied Mace darkly.

Something about the tone of his voice, perhaps it was the confidence with which he spoke—as if he knew everything there was to know about Jeff Carr and his forbidden dreams about his sister Mallory—made Jeff's blood run cold . . .

Books by Ray Garton

Crucifax
Live Girls

Published by POCKET BOOKS

CRUCIFAX

RAY GARTON

POCKET BOOKS

New York   London   Toronto   Sydney   Tokyo

Another *Original* publication of POCKET BOOKS

POCKET BOOKS, a division of Simon & Schuster Inc.
1230 Avenue of the Americas, New York, N.Y. 10020

Copyright © 1988 by Ray Garton
Cover artwork copyright © 1988 Ron Lesser

ISBN: 0-671-62629-9

First Pocket Books printing June 1988

10 9 8 7 6 5 4 3 2 1

POCKET and colophon are trademarks of
Simon & Schuster Inc.

Printed in the U.S.A.

Dedicated to
Paul Meredith

A true friend

Acknowledgments

In many ways, this book was a collaborative effort involving a lot of people who contributed their time, knowledge, and support to its creation. I would like to thank my co-conspirators . . .

Scott Sandin, David Wurts, Dave Yeske (who came up with the word *Crucifax*), David Schow, Kathy and Bill and the crew at Giugni's Deli, Sarah Wood, Joan Myers, Laurel Larson, Jessie Horsting, Richard Christian Matheson, Richard Laymon, Dean Koontz, Francis Feighan, Steve Boyett, Jo Fletcher, Steve Jones, the makers of No-Doz, Ruth James, Debbie Allen, Susan Davis, Cheryl Lormann, Barbara Neiborg, Sue Shelley, Sherry Parker, Chris Waltz, Tracy Heller, Wayne Manning, Jim Potter, Michael Bradley, and my parents Ray and Pat Garton and sister and brother-in-law Sandy and Bill DeWildt, who are always there.

AUTHOR'S NOTE

For the sake of atmosphere and convenience, I have taken a number of liberties with the San Fernando Valley, not the least of which is my grossly inaccurate depiction of its sewer system.

Some of the places of business mentioned actually exist, but, like Dangerous Visions Bookstore, not necessarily in the locations given. Valley High School and the Calvary Youth do not exist and never have. However, while the Laurel Teen Center is fictitious, it is not entirely imaginary; hundreds, perhaps thousands, of similar institutions are currently in operation and doing bang-up business throughout the country.

PART I

The Last Saturday Night of Summer

One

September 3

As daylight faded over the muggy San Fernando Valley the dirty brown of the smog in the sky was deceptively hidden by the soft blood-blister pastels of sunset.

It had been one of the hottest and most humid summers in recent memory. Temperatures and humidity levels reached record highs in the Valley, and Los Angeles residents, normally willing to venture over the hill for one reason or another, took to avoiding the Valley completely.

Three deaths were blamed on the heat: two elderly patients in a small Canoga Park nursing home in which the air conditioner had broken down, and a postman in Sherman Oaks who had been less than a week short of retirement.

The bright, stylish clothes of Valley teenagers, usually spotless and perfectly in place, wrinkled easily and were blotched with perspiration as the kids paraded through the malls and up and down the boulevards. The most-voiced complaints among teenage girls that summer concerned the damage done to their hair and makeup by the insufferable humidity.

Cars overheated on short trips to the market, and fast

food drive-up windows attracted interminably long lines of afternoon drivers in need of a cold drink.

Those without air conditioners sacrificed a few nights out each month so they could afford to rent them; those with air conditioners did the same so they could afford to repair them when they burned out from overuse.

Two women were arrested for tearing each other's clothes off in a fight over who was first in line at the Frostee Freeze on Lankershim Boulevard.

A widower in Sylmar came home from work one afternoon in July to find that his fifteen-year-old daughter had baked some cookies, raising the temperature in the apartment; he caved in her forehead with a rolling pin.

Children did not go out to play in the afternoon, and dogs did not chase cars.

Sirens were the carols of the season day and night.

But the long summer was nearing its close.

It would end officially after the Labor Day weekend when school began and department store windows displayed their new lines of fall clothing.

On this Saturday evening, as shadows lengthened and the smog slowly lost its facade, clouds began to roll in. There were only a few at first, separated by large patches of gray-blue sky, but they were fat with dark undersides. As they crept over the Valley, low and sluggish, they gathered together, slowly closing the spaces between them.

Deejays on local radio stations announced the unexpected cover of clouds over the Valley with a fanfare one might expect to accompany the arrival of royalty; they played songs about rain and dusted off their sound-effects records to play the rumbling of thunder and the spattering of rain.

As the night darkened and the cloud cover thickened, acne-prone young people began to cruise the boulevard with rain songs pounding from their car stereos.

Nightclubs that catered exclusively to teenagers geared up for a night of heavy traffic, knowing that the last Saturday night before the beginning of a new school year—especially if it cooled off and rained—would be a busy one.

The fat, dark clouds blocked the starlight and glowed with soft swirls of color from the lights of the Valley. They stopped their crawl across the sky and remained, hovering over the Valley like an enormous, fragmented, cottony ghost.

But it did not rain. . . .

Two

Jeff Carr blanched at the heat when he stepped out of the Studio City Theater on Ventura Boulevard. The moist air clung to his flesh like honey.

The movie was not over, but he didn't care how it ended. He hadn't really wanted to see it; he'd just come along with the others because his sister Mallory had picked it, and he wanted Mallory to enjoy herself tonight.

To the left of the theater entrance was a small group of conservatively dressed teenagers. The boys wore ties and dress shirts with the sleeves rolled up and dark slacks with perfect creases down the legs. All the girls wore knee-length skirts and loose-fitting tops, some with buttons down the front, fastened all the way up to the throat. Each of the eight group members carried a stack of pamphlets and wore a button with CALVARY YOUTH printed below a stylized cross. They were all smiling pleasantly.

Standing in the middle of the group was a wiry blond man in his fifties. He wore a dark suit, and there were sweat stains on the collar of his white shirt. Beneath the light of the marquee his cheeks looked hollow, and below his brows were deep caves of shadow. He carried a Bible under his left arm and he smiled at Jeff with a birdlike tilt of his head.

Jeff turned away from him. He'd seen them before, the Calvary Youth. They waited outside theaters and night-clubs, places where high school students gathered, dressed like Sunday school teachers, trying to recruit a few more souls for the Lord's work.

He walked to the curb and slipped his fingers into the back pockets of his baggy white pants, watching the traffic. The boulevard was backed up from the intersection of Ventura and Laurel Canyon, and the smell of exhaust was heavy in the air. Music blasted from open car windows and clashed, sounding like construction work. Looking up past the lights of the street, Jeff saw that the clouds that had rolled in earlier were still there.

"Some clouds," he muttered disgustedly, turning away from the street.

"Hey, Jeffy!"

He looked back at the line of cars and saw Larry Caine standing up in the back seat of a red Rabbit convertible, waving a hand over his blond head. He wore a yellow muscle shirt that showed his hard, tanned arms. There was one other guy in the car and a bunch of girls. Figured.

"Where is everybody?" Larry asked.

Jeff gestured over his shoulder toward the theater.

"Your sister, too?"

Jeff nodded.

"I thought she was going out with Kevin tonight."

"He stood her up."

"Yeah?" Larry flashed a pleased, straight-toothed grin. Jeff hated him, knowing what was going on behind those bright blue eyes. The light at the intersection changed, and the cars began to move. Nodding, Larry said, "Well, bring her over to Fantazm later and we'll show her a good time." He waved again, then sat down as the car moved on, putting his arm around one of the girls.

Jeff walked away from the curb and leaned against the wall of the theater.

Larry Caine had been after Mallory for months, but she

wasn't interested—something Larry found rather confusing, Jeff was sure. Mallory had been seeing Kevin Donahue for the last month or so, probably a source of further confusion for Larry. Why would Mallory ignore the sun-bronzed physique and movie-star smile of Larry Caine in favor of a scrawny, sneering punk like Kevin Donahue?

Jeff didn't know the answer to that question either, but as much as he despised Larry, and as much as he enjoyed seeing the puzzlement in Larry's eyes each time Mallory turned away from him, he would rather have his younger sister spend time with him instead of someone like Donahue.

Normally, Larry would not take such rejection quietly, without performing what he seemed to consider some sort of mating dance. He and his grunting entourage of bench pressers would begin to frequent places where Donahue hung out. They would talk to one another in booming voices, making sure Donahue could hear them as they made profane remarks about his clothes or his jewelry or his black scraggly hair that sometimes shone with a hint of grease when he went a few days without bathing. If that got no reaction, they would direct their insults to Donahue until he made a move. Then they would probably take him outside and beat him senseless. That's what they would *normally* do. But they didn't.

Because they were afraid. And with good reason.

Kevin Donahue and his friends would fight back without hesitation. They wouldn't use their fists because, like Donahue, most of them were very skinny and rather pale. They would use knives and clubs and—Jeff wasn't positive, but he suspected—guns.

Larry Caine was not smart by most standards, but he wasn't stupid; Jeff was sure he was willing to let a girl, maybe even a couple girls, slip through his fingers to avoid that kind of trouble.

Mallory was fifteen, a year younger than Jeff, and Donahue was her first *real* boyfriend. She'd dated a guy named Rich for a couple weeks the previous spring, but she hadn't slept with him. Jeff knew it was different with

Donahue. Mallory had not actually told him, but he could tell.

Their mother knew Mallory was seeing Donahue, but she didn't know anything about what kind of guy he was, nor did she know how serious it had become. She and Mallory weren't talking much these days—their conversations had been fluctuating between flat, polite exchanges and icy periods of silence, occasionally punctuated with a brief time of reconciliation, ever since Dad had left two years ago— and Jeff didn't think it was his place to tell her anything.

"Don't worry about it," Mom had told him over breakfast when he had skirted the subject of Mallory and Donahue a few days earlier. "She'll get tired of that crowd and find another one. I swear," she'd said, ruffling his hair and giving him a smile that seemed wearier than it had two years ago, "you almost sound jealous of your little sister!"

No, Jeff told himself, flattening his palms against the warm cement wall behind him, *not jealous, really. Just . . . worried.*

But he knew better.

When Donahue had stood Mallory up earlier that evening, Jeff had decided to get her out of the apartment, cheer her up a little, and, if he thought it was appropriate, maybe talk with her about Donahue. He didn't want to sound naggy about it, but it probably wouldn't hurt to drop a few words of caution.

He knew what her reaction would be. She would smile softly, put her hand on his, and say something like, "My knight in shining armor. Are you going to follow me through life, fighting for my honor?"

Jeff fidgeted against the wall, looking down at the sidewalk. He wasn't about to fight for *anything.* He was far from the fighting type. His arms and legs were long and skinny. He had never been any good in sports, mostly because he had never been interested in them—something his father had always resented. Jeff was all too aware of the fact that what he lacked in build he did not make up for in looks. He had straight, light brown hair and a few freckles on his cheeks; he wore tan tortoise-shell-framed glasses for his astigmatism, and, worst of all, he had crooked teeth.

"Even if we had enough money to afford braces for your teeth," his father had told him a few years ago, "there are plenty more important things to spend it on." He'd said it in that clipped way he had of making everything sound trivial and annoying. "It'd be cheaper if you just didn't smile as much."

Jeff lifted his head and watched a laughing couple walk by, noticing how the girl's body moved in sync with the guy's, the way they touched one another at just the right times and in the right places with no clumsy fumbling or bumping. The guy slipped his arm around her waist as he leaned over to say something, and she propped her elbow on his shoulder for a moment, listening; she tossed her head back and laughed, they parted a moment, then she slid her hand beneath his shirttails and tucked her fingers into his back pocket.

It amazed Jeff the way most people were able to be couples so well, as if they had practiced a lot or taken a course. Maybe they were teaching that over at Northridge now. Summer classes. *Introductory Being Together—Learn to move right and look good as a couple. You can't be it if you can't do it!*

Jeff tried to force a smile, but the thought just didn't seem funny.

"When're you gonna get yourself a girlfriend, Jeffy?" Brad Kreisler had asked him a few days ago, thumbing through a *Playboy* at the Van Nuys newsstand.

"I check the papers every day for sales," Jeff replied, scanning the shelves of magazines.

"Well, pretty soon people are gonna start thinking you're a floater. You want people to think you're a floater, Jeffy?"

Jeff hated being called "Jeffy." "You know it's what I live for, Brad."

"Smartass," Brad laughed. "What about that girl who works at the Cookie Jar? In the Galleria. Lily something? You two seem to get along. Why don't you go for it?"

Jeff said nothing.

"Well, you know, if you keep hanging around with your sister"—Brad replaced the magazine and held out a hand, palm down, tilting it back and forth—"people are gonna think something funny's going on."

If you keep hanging around with your sister . . . keep hanging around with your sister . . . hanging around with your—

The theater doors opened, and the crowd spilled out onto the sidewalk, most of them grumbling about the movie. As Jeff stepped away from the wall he heard Brad Kreisler's voice rise above the others.

"Whatta shitty movie!" he barked, taking his pack of Yves St. Laurents from one of the big pockets of his blue shorts and lighting up. "And where's the fuckin' rain? I thought it was gonna *rain!*"

"I wanna go back to Oregon," Bobbi Cheever whined, brushing plump fingers through her short, orange-tinted hair as she shouldered through the crowd. "It's cooler, and I think the movies are better."

"Yeah," Nick Frazier said, a step behind her, "but you'd have to stop shaving your legs again."

"Fuck off and die, Nick!" she snapped.

They had been fighting all week, and Jeff figured they would break up before school started on Tuesday.

"Where's Mallory and Tina?" Jeff asked.

Brad jerked his head back toward the theater, tossing his red curls, and said, "Bathroom."

The sidewalk became congested as the theater emptied, and the Bible-carrying man in the suit stepped forward. Still smiling, he gently touched his fingertips to the perfectly straight part in his hair and said loudly, "Friends, just as this long and miserable summer is coming to an end, so is the long and miserable existence of this sin-sick planet. Every headline and every newscast is a road sign, and our journey is almost over. Our Lord Jesus Christ is preparing for His return, and He wants all of us to be ready, friends, *all* of us."

A boy in bermuda shorts and a torn T-shirt shouted over his shoulder as he walked away from the theater, "I'm not your fucking friend!"

Jeff glanced at the preacher; the man blinked as perspiration trickled down his forehead, but his smile did not waver.

"My name is Reverend James Bainbridge," he went on, holding up his Bible, "and these young people are the Calvary Youth. They have been set free by the Truth, friends—free of the addiction to drugs, free of the deceptive promise of sex and the seductive beat of rock and roll. They've brought that Truth to you tonight."

He nodded without turning from the crowd, and, in unison, the Calvary Youth stripped the rubber bands from their stacks and began passing out the pamphlets. Most of the crowd ignored them.

A small hand came to rest on Jeff's shoulder, and he turned to Mallory. "I think I'd like to go home now, Jeff," she said quietly, the glaring light from above softened as it was reflected in her golden hair.

"Why don't you come down to Tiny's with us for a bite to eat?" he said. "You haven't eaten anything all day."

"I don't think so." She had a tight look around her brown eyes, as if there were a pebble in her shoe or something. That look always made Jeff want to take her hand.

"C'mon, just for a while. Then, if you want to go, I'll take you home."

She shrugged indifferently.

Tina Shephard came out behind Mallory and went to Brad's side, snaking a thin arm around his waist.

"We going to Tiny's?" she asked.

"Yeah," Jeff said, putting his hand on the back of Mallory's neck and squeezing encouragingly.

". . . don't have much time," Reverend Bainbridge said, his voice fuller than before, the Bible held high over his head. "The Bible says He will come like a thief in the night, and our world is *now* in its *darkest* night! Just look *around* you, friends, and what do you see?"

"Nocturnal emissionaries!" Someone laughed.

Brad took Tina's hand, and they led the way down the walk to Tiny Naylor's. Bobbi and Nick walked with a couple feet of cold space between them.

"I really don't want to stay very long," Mallory said. "If you want, I can walk home."

"No, I'll take you." Jeff had to slow his pace so he

wouldn't leave her behind. "I just thought it'd be better than hanging around the apartment."

". . . bled on the cross for *our* sins . . ." Reverend Bainbridge droned on, his voice fading behind them.

"Yeah," Mallory smiled up at Jeff. "I guess so."

She stopped.

Her smile fell away.

Jeff stood beside her, frowning, although he wasn't sure why. He looked ahead at the others; they had stopped, too, and were looking around.

Despite the sounds of the traffic, the boulevard suddenly seemed quiet, and everything around him seemed to slow to a liquidy, dreamlike crawl. There was a low, almost imperceptible buzz in Jeff's head, as if the roots of his crooked teeth were vibrating. The skin on his back tingled as a gentle balmy breeze began to blow, and when Jeff looked back at the Calvary Youth, he saw them standing oddly still as the pamphlets slipped from their soap-scrubbed hands and skittered down the sidewalk.

The stragglers still coming from the theater slowed and looked around at the dazed teenagers.

Reverend Bainbridge paused, lowering his Bible hand, and then raised it again, speaking even louder than before, trying to regain what little attention he'd had.

"There will come a time of trouble as no man has known before, my friends, and that time has already started," he said. "The clock is ticking and . . . and . . ." He leaned toward one of the young women who had dropped her pamphlets and was slowly turning her eyes upward. "Pick them up!" he hissed.

She did not respond.

Mallory tilted her head back.

So did Nick and Bobbi, Tina and Brad.

And the Calvary Youth.

Jeff looked up past the lights and the buildings to the dark and cloudy sky and saw nothing.

There was a break in the clouds, a narrow, crooked opening, like a crack in a giant plaster ceiling. Something flickered. Jeff couldn't tell if the flickering was in the clouds or somewhere deep inside his head, way behind his eyes.

He squinted, shaking his head.

A plane, maybe? he thought. The Burbank Airport was nearby, and planes flew over all the time, their lights blinking.

A shriek came from the group of young Christians, and a girl squealed, "It's *near!* It's *coming!* The *end* is *coming!*"

Lightning, he thought, craning his head forward. But when he closed his eyes for a moment, the flickering seemed to continue.

"The Holy Spirit is *here,* my friends!" Reverend Bainbridge shouted. "These young people have been moved by the Holy Spirit to come to you tonight—"

Eyes open again, Jeff thought, *It probably* is *lightning, and it's finally going to rain, and I wish that guy would shut up!*

"—*not* by personal gain, *not* by pride—"

Maybe the rain will make Mallory feel better, and then maybe, then maybe this guy would shut the fuck up because—

"—or a need for recognition, but by the soft murmurs of the voice of God Himself!"

—because there is *no God; if there was a God, there wouldn't be any heat waves, and—*

"They are here because they live in fear for the souls of their friends, their families, and the souls of each and every one of *you!"*

The voice faded a bit and, in the edges of his vision as he looked upward, Jeff thought he noticed a dimming in the lights of the boulevard—

Maybe . . . maybe it's a helicopter or—

—and a cold hand slid into his brain and began to rummage around.

—or assholes like my father, *there wouldn't be any of* those *if there was a God, and there wouldn't be any slutty sisters, no slutty sisters with revolving doors between their—*

Jeff's head jerked back suddenly as if dodging a swinging fist. His eyes stretched open wide, still on the sky but seeing, for a heartbeat, his sister's warm smile. Guilt sliced through his chest like a just-sharpened razor.

Then it was gone.

The clouds were dark.

A car horn honked as the traffic slowed for another red light.

Jeff turned to see the Calvary Youth slowly moving about, picking up their scattered literature; one of the girls was on her knees, bent forward, her hands clasped before her face, rocking back and forth as she mumbled frantically into her hands. One of the pamphlets whispered over the cement and came to rest at Jeff's feet as the breeze gently backed off.

". . . Spirit is *speaking* to you through these young people, my friends," Bainbridge was saying, pointing to the girl with his Bible, "for a little child shall lead them, and if you ignore the Word . . ."

Jeff looked at Mallory; she was still staring at the sky. Her mouth was open and her brow was creased, but it was more a look of wonder than a troubled frown.

She whispered, "Did . . . you . . . see something?"

Jeff looked up again. Nothing but clouds and darkness. A knot had tied itself in his stomach, and a dull ache was coming up in his head, like mud from the bottom of a stirred-up pond. His hands were trembling, and he wasn't sure why.

The others were moving haltingly toward Tiny Naylor's; they took a few steps, stopped, looked up; Brad shook his head, Tina folded her arms across her breasts, Bobbi grumbled something, and they moved on.

"No," Jeff said, his mouth dry. "I didn't see anything. Come on." He took her elbow and led her toward the restaurant.

He suddenly felt as if he had lied to his sister. But he hadn't; there had been nothing to see. Nothing.

And although it was a hot, damp night, he suddenly felt a chill. . . .

Three

A few minutes before Jeff Carr walked out of the Studio City Theater, his mother, Erin, was holding the head of a fat man between her hands, pressing her thumbs down hard on his eyes. His smiling mouth opened and closed when she tugged the string she'd threaded through the small hole in the top of his skull.

The arms of his headless body dangled limply as she lifted it from the table and attached the head. Pushing her chair back, Erin stood and lifted the T-shaped handle to which the little man's strings were attached. She carried him to the full-length mirror on the broom closet door and lowered him until his feet touched the floor. Manipulating the strings with her fingertips, Erin made his arms move up and down, then close together in an embrace; smiling, she put him through a gentlemanly bow, a little of the old soft shoe, a belly-jiggling laugh—and his left eye popped off.

"Shit!"

Bending down, Erin plucked the staring eye from the carpet with thumb and forefinger and returned to the kitchen table with a sigh.

She had been working on Mr. Spiropolous for days, and

he *had* to be ready by noon tomorrow. First his jaw had been loose, then his head wouldn't nod. Next his belly didn't jiggle properly—now the eyes were popping off.

Fine, she thought, *so I'll be up awhile longer.*

She probably couldn't sleep anyway, hot as it was. Her temples were damp with perspiration, and her salmon-pink top, though light and sleeveless, was spotted here and there. She could only afford to run the air conditioner during the day, when the heat was at its worst. At night she opened the doors and windows and hoped for a breeze; mostly she got flies.

Erin poured herself a glass of ice water and took it out on the patio.

It wasn't a patio, really, just a small rectangular space, a folding chair, a waist-high wooden railing with a window box on it. But it was all the patio she needed.

She touched the cold water glass to her forehead and rolled it back and forth. It left beads of cool moisture on her skin; she didn't wipe them off. Leaning back on the rail, she looked through the sliding screen door at the round and lifeless form of Mr. Spiropolous and smiled a little, pleased with the little man, even though he wasn't holding together just yet.

Erin had been holding three jobs for almost two years; one of them paid better than making puppets, but neither of them made her feel as good as she felt when a puppet was finished and she had transformed an assortment of cloth and screws and hinges and a few pieces of wood into a little person. Some were better than others, but they all gave her a sense of accomplishment and satisfaction that she didn't get from her other jobs. She would gladly devote all of her time to making puppets and drop the other work, but two kids, rent, utilities, and a dozen other expenses kept her from it.

When Ronald left, he had taken not only the television set, the VCR, and the car, but also the only income Erin, Jeff, and Mallory had. The three of them had moved into this smaller apartment in North Hollywood, and Erin had immediately taken an old friend, Kyla Reilly, up on a long-standing offer.

When Mallory was a baby, Erin had made a few dolls.

Erin's friend Kyla saw them one day and had gasped enthusiastically.

"Erin! These are beautiful! I didn't know you did this. These are *gorgeous!* You should make puppets for the theater! We could pay you. Not much, but we could pay you something."

At that time, Kyla had been working nights as a stripper at the Playland Bar in Van Nuys. During the day, she and a couple friends ran the Holiday Puppet Theater. Parents hired them to perform at their children's birthday parties and at Halloween and Christmas parties. Kyla started the business with a great deal of doubt, but it had been more successful than she'd expected. Despite the growth of the Holiday Puppet Theater, Erin continued to turn down Kyla's offers.

When Ronald left, Erin not only started making puppets for Kyla but took a job as a stripper at the Playland. Not long after that, Kyla gave up stripping in order to satisfy the growing demand for the Holiday Puppet Theater throughout the Valley and Los Angeles and even rented a small building in which to give regular afternoon performances during the summer.

The pay for Erin's puppets was minimal, to say the least, so she was still working nights at the Playland. She wasn't crazy about it, but if the men who gathered there were willing to give her ridiculously large tips for getting on stage and taking her shirt off, she wasn't going to deprive them of whatever fun they managed to derive from grabbing their crotches and making loud zoo noises.

She worked seven-hour shifts four nights a week, and so far she had managed to keep it from Jeff and Mallory. They thought she was waiting cocktails. Although Erin did spend half her time at the bar waitressing, she was uncomfortable with the untruth. She didn't like keeping things from them, but she'd like it less if they knew she was stripping.

Jeff would . . . well, Erin wasn't sure *what* Jeff would do. He was a sensitive boy. No—young man. Jeff had passed up boy some time ago. His initial reaction would probably not be strong, but she suspected that something—maybe something within Jeff, maybe something between them, maybe both—would change. She didn't want that. Jeff was much too important to her; she needed him too much.

Mallory, on the other hand . . .

Oh, wouldn't Mallory be tickled pink to find out, Erin thought, wincing at the bitterness of the words as they were spoken in her mind.

No. She wouldn't do that, wouldn't be that way. It was true, Mallory would be pleased because it would, in Mallory's eyes, confirm everything she thought of Erin. But Erin didn't want to handle it with bitterness. She was biding her time, knowing that, once Mallory had grown a bit and was able to see things from a different angle—like how some husbands don't just leave their wives, they leave their kids, their whole lives behind, not because the little woman burns the roast or doesn't particularly enjoy performing fellatio, but simply because they *want* to leave, goddammit!—once that happened, things would change between them.

She hoped for that, anyway.

Erin finished the ice water and stretched her arms and legs, twisting around till her spine cracked like distant gunshots. She hadn't gone for her regular swim in a couple days, and she was getting stiff.

Tomorrow, she thought, looking up at the rainless clouds. *I'll go for a swim tomorrow, right after delivering the puppets.*

At thirty-seven, she was in good shape; not too tall, but very trim, with a minimum of noticeable lines on her face and, so far, no sign of gray in her long auburn hair. She had no trouble with aging, but the management of the Playland Bar did. It wasn't the most respected of jobs, but it paid very well, thank you, and it was better than nothing, which was what she was afraid she'd have otherwise. She hadn't finished school, had no skills, and couldn't afford the time it would take to go back to school and learn to *do* something.

When her mother called from Michigan twice every week, she always asked Erin, "So, are you still making those dolls?"

"Puppets, Mom. Marionettes. Little people with strings?"

"I know what they *are,* I just don't understand how anyone can possibly support two teenagers by—"

"Mom. Please. We're okay. Really. We're o . . . kay."

It made her feel good to say that and mean it. They were okay. They weren't great, things got tough sometimes, but they really were okay.

As she went back into the apartment Erin thought, *But we would be a lot better if things were different with Mallory. . . .*

She went into the living room, turned on the radio, and found a station that was playing something old and easy. Humming along with the music, she was about to return to Mr. Spiropolous's eyes when the phone rang.

Erin looked at the clock on the stereo; it was after eleven. She'd forgotten she was on call tonight.

Job number three.

"Hello?"

"Bunny?"

"Yes."

"Pen and paper?"

"Mm-hm."

"George would like you to call him back at eight-one-eight, seven-five-nine, sixty-one, sixty-one."

"Okay. What's he want?"

"The standard."

Erin had heard about Fantasy Line Phone Sex from Jess, her boss at Playland. She'd needed extra money to buy Mallory some new clothes and supplies for school. Jeff had a job at a bookstore in Sherman Oaks and pretty much took care of himself, God bless him.

She'd taken the job only two weeks ago and had no intention of keeping it much longer. It was a good way to make some quick cash, though. She was on call from twelve to four three nights a week and got fifteen dollars for each twenty-minute call. Not bad, especially considering most of them took much less than twenty minutes.

Erin carried the phone from its stand by the kitchen door to her bedroom. She closed the door in case the kids came home, sat on her bed, and dialed George's number.

"Hello?" It was a young male voice.

"Hello, is this George?"

"Yeah."

"Hi, George. This is Bunny. How are you?"

"I'm, oh, I'm fine." Very young. Probably underage. "So, your name is Bunny, huh?"

Erin heard a chorus of stifled laughs; someone hissed, *"Bunny?"* She knew immediately. It was a bunch of high school kids having a little fun. Probably charging it to Dad's credit card. *And,* Erin liked to imagine, *after Dad sees the bill, he and Mom have a little talk with Junior and ask how dare he call such filthy numbers on their phone, and Junior smiles and says, "I didn't think you'd mind, Dad, I found the number in your wallet."*

"That's right, George," she said, smiling at her little scenario. "What are you up to tonight, hmm?"

"Oh, not much. Just kinda hanging out, y'know?"

"Sounds like you've got company. Having a little party, George?"

"Well, yeah, I guess." George swallowed a giggle.

"Guess they'll just have to take care of themselves tonight, huh, George? What do you want to talk about?"

"Um, I guess about you."

"'About *you'?*" someone in the background croaked. "Tell her to suck your fat one, dude! *Sheezis.*"

"Okay," Erin said, trying not to laugh, too. "You want to know what I'm wearing, George?"

"Yeah."

"I hope you like lace, because I'm wearing a lace bra. Black lace. You can almost see my nipples through it. If I touch them and make them hard, maybe . . . you want me to do that, George?"

"Yeah, touch 'em."

"'Touch 'em'?" someone rasped.

"Radical!" another said.

One of them guffawed.

The voices were suddenly silent.

Erin pressed the receiver a bit harder to her ear because she couldn't even hear George's breathing anymore.

One of the boys said quietly, "What . . . was that?"

Another: "Did the lights just . . . dim?"

Their voices were so hushed that Erin frowned and sat up a bit straighter on the bed.

"Something's . . ." George said, swallowing hard, "something's over . . ."

Erin's grip tightened on the phone, and for some reason it suddenly occurred to her that she had left the sliding glass door open, the *front* door, too, and all the *windows*. . . .

"George," she finally said, "is anything wrong?"

George said, "Something's . . . over the . . . house. . . ."

The receiver clattered to a hard surface, and the pinched sound of hurried movements came through the earpiece: thumping feet and bumped furniture. No voices; they were silent.

"Hello?" Erin said, her phone voice gone; she sounded timid.

There was no reply.

Her next thought entered her head like a bullet, with such suddenness and ferocity that for a brief instant she thought she was having a heart attack and clutched her chest with one hand, sucking air into her lungs:

Sweet Jesus, something's happened to the kids.

The receiver slipped from her hand as she shot from the bed and out of the room, not really sure where she was going, just needing to move, just move because a snake had just crawled through the middle of her; that's what it had felt like, a snake.

She went to the patio with visions of mangled cars and fractured bones jutting through torn flesh. Leaning both hands on the railing, she took deep, slow breaths, thinking, *Please, God, let them be all right, let them both be all right, they're all I've got, please . . .*

Erin thought she should probably call somebody because something—she didn't know what, but *something*—had just happened to her—anxiety, maybe?—that was making her think stupid things and scare herself. She would call someone and just talk, that's all, she just needed to . . . but she'd already called George. . . .

Her thoughts took on a hazy glow for a moment, and she felt vaguely confused.

Something's . . . over the . . . house, George had said.

Erin looked up at the sky.

Nothing.

When she went back in the bedroom and lifted the receiver to her ear, she heard a dial tone and felt, for a second, as if she'd just bitten down on a lump of aluminum foil.

She hung up the phone and sat on the bed again. Her hands were still trembling.

Erin picked up the phone again and dialed Kyla's number.

Just to talk . . .

Four

As Erin listened to the endless *burr*ing of Kyla's telephone eleven teenagers came to a silent halt in the parking lot of Fantazm. A couple holding hands unlaced their fingers and stepped away from one another; two broad-shouldered guys, whose laughter had boomed across the lot as they got out of a big four-wheel-drive pickup truck, seemed to forget what had been so funny as they turned their eyes upward; their smiles melted away to frowns as their heads leaned back.

Kevin Donahue was sitting on his motorcycle surrounded by six of his friends—his only friends, really, not counting Mallory, and she was different—when the buzzing started. One of the guys—either Mark or Trevor (Kevin wasn't sure because remembering had suddenly begun to feel like looking down the wrong end of a telescope)—had just asked him something about the band, something about getting a gig at Fantazm, and Kevin had been about to say . . . what *had* he been about to say?

Well, I've got this friend whose brother's wife has a cousin who's the booker here at Fantazm, Kevin thought, *but even if he gets us in, we'll just be playing for a bunch of goddamned even-tanned daddy-bought-its when what we really wanna do, I mean what we really fuckin' wanna do, is blow this valley off the map, make this fuckin' valley EAT MET-ALLLL!*

He shook off his screaming thoughts as he got off his motorcycle. At first he thought the buzzing was from the lights that were shining down in pools on the parking lot, but it seemed to be inside his head. He stepped away from his bike, slowly looking around at his friends and at the few others on their way into the club. They were all looking up, and it seemed perfectly natural to Kevin that they should be doing so. He did the same—

—and flashbulbs began going off in his skull, faster and faster until the flashbulbs became two blinking strobe lights, and the strobe lights became two piercing golden eyes, unblinking, searching, probing his mind, examining it like the eyes of a jeweler on a diamond.

Kevin didn't realize he was walking farther away from his friends, crossing the parking lot with long, slow steps as he looked at the sky; neither did he notice the gentle, balmy breeze that was shifting his shaggy black hair. He kept his eyes on those clouds.

The wings in his head were gone, and he glimpsed Mallory's face, her breasts, he heard his mother's voice—

—*can't you be like your little brother, he's only twelve and already he outshines you like you aren't even there*—

—saw his father slipping a stick of gum into his mouth to fight the urge to light a cigarette, not because he was worried about lung cancer or heart disease, but because "everybody at the office seems to be quitting—everyone in town, in fact."

And he glimpsed their new car, that shiny fucking silver Mercedes Benz they'd just bought, not because they needed a new car, but because it was time to get a new one, every couple years without fail they bought a brand-new car, an expensive car, just so all their friends, all those doctors and directors and lawyers and producers, would know that they could, that they were *af-fucking-fluent*. Suddenly Kevin was filled with such tangible hate for them that it seemed if he leaned forward and vomited, it would all slap to the pavement in a steaming, viscous heap. But he didn't do

25

that. Instead, he pivoted, kicking up one foot until it connected with something—*anything,* he didn't care what —and something cracked; he kicked again, still looking at the clouds, his teeth clenching hard now, burning in his gums, and something shattered, plinking in pieces to the ground.

And it was gone, all of it; the buzzing, the images that had been shooting in one side of his skull and out the other, the hate for his parents that, for a moment, had burned hotter than ever before. Gone, too, was whatever reason there had been for staring at the sky.

Kevin lowered his eyes and saw that the others were doing the same. He looked down and saw the frosty pieces of glass around his feet, saw the shattered headlight, and saw that it was attached to a brand-new shiny silver Mercedes Benz. No, it was silver only for an instant. It was really white.

Just like theirs, though, Kevin thought, the flames of his hate flaring up for a moment.

"Hey, Kevin," Mark called.

They were walking toward him.

The couple was holding hands again, making their way to the entrance of Fantazm; the two guys from the pickup truck were going in, too, glancing nervously over their shoulders.

"The fuck you doing, dude?" Mark asked, closer now.

Kevin's fists opened and closed at his sides. He didn't know what he was doing or what had happened. He didn't know . . . well, at the moment, he didn't know much of anything. There were clouds in his head just like those in the sky; they weren't moving, they were just sitting there making everything dark.

But he felt different. He felt as if . . . yeah, as if everything was okay, or was going to be okay. It had finally happened.

What's happened? he thought, unable to find an answer.

It didn't matter. Everything was going to be okay.

He took a wrinkled cigarette from the pack he kept tucked beneath the belt around his blue jeans, and, poking it between his lips, he said, "Let's get the fuck outta here."

"What?" Trevor snapped. "I thought you were gonna talk to the booker! Get us a gig!"

"Not tonight."

"Why?"

Kevin left a swirling trail of smoke as he walked back to his bike, taking long strides.

"We don't need him," he replied.

"*What?*" Trevor stepped in front of Kevin, but the others remained behind. "I thought you knew the guy, you said you knew his brother-in-law and he could get us a gig here—I thought you wanted the band to play, man. Or are you just gonna keep talking about it and not do nothing?"

Another wave of anger swept through Kevin, and he bent down, slapped a hand to his boot, and, with a solid *click,* sliced the air in front of Trevor's face with his switchblade.

Trevor held up both hands and backed up.

"Hey, no, no, okay, Kev, okay, you say we don't need him, okay, man, but . . . we all wanna play, Kevin. You know?"

The anger fell away in an instant, and Kevin slowly lowered his knife, folding the blade back in and slipping it into his boot again, blinking with confusion. He took a long drag on his cigarette and went to his bike.

"Look," he said, putting on his glossy black helmet, the dark visor raised, "we're just . . . not ready yet, okay? We've gotta rehearse some more."

"Not ready," Trevor muttered angrily.

"That's right, not ready. We don't even have a fuckin' name yet." The bike started with an angry roar.

"Where you going?" Trevor asked.

Kevin slid his visor down. "I don't know," he replied as he drove away, putting behind him the arced neon sign that read FANTAZM.

Five

J. R. Haskell was torn from a peaceful dream of his dead sister with a scream lodged in his throat like a lumpy gob of phlegm and the echo of an unuttered cry in his head. He sat up in bed, his fists closed around clumps of the single sheet that was spread over him, his eyes wide, his chest filled with the feeling of something massive, enormous beyond his imagining, hurtling toward him, rushing over a vast distance at an incredible speed, leaving him nowhere to run, to hide, to find safety—

—then it was a memory.

He looked around his dark apartment, swallowing hard several times in succession; he knew that if his throat remained open for more than a second, his voice would tear from his chest in a desperate wail.

And he didn't know why.

There were no unusual sounds; the fan in the window was whirring quietly, and the refrigerator was humming, but nothing more.

As he sat in bed the feeling disappeared quickly, like water being sucked down a drain. It left him weak, but wide-eyed and alert.

J.R. got out of bed and went to the window. The fan blew warm air from outside over his bare chest. He was disappointed to see that it had not rained. Leaning a hand on the windowsill, he looked over his shoulder at the bed again. Any sleepiness he'd felt was gone. With a sigh, he went to the kitchen in his undershorts, took a can of beer from the refrigerator, and popped the tab.

He leaned against the counter and stared at his bed through the kitchen door. He was anxious, that's why he couldn't sleep—because he was anxious about Tuesday.

"J.R. the high school counselor," he muttered, lifting the beer in a toast to himself.

He'd taught English and literature for three years at Santa Rosa High School in Northern California but quickly grew tired of faculty politics and the tedium of paperwork, the tap dance to avoid this irate parent group or that messy lawsuit. He didn't grow tired of the students, though; they were the reason he'd gone into education in the first place. He still wasn't sure why he'd left Santa Rosa, though. He missed the crisp air and the green surroundings. The pay was better in Southern California, however, and he liked the school.

He wasn't sure he was going to get the job at first. The principal, Mr. Booth, a round-faced man with thinning rusty-red hair, had seemed uncertain of J.R.'s ability to handle the job. Booth was a bit put off by the fact that this would be J.R.'s first counseling job, and although he tried to be as diplomatic as possible, he pointed out to J.R. that he seemed a little too soft-spoken and passive to hold a position of any authority.

J.R. was used to that sort of thing; he was five-foot-eight and had a wiry build and a boyish face with short, curly brown hair; people frequently underestimated him in many ways. He usually surprised them. He had managed to convince Booth that he was more than capable of taking on the job, though. Now he wasn't so sure.

He sipped his beer and stared out the window at the murky night, confused by his sudden wakefulness. He knew he'd been dreaming but didn't remember the dream.

Something about Sheila, he thought vaguely.

29

He usually dreamed of Sheila when he was having doubts about something. Uncertain situations, such as his new job, reminded him that he had been unable to help her when she had needed it most. So what made him think he would be any use to a bunch of frustrated, horny, and maybe even desperate teenagers whom he was supposed to counsel?

While J.R. was a student at Berkeley, his little sister was living at home and going to high school in El Cerrito, about thirty miles away. Sheila had been a rebellious girl, always coming home with a strange new hairdo, outrageous clothes, questionable friends, and once with a black rose tattooed on her shoulder. J.R. liked her because of her rebellious nature, rather than in spite of it, because he understood it. While their parents had always been regular churchgoers, they embraced their religious beliefs with greater fervor as they grew older, and they pushed them on Sheila. She was simply trying her best to maintain a distance from her parents' rigid beliefs and keep an identity of her own. When J.R. tried to explain that to Leonard and Marjorie Haskell, his words fell on deaf ears. So he tried to let Sheila know *he* thought she was okay and that she could be whatever she wanted if she stayed out of trouble.

One night, J.R. was awakened by a phone call from his mother. She was in tears, babbling about Sheila being out of control. He got dressed and drove to El Cerrito. He heard the shouting before he was halfway up the front path.

Marjorie Haskell had found her daughter in bed with a girl. The girl had been kicked out, and Sheila was on the sofa getting a loud and tearful lecture from her mother about what an evil sickness homosexuality was and how much damage she had caused by bringing it into their God-fearing home.

Sheila was sleepy-eyed and half-smiling, obviously on something. J.R. assumed it was marijuana.

"Oh, J.R., she was vile!" Marjorie said to him. "Absolutely vile, that woman who was here. She laughed—if you'd only heard her—she laughed when I found them! Black shaggy hair, and those tight leather pants, she was . . . she . . ." Marjorie burst into more sobs.

"Where's Dad?" J.R. asked.

"He's in the bedroom praying."

Jesus, he thought.

He took Sheila to a nearby Denny's, wanting to get her out of the house before Mom and Dad realized she'd been taking drugs. She sat across the table from him in a sleepy haze.

"What've you been taking, Sheila?"

"Mm, nothing much."

"What?"

She wouldn't answer.

"Look, Sheila, I know I told you to be your own person and all that, but come on—be realistic. You're living in their house."

Her face wilted. "Do you think I'm sick and evil?"

"No, of course not. I'll admit, it was a surprise to find out that . . . you're . . . "

"A lesbian."

"Yeah. But I don't think anything is sick and horrible if it makes you happy, as long as it doesn't hurt anyone. Now, whatever you may think of Mom and Dad's beliefs, that's the way they are, and this hurts them. Why didn't you do it somewhere else, for Christ's sake?"

"We couldn't go to her place."

"Why?"

"Her . . . well, her boyfriend had company."

"Her . . . she has a . . . I don't understand."

Sheila smiled, became more animated. "They're so cool, J.R. They don't care that I'm just a teenager, that I hate school—they think I'm *okay!* They're like that with all the kids."

"Kids? How old are these people?"

"I don't know. In their twenties, I guess. Hard to tell."

"What did they give you? What kind of drugs?"

She shrugged. "Some kind of hash, I think."

"You're not even sure?" He paused to choose his words carefully. "Look, Sheila, you know I love you, right? I'm not telling you this because I think you're a bad kid, but because I care about you. Lay off the drugs—be really careful, okay?

31

And I think it might be a good idea to stay away from these people. They don't sound so cool to me."

"But they're *fun,* they're—"

"Sheila. Until you're on your own, you're going to have to make some compromises."

She looked away from him and muttered, "You're just as bad as they are."

J.R. didn't want to leave her, but he had to go back to school. He could see both sides of the problem but thought Sheila was the more vulnerable. He stayed in close contact with her for a couple weeks, but after that she was seldom home when he called.

"I don't know what we've done wrong, J.R.," his father said on the phone one evening. "Maybe we're being punished for something, I don't know. She's hardly ever home anymore, refuses to go to church, and sometimes she doesn't even go to school. She won't talk to us anymore, so we don't know what she does when she's gone. We've left it in the Lord's hands. That's all we can do."

J.R. tried to tell them that wasn't all they could do, but they wouldn't listen.

During the following weeks, J.R. read reports in the newspaper of violence at Sheila's high school: students attacking one another as well as faculty members. One boy was killed in a fight. A girl killed herself, and after that, a boy—a very popular boy who had been involved in school politics—slashed his wrists. Two others followed. The night J.R. read a headline that shouted OUTBREAK OF TEEN SUICIDES IN EL CERRITO, he decided it was time to do something about his family's problem. He would get them into counseling if he had to drag them, and he would do it that weekend.

That same night he was awakened again by another hysterical phone call from his mother.

"She's leaving!" Marjorie shouted. "She's taking her things and leaving with those people, that woman, and Leonard won't do anything, but you can talk to her, she'll listen to you, so will you come, please come!"

When he arrived, he found Sheila carrying an armload of clothes across the yard toward a large black car parked at the curb. He called her name, but she ignored him, tossing the clothes into the back seat and heading back into the house.

"Wait!" he shouted, grabbing her arm. She wore a white sleeveless top, and as he held her arm he saw in the yellowish glow from the porch light the needle marks that bruised her inner elbow. "Jesus," he muttered, "what have you been doing to yourself?" She jerked away from him. "Just wait a second and talk with me!"

"No. You're just like them. You don't want to talk *with* me, you want to talk *to* me." She stormed through the door and into her room.

J.R. found his father in the living room rocking gently in his chair, staring out of the window.

"Where's Mom?" J.R. asked.

"In the bathroom crying."

"Well, aren't you going to do something? Talk to her? Anything?"

Without looking at his son, Leonard said, "In the Old Testament, God told Abraham to take his son Isaac into the land of Moriah and up on a hill, where he was to kill Isaac. Sacrifice him. Abraham loved his son, but he loved his God more, so he did as he was told. As he held the knife over his son, ready to put it through his heart, the Angel of the Lord held his hand and said he didn't need to kill Isaac. It was only a test of his faith, his devotion." Meeting J.R.'s eyes, he said, "God is testing us now. It's in His hands. His will be done."

Furious, J.R. followed Sheila back out to the car. She tossed her last load into the back seat and started to get in.

"Wait, Sheila, don't do this!" he pleaded. "You can come live with *me* if you want, I've just got that tiny apartment, but if it'll—"

"Yeah, *then* how would I have to live, huh? Your way instead of *theirs?* Big difference." She slammed the door.

"Sheila, please! Where are you going?"

She opened the window a crack and said, "Someplace better than this."

The window on the driver's side slid down smoothly, and a woman with bushy black hair, pale skin, and dark eye makeup smiled out at him.

33

"You lose, big brother," she said as she drove away. J.R. was sure it was just reflected moonlight, but her eyes had shimmered in that last moment before she was out of sight.

J.R. rushed into the house, angered by the woman's cockiness, and called the police, since his parents wouldn't.

"Is she a minor, Mr. Haskell?" the officer asked.

"She's seventeen."

"And she just left tonight, huh? Well, apparently she wasn't taken against her will. You don't know where she went?"

"No."

"Well, if you haven't heard from her in twenty-four hours, give us a call. But as far as I can tell, there's not much we can do."

Three days later, Sheila was found hanging in the closet of a cheap motel room just outside of El Cerrito. She had taken her own life and left a note that read simply, "I'm going to someplace better."

Nine days after Sheila's death, a restaurant that had been abandoned for nearly five years, the Old Red Barn, had caught fire. The building had been in very poor condition, and no one was surprised by the news of the fire. All had been shocked, however, by what was found inside the building.

The restaurant had been designed to look like an old barn with a high ceiling and rafters. Most of the rafters collapsed during the fire. Tied to the rafters were twenty-two ropes. Each rope ended in a noose, and each noose was wrapped around the neck of a dead teenager.

It was later determined that the teenagers had been dead at least two hours before one of the ropes had snapped and the corpse of a sixteen-year-old boy from Richmond had fallen on lighted candles that had been burning in the building, starting the fire.

The following week was filled with funerals, long processions of slow-moving cars with headlights shining, flags flown at half-mast, and a fruitless attempt to understand why twenty-two teenagers had ended their lives.

J.R. recognized many of the dead as former friends of Sheila's, and when he heard that several teenagers claimed that their friends had been involved with a couple named John and Dara, he became suspicious. They claimed the couple had encouraged the students to take drugs and engage in promiscuous sex, and they had spoken of suicide as if it were some kind of elevation of the spirit to a higher plane. They believed John and Dara were responsible for the deaths. J.R. had considered speaking up, supporting them, telling of Sheila's association with John and Dara, but when he saw the reaction they got, he decided there was already enough misery in his life.

While going through their dead children's belongings, some of the parents found rock lyrics written down in notebooks, letters, even on napkins—lyrics that made explicit references to sex, drugs, and violence. The parents organized and began fighting for the censorship of such rock records, claiming the lyrics had confused and desensitized their children, leading them to suicide. When the teenagers protested the group's ideas, the parents fought back with a very parental response: "It's for your own good."

The suicides made national news, were analyzed and reanalyzed by television and radio psychologists, written about in magazines and psychology journals, and preached about in churches.

All J.R. knew was that he'd lost his little sister. If she hadn't killed herself in that dingy motel room, she probably would have joined her friends in the Old Red Barn and, as morbid as the notion was, he was rather glad that she'd avoided being a part of the whole big media sideshow. Her death might have been prevented—as, he was sure, the other twenty-two might have—had her problems been dealt with in a more supportive and loving fashion by her family. He wasn't blaming his parents; he knew he could have done more, too.

The loss of his sister had not been brought about by rock lyrics, not even by drugs or a man and woman named John and Dara. It had been brought about by ignorance.

J.R. turned away from the dark thoughts of his sister and tried to feel confident about facing those kids on Tuesday and the days to come. His eyes locked on one of the fat dark clouds in the sky as he stared out the window. Its puffy underside glowed with reflected neon. He frowned and stepped toward the window, watching the cloud slowly ooze across the sky. He hadn't been paying much attention, but he could have sworn that, just a moment ago, the cloud had been holding perfectly still, like a painted cloud on a stage backdrop.

It was moving now, though, along with the others, moving at the speed of pouring honey.

J.R. took a few steps back, leaned on the counter, and took another drink of beer, frowning out the window, but not sure why.

His small apartment suddenly seemed rather cold. . . .

Six

Mrs. DiPesto was already hurrying down the walk in front of her house on Whitley Drive as the squad car parked at the curb. Officer Bill Grady saw her first as he got out from behind the wheel and shut the door.

She was plowing toward them, her hips wider than the narrow path, her large, sagging breasts dancing beneath her green terrycloth robe. Curls of gray hair stuck out from beneath the black spider-weblike net she wore on her head, and one liver-spotted hand was pressed just below her throat.

"What took you so long?" she panted. She wore big, round, thick-lensed glasses that had slid down her nose. "He coulda come back and raped me in the time it took you guys to get here!"

"We got here as fast as we could, ma'am," Grady said, lifting a calming palm and giving her a reassuring smile. His partner, Harvey Towne, stepped up beside him.

Grady was fifty-three years old, a tall, barrel-chested man with thick hair the color of desert sand. He planned to retire next year; he'd had enough, thank you very much. The last of his four daughters had graduated from college. All four of them had pretty much paid their own way through school, leaving Grady and his wife Marge a good-sized nest egg. They hoped to use that to find a place in Monterey.

"You are Clara DiPesto, aren't you?" Grady asked.

"Of course I am." She smelled of stale cigarette smoke and gin.

Towne flipped open his notepad and held his pencil, ready to write.

"You say you have a burglar, ma'am?" Towne asked, his voice mechanical and emotionless.

Sounds like one of those clowns on Dragnet, Grady thought, wanting to chuckle. Towne was a rookie and had been assigned to him a little over a week ago.

"Had," Mrs. DiPesto snapped. "He's long gone by now. I caught him on my back porch trying to break in."

"Can you give us a description?" Grady asked.

"Well . . ."

"Try."

"Umm, let's seeee, he was young," she said, closing her eyes to remember. "A kid, maybe sixteen. Had long hair, of *course,* dark brown, maybe, but it was hard to tell. And he was wearing one of those T-shirts—it was black—with the sleeves cut off? Torn off, more like it," she added, opening her eyes. "I don't understand why they do that. It looks so sloppy."

Grady patted Towne's arm with the back of his hand and said, "I'll go take a look around."

He went to the car, got his long black flashlight, then walked between Mrs. DiPesto's house and her neighbor's to the alley that ran behind them. He shone the light first to the right, toward Ventura Boulevard, then to the left, and decided to go that way.

Grady was in no mood for someone like Mrs. DiPesto tonight and he figured Towne could use the practice. Rookies were always shocked to find that most of the people they dealt with were Mrs. DiPestos, and not rapists and serial killers like on television.

To Grady's left were the back fences of the houses along Whitley; to his right was a tall Cyclone fence crawling with vines and shrubbery and lined with garbage cans.

The alley itself was quiet, but there were sounds in the distance: cars, music, shouting, a barking dog, a siren. Above the trees on the other side of the fence, Grady could see the glow from the lights of Studio City. The thick, balmy air seemed to pour into his lungs when he inhaled.

Something clanged behind him.

Grady spun around.

His flashlight beam caught the jittering movement of a garbage can lid that had fallen to the pavement.

Probably just a cat, he thought, but he headed back that way just in case. He doubted he would find the guy, but he wanted to give Towne enough time to finish up with Mrs. DiPesto.

He started toward Ventura, shining his light between garbage cans and behind trash bins where flies buzzed hungrily. As he neared the boulevard the alley brightened, and he flicked off the flashlight.

A cat dived from a fence and crouched before him, then darted by him with a low, throaty *meeeoowww.*

Tapping the long flashlight against his thigh, Grady stopped and looked around him. The kid was probably in another neighborhood by now, trying to hit another house. Or maybe he was on the boulevard, lost in the waves of other teenagers prowling the sidewalks like stray cats in a wrecking yard. With one more glance toward Ventura, Grady passed between two houses, got back on Whitley, and headed for Mrs. DiPesto's.

Then he stopped.

He craned his head around and looked over his shoulder.

At the end of the street to the right was the corner of a large building. It used to be the Studio City Fitness Center. Before that, it had been a nightclub for a decade or so. When that had closed four years ago, some Arab had bought it and turned it into a health club. A "deluxe health club," the ads had said. He'd bought the lot next to it and expanded the building, put in a huge underground swimming pool and racquetball court—the whole nine yards—then launched an expensive ad campaign to convince everyone that they weren't really in shape unless they were paying an arm and a leg to exercise at his club.

The place had attracted a lot of movie and television people from the nearby studios, as well as a lot of yuppies who wanted to watch the stars sweat and maybe even find a hard body to curl up with that night.

A year and a half after the grand opening, "faulty wiring" (according to the papers) had gutted the place with fire.

Instead of rebuilding, the Arab let the place sit. Eventually, FOR SALE signs showed up on the walls of the building, their red and blue letters seeming bright next to the yawning, blackened windows.

A few months later, some of the local teenagers had adopted the abandoned building as a meeting place where they went to listen to those damned noise boxes they carried, take drugs, and fuck like rabbits. Grady was one of the three cops who had busted them one night after a series of complaints from nearby residents. They'd had quite a setup: cushions and blankets spread over the bottom of the empty pool, iceboxes for beer and wine, a complete stock of hard liquor—everything a bunch of horny teenagers could want. When Grady and the other uniforms had gone in, the large rooms downstairs where the kids had set up house reeked of marijuana, and the floor was littered with cigarette butts and used condoms.

After the teenagers had been kicked out, the building had been boarded up and locked more securely than before. Since then there had been no problem.

Until, perhaps, now.

Something caught Grady's eye. It might have been the reflection of a passing car's headlights, but he thought he saw a flicker of light through a space in one of the boarded side windows of the empty building.

Grady turned and headed in that direction again.

There it was again; it looked as if a light were being passed back and forth on the other side of the window.

Grady picked up his pace.

It made sense; the kid got caught trying to break into a house, so naturally he'd want a place to hide. Grady couldn't figure out how he'd gotten in, though. The building was locked like a safe, as far as he knew.

Grady approached the window quietly and leaned toward it, cupping a hand to his face as he peered between the boards.

He could make out a fire-ravaged wall with a large chunk missing. A soft yellow glow, like candlelight, flickered in the darkness, shimmering over the wall, shifting back and forth, as if someone were walking around inside with a candle.

"Gotcha," he breathed, walking around to the front of the building.

The glare of neon and fluorescent lights and the bright headlights of the cars on the boulevard made Grady squint. What used to be the glass double doors of the entrance was now a wall of boards and locked chains. No one had gone through here. He kept walking, passing the front windows, all of which were still secure.

He turned right at the faded, crooked sign that read PARKING below a painted arrow and walked along the side of the building to the parking lot in back. His shoes crunched on gravel and broken glass as he switched the flashlight on again.

There were no windows on this side of the building for Grady to check, so he hurried along the wall and rounded the corner. Shattered beer bottles and empty six-pack cartons were strewn over the parking lot; there was a pile of cigarette butts where someone had emptied a car's ashtray. Apparently the kids used the lot for partying. There had been no complaints, though, so Grady figured they were keeping a lid on it.

He went to the rear entrance. It was still firmly boarded. He pounded the heel of his palm against the boards once just to be certain. They thumped solidly, and Grady heard a quick shuffling inside the building. He hurried to the nearest window and peered between the boards.

This window looked into a different room than the last, but the golden shimmer of light was still dancing on the walls. He heard the shuffling again, and the glow became brighter, as if it were drawing nearer the window.

In an instant, the room became dark. It was more than just dark; it suddenly seemed to be gone.

Grady lifted the flashlight and shone the beam between the boards, nearly dropping it when he saw a wide, glistening, golden eye gazing back at him.

"Okay," Grady barked, stepping away from the window and unsnapping the flap of his holster, "come on out of there slowly, and let's see some I.D. This is the police."

He waited, his hand resting lightly on his holstered gun.

Someone inside laughed at him. It was a quiet, dry laugh, like the sound of a small animal slowly being crushed.

Grady swept the beam back and forth over the wall until it landed on a half-open door. It was the employee entrance. The boards that had been nailed across the doorway were lying on the pavement, broken and splintered. As he approached the door he saw that the steel eyelet through which a padlock had been fastened had been torn from the door and lay on the ground beside the broken lock.

"Jesus," he muttered, carefully pulling the door open. The door hung loose from the top hinge and scraped against the pavement as it moved.

The doorway opened on a dark corridor with a door on each side. Grady took one step and froze when he heard a voice whisper softly in the darkness.

Two people? he thought, taking his gun from the holster and holding it cautiously at his side.

"One more time," he said loudly. "Come out slowly and identify yourself. I've drawn my gun."

Another low chuckle.

Yellow light flickered beyond the doorway to his right.

Grady moved forward, lifted his gun, and sidled into the room, bits of rubble making crackling sounds beneath his shoes.

Across the room, a lighted candle in a small holder stood on a wooden crate.

He took two steps into the room, sweeping his flashlight beam back and forth across the blackened walls. Something shuffled before him, but he could see no movement.

—until he looked down.

The floor was shifting.

Specks of light glistened up at him.

He shone the beam at them and quickly realized that the specks of light were really eyes.

Hearing footsteps behind him, Grady spun around to face a tall, dark figure in the doorway. *"Holy—"* he blurted. A hand knocked the flashlight to the floor. It hit with a crack, and the beam disappeared.

Grady held the gun before him protectively, his skin crawling at the thought of what was at his feet.

"Back up!" he growled.

Must be fifty of 'em, he thought, *whatever the hell they are!*

"I said back up, goddammit, the room's full of—of—of . . . goddammit, outside now!"

"I heard you." The voice was low, firm, and very deep. Deathly pale light outlined the tall man in an eerie glow, seeping through the sunburst of spiky hair that surrounded his head. "They're mine," he said with a smile in his voice.

"Don't fuck with me, man, now back the hell up!"

Grady lifted his thumb to cock the gun, but cold fingers wrapped around his wrist in a steel-like grip, tightening until his fingers loosened on the gun, dropping it to the floor. Grady made a small grunting sound in his throat, expecting to hear the thick crack of his wristbone breaking when the icy grip tightened even more. The stranger stepped forward, pushing Grady back into the room.

"No," Grady whispered, the image of those small, glistening eyes flashing in his mind. He felt something brush his pantleg, and he sucked a sharp breath into his lungs.

When the grip on his wrist loosened slightly, Grady opened his eyes.

The man's thin, finely sculpted face was bathed in the soft light of the candle, and he smiled before opening his mouth wide—wider than seemed possible—and Grady knew he was going to die, it was a feeling that cut through his gut like a razor as something shot from the stranger's mouth, something long and wet, bursting into Grady's mouth, knocking two of his front teeth from his gums with a sickening crunch as it went down his throat, deeper and deeper inside him, squirming like a fat, agitated worm, making him gag, lose his footing, and tumble backward. His arms flailed as he tried to regain his balance, but he continued falling as he heard the creatures shuffling over the floor below.

Bill Grady's last sensation was that of warm, baby-sized bodies wriggling beneath his back. . . .

PART II

Crucifax
Genesis

Seven

September 6

Jeff seated himself at the breakfast table and poured Wheat Chex into the empty bowl before him.

"Morning," Erin said sleepily, her slippered feet *shoosh*ing over the kitchen floor, then falling silent on the carpet as she brought a plate of toast to the table.

"Hi, Mom."

"Mallory still in bed?"

"She just got in the shower." He poured milk over the cereal.

"She's slow this morning. Was she up late last night?"

A spoonful of cereal froze halfway to Jeff's mouth. "Yeah," he said, then he scooped the bite in and chewed hard.

It wasn't a lie, but it wasn't the truth, either. If he could have told his mother the truth without setting off fireworks between her and Mallory, he would have. He wasn't in the mood for the shouting that would ensue. Even worse would be the days of chilly silence that would follow.

As Erin returned to the kitchen for a cup of coffee Jeff nibbled a slice of toast and let his weary eyes close.

Mallory had gone out with Kevin the night before.

"We've made up," she'd told him, "and he wants to take me out."

"Where are you going?" he'd asked, hoping she'd say they were going to a movie or out for a pizza. Something safe.

"I don't know. Out with his friends."

Her last words had kept Jeff awake all night. Lying in bed staring at his ceiling, he kept expecting the worst: a phone call from the police department maybe, or, even more horrible, from the hospital. He'd known that, if Mallory went out with Kevin *and* his friends, they wouldn't be having a burger and fries at DuPar's. That just wasn't Kevin's style.

Erin had come home from work around three and gone straight to bed. Jeff had heard Mallory sneak in at about five.

He'd slept for little more than an hour, and even then he'd passed through foggy dreams of his sister and Kevin Donahue rolling naked and sweaty over a dirty floor in some dark, hidden room as Kevin's leering friends looked on.

"Feel like driving?"

Jeff's eyes snapped open as Erin sat across from him with her coffee.

"What?"

"Well, I figured I'd let you take the car today. I won't need it, I'll be here working. You and Mal can drive to your first day of school in peace, skip the bus. Sound okay?"

"Sure. Thanks, Mom."

"Just make sure you lock it up."

"I will."

Erin finished her coffee, gave Jeff the car keys, and went to her room. A few minutes later, Mallory came out, hurriedly buttoning her baggy yellow shirt. It hung well below the waist of her turquoise pants, gathered in the middle by a slanted, loose-fitting black belt.

"Grab some toast," Jeff said, standing up from the table. He didn't look at her as he stuffed his wallet in the hip pocket of his blue jeans and grabbed his books and the car keys.

"You're driving?"

"Yeah. Let's go."

Mallory made an annoyed sound—a short burst of air through her nose—and followed him out of the apartment with her bag.

As Jeff pulled the car onto Laurel Canyon, the radio playing loudly, Mallory asked, "What's wrong with you?"

Jeff turned down the radio. "What?"

"I said, what's wrong with you? You're awful quiet."

"I didn't sleep very well last night."

"Yeah, well, neither did I." She sounded testy.

"Get back late?"

"Mm-hm."

"What time?"

"I don't know. Late."

"About five."

From the corner of his eye, Jeff saw her turn to him suddenly, suspiciously.

"You were awake?" she asked.

He nodded.

She turned away and looked out the window, shaking her head. "Jesus," she breathed.

The song on the radio ended and the morning disc jockey went into his Sylvester Stallone impression, getting some muted background chuckles from his A.M. Wake-Up Crew.

Mallory stared out the window silently for a few moments, her jaw working slightly. Jeff had seen her do that before, but only during heated conversations and shouting matches with their mother.

She finally turned to him and asked, "Did Mom stay up waiting for me? No. She wasn't worried, so why should you be?"

"Mom didn't know you were out when she came home, but even if she did, she doesn't know anything about Kevin Donahue."

"Neither do you," she snapped quietly, turning to the window again.

"I know enough to be worried."

Jeff suddenly wished they weren't talking about this. He was tired and could tell Mallory was more than a little annoyed. He was more concerned, at the moment, with the first day of school and being unable to stay up for the Letterman show every night. He didn't care about Kevin Donahue anymore. Mostly because it reminded him of his dreams the night before.

"You know," Mallory said without turning to him, "you really don't know *anything* about Kevin. You *don't.*"

I know what you do with him, he thought, immediately regretting it. He gripped the wheel a little tighter as the memory of last night's dream came to him suddenly: boys clutching Mallory's round breasts, burying their faces between her legs and slurping like dogs, holding her hair in their fists as they plunged their stiff cocks into her mouth. . . . And worst of all was the warm moisture he'd felt against his legs when he woke.

Guilt washed over him in a thick, black wave, and he wrung his fists around the wheel. It was a familiar guilt, one that had first visited him two years before and returned with increasing regularity. It was beginning to feel like a constant, despised companion.

The week his father left had been one of the worst of his young life. It had been a bad one for Mallory and their mother, too, of course. But for Jeff, it had brought something more than just the disruption of his family.

The night after his father left, Jeff could not sleep. It was a hot summer night, and he lay atop his covers in his undershorts listening to his mother's pacing footsteps and stifled sobs in the next room, thinking that his father's absence would probably be a good thing. It would be a good thing for him, anyway; Jeff hadn't been on the best of terms with his father since he was a small boy. Dad's attention had been focused on Mallory; he'd doted on her, showered her with affection, bought her loyalty with gifts he couldn't afford. Jeff was surprised he didn't try to take Mallory with him. Jeff knew she was hurting much more than he and probably would for a while.

A timid knock on his bedroom door made him sit up on the bed. Mallory opened the door a crack and looked in.

"Can I come in?" she whispered. Her eyes were puffy and her cheeks wet.

"Sure."

She closed the door quietly and stood there a moment, her face turned down. She wore a blue nightshirt that went to her knees and was split up both sides to her waist. Jeff had not noticed, until that night, how well she was filling out. The material of the shirt was stretched taut across her breasts, and her body had developed curves in places that, not long ago, had seemed boyish.

"I can't sleep," she said, crossing the room and sitting on the edge of his bed.

"Neither can I."

"Can I . . . stay here awhile?"

"Sure."

She bunched a corner of his sheet between her hands and sniffled.

"Why do you think he left, Jeff?" she whispered. "What could she have done that was that bad?"

"Don't blame Mom. She's taking it pretty hard, too."

"She should," she breathed, wringing the sheet around and around in her fists.

"C'mon, don't—"

"Well, it wasn't us!" She turned her teary eyes to him as her face twisted into a mask of pain. "Was it?" she sobbed. "I mean, do you think it was because of *us,* Jeff?" She let go of the sheet and slowly eased toward him, suddenly falling into his arms and pressing her face to his bare shoulder. Her tears rolled down his back.

"No, it had nothing to do with us," Jeff whispered in her ear. She smelled of shampoo and toothpaste and felt warm, even feverish, in his arms. "Don't think that. And it wasn't Mom, either. He just . . . left. That's all."

"But he didn't even say goodbye. He didn't even—"

"That wasn't because of anything we did or didn't do. He just . . ." Jeff stopped to weigh his words, wondering if they would sound too harsh. "Did it ever occur to you that maybe . . . maybe he just didn't *care* enough to say goodbye?"

"How could he not care? After all the things he used to . . . to t-tell m-me . . ." Her words were lost in a storm of sobs that made her body quake in his arms.

They didn't talk any more that night. They lay on the bed, Mallory huddled in Jeff's arms, her head resting on his chest, her sobs slowly dissolving into slow, regular breaths of sleep. With each inhalation, her breasts gently pressed against Jeff's side, then slowly pulled away. Her breath was hot and moist on his skin.

As Mallory slept Jeff tried to remember their childhood summers together, the camps their father sent them to and the year they'd gone to Disneyland, Magic Mountain, and Knott's Berry Farm all in one week.

He remembered the biggest fight they'd ever had. It had been over a block of clay they'd had to split between them; Mallory wanted more than half because she was making a miniature backyard fountain for two of her dolls who had just married, and Jeff wanted more because half the block wasn't enough to make a voodoo doll of Mrs. Rhodes, his fourth-grade teacher. Their quarrel went on for days until their mother threatened to ground them if they didn't forget it.

He tried to remember Mallory and himself as children, a brother and sister who got along unusually well and depended upon one another for support, companionship, and sincere, innocent affection.

But something changed in Jeff that night. His crystal-clear vision of Mallory the child had gone from library paste and bubble gum to perfumes and powders and a subtle, darkly enticing smell that, when noticeable, made him feel warm inside, warm and guilty. *This* Mallory was different than any other girl; she thought differently, even spoke differently. He knew more about her—about the things she'd done, the thoughts she had, and the things she felt—than anyone else. She was his best friend, his closest companion, and he loved her more at that moment than he'd ever loved her before.

But a shadow had fallen over his love for Mallory, a shadow that made their physical closeness on the bed that night more exciting than it should have been, more intimate, and, ultimately, more shameful.

Jeff was unable to close his eyes as Mallory slept beside him. Where her breasts touched him, his skin burned.

Mallory moved her leg over his knee, his thigh, until it was resting against the hardening bulge beneath his shorts. The sensation of her bare skin sliding over his made Jeff dizzy until the dark room seemed to tilt a bit.

A shaft of bluish moonlight from the window fell over them, glowing on the curve of Mallory's hip where her shirt had hiked up. Jeff's hands trembled to reach down and touch her smooth skin. He ached to press his erection against her thigh, just a little. . . .

After lying there for a long time, Jeff slowly moved his arm across his body and held his hand an inch above her breast, cupping his palm as if he were actually touching the mound of flesh. He lowered his hand slightly, then a fraction more. He did not touch her, but after several minutes of holding his hand there, he thought he could feel heat rising from beneath her shirt.

Before he gave in to his temptation, Jeff eased out from under her. She mumbled in her sleep, rolled over, and curled herself around a pillow. Jeff put on his robe, went to the living room, and watched television until dawn.

Things had never been the same since that night. At first, it was difficult for him to be around her. He often found his eyes wandering over her body and quickly made excuses to go away. After a while, though, he learned to bury his thoughts so deep they didn't show on his face. He shared them with no one and savored them only in his dreams. He always awoke with a pounding erection, a hard, cold lump of guilt in his stomach, and one thought. It was a dreadful thought that terrified him: *There's something wrong with me.* . . .

As he took a right on Chandler Jeff said, "I'm sorry. It's none of my business, really. I just . . . worry too much, I guess."

After a pause, he felt her eyes on him. "I know," she said quietly. "I kinda like that. But Jesus, Jeff, it's like you don't trust me at all, like you have to have your eyes on me all the time."

"It's not you I don't trust, it's—"

"I know, you don't trust him. But that's only because you

don't know him. If you knew more about him . . ." She gave up and faced front with a sigh. "I'm meeting him after school, so I won't be going home with you. Don't wait for me."

Jeff tapped his thumb on the steering wheel as he waited for a traffic light to change. His breakfast was sitting heavily in his stomach and he looked forward to getting to school and out of the car.

When they got to school Mallory opened the car door and stepped out before Jeff turned off the ignition. She almost stopped to say goodbye and wish him a good day but decided she didn't want to give him the chance to make some remark about her after-school plans. Slamming the car door, she started across the school parking lot with her bag slung over her shoulder.

Sometimes Jeff worried her. She expected her mother's meddling and concern, but Jeff was her brother. He was supposed to be on *her* side. He usually was; that's what seemed so odd.

Unlike most of her friends, Mallory's strongest source of support was her brother. Most of the kids she knew couldn't stand their siblings. She and Jeff had always been close. When they were children, he defended her if she was being treated unfairly, and he was the first to let her know if he thought she was being unfair. She'd always liked that; it made their relationship special because it was so different from those of the other brothers and sisters she knew. Jeff was like a built-in boyfriend.

That was the problem. Now she had a real boyfriend, and Jeff couldn't handle it.

Someone called her name, and she stopped on the steps in front of the school. Deidre Palmer was hurrying up the steps toward her, a fat notebook held against her chest with both arms.

"So how come you look so pissed?" Deidre asked.

"I look pissed?"

"Mm-hm."

"I just had a bad morning, is all."

"Your mom?" .

"My brother."

Deidre blinked with surprise. "Your brother? What's wrong?"

Mallory found her locker and began spinning the combination lock back and forth.

"Jeff doesn't want me to see Kevin," she said, jiggling the latch. The locker wouldn't open.

"What? Why, as if it's any of his business?"

"He thinks I'm gonna get into trouble." She began spinning the lock again.

"You mean, like, *pregnant?"*

"Well, that, too, probably, but"—she jiggled the latch again, but with no success—"mostly he just thinks I'm gonna get into, you know, trouble. This damned locker . . ." She tried the combination a third time.

"What, like *police* trouble?"

"Oh, I don't know," she said impatiently. "Did they change the damned combination on this locker?" Clenching her teeth, she jerked on the latch a few more times until a hand reached over her shoulder.

"Here," Larry Caine said, his breath warm on her ear, "sometimes you just have to give it a really hard pull like . . . this." He gave it a strong downward jerk, and the locker clattered open.

Mallory looked at Deidre. Her wide-eyed smile was directed over Mallory's shoulder as she hugged her books more tightly to her chest.

"How'd you do that?" Deidre asked.

When Mallory turned around, she caught Larry sweeping his fingers through his golden hair, one side of his mouth cocked up. There were two other guys behind him; one was Randy Scheckley, but the other was new. She didn't care, didn't want to know him, and turned away, taking books from her bag and arranging them in her locker. She knew Deidre's heart was probably doing backflips, but Mallory was merely annoyed. Anyone could have helped her open the locker; why did it have to be Larry Caine?

"Thank you, Larry," she said flatly, slamming the locker.

"No problem." He slipped the fingers of his right hand into the back pocket of his jeans and leaned his elbow on the wall of lockers, trying to get her to look at him. "What class're you going to?"

"My first one." She turned and walked away.

Still hugging her books, Deidre stepped around Mallory as she passed and said, "Hi, Larry." When there was no reply, Mallory heard Deidre say, "Hi . . . Larry?"

Mallory felt his hand on her shoulder and turned. He'd walked away from Deidre without so much as a hello and followed her. His buddies stayed where they were, watching him as they smirked into their palms.

"Hey," he said, "all I get is a 'thank you, Larry'?"

"Okay. Thank you very *much,* Larry." She started to turn away again, but he tightened his grip on her shoulder.

"Wait a sec," he said. "I thought I could, you know, take you out tonight. A movie? Dinner, maybe? At least let me take you to Tiny's."

"No, thank you." She glanced over Larry's shoulder at Deidre, who was rolling her eyes, exasperated with Mallory for turning down yet another opportunity to go out with Larry Caine.

He reached behind his head and rubbed his neck. "Jeez, you know, if you don't want to go out with me, that's one thing, but you could at least be, like, friendly, you know?"

Mallory turned and started down the corridor.

"Still seeing that leather fag?" Larry shouted.

A gust of breath came from Mallory's lungs as she picked up her pace. A few of the students in the hall slowed and turned to Larry, then to Mallory. Her face began to feel hot. She kept walking, hating Larry a bit more with each step for acting as if he was doing a favor by asking her out every few days; she even hated Deidre for being so crazy about him, and for acting as if there was something wrong with Mallory because she didn't feel the same.

"Know what's gonna happen?" Larry went on, louder now that he had an audience. "You're gonna catch some disease from that slug, that's what's gonna happen. You won't be able to *buy* a date then!"

She rounded the corner, trying to get away from the eyes that surrounded her, and away from the sound of Larry Caine's voice. When she felt the tears welling in her eyes, she clenched a fist at her side, angry at herself. There was a side exit up ahead, and she hurriedly dodged a group of girls babbling to one another in Spanish and pushed through the door.

She felt much better on the sidewalk and took a deep breath of the cool air, but the burning sensation in her stomach wouldn't go away.

Mallory and Kevin had been dating for almost a month, and during that time her friends had not given her a moment's peace. "He's five miles of bad road," Deidre had told her, and at first Mallory had been inclined to agree. She hadn't planned to see him more than once or twice.

On their first date, he'd taken her to his garage and played his guitar for her, then handed her a set of headphones and played a demo tape he and his band had made. The music was her first clue that Kevin Donahue was not the guy she'd thought him to be. When he played the guitar, his face tightened, becoming intense and withdrawn, as if he were no longer in the garage with her. As she listened to the tape he paced like an expectant father, awaiting her opinion of the music. He was quietly passionate as he talked about writing songs, and when she told him how much she liked his music, she spotted a glimmer of fierce pride in his dark eyes. He had reason to be proud; the music was dark, angry, and provocative. She'd been very impressed.

His parents and brother had been gone that weekend visiting relatives out of town, so he'd taken her in the house and shared a joint with her, played some records, danced a little. She kept expecting him to make a pass, but he didn't. Until the second record was over.

"Hey," he'd said, taking her hand, "let's fuck."

It was a shock at first, but intriguing. No one had ever come right out and said it like that before. They fooled around a little, but she wouldn't go all the way that night. He'd become so angry, she thought he was going to hit her.

The second time they went out, it was to a movie. She'd expected him to come on to her again and was ready to say yes, but he didn't.

On their third date, he'd taken her up to Mulholland, spread a blanket over a patch of weeds well off the road, and taken off his pants, all without saying a word. When she asked him to be careful because it was her first time, he'd acted as if he hadn't heard her.

It hurt, but it felt pretty damned good, too, especially the way he used his mouth on her. He softly growled obscenities in her ear while he moved inside her.

"You could do so much better," Deidre told her almost every day.

Mallory felt differently. There were guys who dressed better—although Mallory enjoyed the smell of Kevin's scuffed leather jackets—guys who were more popular, better-looking, but none she knew who were as . . . unpredictable as Kevin. They didn't have the edge, the electricity she felt when she was with him.

Okay, she thought, *so they don't have the criminal record Kevin has, either, but that's no big deal.*

He'd been in trouble with the police last year. From what little he said about it, she gathered he'd stolen something. At least it wasn't rape or murder. She couldn't understand what he needed to steal for, though; his parents were definitely not poor.

Maybe that's why, she thought. *Maybe stealing was the only way he felt he could get something on his own, something that wasn't handed to him by his parents.* He didn't talk about his parents often, but when he did, he had nothing good to say.

Beneath his abrasive surface, though, Kevin had a soft side. It was buried deep and she'd only seen glimpses of it a few times, but it was there. And it seemed that maybe, just maybe, it had come out a bit more in the last couple weeks, that maybe she was having an effect on him. Perhaps, with a little time, she could cool the angry fire that seemed to burn in his eyes.

He hadn't said so, and probably wouldn't, but Kevin Donahue *needed* her.

Dating Kevin came with a price, though. The reactions from her friends hurt her, made her feel isolated, cut off, and, most of all, let down. They also made her more determined to stay with him, to show them she wasn't going to knuckle under just because they didn't approve.

That did not, however, diminish the disappointment she felt, as if she'd been betrayed or abandoned.

Her shoulders suddenly felt heavy, and she wanted to talk to Jeff. He always cheered her up when she was down, made her feel better, or at least took her mind off things.

Not this time.

Maybe, she thought, *he can't do it anymore at all. Can't or won't. Maybe those days are over.*

That only made her feel worse.

She stopped at the side entrance to the building and stared for a moment at the door. If she went to class, she would run into Jeff; their first classes were next door to each other. If she didn't, she could get the assignment from Deidre later, and she could go find Kevin.

Mallory picked up her pace as she walked by the door. . . .

Eight

Kevin Donahue opened his eyes and quickly squinted against the sunlight shining through his bedroom window. His headphones were still on, but the music had stopped. He sat up in bed and looked around. Something had awakened him.

"Kevin!" his mother snapped, pounding on the door again. "I have got to go to work now—will you get *up?*"

He took off the headphones and sat on the edge of the bed, staring at the ragged sneakers that were still on his feet. His jeans and T-shirt clung to his skin.

"Kevin?"

"Yeah, I'm coming," he said hoarsely.

He ran his hands through his bushy hair as he stood and stretched. His eyes were bleary with sleep, and he rubbed them hard for a moment, then crossed the room and turned off the stereo.

After dropping Mallory off the night before, he'd come home to his room to write for a while. Music thundering in his head, he quickly jotted down the lyrics of a song he hadn't touched in months. When he finished, he read it over quickly and realized the song was about Mallory. No surprise. He'd never had that much sex in one night. Trevor's brother was gone for the week, and Trevor had lent them his key. It had been a small and sloppy apartment, but it had a big bed.

After finishing the song, Kevin had gone downstairs to the back yard, smoked a joint, and returned to his room to enjoy the high with some music and to relish the lingering, throbbing warmth in his genitals.

He went to his desk and looked at the lyrics of the song again. Sometimes they didn't seem so good the next day. This time, they did. He played the tune in his head, singing the words under his breath.

"Kevin!"

He reached under his shirt and scratched his flat belly, wishing he hadn't fallen asleep.

He opened his bedroom door on his mother, who was standing at the mirror in the hall, tugging her coat into position, turning this way and that, looking at her reflection.

"You know, Kevin," she said, adjusting an earring, "I don't think putting that lock on your door was such a good idea. I've been standing out here knocking on your door for the last ten minutes. If you can't get yourself up when you're supposed to, the lock *goes,* do you understand?"

"I thought you were late for work."

"I am, but I wanted to make sure you were up before I left." She turned to him, running a hand down the side of her shoulder-length ash-blond hair. "Things are going to change this year. You're going to school *every day* unless you're sick, or there will be some serious changes in this house." She spoke quickly and crisply with her face tilted downward, looking up at him from beneath her carefully plucked eyebrows. "Why are you dressed? Did you sleep in your clothes? When did you get home last night?" The questions poured out in one breath as she looked him up and down.

"I fell asleep with 'em on, yeah." He turned away and started down the hall. He could smell bacon frying downstairs.

"Sylvia has breakfast for you downstairs. Cold by now, probably. Get to school today, Kevin. I mean that."

Her voice faded behind him as he went down the stairs wearily, then caught up with him again as she hurried by from behind, saying, "I was supposed to be at the studio five minutes ago, dammit. Your dad's in the kitchen, tell him I had to go." And she was gone, leaving behind an invisible cloud of musky perfume.

As he neared the kitchen Kevin heard his little brother Michael talking. Probably to Sylvia. She'd been their housekeeper and cook for as long as Kevin could remember. He stood at the doorway and saw her pouring a cup of coffee at the counter. She was a short, round woman with graying hair tied in a bun and a smiling, rosy-cheeked face. She nodded as Michael went on about school. He was skipping this year from fifth to seventh grade, and it had been his favorite topic of conversation most of the summer.

On the far side of the kitchen, Kevin's father stood at the bar, the telephone receiver cradled between his ear and shoulder, his hands shuffling through his briefcase as he spoke quietly into the phone. His posture was perfect in his dark suit; his styled brown hair looked appropriately wind-blown resting on his wrinkled forehead. He looked important.

No, no, Kevin corrected himself. *He looks like he thinks he's important.*

Kevin watched them for a while, thinking how distant they seemed from one another. Sylvia was nodding and smiling as Michael spoke but seemed preoccupied. She had a home and a husband, too; there were other things on her mind than the Donahues and their breakfast.

Michael would talk endlessly to anyone who didn't tell him to shut up; it made no difference to him who it was.

And Kevin's father could just as well have been in his office. In a few minutes he would leave in a rush without even noticing that his wife had already gone.

The bacon smelled good, and the marijuana had left him hungry, but Kevin didn't want to be in the kitchen with them. He turned and went back upstairs. In his room, he

62

quickly changed his T-shirt, went to the bathroom, washed his face and brushed his teeth, grabbed his coat, and went back downstairs.

The morning air was cooler than it had been in a while, and the sky was slightly overcast. It seemed summer was finally giving in.

With the visor of his black helmet down over his face, leather jacket zipped up halfway, Kevin sped his motorcycle out of the neighborhood, past the large houses with two-car garages, exquisitely manicured lawns, and ornate mailboxes. He turned right on Ventura and drove out of Encino, past the tall, smoky-glassed building in which his father's law firm was located, and into Sherman Oaks. At Woodman, he took a right and headed for Sam's.

Sam's Stop was a small outdoor diner. Six round-seated stools lined the counter beneath a dirty black-and-white-striped awning at the corner of Woodman and Moorpark. The menu was limited, and the food wasn't great, but the prices were ridiculously low. But price made no difference to Kevin. With the money his parents gave him every week, he could afford to eat in stylish, expensive restaurants three times a day if he wanted, and still have plenty left over.

His mother, a television set designer, was always trying to coax him into hanging out with the sons and daughters of her coworkers.

"Here," she'd say, handing him some money, "why don't you get dressed up and go out? Or go to the country club a couple nights this week. Krystal and Zona—I've told you about them, haven't I?—they go there all the time, and they'd love to meet you. You know, they're reading for parts all over town. It's only a matter of time."

Kevin had no desire to get to know any of them. He knew they were just clones of their parents, who were just like his parents, and he didn't like their company, either.

Kevin preferred the uncomfortable stools of Sam's Stop, the greasy food and the smoke from the grill as it blew in his face. He liked the activity of the street and the sidewalk behind him as he ate and visited with his friends—friends he chose for himself. He liked Sam, too, a wiry sixty-year-old man who hated Los Angeles but stuck around because he couldn't think of any place he hated any less.

As he drove down Woodman Kevin squinted ahead through the smoky haze of his visor to see who was at Sam's this morning.

Sam was standing behind the far end of the counter, his face hidden by the morning paper.

A tall slender person with long platinum hair and sunglasses stood at the opposite end facing the street, elbows on the counter, booted ankles crossed.

As he got closer, slowing down the bike, Kevin looked at the stranger's face. It was narrow with very fair skin, almost porcelain. The mirrored shades rested on high, pronounced cheekbones. Shadows carved hollows in each side of the long face.

Kevin thought, at first, that it was a woman, but as he drew nearer he spotted the bulge of an Adam's apple below the razorlike jaw. He seemed to be watching as Kevin approached, but through the dark glasses it was hard to tell. His hair was short and spiked on top, disappearing behind his shoulders in flowing strands of glaring platinum. The breeze shifted the ruffles that went down the front of his blousy white long-sleeved shirt; it was tucked into the black jeans that clung tightly to his long, narrow legs.

Kevin kept his eyes on the stranger as he pulled his bike up to the curb, watching him inconspicuously through the edge of the visor. The man reached up with his right hand, curled his long and slender fingers around the sunglasses, and slid them off his face.

Kevin froze.

The stranger's smiling eyes seemed to gaze through the visor, straight into Kevin's. He propped his elbow on the counter again and let the glasses dangle from his fingers.

Kevin killed his engine and swung his left leg up off the bike, keeping an eye on the man. As he walked toward Sam Kevin pulled off his helmet and tucked it under one arm. Without moving his head, the man watched Kevin, a slight smile resting on his thin lips.

"Hey, Sam," Kevin said, perching himself on a stool. "How's it hangin'?"

Sam peered over the edge of the paper, a frown crinkling his stringy features.

"This fuckin' city," he growled, crumpling the paper into a heap on the counter.

"What's the matter now?"

"Ah, somebody killed a cop and dumped the body in a garbage bin in North Hollywood. You believe it? Didn't even leave a mark. Just a few bites where the rats nibbled on his corpse."

"I thought you didn't like cops, Sam."

"Don't. Hate 'em. What'll you have, kid?"

"Eggs over easy, bacon, and white toast."

Sam switched on a portable radio that sat on a shelf above the grill; tinny Top 40 music began to rattle from its battered speaker as he cracked open a couple eggs.

Kevin pulled the paper across the counter and scanned the headlines, turning slightly to his right to get a better look at the stranger from the corner of his eye.

He was facing Kevin now, one elbow still propped on the counter. The breeze shifted his spiky platinum bangs back and forth over an arched brow.

"Hey, man, you gotta problem?" Kevin snapped, turning to him suddenly.

The stranger's mouth curled down slightly into a poorly concealed smirk. He shook his head slowly.

"Then what the hell're you staring at me for, huh? Why don't you go stare at somebody else, find a mirror and stare at yourself, okay?"

The smirk disappeared and the lips pursed as he nodded ever so slightly, averting his eyes.

Kevin looked down at the paper again.

"Hey, kid," Sam said over his shoulder as he cooked, "Paco tells me you didn't get that gig at Fantazm. Zat true?"

"Yeah." He hunched over the paper, staring blankly at the small, blurred print. The stranger was making him very uncomfortable, and as hard as he tried, he couldn't pretend the guy wasn't there.

"So what happened, huh?"

"I just haven't talked to the booker yet."

"Thought you knew the guy."

"Sort of. I know his brother-in-law."

"I hear your buddies are pissed at you for not goin' in the other night. Why didn't you?"

Kevin started to reply but realized he didn't know what to say. He squinted at the headlines but did not bring the letters into focus. He couldn't remember exactly why he hadn't gone into Fantazm on Saturday night. He remembered going there . . . crossing the parking lot. . . .

Kevin suddenly got a bad feeling, a tight feeling in his gut like a cramp without the pain. The sizzle of food frying on the grill diminished to a mosquitolike hum as he stared at the newspaper and vaguely, hazily remembered the sky on Saturday night. . . .

The newspaper disappeared beneath a plate of eggs, bacon, and toast that slapped onto the counter with a jarring clunk.

Kevin's head snapped up, and he blinked at Sam.

"Kid," Sam barked, "I asked you how come you never went in?"

"Um . . . I just figured the band wasn't, you know, wasn't ready yet. We need to rehearse a little more."

"Wasn't ready? Jesus Christ, all I hear for a year is 'the band's gotta play, the band's gotta play.' Now you say they wasn't ready? The fuck you waitin' for, kid?"

Kevin began poking at his eggs with his fork; the eggs were runny, and the bacon seemed undercooked. He glanced down the counter.

The stranger was smiling at him.

"Course," Sam went on, the toothpick bobbing up and down between his lips, "I never heard you play, but I figure, shit, the stuff they call music these days"—he cocked a thumb over his shoulder toward the radio—"my dog could bark through a tube and be a fuckin' star."

A large black man lifted himself onto the stool next to Kevin with a throaty grunt and slapped a beefy hand onto the counter.

"Leland!" Sam said with a grin, stepping away from Kevin and wiping his hands on a towel. "The usual?"

Leland nodded with a gravelly mumble.

Kevin was looking at his breakfast but thinking about the

stranger's smile. It had been a pleasant one, the kind of smile you give somebody you haven't seen in a while, the kind of smile you see in airports and bus stations.

Leaning back slightly, Kevin looked around the back of the big man sitting beside him.

The stranger was gone.

Kevin stared for a moment at the empty stool, then took some cash from his jacket pocket.

"You leavin', kid?" Sam blurted. "Without eatin'?"

"I don't feel so well, Sam."

"Jesus. And to think I spent all those years in France goin' to fuckin' chef's school."

Leland cackled and turned, grinning, to Kevin; most of his teeth were gone.

"Hey, Leland," Sam said, "you read the paper yet? This fuckin' city . . ."

Kevin put a five by the plate, took his helmet from the counter as he stood, and turned to look into the mirrored sunglasses of the smiling, platinum-haired stranger.

"You're a musician," the man said, gently fingering the ruffles of his shirt. His voice seemed to come from deep within his chest, soft but resonant. Somehow, he sounded much older than Kevin had thought.

"Yeah, so what?" Kevin snapped, tucking his helmet under one arm.

"I heard you talking with the old man. You have a band?"

"Why?"

His smile grew with amusement. "Because I'm interested. I just got into town, and"—he removed his sunglasses— "I'm a musician, too." His eyes did not squint in the harsh light of the overcast sky; they seemed relaxed and unaffected. They were gold, scattered with flecks of caramel-brown, and the lashes above them were thick and light-colored. "What do you play?"

"Lead guitar." Kevin tried not to stare at his eyes, but it wasn't easy. When the man moved his head and the dull sunlight filtered through his platinum bangs, the lashes seemed to glow, and the caramel flecks appeared to shift about the pupils. "And, um, I sing a little, too. Me and one of the other guys."

"Play any clubs around here?"

Kevin was finally able to look away from him; he put the helmet under his other arm.

"Well, uh . . . not yet. We don't get to rehearse as much as we need to."

"Do you have a place?"

"Garages, when we can get them."

The man nodded and ran the edge of his sunglasses back and forth over his lower lip, his eyes wandering beyond Kevin for a moment. Then he smiled again and held out his right hand.

"My name is Mace."

Kevin took his hand, and they shook. Mace's grip was firm; his long fingers wrapped nearly all the way around Kevin's hand.

"Would it help if you had a place to rehearse?" he asked. "A place you could use whenever you wanted?"

Kevin let go and dropped his hand to his side.

"Why? You got a place?"

"Maybe. It depends."

"On what?"

"Do you write music?"

"Yeah."

"And the band plays only *your* music?"

"Mostly."

"Does the band have a name?"

Kevin glanced at the diner a few yards away. Sam was serving up Leland's breakfast, grumbling about something.

"Look, man, whatta you want?" he asked, looking into Mace's golden eyes again.

Mace held up a long, narrow palm, as if to put him at ease.

"You don't have to be suspicious," he said. "I don't blame you. In fact, I admire that. I just think we might be able to help each other out." He turned and started up the sidewalk toward Ventura at a slow, thoughtful pace.

Kevin fell into step beside him without a thought, his head cocked so he could see the man's face.

"I write music, too," Mace said. "And I sing. I'm not from around here, so I don't know anyone, I have no connections. But I know a few things about music and the business. And I have a large place. A place that would be perfect for rehearsal." He looked at Kevin from the corner of his eye.

"But . . . there's a but, right?"

"I'd want to hear you play first. If you're good, I'd like to join the band. Lead guitar and lead vocal. I would also want to handle the business end."

Kevin stopped, but Mace kept walking. With a slack jaw, he watched the tall man for a moment.

"Who the hell do you—what do you—you mean you just wanna—" He caught up with him, chuckling sarcastically. "You just wanna take over my fucking band?"

"No."

"That's what it sounds like!"

Mace stopped and faced him.

"It would still be *your* band, of course," he said congenially. "But I think you could use some help. And that's what I'm offering."

"And just what would you do to help us?"

He took one step toward Kevin and said, "I would help you shape the band, give it character, personality. I'd get you some work when I felt you were ready." Another step. "I'd help you with the music you wrote and played, make sure it was strong. Powerful." He took one more step. "And, if you let me, I would help you turn this band—"

He slowly lifted his right hand—

"—into a band—"

—raised it above Kevin's head—

"—that would make this valley—"

—and lowered it, his palm on top, his fingers curling down over Kevin's skull like spider's legs.

"—*eat metal.*"

Kevin's eyes were locked onto Mace's, and his head was filled with images of the band playing on a stage, ripping the smoky darkness of a nightclub in half with its loud, rumbling music. A thrill rippled through him when he saw the confidence in Mace's eyes, the faith Mace seemed to have in Kevin's ability to turn the band into something successful, something, as he had said, powerful. It didn't seem to matter that Mace had not yet seen the band play. It was Kevin in whom he had faith, not just the band.

"We have a . . . a demo tape," Kevin said.

Mace took his hand away. "Good. Tonight at seven?"

"Where?"

"There's an abandoned building on Ventura and Whitley. Do you know it?"

"The old health club?"

"Yeah. Bring the others. I'd like to meet them. Come to the parking lot in the rear. I'll let you in."

"Okay. Seven o'clock."

Mace cocked a brow. "You have to trust me. Do you trust me?"

Kevin nodded slowly.

"Good. I'll see you tonight, Kevin."

Kevin watched Mace walk on toward Ventura. The confident swing of his arms made Kevin think this stranger was someone important. It seemed more obvious now than it had at first.

As Mace rounded the corner and walked out of sight Kevin felt something building inside him, something he couldn't identify at first but soon recognized as a sense of accomplishment, as if a bridge had been crossed, a doorway passed through. He felt as if he'd done a good thing, a *great* thing, although he'd done nothing at all. He still didn't know what Mace had in mind for the band, but he felt good about it.

Something was about to happen, he could feel it. Something positive that would change things for him, make everything okay. He felt excited as he went back to his motorcycle and slipped on his helmet. He knew the others would be skeptical, maybe even angry with him for not consulting them first.

Consult them about what? he thought. He'd agreed to nothing yet, signed nothing, made no deals. *Fuck 'em.*

As he started his bike with a roar Kevin realized Mace had called him by name.

But he couldn't remember introducing himself. . . .

Nine

J.R. went to the end of the hall in the counseling center and poured himself another cup of coffee, then headed back to his office. He met Faye Beddoe in the hall.

"So," she said, her voice thick with a smoky Jamaican accent, "how is the new boy on the block?" Faye seemed to fill the hall; she stood six feet tall and had big bones and skin as black as night. Her long hair was tied in a bun, and a red sweater draped her shoulders. At fifty, she was a strikingly handsome woman. The moment he met her, J.R. knew he would have enjoyed high school more if she had been his counselor.

"Okay so far," he said.

"You have a full schedule today?"

"Yeah. Next appointment's in about five minutes. A girl named Nikki Astin."

Faye's smile melted from her face, and she pulled her head back slowly, frowning. "Oh?" she said quietly. "They let her out this year, eh?"

"Let her *out?*"

Faye's laugh was deep and musical, and her whole body moved with it as she put a reassuring hand on his shoulder.

"Just ragging you, boy," she said through her laughter. "Never met the girl, I'm sure she's an angel." She laughed at that, too. "I'll let you get to it. Perhaps I'll see you at lunch." She walked away, tugging her sweater around her shoulders a little tighter. "You feel a chill in here, or is it just my imagination?"

"Yeah," he said, still smiling, "it's a little nippy. Summer's over."

"Ah, yes," Faye agreed, almost grimly. "Summer is over."

J.R.'s small office had a desk, two chairs, a metal file cabinet, and one window that faced the parking lot. He'd pinned up a few of his favorite "Far Side" cartoons and a poster of Sylvester Stallone in ballerina garb titled "Rocky Tutu." Nothing too stuffy; he wanted to make the kids comfortable.

During the minutes that remained before his next appointment, he sipped his coffee and thumbed through Nikki Astin's file.

Her grades were not good, to say the least. Two years ago she'd been held back a grade and had gone to three special education classes. Her parents had been divorced four years earlier, and according to the records, there had been a custody battle, which Mrs. Astin had won.

"Mr. Haskell?" a breathy, timid voice asked.

J.R. stood with a smile and said, "Nikki Astin? Come in, have a seat."

She filled his office with the aroma of White Shoulders perfume and grape bubble gum. A surprisingly conservative gray skirt and black blazer failed to hide her voluptuous curves, although the suit displayed very little of her smooth, tanned skin. Her full brown hair was pulled into a ponytail; she wore no jewelry and a conspicuously small amount of makeup. She sat with her knees together, her posture rigid, and her hands folded neatly over the notebook on her lap.

"First of all," he said, "you can call me J.R. I don't feel much like a Mr. Haskell." He tucked her records back into the file folder. "How has your first day gone so far, Nikki?"

"Fine. I've had two classes already. American History and Music Appreciation."

"Music Appreciation, that's good. Have a good summer?"

Her smile expanded into a warm grin. "Oh, yeah," she said. "I had a wonderful summer." Her entire demeanor changed; she relaxed in the chair a bit, and her eyes seemed brighter as she nodded with enthusiasm.

"Great. What did you do?"

She was hesitant for a moment, sucking her lips between her teeth.

"I accepted Jesus Christ as my personal savior," she said, nearly in a whisper.

Don't lose the smile, J.R. told himself firmly, not wanting to put her off. He took a long, slow sip of his coffee. J.R. had not entered a church or opened a Bible since he'd left his father's house at the age of eighteen. He'd had a few born-again students in Santa Rosa, but as a teacher, he hadn't needed to deal with their spiritual beliefs as he would in a counseling position. He was determined not to allow Nikki's beliefs to influence his relationship with her. But whenever someone started talking religion, J.R. heard his father's soft, resigned voice and imagined his sister's swollen corpse hanging at the end of a rope. . . .

"Mmm," he said, touching a knuckle to his lips, "when did that happen?"

"When I joined the Calvary Youth. Have you heard of us?"

"I'm afraid not."

She put a hand on his desk and leaned forward, saying, as if she were reading the words from a book, "We're a group of Valley teenagers who have dedicated our lives to Jesus Christ and His work."

"Well, that's . . . good. It sounds like a, um, worthwhile organization. Do you have any literature or—"

She quickly opened her notebook and removed a pamphlet, handing it to him with a smile. "I helped design these."

J.R. glanced over it briefly. "And who's in charge of your group?"

"Reverend James Bainbridge."

Something about her changed when she said the man's name. It was subtle, but obvious enough for J.R. to notice. Her eyes seemed to pull out of focus for just an instant, the lids became heavy, perhaps, and her mouth pulled downward slightly. Trying to be inconspicuous, he picked up a pen and jotted the name down on the pamphlet.

"Can I keep this?"

"Oh, please. Are you interested? I mean, the group is made up of teenagers, but we hold meetings for anyone who wants to come. Every Wednesday night."

"Well, I'm sure you—"

His phone purred softly.

"Yes?"

"There's a Mrs. Donahue on line one."

"I'm with a student right now, Miss Tucker."

"I tried to tell her that, but she insists it's important. She says you're her son's counselor. Um, Kevin Donahue?"

"All right, thank you." He turned to Nikki and said, "Hold on just a second, here." When he was connected, Mrs. Donahue was speaking to someone else in a loud, impatient voice.

"—don't care how much he said it would cost, I'm telling you, Fran, it won't work!"

"Uh, Mrs. Donahue?"

"Yes, I'm sorry, Mr. Haskell? This is Renee Donahue. You probably know my son, Kevin—they told me at the desk that you're his counselor—and I thought you would be the best person to speak with."

"Well, I'm pretty busy at the moment, so it'll have to be quick."

"I'm at work, too, which is one of the reasons I'm calling. Last year, Kevin had a real problem with attendance."

"How do you mean?"

"He never went to school! My husband and I both work, we're very busy, and we can't watch him every minute. I thought maybe you could keep an eye out. He's promised me he'll do better this year, but I don't know. If you could just see if he's been there today, maybe give me a call this evening or tomorrow—"

"Mrs. Donahue, let me make a suggestion. Usually, in

situations like this, I think it's best if you and your husband and Kevin met with me. The four of us could talk about—"

"I don't have time for that, Mr. Haskell. If I did, I wouldn't have to call you."

J.R. sighed. "Okay, Mrs. Donahue. According to my calendar, I have an appointment with Kevin, um, this afternoon. If he doesn't show up, I'll let you know. All right?"

"Leave a message with our housekeeper. I probably won't be home."

"I'll do that." He tore a page from a notepad on his desk, inadvertently showing his annoyance with the woman; he tore it so hard that the pad flipped off the edge of the desk. "Can I have your number?"

"You don't have that information?"

He sighed again. "Just in case, Mrs. Donahue."

After hanging up, he took a deep breath and turned to Nikki with a smile. "Sorry to take up your time like that. Now, why don't you let me see your schedule."

Her eyebrows rose. "I was supposed to bring my schedule?"

"Uh . . . yeah. See, I need to look it over and make sure you've got all the classes you need. Can you get it? I mean, is it in your locker?"

"It's in my locker, but I'm sure it's okay, Mr. Has—I mean, J.R."

"Oh, it probably is, but I'd like to—"

"I prayed about it."

"—take a look at it just . . . I'm sorry?"

"Before I organized my schedule, I prayed about it. The reverend says that everything in our lives is important to Jesus, including a class schedule."

J.R. took another sip of coffee.

"Well, Nikki, if you don't mind, I'd like to take a quick look anyway."

"No, I don't mind. I'll be right back."

While she was out, J.R. read through the pamphlet. He looked at the blurred illustrations and read the scripture quotes, and the more he read about the Calvary Youth, the less he liked it. . . .

Ten

At lunchtime, Kevin drove to school and found Mallory in the cafeteria with several of her friends. When he patted her shoulder and gestured for her to come with him, he felt the disapproving glares of the others. Mallory took her tray and followed him to another table.

As she ate Kevin explained that he couldn't see her after school but would pick her up at her place around six. He told her he'd met someone who wanted to help the band get some work and that they were to meet with him that night.

"An agent?" she asked, touching his hand, her face brightening with excitement.

"Not really. I'm not even sure he can help us."

"Yeah, but he wants to! That's something. What does he do?"

"Well, I'm not sure."

He could be a fucking escaped convict, for all I know, Kevin thought bitterly, frustrated by his inability to explain why he was so certain Mace could give the band the support it needed. How could he explain something for which there was no solid, logical reason?

"He knows what he's talking about, though," Kevin went on. "I can . . . well, I can feel it."

"Kevin, that is so cool! That's fantastic!" She handed him a celery stick from her tray and said, "I told you, someday someone will see how talented you are."

He stayed a few minutes more, then stood and looked at the other table. When he was sure Mallory's friends were watching, he put his hand behind her head, leaned forward, and pulled her face to his, kissing her hard and briefly cupping one breast with his hand. He laughed as he left the cafeteria, feeling good.

Kevin spent the first half of the afternoon tracking down the others in the band. They all agreed to meet him at Trevor's brother's apartment at six-thirty sharp. When they asked him why, he simply replied, "It's about the band."

He stopped at a gas station, rolled a joint in the restroom, and took a few tokes as he sat on the toilet. He wanted to get in and out of the house before either of his parents got home. They would rag him if they saw him leaving so soon after getting home; they'd want to know where he was going and with whom. He usually lied to them, but tonight he didn't even want to deal with them. They would be especially upset if they knew he was doing something for the band.

"If you'd get serious about music and study it," his father often said, "maybe you could make something of it. But this garage band nonsense isn't going to get you anywhere."

They didn't understand how he could love his music so much when he couldn't read or write a note. They wouldn't listen when he tried to explain that the melodies formed in his head and, once they were there, never went away. He put the lyrics on paper as they came to him and then played the songs for the band until they worked out their parts. It wasn't conventional, but it worked, and Kevin thought they were pretty damned good.

His parents had never heard them play.

It was a little after four when Kevin turned off of Ventura Boulevard in Encino. He was feeling just fine. The pot massaged his brain, and he looked forward to his meeting with Mace.

A soft voice deep inside him whispered, *But you don't know who the fuck this guy is, what he wants from you, why he's—*

Kevin silenced the voice.

Do you trust me? Mace had asked.

Yes. He did. He would, anyway.

He needed to.

Kevin saw his mother's BMW parked in the drive. As he went to the front door he braced himself for the quiz he would get about his first day at school.

She was talking on the phone in the kitchen. From the tone of her voice, he could tell she was upset.

Trying to avoid her completely, Kevin hurried up the stairs and met Michael in the hall.

"Boy, is Mom pissed at you," the boy said with a grin. "You're up shit creek."

"Fuck off," Kevin snapped, brushing by him. He came to a lurching halt at his bedroom.

The door was gone.

"What . . . in the . . ." He stepped into the room. Some of his dresser drawers were half open. The closet light was on, and a box had been taken down from the top shelf and emptied.

Michael laughed in the hall.

Anger burned in Kevin's throat like bile. His vision blurred until he had to swipe his hand over his eyes to see.

"Your father's coming," his mother said.

He spun around and faced her in the doorway. Her face was streaked with tears.

"I called him," she went on, "and he said he would—"

"What the hell is this?" he screamed, waving his arms around.

"You didn't go to school today, and I told you—"

"How the fuck do you know?"

"I talked to your counselor. You didn't show up for your appointment, and—"

"So what? That doesn't mean I didn't—"

"—I called attendance, and they said you hadn't been to any—"

"Don't you have anything better to do with your fucking time? Jesus Christ, I thought you had to work!"

Tears came to his eyes as he looked around the room again.

"Where have you been getting the drugs?" she asked, sounding suddenly angry.

He opened his bottom drawer. The plastic bag of marijuana that had been there that morning was gone. He stood and kicked the drawer closed. Slamming his fist on the dresser, he screamed, "Who the fuck do you think you are?"

"Kevin, I warned you. I said there would be changes unless you cleaned up your act. You haven't. So we're cleaning it up for you."

He began pulling drawers out, tossing them to the floor and kicking them.

"Stop it, Kevin, *stop!*"

He slowly turned to her, his back stiff.

She was fingering the gold chain around her neck, her hand trembling, her chest rising and falling quickly, her mouth a straight line twitching at the corners. Her makeup was smeared around her eyes, and her hair was mussed.

"Now listen to me," she said in a low, unsteady voice, her lips hardly moving as she spoke. "If you want to live here, if you want us to support you, you're going to go to school every day, get passing grades, and, most of all, you will follow the rules set down in this house. We haven't had any rules here, I know, and that's been a big mistake, but we have them now, and the first one is there will be no drugs . . . in this . . . house. If you want to do that when you're on your own, fine, but—"

Kevin began searching the scattered drawers for the demo tape.

"—listen to me, you will not do that sort of thing while . . . Kevin, what are you doing?"

The tape was beneath a stack of underwear. He swept it up in his hand and faced her, growling, "I'm getting the fuck out of this shithole!"

"Kevin, your father is coming, and we're going to talk about—"

He stepped around her and left the room, but she followed him down the hall.

"Kevin!" she called through an angry sob. "If you don't shape up, you're not staying in this house. There are places we can send you to, places that will keep you until you learn how to—"

"Shut up!" he cried, hurrying down the stairs. His mouth was dry, his voice hoarse and ragged, and he hated himself for the tears in his eyes. "Just shut the fuck up!" He burst through the front door and jogged down the walk to his motorcycle at the curb. He took his helmet off the seat and put it on, ignoring his mother as she called him from the porch.

The bike's engine drowned her voice. Slapping his visor down, he looked at her through the darkly tinted plastic.

Her face was a twisted mask of anger. The runny makeup in her tears looked like bruised, melting flesh as she waved an arm toward him, her mouth silently opening and closing and curling furiously around her teeth.

Kevin had never felt such hate.

He drove his motorcycle over the curb, across the sidewalk, and onto the front lawn, where he spun a fast figure eight, kicking up dirt and patches of green, well-tended grass.

As he sped onto the road away from the house he screamed his anger into the shiny black helmet on his head.

Eleven

Pale moonlight shone through the window of Reverend James Bainbridge's motel room on Pico Boulevard in Los Angeles as he lay in bed, praying in advance for his Lord's understanding and forgiveness. The room was dark except for the sliver of light that came from beneath the bathroom door. The shower was hissing on the other side.

He'd come over the hill this time to avoid any chance of being discovered. The time before last, the first time, had been unexpected and had taken place in his bedroom in the Calvary Youth House. He'd sworn that it wouldn't happen again. But it had. And now it was happening a third time.

He felt like crying tears of shame, and at the same time he was trembling with anticipation.

She was a slow girl, but kind and loving. Calvary Youth had been good for her. She was one of the group's most enthusiastic members, happy to share her new-found beliefs with everyone around her, not caring how they treated her in return, how they might laugh or ridicule.

Bainbridge wondered if their relationship might have long-lasting negative effects on her. He prayed that it wouldn't.

Then stop it, he told himself.

But he couldn't. He was a lonely man, hungry for affection. It was a part of himself that he hated but could not ignore.

Bainbridge had been born on the road and had spent his first eighteen years traveling with the Meredith Brothers Carnival with his parents. Growing up, Bainbridge gambled with the other carnies, learned to drink hard and often, and went on troublemaking binges in the towns they passed through. He developed quite a love affair with whiskey—not only its effects, but its taste. On the rare occasion when whiskey was not available, he would drink something else—vodka, gin, even beer—but in his mind, he tasted whiskey. The word *alcoholic* was not in his vocabulary then; everyone he knew, including his father, drank just as heavily, if not more so. Then, in Ely, Nevada, he met Reverend Mortimer Bigley, a massive, silver-haired circuit preacher. For a week, Bigley took him under his ample wing, inviting him to participate in the meetings, even feeding him hot meals and subtly beginning the process of weaning him from liquor, finally convincing him to leave the carnival and join up with the traveling tent revival. It wasn't an easy decision; the carnival was the only life he'd ever known. In meeting Bigley, however, an emptiness Bainbridge had hardly been aware existed in himself had been filled. When he told his parents of his newly adopted convictions and his decision to leave, they laughed.

"Aw, Christ," his father sneered, "he's found Gaaawwd!"

Bainbridge neither saw nor heard from his parents again.

As he traveled with Bigley's revival Bainbridge met a lot of other teenagers who seemed to have the same emptiness in their lives that he'd had. It was then that he noticed the need for someone to reach out exclusively to young people, and he planned to do just that.

On the road with Bigley, Bainbridge had learned a lot. One weekend, during a break between revivals, Bigley had disappeared from the motel they were staying in. He left a note saying he'd be back in a day or so, and ten dollars for food. He returned two days later. Bainbridge found him in the room staring out the window, hands folded over his enormous belly. He appeared lost in thought but turned to Bainbridge and smiled. When he asked Bigley where he'd been, the man replied, "I've been away." Then, after a moment of silence, and with a tear in his eye, Bigley said, "Son, always remember that God knows everything you do, and you can't hide anything from Him. But He also understands more than we sometimes give Him credit for understanding. Like the needs of a lonely man. He understands, and I believe . . . I hope . . . He forgives."

Bainbridge had not understood him at the time, but he did now.

The shower stopped in the bathroom. There was rustling behind the door, then the knob turned. As the door opened the bathroom light went out, and she stepped toward the bed, her body clean and naked, beads of moisture clinging to her round breasts and sparkling in the moonlight. When she reached beneath the covers and touched him, he grew dizzy and began praying silently again, asking for forgiveness over and over as he spoke her name.

"Nikki . . . oh, Nikki . . ."

Twelve

So far, the evening had been very unsettling for Mallory.

First of all, something was wrong with Kevin. He'd been silent since he had picked her up; silent and brooding. He was being very secretive about this meeting place, too, and she didn't like that. At Phil's apartment, he didn't tell anyone where they were going, only that they were to follow him.

Before leaving the apartment, she'd quietly asked him what was wrong. He replied only with a silent, vague shake of his head, and she knew not to ask again.

When Kevin drove his bike behind the darkened, empty building on Ventura, Mallory began to regret coming. Surely no one legitimate would agree to meet at such a place.

As he got out of his Toyota Trevor sneered, "Wow, we've really hit the big time now, huh, guys?"

The others laughed at his sarcasm but stopped when they saw the angry glare on Kevin's face.

"Shut the fuck up or leave," Kevin said. "And if you leave, you're out of the band."

The heels of Kevin's boots clicked on the pavement as he walked to the back of the building.

"You're early," someone said as the rear entrance rattled open. When the door was fully open, Mallory saw him.

He was silhouetted against the glow of candlelight, which hid his face, but she was certain his eyes were looking into hers.

He stepped outside and let the door swing half-closed behind him as she and Kevin and the others approached.

"I like people who are early," he said. "It shows ambition."

"I brought the tape," Kevin said, reaching into his coat pocket.

"We'll get to that," the man said. "Come inside."

Mallory tensed and took a step back. Something was wrong; she could feel it like a gust of cold Arctic wind that cut to the marrow. She took Kevin's hand and squeezed it tightly. The conversation around her seemed garbled, as if her ears were stuffed with cotton. She started to tell Kevin she didn't want to stay and she *especially* didn't want to go into that building because she had a prickly feeling at the back of her neck, like when she was a little girl and her father took her to Disneyland, where she chickened out seconds before entering the Haunted Mansion because she knew it was going to be scary inside, scary as hell, and she didn't want to be that scared, but then Kevin snapped, "Shut up!" and she closed her mouth.

A siren howled mournfully in the distance.

"No reason to shout, Kevin," the man said calmly. He stepped forward into the hazy glow cast by a street light and smiled at them. It was a warm and welcoming smile, and Mallory felt some of the tension in her neck melt away. She almost smiled back.

Almost. Not quite.

"You must be Mallory," he said pleasantly, taking her hand.

She smiled; the gracious gesture was so unexpected, she almost laughed.

"I'm Mace. And there's no reason for you to be nervous."

Kevin introduced Trevor, Mark, Perry, and Steve, and Mace greeted each of them warmly.

"Let's go inside," he said, holding the door open as they filed in.

Though more relaxed than a moment before, Mallory was still hesitant. When she paused at the door, Kevin took her arm and pulled her inside.

It was stuffy and dark in the building; candlelight flickered through a couple of the doorways that lined the corridor ahead, and shadows danced like dark ghosts all around them.

"Did you buy this place?" Mark asked.

Mace replied, "I own it," as he closed the door behind them and locked it. He stepped into one of the rooms for a moment, then returned holding a candle. Above the flame, the features of his narrow face seemed to writhe over his skull as if small, restless insects were crawling beneath his pale skin. Mallory's fear returned in an instant, pulling her with an almost tangible force back to the door, but Kevin held her arm until Mace spoke again, and her unease left as quickly as it had returned.

"Let's go downstairs," he said happily. He led them down the corridor and around a corner, the light of his candle squirming through the darkness, to a staircase that seemed to spiral down to nowhere.

Their feet clattered on the metal stairs as they followed Mace to the room below.

Jeff hated himself as he parked his mother's car on Whitley and killed the engine. When he rolled down the window, he heard laughter echoing from the hidden parking lot behind the abandoned building.

After school that day, Mallory had met Jeff at the car. She said that she wasn't meeting Kevin after all and needed a ride home. In the car, she told Jeff that Kevin had met someone who wanted to give the band exposure, and that she was going to go with him to see the guy that night. Her mood had changed drastically since that morning; she couldn't sit still in the seat as she excitedly talked about what that night's meeting could mean for Kevin's band.

"They might get some club work," she said, "so you could come see them play. You'll love Kevin's music, Jeff, really," she added quickly, touching his arm and bouncing slightly in the seat. "He's incredible on the guitar, and he's never had a lesson! He loves music—I mean, he's *passionate* about it, you know—it means more to him than anything, and this might—God, I hope so—give him the chance to, like, prove it, you know? Prove that there really is something he works hard at and does well."

Her excitement and enthusiasm nibbled at his insides with sharp teeth. Somewhere deep inside himself, Jeff recognized the feeling as jealousy but wouldn't admit it to himself. He never did.

"Where are you meeting this guy?" he asked.

"I don't know. Kevin's picking me up at six. The guy told him to bring his girlfriend," she added with an almost bashful smile.

It didn't occur to Jeff to follow them until a half hour before Kevin was to arrive. Something about this meeting—

The guy told him to bring his girlfriend.

—didn't sound quite right to Jeff. He left the apartment at five-forty and waited in the car until Kevin picked Mallory up, then followed them at a distance, silently chastising himself as he drove.

They'd gone to an apartment just off Chandler first. Jeff parked across the street and several yards down the block. The building was run-down and not very well lighted, and it definitely did not look like a building in which a mover and shaker in the music business would live. Less than ten minutes later, Jeff was ready to go back home and try to forget he'd been so petty as to follow Mallory like some cheap private detective when he'd spotted them leaving. Kevin and Mallory were followed by four guys in a beat-up old Toyota Corolla.

Jeff had started the car, still halfheartedly intending to drive home and study.

But he couldn't.

When they drove into the darkened rear parking lot of the old burnt-out health club, Jeff turned onto Whitley and parked at the curb, almost, but not quite, glad he'd come.

The lot was surrounded by a fence of tall, thick shrubbery, preventing a view of the lot from the street. The only entrance was in the front on Ventura.

The parking lot was a favorite spot to park, drink, smoke some grass, and make out. Jeff wondered if Mallory had lied to him or if Kevin had lied to her. It seemed pretty obvious that there would be no meeting here about getting club work for Kevin's band.

Whatever they're going to do, he warned himself, *you don't want to see it, do you?*

He remembered his dream. All those groping hands and bobbing heads . . .

Do you . . . ?

Jeff got out of the car, quietly closed the door, and headed for the parking lot entrance. . . .

It was difficult to tell how large the room was because of the poor lighting and blackened walls, but it seemed vast. At the foot of the stairs, Mallory looked around, waiting for her eyes to adjust to the shifting glow that came from kerosene lanterns positioned about the room.

"This is the pool room," Mace said. The room's acoustics gave his voice a hollow, empty sound. Pointing with a long index finger, he said, "The pool is over there, and beyond that wall, or what's left of it, is the racquetball court."

Dripping water plinked monotonously.

The still air was cool and damp.

Mace's feet crunched over the littered floor as he led them deeper into the room, saying, "I've got some cushions over here. Let's get comfortable."

As she walked with the others, taking cautious steps, Mallory heard a thick, moist squeak in the darkness and spun around.

Lanterns glowed and shadows oozed over the walls, but she saw nothing more.

Mace led them along the edge of the rectangular swimming pool. Mallory looked into it but couldn't see the bottom; it seemed to drop into a cold darkness so black it might have been tangible. After a moment, she turned away; it frightened her.

"Here," Mace said, putting the candle on a crate beside one of the lanterns. Several fat pillows and cushions were set up in a half circle facing the light. Mace settled on one of the cushions with his back to the crate.

Mallory, Kevin, and the others stood by the cushions uncertainly.

"Go ahead," Mace said genially with a short gesture of his hand, "make yourselves comfortable."

They shuffled around one another until each had found a seat.

Mace held a small pipe to his lips, lit a butane lighter, and held the flame over the bowl. Mallory hadn't seen him take the pipe from a pocket and wondered if he'd held it all along. He inhaled deeply, held it, then blew the smoke out slowly. Its odor was similar to that of marijuana, but sweeter, almost syrupy. He passed the pipe to Mark, who seemed hesitant.

"You've never had shit like this before," Mace said, still exhaling puffs of smoke with his words.

The pipe made its way around the half circle. When Steve handed it to Mallory, she shook her head and passed it on to Kevin.

"No, no, try some," Mace insisted gently.

Mallory wanted to remain alert; she was too uncomfortable in the building to get high and relax.

"I don't think so," she said.

Kevin put his mouth to her ear and whispered, "Do some, dammit."

Usually grass made her cough, but this went down smoothly, massaging her throat like honey. By the time Kevin took the pipe from her, Mallory was feeling its effects. She'd only taken in a little, just to please Kevin, but even that little bit was too much. The darkness began to seem pleasant, almost comforting; the glow of candlelight became a balm to her eyes, and the shadows it cast became a visual sound—

I didn't take much, she thought.

—that filled her with a soothing, imperceptible, bone-deep thrum.

Just a little drag, not as much as the others.

When she looked at Mace, she thought he was glowing, but soon she realized it was only the light from the candle and lantern behind him. It framed his dark shape with a soft aura.

"Um, here's the . . ." Kevin mumbled, offering the cassette to Mace.

Through the pleasant haze that clung to the inside of her skull, Mallory realized she'd never seen Kevin so ill at ease, so unsure of himself.

Mace took the tape, then watched them for a moment, silently, as if he were waiting for something.

"Oh, yeah," Trevor whispered, half to himself, "I almost forgot." He took a hand-sized tape player from one coat pocket and a small set of headphones from the other, handing them to Mace.

As Mace put on the headphones, Kevin said, "Uh, the songs on that tape were—"

"Let it speak for itself," Mace said, starting the tape.

Mallory could vaguely hear the music, like the whine of a mosquito flying around her ear.

"Hey," Mark whispered, "isn't he gonna tell us what he wants to—"

"Quiet," Kevin snapped.

Even in the darkness, Kevin's glare was strong enough to shut Mark up.

Mace leaned back a bit as he listened.

The others were silent, waiting.

The room was still.

Until Mallory heard another wet, sticky squeak and the gentle whisper of movement in the darkness. . . .

When Jeff got to the parking lot, they were gone.

He stood at the corner of the building and stared at the motorcycle and Toyota parked side by side facing the wall of bushes. Turning to the building, Jeff squinted to see through the night.

They couldn't have gone inside; there were boards over all the windows and chains and locks on all the doors.

All but one.

The main rear entrance was unboarded and unchained. He approached slowly, setting his feet down softly, trying to be quiet, although he wasn't quite sure why; it was pretty obvious there was no one around to hear him.

When he tried the door, gently tugging on it, he found it securely locked.

He looked around again, turning a complete circle to see if he might have missed them the first time.

"Mallory?" His voice was little more than a breath.

He stood in the lot a few moments longer, then headed back the way he'd come, thinking it was none of his damned business what Mallory did anyway. . . .

Just the grass, Mallory thought again. Sometimes marijuana made her ears ring. *That's all it is.*

But there was more movement in the darkness, closer than before.

"Kevin . . ."

"Shh."

Again. The squeak was louder, closer, but there was another that seemed farther away, and a third that came from behind her.

"Kevin, did you hear—"

"I said shut up!" he hissed.

Mallory closed her eyes tight. Rubbing them hard with her knuckles, she took a deep breath, trying to rise above the effect of the grass.

What if it wasn't grass?

Shaking her head with a jerk, she looked around at the others. They were hunched forward on their cushions watching Mace as if he were a television set, their lips slightly parted.

Mace had not moved. His head was still cocked back, his arms at his sides. The light shimmered brightly through his hair.

The first movement Mallory spotted was on the floor to Mace's left. It was so small that for an instant Mallory thought perhaps she hadn't seen it at all.

Until it happened again.

Mallory stiffened, and her hand found Kevin's thigh.

Something's wrong here, she thought, her mind a little—but not much—clearer. *Something's big-time wrong, major wrong, we shouldn't—*

Something else moved in the darkness at Mace's right.

—shouldn't be down here, this is uncool, something's—

Two pinpoints of light eased toward Mace. The moment Mallory saw them, blinders seemed to fall from her eyes, and she saw others, many others; tiny spots of sparkling light shifting in the darkness like fireflies, except they weren't fireflies. She knew *exactly* what they were.

Jesus Christ my God everywhere they're everywhere and they're—

Eyes.

—moving closer my God why did I come why did I come?

Her hand closed hard over Kevin's thigh, and he jerked his leg away as if annoyed.

She saw the glow of an ember in the pipe's bowl as Perry took another hit without taking his eyes from Mace, who was still sitting up straight, head back, but with his arms held out at his sides a bit more, his left hand only inches away from the nearest pair of glittering eyes, which moved a little closer until the thing was able to climb onto his hand and ease its way up his arm, a fat lump of darkness the size of a loaf of bread. It crawled to his shoulder, where, against the light, it became an indistinguishable hump on Mace's back. As it moved Mallory made out a rough shape: small ears first, then the squat head that slowly turned as it made a sound like a jagged bone being dragged across a chalkboard.

When she saw reflected candlelight flicker on two rows of small pointed teeth, Mallory raised a hand to her mouth and screamed. . . .

Jeff whirled around at the corner of the building.

It sounded like a scream, but it was so faint it could have come from anywhere. He faced the building again, looking at the securely nailed boards and the chains fastened with padlocks.

Only the main entrance was uncovered.

He returned to the door and tried it again. It jiggled slightly but did not open, as if bolted on the other side.

That probably meant someone was in the building.

He heard the scream again. . . .

"Wh-what are th-they?" Mallory stuttered, closing her eyes. She didn't want to see those eyes anymore.

"Just pets. They're harmless."

Something touched her arm, and Mallory jerked back, opening her eyes. Mace was leaning forward, offering her the pipe.

"Here. Have some more."

"I I don't th-think so, I . . ."

The thing was no longer on his shoulder.

Mace pressed the pipe and lighter into her hand, then leaned back. It was curled in his lap, and he stroked it gently.

Mallory turned away from Mace and reluctantly took another hit. It tasted even better this time, and she took a third.

"You have some more, too, Trevor," Mace said. "Don't be shy, there's plenty."

Mallory handed the pipe to Trevor, then sank deeper into her cushion. She closed her eyes, listening to the voices and enjoying the high.

"You're good," Mace said, taking off the headphones. "Very good. I'm impressed. Does the band have a name?"

Kevin said, "Well, we haven't decided yet, but we were thinking about Candy From Strangers. . . ."

"Mmm. And you've never played any local clubs?"

"No."

"No one has heard you play?"

"Well . . . a couple friends."

"I'd like to—go ahead, Kevin, have some more and pass it around—I'd like to help you. Help you develop an image, get some work, put together some songs. Nothing wrong with what you've got here, nothing at all. But to start, you need something that's going to hit hard, catch them by surprise. And you need a name."

Mace was silent for such a long moment that Mallory opened her eyes.

"Crucifax," he whispered.

The word was softly echoed by the others as they tried it out.

"I'm willing to do everything I can for you," Mace went on, "and I can do quite a lot."

"What'll it cost us?" Kevin asked.

"Not a cent. But it won't be free."

Mallory looked around at all of them. Mace was still talking, mostly to Kevin, but his words became an aural blur as she brought her eyes into focus—

". . . some songs I've written . . . music with power . . ."

—able to center her attention on no more than one thing at a time.

The guys were all leaning toward Mace, watching him intensely as he spoke—

". . . of our group like a brotherhood . . ."

—their hands in their laps, moving slowly back and forth, back and forth, and at first—

". . . requires loyalty and devotion and trust . . ."

—she thought they were masturbating, but that was silly, so silly she almost giggled. But they weren't doing that, they were stroking, all right, but they were stroking—

". . . think of this place as your home . . ."

—black lumps that were curled up in their laps and when she turned to Kevin—

". . . of me as your friend . . ."

—she blinked again and again, hoping she was not actually seeing the thing that seemed to be hunched on his shoulder facing her—

". . . and I promise you . . ."

—with fierce golden eyes and two small tusks protruding from its lower jaw—

". . . we . . ."

—and she sucked in a deep breath, wanting desperately, more than she'd ever wanted anything before, to scream—

". . . will own . . ."

—but the breath left her lungs without a sound and when

she tried to stand, to move away from Kevin, she couldn't her body would not obey her mind, and she closed her eyes over burning tears, folded her arms across her stomach and leaned forward into a ball, a sniffling, rocking ball.

". . . this valley."

Jeff found a gap between two boards nailed over a window and peered through it, cupping his hands to his eyes. He saw dim light; someone was in there.

He looked around the parking lot again just to make sure he was not being watched, then curled his fingers around the board and pulled hard.

The nails creaked, strained.

He pulled again and again until one end of the board came free and then the other.

The board clattered to the pavement, and the sound ricocheted through the night like a bullet, making him wince.

Jeff put his face to the opening left by the board. He listened for voices, another scream, anything. But what he heard was not human.

Something scuttled over the floor beneath the window and made a belchlike squeaking noise.

Rats? he thought.

He gripped the next board and began pulling, but the noise inside increased, and he stopped to listen.

More of them.

He pulled the second board away and eased it to the ground, catching a whiff of the stuffy air inside, almost backing away, almost leaving.

Instead, Jeff leaned his head into the window.

"Mallory."

She felt his hand on her neck, his wrist on her shoulder, and lifted her eyes to him.

Mace was standing beside her, bending down slightly and smiling.

"What's wrong?"

"I'm . . ." She looked at the others in the dark, holding those things, petting them as if they were puppies. Kevin even seemed to be smiling, enjoying himself. Maybe not; it was dark. "I'm scared."

"Mmm, too much smokes."

"I want to go. Now."

"Where? Home?"

She nodded.

"You like it at home?"

The words were whispered so quietly, Mallory knew only she could hear them. She slowly looked up at him again but didn't reply.

"You don't seem to me to be a very happy girl," he went on. "I'd guess home isn't such a cool place to be."

Mallory didn't reply. She didn't feel the need to say anything; his golden eyes seemed to know everything she might tell him.

The room was alive with guttural squeaks that sounded somehow content.

"Parents giving you a rash of shit?"

She shrugged. "Just my mother," she said, her voice faint. "Dad's gone. Two years now. And Mom and I . . ." She shrugged again.

"What else?" He rested his big hand gently on the crown of her skull.

"My . . . brother. He's so . . . I don't know, he's as bad as her, but in a different way. She doesn't . . . doesn't seem to care what I do. He cares too *much*. He doesn't want me to see Kevin . . . always asks where I'm going, what I'm doing. I love him, but . . ."

Mace's smile stretched into a grin.

"Protective of his little sister, isn't he?"

Little sister? she thought. *How does he . . .* But the thought faded, outweighed by the comfort she found in Mace's eyes. They were the color of melted butter, at once warm and smooth, cool and comforting.

They snapped shut suddenly; his grin dropped away. He raised his head a bit and said in a breath, "Someone's here. . . ."

* * *

When Jeff saw the eyes in the corner, he knew they'd seen him first. There were four of them, unmoving, unblinking, but definitely eyes glinting in the dark.

Okay, he thought, gulping, *I'm outta here, I'm—*

Something moved just beneath the window. When he looked down, it pounced up at him in a flash of sharp teeth and small, snatching claws, making a deep, chitinous sound as it shot out of the dark. Jeff threw himself back from the window, his arms flailing before him, his feet stumbling backwards as he made a staccato *nuh-nuh-nuh* in his throat. The pavement came up and hit him in the back, knocking the wind from his lungs, making him gasp desperately for breath as he crawled backward; watching the window, he saw small claws pulling a dark shape through the gap in the boards, a shape with glistening black lips that pulled back over sharp teeth and two lower tusks that curled upward about an inch and a half, gnashing the air as the creature pulled itself over the sill and down the wall dragging a long, flesh-pink tail behind it. Another came through the window, then another.

The first creature hit the pavement and began skittering toward Jeff, its nose aimed directly between his legs.

Jeff rolled over, crawled on his hands and knees for a few feet, then clambered to his feet and broke into a lurching run toward the shrubbery that ran along Whitley.

Throwing himself into the bushes, Jeff felt the sharp branches scraping over his face and neck, cutting his hands as he clawed his way through, spitting leaves from his mouth; he tore through the thick web of shrubbery until his arms were caught, trapped like a spider's prey.

"Muh-Muh-Mal-Mal," he blurted, trying to call his sister's name.

With a throaty grunt, jagged teeth clamped onto the cuff of Jeff's pants and began to thrash. . . .

Mace's smile returned. His eyes were still closed, but he was *seeing* something, Mallory was certain. The gleeful look on his face seemed somehow malignant, and she felt the comfort of a moment before drain from her like water from a sieve.

"And what's your brother's name?" he asked.

"Juh . . . Jeff."

He opened his eyes and grinned down at her, sliding his hand lovingly over her hair as he whispered, "Yeah, he's protective of his little sister, all right. . . ."

The pantleg tore and branches snapped as Jeff threw himself forward to the sidewalk on the other side.

Behind him, the bushes continued to rustle as the creatures pressed on through.

Jeff crossed the street in a staggering run, falling against the car, pulling the door open and lurching inside. A second after he slammed the car door, something thumped against it, claws scratched the metal, and, for an instant, snapping teeth flashed in the open window. Jeff rolled it up as he started the engine, floored the accelerator, and tore away from the curb.

His lungs were burning, his chest heaving, and his mind was a clean, white blank. He glanced in the rearview mirror, expecting to see the creature in the road behind him. Teeth lashed against the back window, and the creature's small claws slid frantically over the glass, as if it might dig its way into the car.

"Oh Jesus oh God oh Jesus Jesus Christ," Jeff sputtered, at a loss. Bracing himself against the steering wheel, he slammed on the brakes. The tires squealed over the road, the rear of the car swerved to the right, and the creature swept across the back window and out of sight.

Jeff let up on the brakes as he steered into the swerve, looking in the mirror again.

The creature was rolling over on the pavement. It landed on its feet, sat up on its haunches, and sniffed the air, snapping its teeth as it grew smaller and smaller in the distance.

"Oh, God, Mallory," he gasped as he continued down Whitley. He spoke his sister's name again and again, wiping the sweat from his forehead, tugging his collar away from his throat.

What had happened to her? If she'd gone into that building with those things . . .

He took a right on Moorpark and drove into the parking lot of an AM/PM Mini Market, where he parked. Opening the door, Jeff leaned out and vomited onto the pavement.

Mallory felt dizzy as Mace took her hand to help her stand; she stumbled against him, and he put a long arm around her shoulders. She avoided looking at Kevin and the others. She couldn't bear the sight of them holding those animals. Mace led her by the pool again and back to the stairs.

"Tell you what," he said softly into her ear, "why don't you go around the corner to the phone booth and call your brother." He lifted her hand and pressed a quarter into her palm as they went up the stairs together. Halfway up, he stopped and faced her. "Tell him you're okay. Then, if it'll make you feel better, wait in the parking lot."

"Okay."

Mace held her head gently between his hands and looked into her eyes.

"I want you to know that you're welcome here any time, Mallory. If you need a friend, I'm here. Okay?"

Mallory felt a lump rise in her throat—

Just the grass.

—and had to fight back tears. His hands felt good on her head, safe, reassuring. His eyes glistened, too, as if he were struggling with tears. There was still a skeptical voice whispering within her, reminding her that she knew nothing of this man, that she had no reason to trust him or even consider trusting him.

But she didn't even trust her own voice, so she nodded silently.

Mace touched his lips to her forehead, then turned and went down the stairs. She watched him for a moment, liking the way he made her feel—

But those things down there . . .

—the way he seemed to accept her without reservation, so willingly, so warmly. She knew she would be back.

As Mallory continued up the stairs she heard Mace clap

his hands once and say, "Okay, guys, how about a tour of the building? Let's go downstairs and I'll show you the other way in and out."

"Downstairs?" Kevin muttered.

"Yes. In the sub-basement." Mace chuckled. "The sewer . . ."

PART III

Crucifax
Autumn

Thirteen

September 7–October 12

Seasons change with very little fanfare in Southern California. The Santa Ana winds lose their temper and blow away the stifling heat of summer, sweeping much of the smog from the sky and replacing it with spotty clouds. Fashions change more noticeably than anything else. The cheerful ice-cream colors of summer give way to darker earth tones, but perpetually tanned flesh is still visible: midriffs, legs, bare arms and shoulders. Summer seems to relax, but it never quite goes away.

This particular year, however, was different. Through the month of September, summer and autumn engaged in a game of tug-of-war over the San Fernando Valley.

There were days when the sun shone, unhindered even by smog, from aqua-blue skies. On other days, clouds that completely ignored the Los Angeles basin blanketed the Valley, their shadows occasionally cut by blades of sunlight that fell briefly in small pools amid the gloom. Twice, the clouds yielded a light sprinkle of rain.

At times the wind blew in fierce gusts, dry and cool, lifting skirts and mussing hair, skittering dry leaves and litter over the streets and sidewalks. Sometimes the air was still as death.

The local news story of the month was the mysterious death of North Hollywood police officer Bill Grady. The only visible sign of injury had been some blood in his mouth. The autopsy revealed much more. The man's internal organs had been disconnected, rearranged, thrashed. His stomach had been torn open from the inside; and, as the coroner told the press, "his insides were stirred up like a pudding."

When the coroner reported that Grady's death had been caused by "insertion of an unidentified object into the abdomen by way of the throat," the story attracted national attention. The media, however, was not being told how much confusion was being caused by that unidentified object; despite the tremendous amount of damage it had done to the inside of Bill Grady's body, it had left no mark in his mouth or throat except for the clean loss of two upper front teeth.

The investigation was going nowhere, and most of Grady's former colleagues felt the crime would remain unsolved.

The funeral was a large one. Angry editorials were written in all of the Southern California newspapers.

With so much attention focused on the murder, few people noticed a small article that appeared in the back pages of the *Times* and the *Herald Examiner*. It was so brief that its apparent unimportance invited the reader's neglect.

The article stated that there had been a number of recent sightings of what appeared to be large rats roaming the streets in the vicinity of Laurel Canyon Boulevard and Whitley Avenue.

No one cared. . . .

When Jeff got home on the night of September sixth, his stomach burning, his knees still weak, the phone was ringing. He answered quickly and was surprised to hear Mallory's calm, relaxed voice on the other end. He'd planned on calling someone, anyone, for help as soon as he got home, knowing that if Mallory wasn't hurt yet, she would be soon.

She was calling, she said, to tell him she was okay and would be home later.

He knew from her groggy voice that things were not as they should be. He wanted to ask what she'd done in that building, and if she'd seen the things that had chased him to the car, but he held back. If she knew he'd followed her, she'd be furious; worse, she'd be hurt, and whatever trust she had in him would be seriously damaged.

That night, and the nights that followed, his dreams were different than usual. Sometimes he awoke sweat-drenched and gasping, relieved to be in his bed rather than running down dark streets from squat black creatures with fiery golden eyes and snapping teeth. Other times, he dreamed of his sister spread-eagled in jet-black darkness, surrounded by those eyes; the dark creatures licked her flesh, flicking their tongues over her pebble-hard nipples as she cried out in pleasure, writhing and bucking against their fanged mouths.

Each time he woke, one thought was uppermost in his mind: *There's something wrong with me.*

Jeff and Mallory saw one another over breakfast each morning but said very little. Mallory had become very quiet since school had started, since that night in that dark, fire-blackened building.

In the evenings when both of them were home, they usually studied in their own rooms for a while and came out for dinner. Their mother seldom ate an evening meal with them but cooked it before going to work. Jeff and Mallory no longer had their usual dinner table conversations. Mallory had taken to eating her dinner in front of *M*A*S*H* reruns. She did not ignore him; when he asked her if anything was wrong, she smiled and said no, that she was just tired.

But to Jeff Mallory seemed preoccupied, bothered by something rather than intentionally distancing herself from him. Jeff feared that if he questioned her further, she would cut herself off from him completely. So he remained silent, hoping she would open up without being prompted.

She never did.

One of the best things about the new school year was Jeff's assignment to a new counselor, Mr. Haskell. Their first meeting turned into a casual conversation about movies, music, and the rest of the faculty.

"Look out for Mrs. Carmody, the girls' P.E. teacher," Jeff told him. "She's a real barracuda, and everybody on campus is terrified of her."

"Thanks for the warning," he laughed, lowering his voice, "but remember, we never had this conversation. I get caught gossiping about the faculty with a student, I'm dog meat."

Haskell insisted Jeff call him J.R. and told him to drop by the office any time he wanted. Jeff felt he could talk to J.R. if he needed to. He even considered going to J.R. about Mallory, talking to him about her strange behavior, but decided against it, fearing J.R. might think him a nosy brother who meddled in his sister's life.

Jeff told himself again and again that he had to stop being so intrusive; the more he looked into Mallory's life, the more curious he became, and the more worried he became. Her odd behavior was a sign of something. She was different. Changing.

He realized that he wasn't as worried about her as he was afraid for her. That made him worry about himself, because he had no idea what there was to be afraid of. . . .

Mallory was afraid, too, but she knew why.

She hadn't gone back to see Mace since that first night with Kevin. Most of that evening had become a hazy, dreamlike memory.

Except for those *things*.

They remained vividly burned into her memory.

"What *are* those damned things, anyway?" she asked Kevin that night when he took her home.

"Pets. Like he said."

"But what *are* they?"

"I don't know. Rats, I guess. Lotsa people keep rats."

"They're not rats! You got a better look at them than I did. They're not rats, and you know it."

"Well, whatever they are, don't be afraid of them. They're kinda nice. Really."

But she *was* afraid of them.

Especially since they'd started following her.

The morning after her visit with Mace, she'd groggily awakened, rolled over, and heard something move beneath her bed. After the quiet movement came a soft, chittering squeak. She'd wanted to lean over the edge and look beneath the bed, but she knew instinctively what would be looking back at her from the dusty darkness. She didn't look.

She heard them in bushes, beneath cars, moving inside garbage cans, cautious and secretive, but restless.

One morning when she heard a rustling in her closet, she almost called Jeff in to see if he could hear it, too. But then he would start asking questions, wondering why she was so frightened, and if she didn't explain, he would become suspicious. Things had been good between them lately—quiet, but good—and she wanted to keep it that way. Perhaps the little chill that had developed between them was healthy and would give Jeff a chance to turn his attention elsewhere, maybe even to get himself a girlfriend, so he would get off her back.

Kevin, too, had changed. Since meeting Mace, Kevin had become so cheerful and pleasant that he almost seemed a different person. Yet there seemed to be an underlying malignancy to his upbeat attitude, as if he were smiling on the outside to hide something that was brewing within.

He was also attending most, if not all, of his classes because, he claimed, Mace said he should.

Kevin was constantly talking about Mace; Mace said this, Mace did that, Mace is going to get the band some work in October. . . .

"Mace wants you to come back," he told her.

"I don't know, Kevin. . . ."

"Jesus, Mallory, all the other girls come, and they love it. It's like a party every night. I thought you liked to watch us rehearse."

"I do, but I told you . . . I'm afraid of those things."

"You don't need to be."

"Kevin, this'll probably sound crazy, but . . . I think they're, like, following me. Those animals."

He pushed a hand through his thick black hair and laughed. "That's bullshit, Mallory."

"Okay, just forget I said it."

Maybe she would go back. Maybe in the light of the day it wouldn't be so bad; maybe if she didn't smoke any of Mace's killer grass, she would remain alert and see that his "pets" weren't so awful after all.

Then again, maybe not. . . .

The building on the corner of Ventura and Whitley appeared empty and abandoned. Inside, however, there was life. Since Mace had introduced himself to the band, it had become their meeting place. They left their instruments there, and each day after school the guys took their girl-friends down into the pool room, where their instruments were assembled and waiting. Using the generator Mace had set up, they rehearsed—not loud enough to draw attention, but just loud enough to tremble the darkness inside.

The band's performance improved tremendously through the month of September; it became richer, darker, as if shaped by their surroundings. Mace's music, angry and cynical, seemed to have been written explicitly for them, bringing to the surface their strengths and subtly concealing their weaknesses.

After sending Mallory away the first night, Mace had taken Kevin and the others down a steep and narrow metal staircase into the building's sub-basement. It was a dark, cramped, smelly room, damp and cluttered with intestine-like pipes that came from the walls and ceiling. Across from the staircase a hole had been knocked into the wall, just big enough for a man to squeeze through if he hunched down.

"It's important that you're not seen coming into the building," Mace said, holding a lantern before him. "So come through this way."

A draft of bitter sewage odor wafted into the room through the hole, fluttering the cobwebs that stretched from pipe to pipe around the room like wasted muscle tissue, and the boys objected loudly.

"C'mon, guys," Mace laughed, "where's your sense of adventure?" He led them to the hole, through which they could hear the dripping and rushing of sewage. "The sewer system will give us access to any part of the Valley we want without the hassle of being followed."

"Why do we have to hide?" Kevin asked.

With a smile, Mace put his arm around Kevin's shoulders and said, "We're not going to win any popularity contests, my friend."

Kevin wasn't sure what that meant, but he didn't question him. He never questioned Mace; none of them did. There was a wisdom in Mace, an air of knowledge that seemed to hover far above questioning. If asked to explain his nearly blind acceptance of Mace, Kevin wasn't sure he could. Part of it lay in Mace's determination to help the band, but perhaps a great deal of it was due to the fact that Mace seemed to have an equally blind acceptance of Kevin and his friends.

Because of Mace, Kevin had been going to school regularly. After he told Mace what had happened at home, Mace told him to do his best to keep peace for a while, and that included going to school. He didn't need to explain; it made perfect sense to Kevin.

His parents had threatened to put him into a counseling program, even send him to the Laurel Teen Center.

"Our insurance will cover it," his father said, sitting in his favorite chair chewing Juicy Fruit.

His mother added, "And they'll keep you there until you've learned how to handle responsibility, until you've learned how to act like an adult, which you *are,* even though you're only seventeen. That's old enough; you are an adult."

"You'll receive therapy in groups and in a one-on-one situation," his father went on. "There are counseling programs that will teach you how to deal with school responsibilities, home responsibilities. Unless things change, Kevin, that's where you're going."

If he did what they wanted for a while, they would leave him alone so he could rehearse with the band.

"When the time is right," Mace said, "you'll break away from them entirely."

So he'd begun going to school, keeping his stash of marijuana out of the house. He hadn't needed it, anyway, because Mace was so generous with his own grass. He didn't even complain about his lack of privacy, though his parents had refused to replace his bedroom door. After school and in the evenings, he rehearsed with the band. The other band members brought their girlfriends, and he knew it wouldn't be long before Mallory went with him to the building and made herself a part of the group.

He knew because Mace had told him. . . .

Mace walked the streets day and night. When he was not with the band, he was strolling sidewalks, wandering through shopping malls, covering the Valley.

He chatted with teenagers on corners, in bus stations, outside school functions and churches. Sometimes when he returned to the building, he did not return alone.

The group that gathered in the pool room quickly grew. Teenagers from Reseda, Tarzana, Mission Hills, Panorama City—from all over the San Fernando Valley—joined Crucifax. Some of them brought friends, and sometimes the friends brought friends.

At night, when the wind was blowing in precisely the right direction, one might hear the ghostlike riffs of an electric guitar and the pulse of a drum drifting upward like a breeze from some of the manholes around Ventura and Whitley. If one moved close enough to the old building on the corner, one might hear lusty peals of laughter from somewhere inside. If one peered through the cracks in the boarded windows, one might glimpse the shimmer of golden eyes in the darkness.

But the sounds of the boulevard were loud and ceaseless, and, mixed with the sound of rainfall and blowing winds, the noise from inside the building was indistinguishable.

For five weeks, Crucifax and the group of teenagers that grew around them went unnoticed. . . .

Fourteen

October 13

The walkways of the Sherman Oaks Galleria flowed with the usual after-school crowd the way veins and arteries flow with blood.

Teenagers were perched on benches, leaning against handrails, some talking and smoking, others waiting for friends, while still others were there just to see and be seen.

Sugary music played softly from hidden speakers while rock music pounded from a record store. The smell of hot dogs and nachos mingled with the aroma of fresh baked goods.

Escalators silently carried shoppers between floors, and in the center of the mall a glass elevator slid up and down a shaft that was bordered by bright white lights.

In the doorway of a toy store, a stuffed bear was displayed amidst a dozen plastic red-gummed snapping teeth that clacked and jittered endlessly. The bear's arms, mouth, and eyes moved in stiff, mechanical motions as it happily greeted passersby: "Hi, there! I'd like to be your friend . . ."

When the Cookie Jar was in sight, Jeff seated himself on a bench to think a moment. He could see Lily through the window; she was waiting on two small old women carrying shopping bags.

She wore a white visor with the store's name on the bill and a smock with a colorful rendering of an old-fashioned cookie jar on the front. Her sun-streaked brown hair was cut in a pageboy that revealed her slender neck and perfectly framed her unblemished, pug-nosed face. One of the old women leaned over the counter to speak to her, and Lily smiled brightly, her big eyes widening with interest.

A week ago, Brad had pointed her out to him at an afternoon assembly.

"Look!" he hissed. "There she is."

"Who?"

"The girl from the Cookie Jar. In the Galleria. 'Member? We went there a few days before school started, and she talked with you? Lily something."

"What about her?"

"Well, she liked you. She talked to *you*. You didn't even have to start the conversation. A girl like that pays attention to you, you pay a little back. You've gotta ask her out."

"I do, huh? What if I don't want to?"

"Then you better see a doctor right away."

Lily and Jeff were in the same biology class. A few days after the assembly, they dissected frogs in the lab. She was assigned the table directly across from him. He watched her as she manipulated her scalpel over the dead frog, watched her pug nose curl in disgust and her lips pull back in a sickened scowl. She looked up from her frog, their eyes met, and she shook her head, her shoulders bobbing with silent laughter.

After class, she caught up with him in the hall and said, "That is so gross! Don't you think so?"

"I don't mind it so much."

She laughed. "Guys never do."

Jeff walked Lily to her next class that day, and by the time they got to the classroom, they were both laughing.

Since then, he'd been considering asking her out; but holding a pleasant conversation with a girl and asking that same girl out on a date were two entirely different things.

I'd like two of the oatmeal cookies, please, Jeff thought, *oh, and by the way, would you like to go out with me?*

The very thought made him blush. He fidgeted on the bench, looked around, and took a deep breath, trying to tell himself he wouldn't be that clumsy. He looked up absently at the second-story balcony, thinking the worst she could do was say no, and that would be it, when he froze, completely forgetting about Lily.

There was a man leaning on the balcony rail, arms folded, ankles crossed, staring at him with a relaxed smile. He wore a long steel-gray coat that fell past his knees and had long, spiky platinum hair, and he was staring directly into Jeff's eyes.

Jeff turned away for a moment, saw the old ladies leaving the Cookie Jar, then looked back up at the balcony.

The stranger had not moved. He was still watching Jeff. After a moment, he moved away from the rail and walked along the edge of the balcony, his eyes still on Jeff, the hem of his coat fluttering around his legs.

The glass elevator rose swiftly to the second floor, and its doors slid open.

The man stepped inside and smiled down at Jeff through the tinted glass.

After the doors closed again, the elevator began its descent. It seemed to move more slowly coming down than going up, and as the man's face drew nearer, grew larger, Jeff's chest grew tight, as if his lungs were filling with water, and his fingers clutched the edge of the bench until his knuckles burned and, as the elevator came to rest on the first floor Jeff jolted to his feet and moved quickly toward the Cookie Jar, glancing over his shoulder in time to see the man step out of the elevator.

Jeff pushed into the shop. As the door lazily swung closed behind him Jeff stared out the window, his breath coming hard, and watched the man seat himself on the bench facing the store.

"Hi!"

Jeff spun around, startled, and tried to smile at Lily.

"It's Jeff, right?" she asked, pointing an uncertain finger at him.

"Yeah," Jeff said, walking toward the counter. He scratched his head, as if he could scratch from his mind the image of that man sitting outside the shop.

I don't know him, Jeff assured himself, *he wasn't coming for me, this is stupid, I don't know him. . . .*

The breathless panic he'd felt a moment ago slowly melted from his chest.

He rested his elbows on the countertop and said, "How's the cookie business?"

She shrugged. "Pays for my gas, but other than that, I'd almost rather be at school. Hey, how was the biology quiz yesterday? I had to go to the dentist."

"It wasn't bad. If you did okay on the dissection, you'll do fine on the quiz."

Her face withered. "But I didn't do okay on the dissection! You know that," she laughed.

Lily glanced over his shoulder toward the window.

"Don't worry too much about it," Jeff said.

"Want a cookie? On the house."

"Sure."

"Chocolate chip?"

He nodded, and Lily took a cookie from a tray in the display case, wrapped it in a napkin, and handed it to him.

"Thanks."

She looked over his shoulder again and frowned slightly.

"You know that guy?" she asked.

Jeff bit into the cookie. He didn't want to turn around; he knew what he would see.

"That guy at the window," Lily went on. "He's been looking at you. Smiling."

Jeff's mouth became dry, and cookie crumbs began to cake to his lips.

"Just take a look," Lily said.

Looking over his shoulder, Jeff saw the man standing at the window, his long arms folded across his chest. Quickly turning back to Lily, Jeff said, "No, I don't know him."

Lily continued to frown at the window.

"He's weird," she said. "I've seen him hanging around here a lot lately. He goes up to people and starts talking to them like he knows them, and I don't think he does. You ever seen him before?"

"Uh-uh." He chewed the cookie some more, tried to work up some spit so he could speak. "Good cookie."

Her eyes returned to him and she smiled, but only for a moment. She looked out the window again, and her eyes clouded.

"I wish he'd either come in or go away," she muttered.

"Ignore him, and maybe he will." But Jeff wasn't so sure. He felt cold, as if he were standing in a draft, and he was ashamed of his sudden urge to bolt from the shop, to get out of the Galleria as quickly as possible, as if its walls were closing in on him and he would be crushed if he didn't leave immediately.

"Something the matter?" Lily asked.

He blinked, shook his head. "No, I was just thinking—"

Here it is, Jeff thought, *this is it, you've already started, you can't stop now.*

"—that maybe tonight, if you're not busy, we ought to go to a movie or something."

Her face brightened just a little, but enough to make Jeff heave a silent, inward sigh of relief.

"Yeah, I'd love to," she said, "but I can't. Not tonight, anyway."

"Okay. Just thought I'd ask." He wrapped his forced smile around another bite of the cookie.

"Maybe some other time," she said quickly. "Like this weekend. See, I've got this friend. Maybe you know her—Nikki Astin? I'm supposed to see her tonight. We used to be best friends. But this summer she got involved with this religious group. Calvary Youth? She's found Jesus," she said with a roll of her eyes, "and now she's like . . . well, a different person. No parties, no dating, and she hardly ever sees any of her old friends anymore. Anyway, she wants to have dinner with me tonight. I figure she probably just wants to convert me, you know? Spread the gospel, and all that. But it's been so long since we've talked, I'd just like to see what's going on with her. Tell you the truth, I'm a little worried about her." She looked over Jeff's shoulder again and whispered, "Jesus, he's still there."

Jeff tried to keep her attention away from the window, hoping the man would go away.

They talked a while longer about the Calvary Youth, about school and the odd weather, and when Jeff was finished with his cookie, he thanked her again and prepared to leave.

Lily took a pen from her pocket and scribbled something on a napkin. "This is my phone number," she said, handing it to him. "Call me tomorrow night if we don't talk at school, and let's make plans. I would like to see a movie with you."

As good as that made him feel, it was difficult to smile through his apprehension; he didn't want to go out into the mall.

"Is our friend gone?" he asked, wiping the crumbs from his mouth.

Lily peered over his shoulder, looked left and right, and said, "Yep. Gone."

They exchanged goodbyes and, after tucking Lily's phone number into his biology book, Jeff left the Cookie Jar, turned right, and headed for the exit.

"Any luck?"

Startled, Jeff stepped away from the deep voice, nearly dropping his books.

It was him, the stranger, his shiny hair fluttering around his head as he walked beside Jeff.

"What?" Jeff blurted.

"You were asking her out, weren't you?"

"I was . . . well . . . yeah."

"She say yes?"

"Well, she said maybe this weekend we'd—" Jeff stopped and faced the man angrily. "That's none of your business, I don't even know you."

"Just trying to help," the man said with a slinky shrug.

Jeff started walking again.

"I don't think she's your type, anyway," the man said, coming after him.

"What do you know about my type? Leave me alone."

"You know, I think I've got just the girl for you."

Jesus, he's a pimp, Jeff thought. He saw a security guard

116

standing on the other side of the walkway and veered toward him.

"Blond," the man said, "with the prettiest eyes, man, the most gorgeous fucking eyes you've ever seen. Big and brown. She needs someone like you. A knight in shining armor to fight for her honor. Sort of a"—he chuckled—"big brother."

Jeff stopped and faced the man, suddenly filled with an icy mixture of fear and anger.

"I knew you'd be interested," the stranger said, his smile creasing the pale skin around his golden eyes. "I can arrange it. A real dream come true"—he winked—"if you know what I mean."

Jeff felt sick, confused, and afraid. "Stay away from me," he said quietly as he spun around and hurried away.

"My name is Mace."

"I don't give a fuck who you are, just leave me—"

"You shouldn't say that until you know what I can do for you."

"There's nothing you can do for me, whoever you are, so just—"

"Maybe not today."

Something about the tone of his voice—perhaps it was the confidence with which he spoke, as if he knew everything there was to know about Jeff Carr—made Jeff turn to him again.

"But there's a big storm comin', friend," Mace said, curling his right thumb and forefinger into a circle and slipping his left middle finger in and out, in and out with a soft, breathy cackle.

"Oh, Jesus," Jeff groaned, hurrying away, nearly breaking into a run, confused by the lead-heavy feeling that overcame him, as if a part of his mind had fallen away to reveal a black, endless pit that was never meant to be seen.

When he got outside, he drank in the chilled air, stopped on the sidewalk, and looked up at the sky.

The gray clouds had grown darker.

. . . *big storm comin'* . . .

Rain speckled his face and began to fall with a snakelike hiss all around him.

Fifteen

Erin Carr was on her knees searching through a box she'd pulled from the hall closet when she heard something move within the walls behind her.

"Damned mice again," she muttered. They'd had trouble with mice eighteen months ago, and the landlord had taken care of it quickly, assuring his tenants there would be no such problem in the future.

Apparently he'd been wrong.

Unable to find the spool of dark blue thread she needed to sew a policeman's uniform for one of her puppets, she'd taken the box from the closet as a last resort. It was filled with scraps of paper, scores of pens, pencils, crayons, paint brushes, a couple of outdated telephone directories, scissors, balls of twine and rubber bands, paper clips, and thumbtacks, and she hadn't even reached the bottom yet.

While Jeff and Mallory were in school, Erin spent most of her time working on her puppets and talking with Fantasy Line customers. Not long after the kids got home, she'd go to work at the bars. Ten days ago, she'd started working three different bars besides the Playland: Thirsty Jack's, the Playpen, and the Wandering Eye. She was making more money, but working seven nights a week she had little time to herself and even less to spend with her son and daughter.

During the short time the three of them were home together in the evenings, she realized the apartment was just as quiet as when she was there alone. Usually, Jeff and Mallory chattered like two old maids. She'd been too preoccupied to notice, but now, as she sorted through the box, she wondered if there were problems between them.

The weekend was coming up. Maybe it would be a good idea if she made time for the three of them to do something together, go to a movie or play, have dinner.

Erin found the spool of blue thread down in the corner of the box beneath several books of matches. She took it out and put it on the floor beside her and began to load the box up again.

When she lifted an old copy of *The Godfather* to put back in the box, some of the pages fell out, their glue dry and cracked, and with them came a photograph.

Half of the picture had been torn away. In the remaining half, a younger Mallory, about eight years old, was standing in the crook of her father's arm. She cradled Caesar, a stuffed dog she'd kept with her through most of her childhood. She was grinning with the kind of open-armed happiness Erin hadn't seen in her in years.

Erin recognized the snapshot. It had been taken the summer they drove up to Monterey for a weekend. Jeff had taken it. The half torn away had shown Erin standing on the opposite side of her husband, his arm around her shoulders, her face bright with laughter. It had been ripped away, discarded, leaving a tattered edge where Erin had once stood.

Her eyes filled with tears. She wondered when Mallory had torn her from the picture and what had been going through the girl's mind at the time.

Erin remembered Mallory stepping around her father after the picture had been taken and giving her mother a big, grunting bear hug that made Mallory puff her cheeks and clench her eyes shut.

Erin closed her eyes and revived the sensation of Mallory's small arms encircling her, squeezing tight. Tears streaked her face as she pressed the torn picture between her palms.

Since Ronald had left, the only time Erin and Mallory spoke was when they argued or exchanged hesitant apologies. It had been a long while since Erin had taken the time to remember how it used to be between them, and now that she had, she regretted it. Because it hurt.

Erin knew Mallory blamed her mother for the loss of her father; she knew Ronald's absence hurt Mallory most of all, and she had to lay the blame on someone. But Erin didn't know how to bridge the gap that had grown between them. She didn't know how to convince Mallory that she, Erin, had been just as hurt, although not as shocked, by Ronald's sudden departure. Erin wanted to tell Mallory of the sleepless nights she'd spent in her bed wondering what she had or *hadn't* done to chase Ronald away without so much as a "so long" or an explanation. But whenever the two of them spoke, the most trivial exchanges turned into angry, bitter shouting matches. Their relationship had turned into a wound that was never given time to heal; the scab was torn off again and again.

Erin dropped the picture back in the box, unable to look at it any longer, unable even to see it through her tears. She decided she had to do something, anything, about what was happening to her and Mallory. She knew that, as with a decaying tooth, any further neglect would only cause irreparable damage.

As she got to her feet and scooted the box back into the closet she heard the sound inside the wall again, this time accompanied by a thick, muted squeak. Erin pounded a fist on the wall, hoping to scare it, and the gesture felt good. It was a small but welcome release of anger that, she realized, was not for the rodents in her wall but for herself.

Before she could hit the wall again, her phone rang. . . .

After parking his bike on Whitley, Kevin hurried through the rain down a narrow alley, his boots splashing through puddles. Several yards down the alley, he removed the manhole cover and climbed down, pulling the cover back over him; it made a chilling scraping sound as it slid back into place. He descended the metal rungs that stuck out of the dirty, moist cement wall.

The air was damp and thick with the smell of urine and feces. His boots made wet slopping sounds on the grimy puddled walkway that ran along the wall of the sewer. It was wide enough for two people to walk side by side if they were careful; then it dropped off into a swirling, gurgling stream of sewage that flowed in a three-foot-wide gutter. Dirty brown foam licked at the edge of the walkway, pushed to the sides by the stream of black lumpy matter.

Light seeped down through grates and small holes in the manhole covers above, playing deceptively on the pipes and ducts that writhed from the walls like snakes, giving them a sort of peripheral life.

Kevin removed a pocket-sized flashlight from his coat and flicked it on, shining the beam before him. With his back to the wall, he turned right and started along the walkway, sliding his hand over the coarse, wet wall as he walked, carefully ducking pipes.

Kevin was not quite used to going through the sewer yet. While it was not as unpleasant as it had been at first, neither was it any safer. Mace had warned them of the homeless people who lived beneath the streets. They considered the sewer their home, and anyone who went down there was, as far as they were concerned, trespassing; sometimes they became violent.

"Be nice to them," Mace had said. "I want them to know we're their friends."

Once again Kevin had tried to get Mallory to come with him, and once again she'd refused. He was beginning to think that perhaps he was being too nice about it.

He turned right at a corner and came face-to-face with a wet-furred rat perched on a fat pipe. It held something dark and tattered in its mouth, something that glistened in the beam of his flashlight. The rat waddled backward and pressed itself against the wall when it saw him. He stood there a moment, watching, and heard someone laughing somewhere in the sewer; it was a phlegmy cackle that sounded ghostly as it echoed through the tunnels. Gulping back his fear, Kevin tried to ignore the disgust he felt at the sight of the rat's filthy, matted fur and its wet, twitching nose as he ducked down low to pass beneath it. He imagined the rat hunched on the pipe above him, ready to pounce on his back as he moved under it, dropping the dark morsel in its mouth so it could sink its tiny, needlelike teeth into the back of his neck.

The distant laughter of one of the hidden sewer dwellers faded, died.

The hole in the wall that led to Mace's sub-basement was about two feet above the walkway. When he got to it, Kevin climbed up and through, scraping the top of his head on the upper edge. As he entered he could hear footsteps on the metal stairs.

"Kevin," Mace said pleasantly.

Kevin stood up, rubbing his head. He put the flashlight back in his pocket.

Mace was coming down the stairs holding a lantern, his small pipe clamped between his teeth. Two of his pets were following at his heels, and a dark, cross-shaped object hung on a cord around his neck. In his other hand he held a paper bag. He took the pipe from his smiling mouth and handed it to Kevin.

As Kevin inhaled some of the sweet smoke Mace walked around him and crouched in front of the hole in the wall, setting the lantern on a crate. He reached into the bag, pulled out two boxes of Twinkies and a gallon of milk, and set them outside the hole.

"What's that?" Kevin asked.

"A little treat for our less fortunate friends." He stood, took his lantern, and crossed the room to a stack of boxes against the wall. He opened the top box as he asked, "Did you go to school?" He removed something wrapped in delicately thin cream-colored tissue.

"Mm-hm." Kevin slowly exhaled, and tendrils of smoke curled around his face like long, bony fingers.

"That's good." The paper crinkled softly as he unwrapped it. "You're alone. Mallory wouldn't come?"

"No." Kevin took another drag and felt the drug's effect spreading through him, warm and soothing, like liquid sunshine flowing through his veins.

"Too bad." Mace let the paper drop to the floor and turned to Kevin. "The others are upstairs waiting to rehearse. But before we go up, I want to give you something. Come here."

As he crossed the room to stand before Mace Kevin felt as if he were hovering a few inches above the floor, holding perfectly still while the room moved around him. The sensation made him smile. He handed the pipe to Mace, its ember dead and dark, and Mace tucked it away in one of his deep, baggy coat pockets.

"Everyone will get one of these," Mace said softly, lifting his right hand. Something dangled from his fingers, suspended by a cord of leather. "But you are the first. Because you're important to me, Kevin."

The whisper of the flowing sewage behind Kevin diminished until all he could hear was Mace's voice, all he could see were Mace's eyes framed by the leather cord that he now held up before him with both hands. A shiny, heavy-looking object dangled from the cord, but Kevin saw it only peripherally. His attention was intensely focused on Mace's eyes and gentle, lulling voice.

As Mace continued speaking he lifted the cord above Kevin's head, then slowly lowered it until it was hanging around his neck. The object on the cord rested heavily on Kevin's chest. It felt cool through the material of his black T-shirt.

"Don't take this off," Mace said. "Someday very soon, people will know who you are when they see this around your neck. They'll know that you're a friend of mine, a very good, valued friend of mine. That you're important. And powerful." He fingered the object on the cord, lifting it from Kevin's chest for a moment. "And someday," he went on, his voice a mere breath, "this will be your escape from all that you hate, from all the people who don't understand you, who refuse to accept you as you are, as I do. There's a big storm coming, Kevin, and someday this—" he tapped it with his finger—"will be all you have. So don't ever . . . take it . . . off."

Mace smiled as he placed his hand on Kevin's cheek, and his touch had a relaxing, massaging effect on Kevin's entire body, made him feel peaceful, as if all was finally well in his life.

"You're very talented, Kevin," Mace said. "I'm impressed with the progress we've made in the last two weeks. It won't be long now, I promise." He held Kevin's face between his hands. "I have plans for you. For all of you, really, but especially for you. And for Mallory."

Then the long moment ended as if it had never been; Mace's hands dropped, and he turned away, starting for the stairs.

Kevin lifted the object before his face and squinted at it in the darkness. It was identical to the object around Mace's neck.

It was a cross. At first glance it looked black, but a moment later he realized it was a deep, dark red, the color of dried, crusty blood. It was hard and smooth and felt like obsidian. With the exception of the bottom end, each end of the cross flared like the head of an axe, filed to a fine, thin edge. Kevin ran a fingertip along the top edge and immediately jerked his hand away.

His skin had been neatly sliced open, and a tiny bead of blood rose to the surface. He slipped his finger between his lips and sucked on the small cut.

Mace's feet clanked up the first three steps, then he stopped and turned to Kevin.

"Coming?"

"Yeah," Kevin said, frowning at the cross. "But what . . . *is* this thing?"

"That," Mace said with a smile, "is a Crucifax."

Kevin stared at it a moment longer, said, "Oh," then dropped it to his chest and followed Mace.

Halfway up the stairs, Mace bent down and lifted one of the creatures to his chest. It crawled up on his shoulder.

"Why didn't Mallory come?" he asked.

"I don't know."

"Is she afraid of me?" Mace asked, his whisper sounding metallic in the darkness.

A few yards away from them, soft light glowed from the swimming pool; Kevin heard laughter coming from there, too, and music. And frantic sucking.

"Not you. Those." Kevin pointed to the creature on Mace's shoulder. The lantern below it cast shadows over its triangular face, glinting in its almond-shaped eyes.

"Ah," Mace said, reaching up to scratch the creature's head. "She's afraid of my pets."

Whispers, stifled giggles, and soft moans came from the pool; a haze of marijuana smoke hovered over it like a ghost. They began walking around the pool toward the band instruments; behind them, Mace's generator hunkered like a sleeping beast.

"She's never seen anything like them before," Kevin said.

"Neither have I, really. I told her they were rats."

"Rats," he muttered thoughtfully. "Well, they're not too different from rats. Rats have gotten a bad rep, you know. Because they're scavengers. There's nothing wrong with that. They're resourceful, that's all. They feed off what others don't want. That's not so bad, is it? But they're not really rats."

"So . . . what *are* they?"

Mace tucked his forefinger beneath the creature's chin, and a long, thin, black tongue flicked out, licked his finger delicately, then disappeared.

"They're my eyes," Mace breathed. Smiling suddenly, he said, "Don't worry about Mallory. She'll come when she's ready."

Then his face stiffened, his head tilted back, eyes closed, and he remained still for a long while, as if watching something. . . .

"What are you wearing, Lou?"

"Wearing? Um, I'm, uh, wearing an undershirt."

"Is that all?"

"Yuh . . . uh, yeah. That's all."

"Come on, now, Lou, no fibbing. I don't think that's all

you're wearing, is it?" Standing in her bedroom, Erin held the receiver a bit closer to her lips and lowered her voice to a husky whisper. "Is it?"

"Well . . . no. Not all."

"What else?"

"Um, well, I'm . . ." His lips smacked dryly. "I'm wearing a pair of my wife's, uh . . . pantyhose."

"Mmm . . . pantyhose, Lou! Do you know how much that turns me on?"

"It does?" He sounded pleased.

"Oh, yeeaah. That nylon stretched over your legs, over your thighs . . . You know what I love the *most?"*

"Wha . . . ?"

Erin smiled, held back a giggle. It was strictly forbidden to laugh at a client's fantasy, but she couldn't ignore the humor in this one; the image of a man talking on the phone while wearing an undershirt and his wife's pantyhose was extremely funny. She stifled her laughter and concentrated on sounding sexy.

"I love to slowly rub my hand over your crotch," she cooed, "and feel that bulge grow, feel that nylon stretch over your cock as it gets bigger . . . thicker. Are you touching it, Lou?"

"Yeah," he gulped.

"Is it getting bigger?"

"Yeah."

"Mmm, I can almost feel it now. Squeeze it for me, Lou."

"Yeah." He was panting.

"Feels like it's going to rip right through, doesn't it?"

"Yuh-huh . . ."

"Stroking it?"

"Mm-hmmm . . ."

"Wanna rub our nylons together, Lou? Grind our crotches?"

"Oh, God, yeah, yeah . . ."

"Press 'em together reeeaaal hard . . ."

"Yeah . . ."

"Make 'em feel like—"

"You slut."

Erin nearly dropped the receiver as she spun around, hitting her knee on the nightstand and sucking in a deep, ragged breath when she saw Mallory peering through the two-inch opening in her bedroom door.

Mallory's eyes were narrowed to ice-cold slits, her mouth curled into a hateful sneer.

"You . . . miserable . . . *slut.*" She turned and stalked away from the door, her footsteps heavy in the hallway.

"Mallory," Erin called, her voice hoarse. The receiver slipped from her hand and clattered on the nightstand, then hit the floor.

Lou's antlike voice whined, "Hello? Hello? Bunny?"

Erin felt dizzy as she pulled her bedroom door open, tears filling her eyes. She wondered how long Mallory had been standing there. The torn photograph filled Erin's mind with unbearable clarity.

When she got to the living room, Mallory was putting on her coat.

"Mallory, wait."

She grabbed her bag and started for the door, but Erin stepped before her and put her hands on Mallory's shoulders.

"Don't touch me," she spat, pulling away.

"Wait, Mallory, please."

"For what? So you can explain, I suppose?" She dropped her arms at her sides, letting her bag dangle against her leg.

"I don't know what you're thinking right now, but I want you to know—"

"I'm thinking I know why Dad left."

"Now wait a minute, I didn't do this while your dad was here."

"Oh? What did you do?"

Erin stepped back, shocked by the hate in her daughter's face. She fought to steady her voice.

"Mallory, we've screamed and shouted about this enough. I think it's time we just talked, don't you?"

"Like you were talking to your friend in there?" she snapped, stabbing a thumb over her shoulder toward Erin's bedroom.

Clenching her teeth, Erin said, "That helps pay the rent and buy groceries and clothes, and if your father hadn't left in the first place, I wouldn't have to do it!"

"Maybe that's why he left, you ever think about that? Maybe he didn't like living with a *whore!*"

"I am *not* a whore!" Erin shouted, her voice cracking. "I was never unfaithful to your father. Not once. But whether you want to believe it or not, he was sleeping with every goddamned—" Her words were garbled by a sob as she turned from Mallory. She wanted to hit something, break something, to get rid of the rage that was ripping through her chest.

"Does Jeff know?" Mallory asked with a snide chuckle.

"Oh, God, Mallory, please don't tell him," she whispered.

"'Don't blame Mom,' he says, 'She's doing her best,' he says. But does he know what Mom is best at?" She made a snorting sound and growled, "I think somebody's waiting for you on the phone."

Erin heard her sling the bag over her shoulder, heard the door open, then slam. She let out her pain in a hoarse, wordless cry, leaning her hip against the back of the sofa. Her face felt hot with shame, and she clutched her cheeks with her hands, thinking she would have to pull herself together before Jeff got home.

Something squeaked and scuttled inside the apartment wall. . . .

Kevin watched Mace curiously until his eyes finally opened again. Smiling down at him, Mace put his hand on Kevin's shoulder and said, "She's ready now. Bring her tonight."

Sixteen

October 14

It was Friday, and the hall outside the counseling center was filled with loud and hurried students eager to start their weekend. In J.R.'s office, however, it was quiet as J.R. sat at his desk listening to Jeff Carr. For twenty minutes Jeff had been telling J.R. about his sister, about her unusual behavior lately.

"I wasn't going to bring it up," Jeff said, "but she didn't come home at all last night. When I got home, my mother was really upset, she'd been crying, but she wouldn't tell me what was wrong. I think something happened between them. And I don't think Mallory came to school today, either."

"Does your mother know?"

Jeff shook his head.

J.R. was fascinated by the changes in the boy's face as he spoke of his sister. He was obviously worried about Mallory, but there seemed to be more than that.

"Why weren't you going to tell me?"

"Because I didn't want you to think I was, you know, prying, being nosy about my sister's business."

"Well, there's nothing wrong with being concerned about your sister, Jeff."

"But she hates it."

"Doesn't mean she hates you."

"But she hardly talks to me anymore." Jeff's face was pensive, clouded; the patch of skin between his brows was creased.

"Do you think she's with Kevin?"

"Probably. I don't know."

"Has Mallory had any other boyfriends before Kevin?"

"One last summer, but they never—" Jeff stopped himself, pressed his lips together as he blushed.

"Never what?"

"Well, I don't think they, um . . . were as serious." Jeff wouldn't meet his eyes; his face remained red for a moment.

Realization slowly began to dawn in J.R.'s mind. He saw more than guilt in Jeff's face; he saw shame.

This guy's jealous of his sister, he thought. *He's got a crush on her.*

That explained the way Jeff had been acting. Normally, he seemed quiet, but with a sharp wit that he used well. He was a good student, involved in school activities, and seemed to have a good number of friends. Today he seemed closed in on himself. The change was subtle; his posture was tense, his arms crossed in his lap. He'd even been rocking himself slightly in the chair, as if to comfort himself.

Perhaps there was just as much reason to worry about Jeff as there was to worry about Mallory.

Scribbling on a scrap of paper, J.R. said, "Here's my home phone number. If she doesn't show up this weekend and you think something's really wrong, give me a call. Otherwise, I'll try to talk to her on Monday."

"If she knew I'd told you about—"

"Don't worry. She won't. We'll just talk. In the meantime, Jeff, don't take all of your sister's problems on your shoulders. I'm speaking from experience here. She's going to do whatever she wants, no matter what you think."

Jeff nodded as J.R. handed him the phone number.

After they wished each other a good weekend, Jeff left. His concern for his sister stirred some unpleasant memories up from the bottom of J.R.'s mind. He tried to imagine how much more complicated his situation with Sheila would have been had he felt more than just a brotherly interest in her welfare. If that was really the case with Jeff, J.R. didn't envy him. . . .

As the Calvary Youth House slowly filled with smiling, chattering teenagers, Reverend James Bainbridge closed his Bible and stood from his desk in the main room. A small bell hanging over the front door jingled each time someone came in, and Bainbridge looked up with a smile.

The house was always busy with activity—some of the kids even lived there—but it came to life around midafternoon as they finished up their classes and began to gather for the afternoon meeting.

It was a large four-bedroom house in a quiet neighborhood on Lamona Street in Sherman Oaks. Bainbridge knew the property manager well; he was a Christian who strongly supported Bainbridge's work with teenagers, so he'd offered the house at half the normal rent, which was easily paid with each month's acquired donations. Mrs. Wanamaker, a widow from Northridge, spent most of her time at the house cooking for them, keeping it tidy, and helping Bainbridge with organizational details. She was constantly smiling. She was of medium height—nearly as wide as she was tall—with rosy cheeks, fluttering hands, and graying hair. Lately she had been complaining of noises in the walls, frightened by the possibility of encountering a mouse. Bainbridge had set out poison, but Mrs. Wanamaker insisted she still heard them. He feared he might have to call an exterminator, an expense the group could not easily afford.

Bainbridge sat on the edge of his desk as the teenagers came in and found seats on the chairs and beanbags and cushions that were arranged in a half circle. Most of the furniture had been donated by parents or collected at garage sales and Goodwill stores, but it served its purpose.

His chest filled with pride as he watched his kids gather in the main room. They were clean, neatly dressed, healthy, and brave enough to surrender their lives and souls openly to their Lord, willing to risk the ridicule and rejection of their friends and families. In this day and age, Bainbridge often thought, that was an act of bravery.

He counted fourteen kids in the room and decided to get started.

"Good afternoon," he said with a smile.

Scattered greetings came from the group.

Bainbridge stood and pulled up a chair, seating himself at the front of the semicircle with his Bible in his lap. He leaned toward a chubby black girl to his left and said, "Brenda, could you go in the back and get the others?"

She stood and headed for the bedrooms to get the five teenagers—three boys and two girls—who lived in the house.

The bell over the front door jingled again, and Bainbridge quickly swept his eyes over the group to see who was missing. Calvary Youth had a membership of thirty-one, but he'd split them up into two groups for convenience. They gathered together each weekend, but today there were to be only fifteen, not counting the residents. When he realized who was missing, his throat tightened just a bit because he knew who was coming in the door.

Nikki Astin.

She stood in the doorway a moment, her usual warm smile gone. Her face looked long, her eyes worried as she slowly closed the door, avoiding his eyes as she crossed the room. As she drew closer, sitting across from him, he realized her eyes were red, as if she'd been crying. He wanted to ask her if anything was wrong but couldn't bring himself to speak to her.

Bainbridge's stomach ached with guilt. Since last July, each time he saw her he sent up a silent prayer for forgiveness, at the same time remembering with a shiver of pleasure that first muggy night he'd taken her into his bed. . . .

And the second . . .

And, a little less than a month ago—

Please, God, forgive me my weaknesses, my loneliness. . . .

—the last time in that wretched motel room.

He took a deep breath and smiled at her, trying to keep his lips from trembling and his eyes from wandering.

Brenda returned with the others, and Mrs. Wanamaker came out of the kitchen, wiping her hands on her apron, and took a seat.

"All right," Bainbridge said, "I think that's everyone. I hope the week has gone well for all of you so far. Uh, today we're going on a field trip. I expect we'll be gone for a couple hours or so. Is that a problem for anyone? Do you have any other plans?"

They responded with "no's" and "uh-uh's" and shaking heads.

Four or five times each week they went to different locations in the Valley where teenagers were likely to be found—sometimes in the afternoon, sometimes in the evening—and passed out literature, spread the Word, and, if nothing else, tried to make the community more aware of Calvary Youth.

"Before we go," Bainbridge said, "I think we should turn to the scriptures for some guidance and encouragement. Today I've chosen a verse from Corinthians. It's one we've read and talked about before, but I think it's a good one to keep in mind as we go about our work. It's from the second book, verse eleven, King James. 'For we which live are always delivered unto death for Jesus's sake, that the life also of Jesus might be made manifest in our mortal flesh.'" He looked from one young face to another and said, "Any ideas as to what that might mean? How about you, Jim? You're very literary. Any thoughts?"

Jim was curled up in a worn, overstuffed chair, frowning. After a moment of silence, he said, "Sounds like it wants us to kill ourselves so Christ can replace us. Take us over. Like in *Invasion of the Body Snatchers* or something."

Bainbridge coughed behind a knuckle and said, "Well, I think you're on the right track there. You see, in order for Christ to be able to live within us, we must let our earthly life end. We must 'die,' so to speak, so that He can enter us fully and live within our mortal bodies."

"So we die," Jim said, sitting up straighter in the chair. "Our, um, personalities, like, die, right?"

"Well . . . once we surrender ourselves to Christ, we have new personalities, pure and—"

"So, like, what's wrong with the personality we started with, huh?"

"Jim. You're raising your voice."

"Well? If God wants us to kill our personalities, why'd he put 'em there in the first place?"

"Jim. Please go to your room until you've calmed down."

Bainbridge watched the boy stubbornly make his way down the hall, wondering what had gotten into him.

"Well, then. As I was saying. Let's keep that thought in mind as we go out to witness for Him today and in the days to come.

"Now, I know it's raining outside," he went on, "but we can't let a little bad weather stand in the way of God's work, can we?"

The teenagers shook their heads; some replied, "No"; Mrs. Wanamaker replied with an enthusiastic "A-*men!*"

"Make sure all of you have your Calvary Youth badges. If you didn't bring yours, we have spares. Now, today we're going to the Ventura Care Center, a clinic that performs scores of abortions every month. Most of these abortions are performed on teenage girls." He looked from one face to another, pausing for effect. "This is a very controversial subject, as I'm sure you know, and we're not going to please some people with our stand against it. It has become a powerful tool for the devil in our society. It's an easy way out, a way of committing the sin of premarital, or even extramarital, sex without having to face the consequences. Before we go, I want you all to be aware of—" He stumbled on his words when he glanced at Nikki. Her face was red, her eyes glistening, nostrils flaring; she was looking directly at him. "—of our feelings on the issue of abortion." He opened his Bible. "We've gone over this before, but I think it's a good idea to—"

Nikki stood and left the room quickly, heading down the hall.

Bainbridge exchanged a glance with Mrs. Wanamaker. She sniffed and started out of her chair to follow Nikki.

"No," he said quietly, "let me." He turned to a boy with tightly curled red hair and handed him the Bible. "Here, David, you're familiar with this material. The pages are marked, and the verses are underlined. Just read them, maybe talk about them a bit. I'll be right back."

"Sure," the boy said.

Bainbridge went down the hall, looking in each door as he passed.

"Nikki?" he called softly.

The bathroom light was on; the door was open a crack. He knocked with one knuckle.

"Nikki? What's wrong?"

He heard her sob and pressed the door open, peering in.

She was sitting on the edge of the tub, leaning against the wall with her face buried in a hand towel.

"Nikki?"

"Please go away."

"Tell me what's wrong." His throat was suddenly dry, and he wished he'd let Mrs. Wanamaker handle this. He had a bad feeling about it. "Would you like to stay here today instead of going on the field trip?"

She sobbed into the towel again.

"Are you ill, Nikki?" he asked, stepping toward her.

"I can't go today," she muttered.

"All right. But what's wrong? Are you sick?"

Her sob turned into a bitter laugh. "I can't go because I . . . it wouldn't be right."

"What wouldn't be right?"

"Me going to an abor—abortion clinic."

His blood chilled; he couldn't find his voice.

Something chittered within the wall facing Bainbridge.

Nikki raised her eyes to him. They were swollen and red; some of her brown bangs clung to her eyelashes and bobbed when she blinked.

"I'm pregnant," she whispered. "I wasn't sure at first, but now . . ."

Bainbridge leaned against the edge of the sink, feeling weak. "How long?" he asked, thinking it was a stupid question.

"About eight weeks . . . or so."

"Dear Lord," he muttered. Tugging at his lower lip nervously, his words were slurred when he asked, "Who . . . who is the father?"

Nikki laughed humorlessly, squeezed her eyes shut, and began crying again as she said, "Who do you think? I haven't been with anyone else!"

Bainbridge put down the toilet lid and slowly lowered himself onto it, shaking his head as he prayed silently:

Father in heaven, please let this be a mistake, please don't let this be the truth, dear Lord, I know I've sinned and I am dreadfully, dreadfully sorry and I beg your forgiveness, but Father, please don't let this happen now that I've come this far with the group, with these kids, don't . . . let . . . this . . . happen.

Nikki said, "I . . . I can't have the . . . the baby."

"What do you mean, you . . . oh, Nikki, no, you can't do that. You can't. It's a horrible sin, Nikki, a moral crime."

"What we did . . . wasn't that a sin?"

"Well, yes, but—"

"You said God would be forgiving, understanding, because you've done so much work in His name, that He would understand you were a lonely man, too busy with His work to find a wife, and—"

"I know, Nikki, I know what I said, but—"

"Well, He didn't understand, and now He's punishing us. Me, He's punishing *me.*" Her words were strangled with her effort to keep her voice down.

Bainbridge reached out to her, held her shoulder in a firm grip.

"Nikki, listen to me. Get yourself cleaned up, take your time, but make yourself presentable. Then come with us to the clinic. Listen to us, think about what you would be doing if you went through with that. Think hard. You don't have to participate. We'll talk later, you and I, we'll pray about it. We'll ask the Lord's guidance."

"No, I can't go, I can't—"

"Yes. *Please.*"

She rubbed the towel up and down over her face, pulled her shoulder away from him, and stood, saying, "Okay."

J.R. remained in his office after his last appointment of the day, elbows on his desk, face in his hands, staring at, but not seeing, the sports section of the *L.A. Times,* burning with frustration. He looked up when he heard a knock at his door and saw Faye Beddoe smiling through the glass pane. He gestured for her to come in.

"You don't look so good, Junior," Faye chuckled, closing the door behind her. She'd started calling him Junior the first week of school because, as she said, "That's what J.R. spells, no?"

"Bad day," he said.

"Yes, I heard the shouting all the way down the hall. Were the parents shouting at their son, at you, or at each other?"

"All of the above."

"Ah."

"Jesus, Faye, the kid's upset about his parents getting a divorce. *Naturally* his grades and attendance are going to be affected. But they think it's MTV, too much rock and roll, too much sex in movies—Christ, the only people they didn't blame were God, the Russians, and—"

"And themselves, of course."

"I suggested some family counseling, maybe, but no. They want to send him away."

"Away?"

"To the Laurel Teen Center." J.R.'s voice was ripe with bitterness.

"Ah, yes, Laurel Teen Center. Are you familiar with it?"

"Not exactly, but I have a pretty good idea what it is. When I was teaching up north, it wasn't uncommon for parents to send their kids to a place called the Walston Care Unit, one of those institutions that labels everything, including the most perfectly natural problems of adolescence and growing up in general, as mental illness. I assume this is one of those places."

"Exactly," Faye said, taking a long, brown-wrapped cigarette from her purse and lighting up. "Most of their programs are covered by insurance. An easy way out for parents who are not willing to deal with their children's problems. Sometimes their *own* problems." She glanced around the small office. "Ashtray?"

J.R. put an empty Styrofoam cup on the corner of the desk and cracked the window open.

"Those institutions have become quite a big business,"

Faye went on, exhaling a plume of smoke. "In fact, around here they've become chic. And as distasteful as you may find them to be, my friend, there is nothing you or I can do. It's in the hands of the parents."

"And they're passing it to the hands of the Laurel Teen Center. You know what the mother said before they left? She said, 'Our insurance is so good, we can keep Mel in there until he's nineteen.' That's almost four years!" He stood and leaned against the wall beside the window. "Most of those kids . . . all they need is a friend. Whether it's a parent, a teacher, or a counselor—hell, even a janitor—just a friend, an adult they can respect and trust, who will accept them without conditions. But when *I* try to be that friend, something always gets in the way."

"And if something didn't get in the way, it still wouldn't be any easier. By the time those kids reach high school, they're suspicious of adults who want to be their friends." She chuckled sardonically. "You get stung by the bees enough times, you stay away from the hive."

For a moment, the office was silent but for the sound of rainfall outside the window. J.R. pressed his back against the wall, chewed his lip, and stared at the floor, shaking his head, feeling angry and a little defeated.

"Don't let it eat you, Junior," Faye said. "Because it will. You're doing the best you can; that's all you can do."

"Yeah," he muttered, "I suppose so."

"You can also let me buy you a beer. Let's get out of here; it's Friday."

Jeff worked three days a week at Dangerous Visions, a science fiction bookstore on Ventura in Sherman Oaks. Sometimes he helped his boss Lydia sort through incoming used books, sometimes he stocked shelves with new arrivals. Today he was slumped in the chair behind the cash register thumbing through a copy of the *L.A. Weekly*. Lydia was in the back room going through a box of old pulp magazines that had arrived yesterday. A Eurythmics album was playing on the stereo with the volume low. Two little boys who reeked of grape bubble gum were at the shelf across from the register browsing through the comic books, laughing at the busty, scantily clad women on the covers.

To Jeff's left was the store's entrance, a glass door with a large window on either side. Outside, the day was cold and wet and gray as old, dead skin. Wind blew in gusts, tossing the rain in every direction, splashing it against the windows so it ran down the panes in small, restless waves, casting liquidy shadows through the store.

When the door opened, Jeff looked up with his usual come-on-in-and-browse but immediately straightened up in his chair and put the magazine down when he saw it was Lily.

"Hey," she said with a big smile, closing her umbrella as she came inside. "How's the book business?"

"Pays for my gas," he said. "What are you doing out in the rain?"

"I promised my friend I'd drive her home. My friend Nikki? She called about an hour ago and wanted to know if I could come get her. I thought I'd come in here and see you."

"Where is she?"

Lily pointed out the window.

Jeff walked around the counter to the door and looked diagonally across the street.

A white van with CALVARY YOUTH painted on the side was parked at the curb in front of the Ventura Care Center. Reverend Bainbridge stood on the sidewalk beneath an umbrella, his small frame swallowed by a dark green raincoat. Standing around him, holding umbrellas in one hand and literature in the other, were more than a dozen young members of Calvary Youth.

"They're harping on abortion today," Lily said. "See the girl standing at the back of the van? That's Nikki."

"Did she try to convert you over dinner last night?"

Lily rolled her eyes. "God, she's got problems."

"Oh?"

"Yeah, she . . ." Lily hesitated. "I probably shouldn't . . . oh, well, you don't know her, right? She's pregnant." She folded her arms, watching the group across the street,

139

shaking her head sympathetically. "She hasn't told the father yet, whoever that is. She wouldn't tell me."

"What's she gonna do?"

"She wants to have an abortion." She chuckled humorlessly. "And there they are in front of the clinic. She felt guilty enough already. An abortion is just gonna make her feel worse, 'cause *they* think it's a horrible sin. That's all he does, you know? That Calvary guy, what's-his-face? Makes them feel guilty about everything, then promises them heaven. I'm so sure."

"What'll they do if they find out?"

"Probably tell her she's gonna burn in hell. Pregnant girls aren't allowed in heaven. Neither are girls who've had abortions. You know, she told me they . . ." She squinted, leaning toward the door. "Well, look who's here."

Jeff followed her gaze across the street to the van.

Mace stood at the back of the van beside Nikki. The wind blew his hair around in long strands, like white worms squirming from his skull.

"Oh, shit," Jeff muttered.

"What's the matter? Oh, yeah, he followed you yesterday, didn't he? I saw him. Is he, like, selling something?"

Jeff said nothing, just watched.

Nikki wore a long tweed coat, which she held together in front with her fists. Mace was leaning toward her, one arm propped against the back of the van. He wore a shiny white rain slicker and long black boots.

Nikki looked as if she was trying to ignore him, but as he talked to her, smiling all the while, he seemed to capture her attention. She slowly turned her face toward him as he leaned closer to her ear.

"I wonder what he's . . ." Lily began, then she put her hand over her mouth. "Oh, Jesus, I wonder if that guy's the father? No, no, she wouldn't . . . not with . . ."

Mace's arm moved slowly, and he placed his palm over Nikki's belly, saying something. She nodded jerkily.

Bainbridge was gesturing emphatically as he continued his attempts to get the attention of pedestrians, but he stopped when he spotted Mace and his hand on Nikki's belly. He moved toward them and said something. Mace replied, patting Nikki's belly. Bainbridge took a step back, as if shocked, and Mace threw back his head and laughed, putting a hand on top of Nikki's head. Bainbridge waved an arm at him, as if he was telling him to go away.

"What the hell is going on?" Lily wondered aloud.

Bainbridge spoke again, and Nikki shook her head, looking as if she was about to burst into tears. Mace smiled at her, gently touching her face, and Bainbridge pushed his arm away.

"Something's wrong," Lily said. "I'm going out there."

"Hold on a sec." Jeff went behind the register and got his coat, calling, "Lydia?"

"Yo!"

"I've gotta step out a minute, okay?"

"Gonna be gone long?" she shouted from the back room.

"Just a couple minutes." He slipped on his coat as he pulled the door open for Lily. She opened her umbrella and shared it with Jeff.

By the time they got outside, Mace was starting across the street, and Bainbridge was standing close to Nikki, speaking rapidly; Nikki's face was in her hands, her shoulders hitching with sobs as she turned away from him.

"Wait," Jeff said, taking Lily's arm and holding her back. Mace passed through the busy traffic with startling ease, whistling a tune as he walked, his eyes front, his arms swinging in long arcs at his sides. He stepped onto the sidewalk and strode down Grayce Street, disappearing behind the flower shop on the corner.

Jeff waited a couple seconds, then headed for the corner.

"What're you doing?" Lily asked.

"I want to see where he goes."

"Oh. Okay." She followed him.

With Lily right behind him, Jeff peered around the corner. Mace passed the RTD bus stop bench, the parking lot behind the bookstore and flower shop, then turned left down an alley that cut through to Woodman.

They followed his path down the sidewalk, pausing at the corner of the building to make sure he couldn't see them, and caught a glimpse of Mace going down the alley, out of sight behind a garage.

When they got to the corner of the garage, he was gone.

"Where the hell did he—" Jeff began.

"Look!" Lily pointed toward the ground.

Mace's head was sinking into a manhole, facing away from them, his hands pulling the cover over him as he disappeared. The round, flat, thick piece of metal made a heavy clank as it fell into place.

"What's he doing?" Lily hissed.

Jeff hurried across the parking lot and down the alley to the manhole, hunkering over it and squinting through one of the three holes in the cover.

Mace's platinum hair stood out in the darkness below; Jeff watched his head bob as he went lower and lower, whistling all the way. When he reached the bottom, he headed toward Grayce Street, disappearing from sight, his cheerful whistle fading.

"I don't like this, Jeff," Lily said nervously, touching his shoulder. "I'm gonna see if Nikki's okay."

Jeff went with her. As they waited for a break in traffic so they could safely cross Ventura Jeff saw Bainbridge huddled close to Nikki, his umbrella collapsed and leaning against the van, his light hair soaked and strung over his forehead. As they crossed the street his words became intelligible through the sounds of traffic and rain.

". . . wrong, Nikki, he's wrong . . . could he possibly know about . . ."

Nikki was crying.

"Come on, Nikki," Lily said, her back stiff.

Bainbridge turned to them, tried to compose himself, and smiled. "Excuse me, but I have to talk to her about—"

"I'm her ride home, and I can't wait." She took Nikki's arm.

Jeff didn't know if they'd ever met before, but it was immediately obvious that there was no love lost between Lily and Reverend Bainbridge.

"I'll talk to you later," Nikki said to Bainbridge without looking at him.

"Are you coming tonight?" he asked, somewhat urgently.

"I don't know."

Lily led her away without waiting for Jeff.

Bainbridge watched Nikki go with a lost, almost pathetic look on his face.

"Excuse me," Jeff said.

The reverend blinked, looked at Jeff, and muttered, "Hm?"

"Who was that guy who was just here? The guy with the long hair."

Bainbridge's face darkened. "I've never seen him before."

"Well, did he say—"

"I'm sorry, but we have to be going now." He turned away and began gathering the teenagers around the van.

Jeff caught up with Lily and Nikki. They were getting into Lily's maroon Honda Civic parked behind the bookstore. He told Lily he'd call her that night.

In the store, Lydia was putting several books in a bag for the two boys. She was a small woman, pixieish, with short auburn hair.

"Something wrong?" she asked. "You look like you're about to throw up."

"No, I'm . . . fine." Jeff took off his wet coat. "Lydia, have you ever seen a tall guy hanging around, with long platinum hair, spiky on top? His name's Mace."

"No, uh-uh. Why?"

"Just wondering."

"You back to stay now?" When he said yes, she returned to her work in the back room.

Jeff opened the *Weekly* again but could not focus his attention. He stared out at the wet boulevard, watching the cars stir up clouds of mist from the wet pavement. He had told no one of his encounter with Mace in the Galleria. What was there to tell? That a man approached him and persistently made a few vague, cryptic remarks that could've been interpreted a dozen different ways? Yet Jeff knew—sensed, at least—that those cryptic remarks had only one meaning, that Mace knew things about him that he shouldn't, *couldn't*, know.

Seeing Mace crawl down into the sewer only increased Jeff's uneasiness.

He had the unnerving feeling that he was caught in the middle of something he could not yet see, something that swirled around him violently and yet remained hidden.

For now . . .

J.R. and Faye went to The Depot, a small neighborhood bar in North Hollywood. They left Faye's car at school, and J.R. drove.

The place was quiet, and there were only three people at the bar; the booths and tables were empty. They took a booth in the rear; Faye bought J.R. a beer and ordered bourbon with a twist for herself. J.R. was surprised but said nothing.

"You may have to drive me home, Junior," she said with a smirk as she lifted her first drink. "I had a bad day, too."

When he asked her what had happened, she avoided his question and talked about the weather. But by the time she started on her third drink she was more relaxed, although her mood seemed to darken.

"I should have gotten my degree and set up a practice," she said after a brief pause.

"Pardon me?"

She shrugged, sipping her bourbon. "I was going to be a psychiatrist. Work with kids. But I realized something. I'd be working with kids whose parents could afford it. Whose parents were paying me to listen to their kids' problems. So I went into education. Taught sciences for a while. Shifted to counseling. Don't get me wrong. I think the work I'm doing now is more, oh, effective. I'm closer to the kids, you know what I'm saying? But there are days when the other . . . psychiatry?" She shook her head as she took another sip. "My own office, my own hours . . . good pay . . . it looks good sometimes. A little more . . . I don't know, distant, perhaps. Padded. Safer."

J.R. wasn't sure what she was talking about, but she was frowning, her voice was low, and she seemed troubled, so he let her go on.

"As it is," she said, "I'm so close. Every day I'm around them, five days a week; even when they don't have an appointment, I see them around campus. I can see changes in them, and I know what's causing those changes, what's going on at home, and the troubles they're having, but I can't . . . do . . . a thing. Not a *thing*. I feel so helpless." Another sip. "Not all the problems are at home, of course; some are at school, with the law, pregnancy, depression—do you know how many of those kids are walking around campus like zombies, deeply depressed, hating themselves for reasons that really have nothing to do with them? But most of those problems start at home. Of course, as you said, parents don't see it that way."

"And as *you* said, Faye, you can't let it eat you."

"Ah, I know that up here." She touched a finger to her temple. "But here"—she put a hand on her chest—"it feels different. Don't do as I do, Junior, do as I say," she said with a smile, patting his hand; she ordered another drink.

In the brief pause that followed, J.R. wanted to steer the conversation in a different direction, but he felt that Faye needed to go on talking.

"Remember the Pied Piper of Hamlin, Junior?" she asked.

"Vaguely."

"Little town in Germany was infested with rats. *Thick* with them. A stranger arrives one day, a very tall man with piercing eyes and bright attractive clothes. And a flute. A *magic* flute, he claimed, that could cast—" She fluttered her fingers dramatically. "—I don't know, hypnotic spells. He used the flute, he said, to help people get rid of pests and was known throughout the country as the Pied Piper. He offered to get rid of the town's rats and asked only one thousand guilders as payment, not a lot considering the circumstances. The town officials were thrilled and eager to pay him if he could do what he said. So the piper marched down the street playing his flute—" Her drink came, she paid, took a sip, and went on without missing a beat. "—and the rats *followed* him! Right down the street and out of the town, they followed him. A little later, the piper came back for his one thousand guilders. The town officials postured and chortled and said, 'Oh, we were just joking about the thousand guilders. We'll pay you fifty.' The piper reminded them that an agreement had been made and he asked them to pay as promised. They refused. The piper told them that if they didn't pay, they would be sorry. The officials got a big kick out of *that* and said, 'What are you going to *do,* blow your *flute* some more? Go ahead, blow it till you're blue!'"

She took another sip and J.R. began to feel some concern; he hadn't the slightest idea what a fairy tale had to do with Faye's kids at school and wondered if she'd had one too many drinks.

"So he went back into the street," she continued, "and began playing his flute again. But this time, the *children* followed him. All the way through the town, down the street, right. In front. Of their parents. They watched while this stranger led their children out of town. 'Oh, they'll come back,' the parents said, 'they'll come back.' But they didn't. Neither did the piper. One hundred and thirty children. Gone." She lifted her glass in a halfhearted toast. "June twenty-six, twelve hundred and eighty-four."

"A *date?*" J.R. asked, surprised. "That's a true story? I thought it was just an old folktale."

"It's in the history books. A hundred and thirty children never seen again, taken away while their families watched. While *everybody* watched. Right under their noses." An angry edge was creeping into her voice and she fidgeted in her chair.

"Faye, something's wrong. What is it, what's happened that's upset you?"

"Oh, nothing in particular, J.R. Everything in general."

"Which everything?"

"Well, it's still going on," she said quietly. "They just . . . they don't pay the piper."

"Who?"

"The parents." She touched the drink to her lips and held the liquor in her mouth for a long moment, swallowed, and dabbed her lips with a knuckle. "They have their babies, nurse them along for a while, maybe watch them grow, like an azalea or something. They don't realize the commitment required to raise that person. They seem to think it's something that just happens, this growth, on its own, like the azalea. You water it, sun it, and it grows. They don't realize the toll that extra life is going to take on their lives. Not a bad toll, really; I think it would be quite wonderful. . . ." She looked away for a moment, then nodded slowly, chewing on her lower lip. "Yes, quite wonderful. But not easy. They don't realize that. They just seem to want to watch it grow. Then after a time they just glance at it once in a while. Pretty soon they don't even notice it. Then one day something comes along and takes that child away, and they wonder why! Start throwing blame around like . . . like Frisbees! It's the rock lyrics! Violence on TV! Sex in the movies! Let's clean up this country and save our kids!" With a disgusted wave of her hand and a shake of her head, she finished her drink and nodded to the waitress for another.

J.R. was stunned by the fervor with which she spoke, the fiery anger and conviction in her eyes. Mixed with all of it was a sadness that seemed deeply rooted.

He pushed his beer aside and leaned toward her, saying, "Tell me what's wrong, Faye. Please."

She smiled, chuckled quietly. "Oh, Junior, you're a good person for listening to a drunken old Jamaican mumble into her bourbon. But we came here to talk about you. Don't let me ramble like that. Speak up, boy."

"Not if you want to keep talking. Something's on your mind."

The waitress brought her another drink, and J.R. paid for it. She lifted it with a flourish and said, "Whatever's on my mind can be taken care of by whatever's in my hand."

He didn't want her to stop and thought he should pry a bit to keep her talking.

"Do you have any children, Faye?"

"No. So who am I to talk, right?"

"Oh, that's not what I'm—"

"I was pregnant once," she interrupted. "I was going to have it, too, even though I wasn't married. I was twenty-two years old, and how I wanted that baby, Junior. I wanted so much to be a mother, to have a little person to love. I suppose I see my reasons were selfish. I wanted it for *me*. Not a terribly good way of thinking if you're going to be raising another human being, no? But I wanted that baby so.

147

I was like a little girl at Christmas." She smiled fondly, took another drink, then stared at the table for a moment as her smile disappeared. "I fell out of a moving car. Freak accident. The door just flew open and out I went, rolling under the car behind us. I lost the baby and was unable to have any more."

"I'm sorry."

"No, no. It was probably for the best. I believe there's a reason for everything. Perhaps I would not have been a good mother. Perhaps I serve the young ones better this way." Another sip.

"I think you would've been a great mother, Faye."

She tilted her head and lifted a cautionary finger. "Ah-ah, don't say that, Junior. *Everyone* says that. Thinks that. Then, one day, the piper comes. And he seldom leaves empty-handed. . . ."

Seventeen

By six-thirty that evening the rain had diminished to a weak drizzle, but the wind continued to blow.

Bainbridge carefully steered the van around the narrow curves of Beverly Glen until he got to Mulholland Drive, where he took a left.

Three years ago Bainbridge had come across a spot just off of Mulholland that provided a beautiful view of the San Fernando Valley. Whenever he was under a great deal of pressure, or when there was an especially difficult problem in the group, Bainbridge left the house and drove up to that spot, where he silently prayed as he looked out over the sparkling lights of the Valley.

He pulled the van off the road, got out with his umbrella, and crossed over to the ledge.

The view was not as clear as usual because of the weather, but the lights still twinkled through the mist, like glitter spilled by God.

Bainbridge had been a useless, scattered wreck since his conversation with Nikki at the house, but what had happened in front of the care center had doubled his anxiety.

He had never felt such inexplicable fear, such crystal-pure dread as he had in the presence of the man with those strange golden eyes.

Almost the color of whiskey, he thought.

They had glinted with a kind of corrupt joy, almost winking as the man patted Nikki's belly and said, "Just admiring your work, Reverend."

Worse yet was the peaceful look on Nikki's face as she watched the man with rapt interest, as if she knew him well and was thrilled to see him, although she claimed they'd never met before.

Bainbridge's encounter with the stranger had been so deeply disturbing that by the time he got back to the house he was trembling and perspiring despite the cold; the activity around him made him feel claustrophobic, so he'd left, to get away from the others and to escape the hauntingly familiar taste that was lingering in his mouth, a taste he hadn't known in years, decades, and was craving like never before.

As the drizzle spattered his umbrella he felt the burn of unfallen tears in his throat, and when he closed his eyes he saw Nikki's pain-wrenched face, heard her sobbed words. . . .

You said God would be understanding, forgiving. . . .

You said . . .

You said!

He lowered his umbrella and lifted his eyes, letting the rain fall on his face.

"Oh, Lord, forgive me for failing You," he said, his voice cracking. "And for failing those precious young souls." His words were swallowed by the wind. Tears fell from his eyes and mingled with the raindrops.

In failing Nikki, he felt he'd failed all of his kids. If one of them could not depend upon him, how could the others?

Trying to lift his spirits, Bainbridge thought of the successes he'd had so far with some of the kids, and the successes that were sure to come if he held onto his faith in God and himself, if he did not allow one mistake, however dreadful, to defeat him.

Jim, for example. He'd been arrested a couple times for

possession of marijuana, and his parents brought him to Bainbridge, insisting that he live at the Calvary Youth House for a while. During summer school his grades had improved, and as far as Bainbridge knew, he'd been off the grass for over a month. But he was still very quiet and withdrawn, almost brooding. Jim had very dark interests and was an avid reader as well as an aspiring writer. He spent most of his time reading novels that were pornographic in their depiction of sex and violence and dealt almost exclusively with the occult. Bainbridge had thrown them all out—horrible things with garish, bloody covers and titles like *Evilspawn* and *Blood Curse*—and had confiscated his writing—equally dreadful stuff, obviously influenced by the paperbacks. Then he had tried to aim Jim's writing talents and reading interests in more positive directions. Whenever Jim threatened to run away, which he did frequently, Bainbridge reminded him that he would not only be in danger of imprisonment, but he would also be in danger of losing his soul.

Then there was Ellen, who wore only black clothes, sported a lizard tattoo on her arm, and wanted to be a rock star, "like Joan Jett," she often said. She was, indeed, blessed with a beautiful singing voice, and Bainbridge tried to coax her into using it at the weekend meetings, but she was more interested in singing her own songs about street life and sex than in singing music of a more sacred nature.

Bainbridge had a few more problem kids living in the house, but those two were his biggest concerns because they each had so much potential. New ones came in all the time, either brought by their parents or by social workers who supported Bainbridge's work. And the Valley below him, sparkling like a vast garden of diamonds, was filled with many, many more young people hungry for the truth, for the Lord's love. . . .

Taking in a deep, fortifying breath, Bainbridge wiped the tears from his eyes and said in a full voice, " 'To the Lord our God belong mercies and forgivenesses, though we have rebelled against Him,' amen."

He felt a little stronger, more prepared to look into those young eyes. Most of all, he was ready to face Nikki again. It was not the Lord's will that she end the life growing inside her, so surely He would give Bainbridge the wisdom to change her mind.

He closed his eyes in a prayer of thanks for the strength he felt when he heard two soggy footsteps behind him.

"Bitchin' view, isn't it?"

Bainbridge twisted around toward the long-haired man he'd encountered earlier.

"Who are you?" the reverend snapped. He was suddenly trembling again.

Smiling, the man said, "We weren't introduced. I'm Mace. And you're Reverend Bainbridge, right?"

"What do you want?"

"Hey, hey, chill out. Just here to enjoy the view." His hands were buried deep in the pockets of his raincoat, and he did not look at Bainbridge.

The reverend ground his teeth together for a moment, asking God to help him hold back his anger and calm the strange fear this man seemed to stir in him.

"You followed me," Bainbridge said.

"Why would I do that?"

"I don't know. Just like I don't know why you would take such pleasure in frightening a young girl, as you did today."

"I didn't frighten her. She was upset. I made her feel better."

Bainbridge took a step toward him, his knuckles white as he clutched his umbrella. "You know very well what you did."

Mace grinned at the Valley below them. "So do you, Reverend."

"Look. I don't know how you know the things you do, but they're none of your business. That girl is in the middle of a personal crisis, and you'll only confuse her further by—"

"Aren't you in the middle of that crisis, too, Reverend?" His hair whipped about in the wind. "Haven't *you* confused her, too?"

Bainbridge realized his chest was heaving with angry breaths, and he decided it was best to leave.

"Just leave her alone. Leave all of my kids alone." He turned to go.

"Oh, don't leave, Reverend. Let's talk." He sounded genuinely friendly. "We have a lot in common, you know."

Turning back to Mace, Bainbridge barked an incredulous laugh and said, "What could we possibly have in common?"

"Several things. We've both come to feed the hungry souls of the young people here in this valley, am I right?"

Another laugh from the reverend, then: "Well, I don't know about you, but I'm trying to—"

"I know what you're doing. I'm very familiar with your work. In fact, you might say we're in the same business."

"I am not in any business. I work with young people, I try to—"

"So do I."

It occurred to Bainbridge that this man might be a problem in the future, a stumbling block to his kids. Perhaps it would be a good idea to learn as much about him as possible. Still, Mace unnerved him and gave him the feeling that he was in danger.

"I bet you do," Bainbridge said. "What are you into, my friend? Drugs? Are you a pusher?"

Mace chuckled. "That's always the first thing you think of, isn't it? Blame everything on drugs."

"Whatever you do, I wish you'd do it away from my kids."

"They need me."

"What could they possibly need from you? I've taken those kids off the streets, out of broken homes, away from abusive parents, I've—"

"I do that, too. With one difference." He finally turned to Bainbridge, and for the first time the reverend realized how very tall the man was. Mace towered over him. "I accept them, Reverend. As they are. Flaws and all. I learn their strengths and nurture them. I find out what they want to be, and I encourage them."

A shudder passed through Bainbridge, a shudder so powerful it forced him to stagger backward a step. His mouth worked a moment before any words came out, and then his voice was weak: "I give them salvation."

"Whether they want it or not."

"They need it."

"They need acceptance, too."

Bainbridge felt dizzy, overwhelmed by the need to get away from the man. He spun around to return to the van as the rain began to fall harder, sounding like machine-gun fire on his umbrella, but he lurched to a stop when something moved at his feet.

"Don't go yet, Reverend," Mace said. "We're not through."

He took another step, but something made a horrid, threatening hiss, then a guttural squeak—and the reverend saw the eyes looking up at him from the wet weeds around his feet, from the brush that grew along the road.

Fear sprang up inside Bainbridge like water from a geyser.

"They won't hurt you, Reverend. If you just stay and talk awhile."

Bainbridge slowly backed up until he was standing beside Mace again; he was trembling so violently, his umbrella jittered above him.

"You know, Reverend, I bet that if you changed your methods a little, your group would grow like you never thought it could."

The reverend began to pray silently, his lips moving frantically as he watched the dark, squat creatures move toward him.

"I bet if you and I worked together," Mace went on, putting his hand on Bainbridge's shoulder and turning him toward the sprawling view, slipping his arm around the reverend, "all this"—he swept his other arm over the Valley—"could be ours. All those kids looking to be accepted, looking for someone to say, 'Hey, you're okay,' they'd all be ours, Reverend. If you'd just work for me."

Bainbridge was frozen with fear; he suddenly felt certain of who, of *what,* this man was, of what he wanted. He had to swallow several times before he could find his voice.

"You're evil," he croaked.

"Evil?" Mace laughed. "But I just told you, we're doing the same work. Getting those kids off the street. *Saving* them, as you'd put it."

"But your intentions are . . . are evil. Selfish."

"And yours? You want them to be what *you* want them to

be. And remember, you've got a baby growing inside a girl barely old enough to drive a car. If I'm evil, Reverend," he laughed, "I sure hope you aren't an example of good."

Tears blurred the reverend's vision as he pushed away from Mace, stumbled, and almost fell as he sputtered, "D-don't t-touch me! Don't touch me!" He ran into the cluster of glowing eyes, and they hissed and squeaked, snapping at his feet as he ran toward the road, toward the van.

"Reverend," Mace called.

Bainbridge pressed on as sharp teeth tore his pants, the hem of his coat. He collapsed his umbrella and began swinging at them, praying for deliverance as he felt something crawling up his leg, beneath his coat, up his back.

"'G-get thee hence, S-Satan,'" he cried, falling forward, dropping the umbrella, clawing at the muddy earth, "'for it is written th-thou sh-shalt worship the Lord th-thy G-God and-and-and—'" They crawled onto his back, heavy and wet. "'—and him only shalt thou seerrrve!'"

Mace's feet stepped before his face, and Bainbridge heard the man's dry laugh.

"What's your hurry to get back, Reverend?"

Bainbridge held perfectly still as the creatures squirmed over him, their breath hot on his neck.

"Want to see Nikki? She won't be there. She's at my place."

"Liar!"

Mace offered his hand. "Why don't you give me the keys to your van, Reverend, and we'll go for a ride. I want to show you something."

Eighteen

Jeff called Lily twenty minutes before he was to close the store for the evening. She was so upset about Nikki that at first he had a hard time getting her to complete a sentence.

"She kept saying she didn't know that guy," Lily said, "but she talked about him like she did."

"What'd she say?"

"That she had to talk to him, she *had* to talk to him. He understands, she said, and he would help her. Anyway, I knew she was zoned, so I asked her to a movie tonight, to get her mind off it, you know, and she says she can't and gives me a bunch of bullshit Calvary Youth reasons why spending time and money on movies is a sin, so I told her that if God didn't want her to go to the movies, He never would've, like, made Tom Cruise, so she says okay. *That* was a surprise. Anyway, we agreed I'd come get her after I changed my clothes, then I dropped her off at her place. But I called her before I left my place, and her mom says she never came in! Jeff, I'm scared. I mean, that guy gives me the creeps, and if she's with him . . . But I'm afraid to tell her mother, 'cause, like, what if I'm wrong? Nikki'd shit! She'd never forgive me."

"Maybe she's at the Calvary Youth House."

"Uh-uh, I called. The woman I talked to said Nikki hadn't been in since the group went out in the van. And they're all back."

Jeff thought a moment, drumming his fingers on the counter.

"Are you busy now?"

"No."

"What do you say we go down there?"

"Where? The sewer?"

"Yeah."

"Oh, Jesus, you think they might have gone down there?"

"Maybe."

When she agreed, he told her to come to the back of the store. As he waited on two more customers, then prepared to lock up, he thought of Mallory, wondering if she'd returned home. He called the apartment but got no answer.

I think I've got just the girl for you, Mace had said.

Somehow, he knew Mallory. And somehow—

He was just bluffing, please, God, just bluffing.

—he knew of Jeff's feelings for her.

He *had* to know more about Mace.

The weather had gotten worse. Rain fell with a constant, monotonous purr, and the wind rattled the window-panes.

When Lily knocked at the back door, Jeff opened it, and a rush of wind and rain followed her in. Her short hair was wet and tossed.

As Jeff went through the store turning out the lights he said, "Do you have a flashlight in your car?"

"I don't know. Do you?"

"I don't have a car."

"You were gonna walk home? In this weather?"

He nodded.

"I'm so sure. I'll take you when we're done."

Jeff smiled. "It's gonna stink down there," he said. "Sure you want to go?"

"Well . . . what are we looking for, anyway?"

"I'm not sure. I just want to see if we can find out where Mace went."

"If Nikki might be with him . . . yeah, I wanna go. I'm scared for her."

Jeff was touched by her devotion to her friend. He realized he knew nothing about Lily but hoped to remedy that soon. He liked what he'd seen so far.

While he got his things together, she stood at the front window staring out into the rain.

"This weather," she mumbled. "You know, it's not like fall around here. It's . . . strange. Everything's been strange lately. Like something's just . . . wrong. Ever since that last weekend. You know, that last Saturday night before school started, it was really weird. I was with some . . ." She frowned out the window, scratching her chin with one finger, then suddenly turned to him and smiled. "I'm rambling. Sorry."

But she was right. For the first time since it had happened, Jeff remembered walking on the boulevard with Mallory and Brad and the others, leaving the Calvary Youth behind at the theater. He remembered the odd hush that fell, the way everyone stopped to look up at the sky, as if there was something to see.

But there was nothing there. Nothing he could see, anyway. He wondered if Lily had had a similar experience.

They had no time to talk now, though.

"Okay," he said, putting on his coat. "It's getting late. Let's go."

When they stepped out the back door, the wind nearly blew them over.

They found a flashlight in the tool compartment in back of Lily's car, then hurriedly pressed through the wind and rain to the manhole in the back alley.

Jeff hooked the index finger of each hand into a hole and lifted the cover with a grunt, sliding it to the side.

"I'll go first," he said, shouting to be heard above the rain.

"I know," Lily said with a nervous laugh.

Shining the light into the hole, Jeff saw the rungs, the dirty pipes, and the filthy floor a few yards below. He tried to wipe his wet hands on his jeans so they wouldn't slip on the rungs, but his jeans were soaked. Clumsily holding the flashlight in one hand, he carefully climbed into the hole, shining the light on the rungs for Lily.

Jeff was going to scurry back up when she reached bottom and replace the cover, but before climbing down, Lily reached out and, with effort, dragged it back over the hole.

Once she was beside him, she winced and said, "Jesus, it reeks down here!"

It did, but the smell was not as bad as Jeff had expected. The wind blew through the sewer in gusts, whistling through the grates and manhole covers above like angry ghosts. Water poured from above, and the flashlight beam danced over the black, gushing sewage below them.

"Now where do we go?" Lily asked, her hushed, trembling voice echoing in the darkness.

"He went this way," Jeff said, turning to the right. "This walkway's pretty narrow, so be careful."

"I'm right behind you." She clutched the back of his wet coat and pressed close to him as they walked.

A couple yards ahead they came to an intersection. Jeff shone the light right and left, but the beam was swallowed by the darkness.

"Let's keep going straight," he said.

They crossed a narrow metal plank that spanned the intersecting gutter.

A little farther on, Jeff felt a draft from the right. He shone the light toward the wall.

At first it appeared to be a small, dark, rectangular nook in the wall, but the light fell on nothing—no wall or door—so it was deeper than it seemed.

"Just a sec," Jeff said. He leaned into the opening a bit and shone the light around. Beyond the wall to their right, sound seemed compressed, the darkness seemed thicker. The beam passed over tangled, intestinelike pipes; beyond that was only more darkness.

Bracing himself against the edge of the opening, Jeff leaned in a bit more.

"What is it?" Lily hissed.

"I . . . don't know. It looks like some kind of . . . room."

To the left, at some distance away, Jeff saw a fire flickering in the darkness. Moving shapes hovered around it.

Jeff immediately backed out, but it was too late. Heavy footsteps crunched through the darkness toward them as Jeff reached behind him and grabbed Lily's coat to pull her away, snapping, "Jesus, c'mon, let's—"

A broken baseball bat with a splintered end swept out of the darkness and cracked against the edge of the opening, and a pale, bony hand slapped onto Jeff's head and clutched his hair.

Lily's scream echoed all around them. . . .

Mallory lay on a pile of cushions in the swimming pool, naked from the waist down, her legs entwined with Kevin's beneath a warm blanket. A cloud of smoke was suspended a few feet above them, and more rose from the pool as the group sprawled around her continued to take drags on joints and pipes.

There were lanterns above them on the floor, but in the pool it was dark. A radio was playing somewhere in the room, but it didn't cover the moans and sighs and wet smacking sounds in the pool.

"Glad you came?" Kevin whispered.

"Mm-hmm."

He laughed.

The night before she'd been hesitant, but she certainly didn't want to go home to her mother. The trip through the sewer had frightened her, but the reception she got from Mace made up for it. There were more people in the building than she'd expected. Besides the band members and their girlfriends, there were a couple dozen other teenagers, some of whom she recognized from school. They were all lounging around on cushions and piles of blankets, smoking grass, drinking beer, and, to Mallory's horror, holding and stroking those tusked, almond-eyed creatures that had frightened her during her first visit to the building. She didn't want to go in when she saw them, but Mace was quick to welcome her with a few tokes on a pipe. It wasn't long before she was relaxed, floating, a little drowsy, and in good spirits.

Mace made a big deal of her arrival and ceremoniously

presented her with a strange cross that seemed to be made of red obsidian. He said it was a Crucifax and that she was never to take it off.

A few moments after she put it on, she realized everyone was wearing them.

Mace rolled a joint for her and told her to relax while the band rehearsed. It had been a while since she'd heard them play, and she was stunned by their performance. It was as if she were listening to an entirely different band. Their music enveloped her like a mist, seemed almost tangible, and when Mace sang, his voice, which alternated between low and seductive and high and piercing, with a razor's edge, was hypnotic, totally captivating.

After running through a couple songs, Mace turned to the band, smiled, and watched them silently with what looked like pride.

"I think it's time to show our stuff," he said. "We're playing Fantazm next Wednesday night."

None of them knew how he'd arranged it, and none of them asked.

For a while, Mallory worried that she would make her mother angry by being out all night; she imagined Jeff lying awake, worrying about her. Eventually, though, they fled her memory like strangers.

The group partied the rest of the night; someone went out for burgers and fries; people came and went through the hole in the sub-basement; there was never less than a crowd in the room. Around three A.M., Mallory and Kevin and Trevor and his girlfriend, Tracy, went out in the rain for ice cream.

Mallory could not remember enjoying herself like this.

Back in the pool, they dozed, smoked grass, made love, and, when Mace offered it, snorted some coke.

Time became a blur, and it was impossible to tell if they'd been there a few hours or a few days.

Earlier that Friday evening, Mace had brought in three men and a girl and introduced them to the group. The men were off-duty police officers who, Mace said, were going to be "very good and very important friends." The girl's name was Nikki Astin, and Mace encouraged the others to help lift her spirits. Mace gave them some grass, some coke, and they got in the pool. Two of the officers made fast friends with a couple of girls, the third with a thin blond boy who'd been lying quietly in a corner of the pool. Nikki was shy and took a while to loosen up, but soon she was in the pool with the others.

As far as Mallory knew, they were still there, but it was hard to tell. In the darkness around her she saw slowly moving arms and legs, lumps beneath blankets. She got an occasional glimpse of a mouth sliding down over a glistening erect penis, or a hand gently closing on a pale, round breast. Slanted, glowing eyes peered down over the edge of the pool, and small claws clicked against the cement. Mallory was more comfortable in the presence of the creatures and paid them little attention.

Mace had left over an hour ago, promising to return with company.

Rock music was thumping through the speakers of a portable stereo.

Mallory felt Kevin's hand slip between her legs, and she moaned as his fingers began to move and thoughts of school and Erin and Jeff and everything else in her life were worlds away. . . .

The reverend sat stiffly in the passenger seat of his van as the tires below him screamed around the curves of Beverly Glen. The windshield wipers droned back and forth and, at the wheel, Mace grinned into the night, occasionally glancing at Bainbridge.

The reverend could feel the creatures at his feet; three of them, pressing themselves against his ankles and crawling over his shoes. There were more in the back, squeaking as the van rounded the sharp turns.

Bainbridge's mouth was dry as old felt, and he could not stop trembling as he prayed frantically for deliverance from what he was certain was the devil's henchman.

If not the devil himself.

"What . . . what are you going to—to do to me?" he asked, his voice a froglike croak.

"Do to you?" Mace laughed. "Nothing. Just taking you to a party."

"Why me? Why am I being tried like this?" He closed his eyes as they shrieked around another curve.

"You're not being tried. I'm sorry you feel that way. Why don't you just think of me as . . . oh, how about a buddy? Not friends yet," he chuckled, "just buddies. But later we'll—"

"You're *evil!* This is a trial, a test of my faith!" The reverend clenched his eyes tighter, wanting to cover his ears, but afraid to move because of the beasts at his feet.

Mace's laugh was deep and rich. He punched the dashboard jovially.

"Black and white," he said. "Everything is black and white to you people, good and evil. You're white and I'm black, all black, evil to the bone, right? But Reverend, you live in a gray world, don't you know that? There is no black, no white, only gray. You say I'm evil, but those kids are *nuts* about me, Rev; I make them happy. Now, is that evil? Making them happy? Huh? *I* don't think so. Now you. You're supposed to be good, all white, but you've been sneaking around with somebody's little girl, and now she's pregnant and you won't let her do what she wants with the baby that's growing in her belly. Hah! That's goodness? You see? We're all gray. Some are blacker than others, maybe a few are all black, but I can promise you one thing, Reverend. Nobody . . . nobody is all white."

Taking in a deep, unsteady breath, Bainbridge said, "Satan uses the truth to tell lies, and—and we're told he can—can fool the very elite, and I will *not* listen to—"

"I'm . . . not . . . Satan." His tone was very serious now, almost threatening. "I'm not from hell or heaven. I'm from . . . *nowhere.* And you brought me here. You. Your fellow clergy. All the many, many moms and dads here in this valley." He drove in silence for a while, then said, "There is no place in this universe for gaps, Reverend. I've come to fill the gaps that you have made."

Bainbridge clenched his fists in his lap and continued to pray. . . .

* * *

A hand pulled Jeff's head back hard as a ragged voice cried, "Leave us alone! Leave us *alone!*" Jeff saw the bat lifted high over his face, saw it stop before swinging down again, and he slammed his arm up, knocking the hand away. He felt Lily grab his coat, and they dashed away from the opening, avoiding the bat by inches as they moved on down the walkway in a staggering, swaying run, their hands slapping the wall, their feet scraping over the grimy cement.

"Get away!" the voice cried as the bat smacked against the wall once, twice, again. Footsteps followed them a few feet, then stopped.

They didn't look back, kept moving, passed another intersection and another, their gasps echoing in the darkness. The sewer veered left then right as their feet clanged over another metal plank.

"Wait, wait!" Lily panted, pulling on Jeff's coat.

When he turned and shone the light on her, he saw her tears, and she stepped into the crook of his arm.

"What . . . what was that?" she asked.

"I don't know. A bum, I guess. I hear a lot of them live down here."

"But what was that room in the—"

"Sh!"

In the silence, water dripped and pattered and sewage gushed. And somewhere in the darkness, music played.

"What?" Lily asked.

"Hear that?"

She listened a moment. "Where's it coming from?"

Jeff faced the opposite wall and listened intently. Mingled with the music were distant, garbled voices, laughter; they were coming from his right, from the direction in which they'd been walking.

"C'mon," he said, taking her hand and leading her along the walkway, the flashlight shining before him. Up ahead, he saw a couple rats that quickly skittered out of sight before Lily saw them.

As they pressed on the music grew louder, the voices and laughter more distinct, although they were still faint, ghostly.

"Sounds like a party," Jeff whispered.

The closer they got, the clearer and louder the voices became; the music was replaced by a loud, fast-talking voice that Jeff recognized as a radio disc jockey. Someone was listening to the radio.

"—c'mere before you—"

"—ha-haaaah—"

"—me another one of those—"

The music began again: Robert Palmer.

The louder they became, the more difficult it was to tell exactly where the voices and music were coming from.

Until they found the hole.

He could tell the hole had been knocked in the wall fairly recently because there were still bits of rubble and a few bricks scattered around on the walkway beneath it.

"In here," Jeff breathed, shining the light through the rough-edged hole.

"What is it?"

The light fell on dark, wet walls, stacks of boxes, twisting pipes connected by fluttering cobwebs, and a steep metal staircase. There was a soft, shimmering glow coming from the top of the stairs.

Jeff leaned close to Lily's ear and whispered, "Be very quiet."

He carefully pulled himself through the hole, then angled the light so Lily could see her way through. With Jeff a step ahead, they made their way slowly and silently to the staircase, where Jeff turned off the flashlight; the glow from above gave them enough light to see. As they carefully climbed the stairs, trying to keep silent on the metal steps, the voices crystallized, becoming clear and distinct.

A male voice: "Did you hear that?"

A female voice: "Yeah, it came from up there."

Another male voice: "The door? Is Mace here?"

They hunkered down as they reached the top of the stairs, and something clattered loudly on the next floor: footsteps on metal stairs.

"I'm back!" The voice was loud, deep, booming; it was Mace.

A chorus of greetings replied, and Jeff was surprised by the number of people he heard. He climbed the remaining steps on his hands and knees, peering over the top of the staircase. There had once been a door there, but only hinges remained. The room was large and appeared to have once been two rooms; the remaining portion of a wall jutted three quarters of the way across the middle of the room, then ended in a jagged, broken edge where it had been torn away. Bricks and chunks of broken plaster littered the floor. There were three holes in the torn-away wall; bars of soft light shone through from the other side, cutting the dusty, smoky darkness.

Beyond the wall, Jeff could make out some movement in the hazy light. He saw a couple kerosene lanterns on wooden crates. Murmuring voices were occasionally punctuated by a burst of laughter or a passionate cry.

Reverend Bainbridge was coming down a spiral staircase; Mace was one step behind him, holding a lantern.

"And I have a visitor," Mace said.

Once they were off the stairs, Mace stood beside the reverend and lifted his lantern, illuminating the little man's face.

"This is Reverend James Bainbridge," Mace said. "Some of you may already know him. C'mon in, Reverend."

Bainbridge looked terrified and moved like a bird as he followed Mace deeper into the room, disappearing behind the wall.

A scuttling noise came from the spiral staircase, and Jeff's mouth closed over the terrified groan that rose from his chest when his eyes followed the sound.

The creatures that had chased him from the abandoned health club were milling around the bottom of the staircase, sniffing the floor, their eyes glinting in the lantern light.

Jeff's throat seemed filled with cotton, and he reflexively put his hand over Lily's, needing to touch someone, to reassure himself that he was not alone.

"Take your coat off, Reverend," Mace said congenially. "Get comfortable. We're very informal here."

They were out of sight, hidden by the wall, but Jeff could hear their movements above the music and soft voices.

"Nikki!" Bainbridge wailed as if in pain. "My God, Nikki . . ." Then, angrily: "What have you done to her?"

Lily squeezed Jeff's hand.

"*I* haven't done anything," Mace said.

Jeff felt Lily stiffen beside him, looked to see her staring intently at the wall a few yards away.

Mace said, "You're here because you want to be, aren't you, Nikki?"

Faintly: "Yes."

"She's been drugged!" the reverend barked.

"Oh, she may be high, but I can assure you she hasn't been drugged, Reverend. No one here has been drugged, and no one is here against their will. Nikki . . . why don't you come out of the pool?"

Pool? Jeff thought.

"I'm taking her out of here," the reverend said, his voice trembling.

"I don't think she wants to go."

"I'll call the police."

"Reverend, I'd like you to meet three very good friends of mine. Officers Peter Wyatt, Jake Margolin, and Harvey Towne." Deep male voices, groggy and garbled, greeted the reverend. One of them laughed. "They're off duty right now, but if you feel you need a policeman, I'm sure one of them would be more than happy to help you."

Jesus, Jeff thought, chilled by the fact that Mace was friendly with the police. Jeff didn't know what he was up to, but he knew it had to be bad; somehow, police involvement made it seem worse.

After a long pause, the reverend whispered, "I was right." Something seemed to have left his voice—reason, hope, maybe both—leaving behind a hollow, helpless sound. "You . . . you *are* . . . evil."

Mace laughed and said, "C'mon, Nikki."

The reverend pleaded, "Nikki, Nikki, what are you doing here?"

"Tell him, Nikki. Why did you come?"

"Because Mace is . . . is gonna help me with my . . . my problem."

"Tell him what problem."

"My . . . my baby."

"Oh, God, dear God, don't do this, Nikki." Bainbridge sounded near tears.

Lily put a hand over her mouth and squeezed close to Jeff.

"Nikki," the reverend went on, his voice a desperate hiss now, "think about it, about what you're doing."

"I can't keep it. I . . . I *can't.* I . . . I haven't finished school. My . . . my mother would . . . my mother . . ."

"But it's . . . Nikki, it's a-a-a"—he gulped back a sob—"sin, a horrible sin, a moral crime!"

"Nikki," Mace said, "did the reverend ever mention that what he did to you was a sin?"

"Mm-hm. He said God would"—she giggled—"understand. And forgive."

"Okay, Reverend. God will understand Nikki's reasons, and He'll forgive her."

"But this is murder!"

"Yeah. And what are the words for what you did, Reverend?" Footsteps; rustling movement. "Adultery?" Mace's voice grew softer. "Fornication?" Softer still. "Maybe . . . rape?"

Jeff and Lily turned to one another. He saw the same realization in her eyes that he felt: Reverend Bainbridge was the father of Nikki's baby. Lily put her face in her hands and slowly shook her head.

"Is *this* what you did, Reverend?" Mace whispered. "Did you touch her like this . . . like this?"

Nikki moaned, sighed.

"Did you touch her—no, no, lie down, Nikki—did you touch her here, Reverend?"

Lily's eyes burned with fear for her friend; she looked ready to make a dash across the room and around the wall.

"No!" Bainbridge cried. "Stop! Stop this *now!*"

Mace laughed.

Nikki gasped ecstatically.

The reverend sobbed.

The voices seemed more attentive to whatever was happening on the other side of the wall.

"Is this what you did?" Mace hissed, voice wet, lips smacking. "Is this what it was like?"

"I'm leaving!" Bainbridge shouted, his feet scraping on the cement. "Nikki, if you would only—" Something made a wretched, throaty hiss, and Bainbridge swallowed his words with a gasp.

Jeff recognized that sound. . . .

Lily started to sit up, but Jeff put a hand on her shoulder and firmly held her down.

There were no lanterns at their end of the room; at the other end, with the exception of a few figures shifting in the hazy darkness, everyone had gone behind the wall. If he was quiet, Jeff thought, the lack of light at their end might sufficiently hide him until he got to the wall and could look through one of those holes.

Jeff turned to Lily, laid a finger over his lips, and breathed into her ear, "Stay here."

She frowned at him and cocked her head.

Jeff started across the room, moving in a crouch, his feet crunching softly over the floor, too softly to be heard above the music and the quiet buzz of voices.

As he crept to the wall Jeff heard Nikki's soft murmurs of pleasure grow louder. He heard Mace whispering, chuckling. Amid the voices were smacking, slurping noises.

Speaking with malevolent deliberation, Mace whispered, "Is this . . . what you did . . . before you planted . . . your *seed* in her . . . Reverend?"

Nearing the wall, Jeff felt as if a steel band was slowly tightening around his chest, making each breath more difficult, squeezing his heart within his rib cage. The back of his neck was damp with sweat.

When he reached the wall, Jeff cautiously peered over the edge of the hole on the right end.

To the right, two guitars were propped against the wall, and drums and a keyboard were set up between amplifiers; four of the dark creatures were crawling over the instruments, sniffing curiously. Beyond the instruments in a murky corner, Jeff saw what looked like a generator. About six feet in front of the instruments was the swimming pool. Shapes moved within its darkness. To Jeff's left, Mace stood in the shallow end of the pool, his tall, lean frame rising above the darkness below. Lying before him on two fluffy-looking cushions, her legs spread, naked but for a blue shirt open in front, was Nikki. A lantern shone on each side of her, making her skin look pale. Her nipples were dark and erect, and a dark, oddly-shaped cross rested between her breasts, attached to a cord that went around her neck. Trails of saliva glistened around her breasts and over her belly.

The reverend stood at her head, several of the creatures huddled between him and Nikki; two of them were standing on their hind legs like guards, teeth bared, eyes threatening.

Mace smiled up at Bainbridge, his lips and chin wet; he passed his hands over Nikki's body, caressing and gently squeezing her full breasts, slipping his fingers between her legs.

"Did you do this, Reverend?" Mace whispered, wrapping his lips around a wet finger and licking off the juices. "Or were you too eager to fuck her?"

Mace leaned forward and slowly, luxuriously slipped his tongue between the flowery lips of Nikki's vagina and moved his head up and down, up and down, licking his way up to her belly, her breasts, sucking loudly. Nikki's breaths were thick with moans of pleasure.

Something crunched behind Jeff, and he spun around to see Lily hurrying toward him. Jeff waved for her to go back, not wanting her to see what was happening beyond the wall. She ignored his warnings and kept coming, her eyes and mouth wide with fear as she sidled up to him and peered over his shoulder, her hands gripping his sides just above his waist.

"No!" the reverend snapped, but his voice was weak. "Stop this, *please* . . . stop . . . this. . . ."

Mace stood to his full height and smiled, purring, "Look familiar, Reverend?" Chuckles rolled like ice cubes up from his chest as he ran the tip of his tongue over his lower lip. Mace opened his mouth, sticking out his tongue as a child might at a playground rival. But it kept coming, like a snake easing its way out of a hole.

Jeff heard a strange dry clicking and realized it was the sound of shock in his own throat.

Lily tightened her grip on his sides and whimpered softly as the tongue slid out farther and farther.

Bainbridge frantically muttered prayers under his breath.

The tip of Mace's tongue touched Nikki's left nipple, rolling around it around and around.

The reverend raised his voice: ". . . though I walk through the valley of the shadow of death—"

The tongue, extended a good three feet from Mace's mouth now, moved to the right nipple, lantern light glistening in diamondlike reflections along its moist length.

"—I will fear no evil, for thou art with me—"

It rose to her mouth, and she wrapped her lips around it, sucking it as if it was a rigid penis.

"—thy rod and thy staff they comfort me—"

Lily's nails dug into Jeff's flanks like small knives, but he hardly felt them because he was numb with horror as he watched Mace's tongue return to Nikki's breasts; they swayed as she wriggled with groggy delight.

"Feels . . . so . . . good . . ." she breathed.

"—thou preparest a table for me in the presence of mine enemies—"

The tongue slid down over her belly, leaving a sparkling trail like an oversized slug.

"—thou anointest my head with oil—"

It eased lower still, over her navel, toward the triangle of hair between her legs. . . .

"—my cup runneth over; surely g-goodness and m-mercy—"

Jeff's guts chilled as Mace's tongue continued its descent. . . .

"Holy Jesus," he whispered, turning to Lily and pulling her away from the hole, somehow certain of what was about to happen. Open-mouthed and breathless, Lily resisted at first, but he jerked her hard into his trembling arms and pressed her face to his shoulder, whispering into her ear, "Don't watch, Lily, d-don't look at this. . . ."

Jeff heard a deep moan of pleasure catch in Nikki's throat and turn into a cough.

Soft wet sounds—moist sliding sounds—were buried by the reverend's gibbering voice: "Oh, God, don't do this, dear Jesus, merciful Father in heaven, *don't do this!*"

Jeff felt lightheaded as he closed his eyes and held Lily

tight; he felt as if he had somehow tripped and fallen into someone else's nightmare as Nikki began to make dry, pained retching sounds.

"Nikki?" Lily whispered.

Jeff pressed her face harder to his shoulder. His jaws ached from clenching his teeth.

Nikki screamed. It was unlike any scream Jeff had ever heard; it tore from her lungs like skin from bone.

"Nikki?" Lily's coarse voice was louder, trembling with fear. Jeff pushed her away from him, turned her around, and clapped a hand over her mouth.

Nikki vomited then; the sound was loud and distinct, as if she were emptying her body of everything it contained.

The reverend let out a crumbling, defeated "Ooohhh," and Jeff heard his body collapse against the wall and slide to the floor. He had fainted.

Lily pulled away from Jeff suddenly and screamed, *"Nikkiii!"*

There was a startled murmur of voices and sudden movement beyond the wall.

Jeff pulled away from their hiding place so suddenly he nearly fell. He spun around and pushed Lily, rasping, "Run!" as he heard the chitter and scrape of small claws on the cement floor coming around the wall. "Run, *run!*"

"But N-Nikki's—"

"Just go, goddammit!" He grabbed her arm and pulled her along, stumbling on a chunk of plaster.

As they clambered down the stairs into the sub-basement Jeff heard the sound of snapping teeth behind them and turned on the flashlight. He missed a step and, for an instant, was airborne, limbs sprawled. When he hit the floor, a needlelike pain shot through his shoulder.

He heard shouting from upstairs, hurried footsteps, and another loud cry from Nikki, sounding different now, empty, resigned.

"Get up!" Lily cried, grabbing his arm. "Get up—Jesus Christ, *get up!*"

Jeff rolled onto his back, and the flashlight beam swept upward, reflected in a dozen golden eyes skittering down the stairs.

Lily pulled, gasping, "Now, now, NOW!" and Jeff struggled onto his hands and knees, half crawling to the hole in the wall, gripping the edge, pulling himself to his feet as Lily crawled through.

Claws scratched over the cement behind him, teeth snapped, and the guttural squalls the creatures made sent slivers of ice through his veins as he fell through the hole, nearly tumbling over the edge of the walkway and into the rushing stream of blackness below.

Lily was before him, pulling on his sleeves, babbling, "Get up, c'mon, please, Jeff—get up now, get—"

Her eyes turned to the hole behind him, widening, and she screamed as she backed away. Above her scream, above the wet sounds of the sewer, Jeff heard them coming through the hole and began to crawl, the flashlight beam cutting wildly through the darkness as he felt them at his feet.

Kicking his feet, hoping to hit them, Jeff managed to stand, his hand sliding over the wet wall in search of something to grasp. As he rushed toward Lily he saw her face twist into a mask of horror as she waved her arms, screaming, "Jesus, oh, God—they're—they're right be-be-behind—"

Jeff spun around and swept a foot over the cement, knocking three of them off the walkway, then swept it back again to kick the others rushing toward him.

One stood on its hind legs, hissed, and dived through the air toward him while his leg was still raised. He tried to hop backward, but he lost his balance, flailed his arms, and fell, splashing into the stream of sewage.

Lily screamed shrilly.

Jeff thrashed in the waste, gulping air, anchoring his feet on the bottom and gripping the edge of the walkway, trying to keep the flashlight safely above his head.

"Get out of here, Lily!" he shouted. "Find a manhole and get out!"

"No, dammit, give me—"

"Go! I'm right behind you!" He put his arms on the walkway and started to pull himself up as Lily's footsteps faded.

The sewage was waist-deep; dark lumps washed around

him, clung to his jacket, and the rancid odor filled his nostrils and throat.

Something grabbed his jacket, and he looked down to see one of the creatures hanging by its teeth, flat nostrils flaring, its teeth tearing into his jacket, and Jeff could not hold back the scream. He brought the butt of the flashlight down hard, striking the creature between the eyes as he swayed precariously in the strong current.

The animal fell away.

Jeff tried once again to pull himself out and saw two black-booted feet suddenly standing before him.

"Help me!" he blurted without looking up. "Help me, please!"

A big hand took his arm and effortlessly lifted him out of the gutter and onto his feet.

"You're welcome to stay," Mace said pleasantly.

Jeff flinched, backing away from him. Mace's chin was still dark and dripping; meaty specks were stuck between his teeth. Jeff aimed the flashlight at him as if it were a gun.

"Is she dead?" Jeff croaked. "Did you kill her?"

"Nikki? No, no, course not. She's fine. I just did what she wanted."

Three of the creatures were sniffing around behind Mace; one of them rubbed itself against his ankle like a house cat.

"If you stick around," Mace went on, "maybe there's something you want, something I can—"

Jeff took several steps away from him. "What are you?"

Mace's smile was filled with such warmth that Jeff felt confused for a moment. He thought that perhaps hurrying away was not the right thing to do, that maybe Mace wasn't so bad after all, because he seemed genuine, sincere. But there were still dark, bloody flecks on his teeth, on his lips, and Jeff quickly remembered what he'd heard inside, what Mace had done. Jeff did not yet understand it, but he remembered. . . .

"What am I?" Mace repeated thoughtfully, wiping his chin with the heel of his hand. "I'm . . . a friend. That's all. Just a friend."

Jeff turned and followed in Lily's direction.

"You remember that," Mace called as Jeff found the open manhole, saw Lily's face peering down from the rainy street above. He grabbed the rungs and began to climb.

"You remember that, because you'll need a friend soon. You'll need a friend." With a hollow, echoing chuckle, Mace added, "Big brother . . ."

Nineteen

J.R. was enjoying the sound of the rain against his windows as he thumbed through the *Rolling Stone* he'd bought that day. A Kate Bush album was on the stereo, he had a beer in hand, and he was slumped on the sofa with his feet up, comfortable and content. The rain reminded him of home, although it was pretty early in the year for such harsh weather, even for Northern California.

He'd driven a very inebriated Faye Beddoe home from The Depot, offering her a ride to her car tomorrow if she couldn't find one and promising to tell no one of her condition.

As if sensing his worry, she'd said, "I don't do this often, Junior. I just . . . just needed to tonight. I'll be better Monday."

"You're sure you don't want to talk about it?"

"But . . . I did. Perhaps you didn't hear. . . ."

He wasn't sure what she was referring to but left it at that, hoping to talk with her later when she was sober.

It had done him good to get out. He hadn't made any friends since his move, with the exception, now, of Faye. He had a lot of students in his charge, making for a tight schedule, and at the end of the day he had too little energy left to pursue a social life just yet. It would have to wait awhile.

He found counseling to be a bit more taxing than he'd expected. As a teacher, he'd dealt with groups of students; while it was hard work, it had given him a little more space than counseling, had been a bit more relaxed.

As a counselor, he dealt with one student at a time. They came into his office to talk about their classes and grades, but, more often than not, the conversation turned to other things:

Julio, the chubby Hispanic boy whose grades had plummeted: "I don't wanna live with my dad 'cause he drinks, but my mom's boyfriend, he don't want me in their house."

The black girl named Myra, whose nails had been chewed to the quick, bursting into tears during a discussion about her poor attendance record: "I'm sorry, Mr. Haskell, I'm *s-sorry,* but my d-dad w-wouldn't let me c-come back to school until . . . until the . . . b-bruises were gone and . . . and the c-cuts h-healed . . ."

The painfully thin girl who wore expensive clothes and drove a brand new sports car: "I just did it to lose a little weight at first—sticking a finger down my throat after meals, y'know?—'cause my mother said I was getting fat, and I hate that, being fat, I *hate* it. But now . . . well, I can't stop now. Throwing up, I mean. And I thought maybe I should, well, like . . . see a doctor?"

The boy named Garth who wore lots of leather, had shaved his head, and had been busted several times for carrying knives on campus: "Fuck you, and this fuckin' school, up your *ass.*"

Sometimes as he sat at his desk listening to a student—perhaps it was the student's tone of voice, a glint of desperation in the eyes, or something much less perceptible—Sheila flashed in his mind, her voice echoed in his ears—

Do you think I'm sick and evil?

—and he was overcome with the desperate urge to help the boy or girl in his office, to do something, anything, that would make things better before it was too late. . . .

All he could do, however, was counsel, refer, and listen.

The tape in the stereo came to its end, and J.R. got up to turn it over. Before he got there, the phone rang.

"Hello?"

"Collect call for J.R. Haskell from a Jeff Carr, will you accept charges?"

"Collect?"

"Yes, will you accept—"

"Yes, yes, of course."

"Mr. Has—uh, J.R.?" Jeff said. He was out of breath, his voice hoarse; from the sounds of rain and traffic in the background, he was in a phone booth.

"Jeff, what's wrong? Where are you?"

"Sorry about calling collect, but we didn't have any change, and—"

"Who're you with? What's happened?" J.R. instinctively groped for a pad and pen in the narrow drawer of the phone table.

"I'm with Lily Jaskett. We're at Ventura and Coldwater, in front of Hughes Market."

"Are you all right?"

"Not . . . really." He laughed then, and J.R. thought he detected a chilling shadow of hysteria in Jeff's voice.

"Should I bring help? Police or an—"

"No! No police. Everything's okay, really, just . . . well, if you could come get us—"

"I'll be right there." He slammed the phone down and dashed for his coat . . .

Things calmed down quickly in the pool room after Reverend Bainbridge ran, babbling hysterically, up the spiral stairs and out of the building.

Curious heads that had risen from the pool's darkness in reaction to the unfamiliar and terrified scream lowered again, returning to their beers, joints, sex. . . .

Mallory remained cuddled next to Kevin beneath the blanket, not much caring about what was going on, deciding, as Kevin did, that Mace would take care of it.

Mace disappeared for a few minutes but returned to assure them that everything was just fine. He asked Kevin to go out for food, and Kevin climbed out of the pool, took his crumpled jeans from the floor, and put them on.

"Want us to find that reverend guy?" Kevin asked.

"Oh, no. He won't be a problem, not now that he knows what he's dealing with," Mace said. He gave Kevin some money and told him to bring back pizza.

Kevin peered over the edge of the pool at Mallory. "Wanna come?"

She was about to say no when Mace answered for her: "She'll stay."

Kevin took Mark and Trevor with him, promising to be back soon.

Mallory closed her eyes, breathed deeply, relaxed, smiled at the mild euphoria she was feeling. She could hear Mace's whispers above her.

"Nikki? How do you feel?"

"Mm . . . sleepy."

"Any pain?"

Pain? Mallory thought. *What happened? Was someone hurt?*

"A little," Nikki murmured. "Not bad." A smile in her voice: "Thank you."

"Here. A blanket. Stay warm. Relax. Sleep. Smoke some more of this."

"Mmm . . ."

"And remember. Our deal . . . your promise?"

"I remember."

"Good girl."

Mallory shifted beneath her blanket. The sensation of her thighs rubbing together, her skin smooth and warm, was soothing, a bit titillating. There was a song playing on the radio . . . one Mallory thought she liked but wasn't quite sure . . . it was hard to focus on the lyrics . . . the melody . . . on anything. Everything around her, even with her eyes closed, seemed to run together like spilled paint.

Until a hand rested on her knee.

"Mallory?" It was Mace.

"Hm?" She half opened her eyes.

"You're all alone."

"You sent Kevin away."

"No reason for you to be alone." He sat down beside her, leaning his back against the pool wall. "Enjoying yourself?"

"Mm-hm."

"I'm glad."

Mace gently stroked her hair; it made her smile, reminding her of the way her father used to run his fingers through her bangs, playfully flip them up and down on her forehead, then caress them back into place.

"Are you going home soon?"

"I don't know. Why, do you want me to?"

"That's up to you." He delicately ran a fingertip over her eyelashes. "You're welcome to stay here as long as you want."

"Really?"

"Really. Here." He reached over her head to the edge of the pool and brought down his pipe and lighter. He slipped the pipe between his lips, lit it, and handed it to Mallory.

She inhaled and held the smoke in her lungs.

"Won't your mother be upset?" he asked.

"Probably doesn't know I'm gone."

"What about your brother?"

She shrugged, exhaling, then took another drag.

"You know, Mallory, I think your brother cares about you very much."

"I know he does."

"Do you? Aren't you afraid he'll be upset? That he'll worry about you?"

"He always does."

He traced the line of her jaw with a finger, and Mallory closed her eyes, leaned back her head as he stroked her throat; her skin tingled.

"Would he worry," Mace whispered, "if he knew you were okay? That you want to be here?"

"I don't know."

"Maybe if he knew it wasn't so bad, he'd want to come, too. To be with you." He moved closer to her, easing an arm around her shoulders. "What if your brother came here and neither of you had to go home again?"

"Well, I'd have to go home *some*time. Change my clothes,

180

maybe get a few things. I haven't had a shower since I got here."

"We wouldn't be staying here. Not in this building. I'll be leaving here. I thought you might want to come with me, you and your brother."

"When are you leaving?"

"I'm not sure yet." He traced the edge of her ear with a fingertip. "Would you like to come?"

"I don't know. Where . . . are you going?"

He gently touched his lips to her forehead. "Away from here." He kissed her eyebrow, her eye, then pulled away, fingering the Crucifax hanging from her neck, lightly touching it to the skin of her throat as he gave her a smile that made her feel on top of the world. "To someplace better."

"Is . . . Kevin going?"

"I think he will if I invite him, and I will. I'm going to invite everyone. When I go"—he stroked her lower lip—"I want to take all of you with me. . . ."

Mickey D.'s NY Pizza was crowded with loud, stylish, and pretty daddy-bought-its. That's what Kevin called them: daddy-bought-its. Even the ugly ones were pretty.

Kevin led Mark and Trevor to an out-of-the-way corner to wait for their order. He hated Mickey D.'s, but it was the closest pizza place, and, although he didn't like admitting it, their pizza was the best on the boulevard.

Leaning against the wall, Kevin watched them. They huddled over pinball machines and video games, crowded around tables and lifted their icy beer mugs in loud toasts. Some of them writhed their well-worked-out bodies on the small dance floor in front of the big-screen television that was showing a Lionel Ritchie video.

He felt out of place, almost claustrophobic. He thought of how happy his parents would be if he could fit into that crowd; if he sported one of those tan, perky girls on his arm, drove a sports car, and had his hair styled. He never would—he didn't want to—and for that reason, he would always remain an outsider in his family.

Kevin held the ticket with their order number on it. He turned to Trevor, slapped the slip of paper into his hand,

and said, "I'm gettin' the fuck outta here. I'll wait for you outside."

There was a small patio area in front of Mickey D.'s. Rustic picnic-like tables and benches were set up beneath a turquoise-blue and white striped awning. A curtain of water cascaded down from the awning, giving the busy boulevard a dream-like appearance.

Kevin leaned against one of the tables and lit a cigarette. He hadn't ridden his motorcycle in a couple days, and he thought of the bike parked on Whitley, soaking wet from the rain. Normally, he wouldn't leave it unprotected for so long. That motorcycle was very important to him. Sometimes he got on it and drove even when he had no place to go. It felt good, so unenclosed, and he didn't think he would ever be able to drive a car. He hadn't felt the need to drive his bike in a couple days, and it wasn't just because he'd been so preoccupied with Mace's drugs and Mallory's body. Since Mallory had finally agreed to join Crucifax, a feeling had crept into Kevin's life that he'd never experienced before, a feeling that seemed to grow as he spent more time with Mace.

Contentment.

The door behind Kevin opened, and he turned, hoping to see Mark and Trevor with their pizzas.

It was Larry Caine.

Behind him were three other guys, all with broad shoulders and thick-muscled necks.

"Hey, gay bait," Larry said, grinning, coming toward him fast, "what're you doing here? I didn't think this place was your style. Your friends with you? Where's Mallory, she get sick of you or something?" He stood inches before Kevin.

Not moving, feeling Larry's beer breath on his face, Kevin didn't blink.

"You still smoking?" Larry asked, tapping the side of Kevin's cigarette with his fingernail. "Don't you know how bad that is for you? Don't you read the papers? Or . . . do you read?"

The three guys behind him guffawed, each of them shifting his weight from foot to foot.

Kevin glanced at the door, willing Mark and Trevor to come out.

Larry knocked the cigarette from Kevin's hand.

"Just thinking of your health, dude," Larry sneered.

The others laughed again.

"So how are things going between you and Mallory? You two happy? She, uh . . . she jack you off while you're riding your big bad motorcycle?"

Something ripped inside Kevin, like a piece of fabric being torn down the middle, and he decided not to wait for the others. He'd been wanting to hurt Larry Caine too long to wait any longer.

He brought his knee up hard; Larry's mouth dropped open, and he jerked forward, his knees pulling together and his hands slapping over his crotch as he made a pained retching sound.

Larry's friends rushed around him, their jaws set. Kevin stepped back, reached down quickly, and swept the knife from his boot, opening it with a smooth flick of his wrist, holding it lightly, and slowly waving it back and forth before him as he stepped back.

Larry staggered backward, spitting, "You little cocksucker!"

The others moved fast, their eyes on the knife; two of them flanked Kevin while one moved behind him.

Kevin glanced at the door again, beginning to feel panicky.

Larry straightened up, his face contorted, and moved toward Kevin again.

"You've got a lot of nerve, dickhead," Larry hissed. "In case you didn't notice, you're all alone here."

"My friends are inside."

"I know, I saw them." He smiled maliciously. "But you're out here." He nodded to his friends.

Kevin heard movement behind him and spun to his left, swinging outward with the knife. The blade cut through the sleeve of one of Larry's friends, and Kevin felt it pass through flesh, then pull out as the arm jerked away with a cry.

Larry's fist pounded into Kevin's kidney, and threads of pain shot up his side like a barrage of bullets. Kevin's knees gave way with the pain, and he fell. Someone grabbed his right wrist and squeezed hard. The knife slipped and chittered over the cement.

Another fist slugged him in the stomach as his arms were pulled above his head. He gasped for breath and tried not to vomit as he was dragged to the sidewalk. They pulled him through the rain and around a corner, then dropped him in a puddle. His head smacked the pavement as one of them kicked him in the ribs, knocking out what little air seemed to be left in his lungs. When Kevin opened his eyes, squinting against the rain falling in his face, he saw them towering over him like buildings. Larry hunkered down beside him, grinning.

"What's this?" Larry asked, taking Kevin's Crucifax in hand. He tore it away, and the leather cord burned Kevin's neck. "Some jewelry?" Larry asked in a swishy, mocking, feminine voice, inspiring more laughter from his friends. "Where'd you get this piece of shit, an arts and crafts fair? Venice Beach, maybe?"

"Give me that," Kevin growled through his pain.

"Oh? Is it sentimental?" Larry chuckled as he tossed the Crucifax over his shoulder.

Kevin winced when he heard it scrape and crack over the pavement.

This will be your escape from all that you hate, Mace had said, *from all the people who don't understand you.*

Kevin tried to sit up, but Larry pushed him back down with his foot.

. . . someday, this will be all you have . . .

Mustering all the strength he could, ignoring his pain, Kevin clenched a fist and threw it in Larry's face. It landed so hard, his knuckles cracked and Larry fell over backward. As Kevin sat up he saw Mark and Trevor rounding the corner of the building. Mark held a stack of pizza boxes but dropped them and rushed forward with Trevor, both of them drawing their knives.

Kevin heard grunts and curses, shoes scraping and splashing over the wet puddled pavement, the meaty sounds of fists meeting flesh. He rolled onto his hands and knees, crawling forward, groping for the Crucifax.

A foot slammed into his stomach, knocking him onto his back again.

"You motherfucking little—" Larry swept down on him like a bird of prey, grabbed his jacket, lifted him, and crashed him to the wall, pummeling Kevin furiously with his fists.

The alley was suddenly awash with red, blue, and white light. Tires hissed into the wet alley; brakes lurched, and car doors opened and slammed as voices shouted:

"Hey!"

"Police!"

"Stay right there! Stop!"

"Jesus, cops!"

There was a flurry of running feet and panting breaths as Larry let go of Kevin.

Eyes blurred, body aching, his head pounding with pain, Kevin slid to the wet pavement. Nearly oblivious to the frantic activity around him, he touched his chest where the Crucifax had been and groaned. The pulsing, spinning lights hurt his eyes, and he closed them, closing his fist over the wet material of his shirt.

People will know who you are when they see this around your neck . . .

He felt empty, lost. . . .

They'll know that you're a friend of mine. . . .

. . . helpless . . .

. . . that you're important . . .

"Okay," a deep voice said, cold and official, "let's see some I.D., kid."

. . . and powerful . . .

"I'm . . . I'm . . . a . . . Mace . . . Mace . . ."

"What?"

Kevin felt sick.

So don't ever . . .

"Maybe you better call an ambulance," one of the voices said.

185

. . . take it . . .

"Cruci-Crucifax . . ." Kevin muttered through the blood in his mouth, still clutching his chest.

. . . off . . .

His parents' faces flashed in his mind, tight and angry, as he felt hands lifting him from the ground.

There are places we can send you to! he heard his mother shouting.

"Mace . . ." he gurgled.

"Mace?" a voice barked. "Somebody spray you with Mace?"

"Bullshit," another barked. "Nothing wrong with his eyes, is there? He's not blind."

"M-Mace . . . Cruci . . . fax . . ."

"He's grabbing his chest. Your chest hurt, kid?"

"Oh, he's okay. On something, I bet. I'm gonna go see if they caught the others."

"Okay, kid, suck it up. You're coming with us."

Kevin began to cry. . . .

When Reverend Bainbridge walked through the front door of the Calvary Youth House, Mrs. Wanamaker was at the piano leading the group in a song. The singing stopped and all eyes turned to the reverend.

Mrs. Wanamaker spun around on the piano stool, smiling. Her mouth dropped open and her hands slapped onto her thighs.

"Rev . . . Reverend," she gasped, standing slowly. "What's happened to you? We were so worried, we thought—"

"Lock all of the doors and windows," the reverend said firmly, taking off his muddy, wet coat.

The kids—about thirty or so of them seated on sofas and chairs, on cushions, and on the floor—stared at him with puzzlement and confusion.

"Did you hear me?" he said, his voice loud but trembling. He let his coat drop to the floor, turned, and locked the front door.

Some of the teenagers stood, but only to continue staring at the reverend as if he were a stranger.

"Lock everything," Bainbridge said, "and pull all the shades. Now." He took a steadying breath and tried to sound more relaxed and polite when he said, "Please."

He walked into the living room, mud caked on his face and clothes, and Mrs. Wanamaker came to his side.

"Reverend, what's wrong?" she asked. "What's happened?"

He shook his head, pressed his hands to his temples, and tried to calm his breathing.

"Could you get me some aspirin and a glass of water, Mrs. Wanamaker?"

"But you're filthy! You should bathe and lie down, you don't look well, you should—"

"Mrs. Wanamaker, we are all in a great deal of danger; my health is the least of my worries. The Lord has shown me . . . He's shown me . . ." He realized he was shouting, and all of them were staring at him in shock, with a little fear in their eyes. "Does anyone here," he asked softly, "know a man . . . named Mace?"

Silent stares.

"Anyone? Have you talked to him? *Seen* him? He's tall and thin, with—"

Quiet laughter came from the kitchen doorway.

Bainbridge saw Jim standing there, leaning against the doorjamb with a satisfied smile on his face.

I should have known, the reverend thought, remembering Jim's stacks of hideous novels and the things he'd written, all those dark and wicked stories. . . .

"You," the reverend breathed, moving toward him. "How well do you know him? What have you told him about me? What do you know?" he shouted.

"I've talked with him," Jim said. "That's all. He bought me lunch."

"Bought you lunch. Do you know who he is? *What* he is?"

"He's a nice guy," Jim said with a shrug. "Interesting."

"He's a devil!" Bainbridge shouted, his tears returning. "He's an angel of Satan! And he's claimed one of us, one of this group! Maybe because of you, because you let him in, because you will not accept the truth offered to you here, because you are so in love with evil!" He searched the boy's face for some sign of fear, of regret, but saw only a glib, satisfied smirk, as if he knew something that he was not about to tell. "I want you out of here. Now. Out!"

Jim laughed and shook his head. "Yeah, I'll go."

"Get your things and get out of here now!"

"Okay, okay, I'm going." He crossed the room slowly, giving Bainbridge a knowing glance, muttering, "But *I* didn't fuck anybody." He disappeared down the hall.

Oh, Lord, he knows, the reverend thought, clenching his fists. *How did he find out? Who has he told?*

Bainbridge looked around at the horrified and confused faces, saw the tears in Mrs. Wanamaker's eyes—

"Reverend, Reverend," she was whispering.

—and got down on his knees.

"Pray," he said hoarsely, a desperate sense of urgency coursing through his veins. "Kneel with me and pray for protection and guidance, because he's out there now, laughing at us—"

And what are the words for what you did, Reverend?

"—looking for our weaknesses, preying on them right now, this man, this evil, vicious disciple of Satan—"

. . . for what you did . . .

The reverend felt sick as he knelt on the floor, knowing by the frozen expressions on their faces that he wasn't getting through to them.

"—waiting for us to open ourselves up to him, to make the smallest mistake, to take our eyes from the Lord for one moment—"

We're doing the same work.

"—to doubt His Word for an instant—"

You want them to be what you *want them to be.*

Bainbridge closed his eyes and for a moment began responding to the remembered words in his head as if they were being spoken into his ear:

"No, no, what *God* wants them to be, His will be done, *His* will be—"

I sure hope you aren't an example of good. . . .

"No, that was a mistake, a *mistake,* the Lord *forgives,* He—"

A hand on his shoulder.

A soft voice:

"Reverend, why don't you lie down, please. . . ."

He opened his eyes. Mrs. Wanamaker was standing over him.

The kids were leaving, quietly filing out with their coats and Bibles.

"No! Don't let them go out there! No! He's waiting, that's what he *wants!*"

Ellen and two of the boys went down the hall toward their rooms, whispering quietly to one another.

Bainbridge's head was spinning when he tried to get up. He fell on his stomach, sobbing, fists clenched.

"He's waiting . . . he's waiting for them. . . ."

The door closed.

They were all gone.

Mrs. Wanamaker put her arm around him and tried to help him up.

"You don't know . . . what I've seen," he muttered, his hands still clinging to each other in a prayerful clench. "You don't know what he's done to those kids, what he's done to . . . to Nikki. Poor . . . dear . . . sweet . . . Nikki . . ."

"Reverend. Let me call a doctor. Please."

He smacked his lips several times. "No, there's no reason to call a doctor." Then, after a moment of thought: "Is there?"

It suddenly occurred to him that perhaps—just perhaps—it had not happened. Perhaps that horrible thing he'd witnessed in Mace's dark and damp basement had been a hallucination, a dreadful waking nightmare.

But he knew it could not be. What he'd seen was real, and those kids, as well as others, were in deep and terrible danger. He knew it would be unwise to go to the police; if Mace had told the truth and those three men in there were police officers, how could Bainbridge know there weren't other policemen involved with him, maybe the whole force?

Who *could* he turn to, then? Certainly not his kids, who had just hurried out like house guests fleeing an embarrassing family argument. And Bainbridge could tell, as he looked up into the confused and pitying eyes of Mrs. Wanamaker, that the poor woman feared he was suffering some kind of breakdown.

Bainbridge's only source of help and guidance was the Lord, and that made him laugh out loud. After what He'd allowed to happen to Nikki, the reverend had no reason to think the Lord would lend him an ear.

"Can I call someone, Reverend?" Mrs. Wanamaker whispered. "I think you need help."

The reverend got to his feet and stood on wobbly legs, trying to compose himself.

"No, Mrs. Wanamaker. Thank you, but no. I . . . I'm sorry for disturbing the group. Terribly sorry." He felt himself slipping again, ready to release another sob, but he sucked it in and scrubbed a hand over his dirty face. "I think I'll take a hot bath; why don't you, um, go home for the night?"

"Heavens, no. I have to clean up yet, and I'm worried about you. Maybe you shouldn't be alone, maybe I should—"

"That's very kind, Mrs. Wanamaker, but unnecessary. Thank you anyway." He seated himself on the sofa and waved at her to go away. He remained there as she gathered her things up to leave.

The reverend sat there smacking his lips, deep in thought. He truly did have no one to turn to . . . except for one very old and long-neglected friend. . . .

He could taste it.

After Mrs. Wanamaker left, the reverend went to his room, browsed through his phone book, and made a call to Duffy's Liquors. The ad in the phone book said: "WE DELIVER!"

J.R. leaned against his kitchen counter facing Jeff. A section of the fluorescent ceiling light buzzed and flickered, in need of repair. Jeff was standing against the wall by the window, his hair wet from the shower he'd taken earlier. He wore J.R.'s white terrycloth bathrobe. His clothes, along with Lily's, were in the wash downstairs.

J.R. had not been able to get anything out of them as he drove them to his apartment. Both had been near hysteria, especially Lily. She'd been so upset that, against his better judgment and with visions of lawsuits dancing in his head, J.R. gave her some brandy to calm her down and warm her up while Jeff was in the shower.

Once Lily was in the shower, Jeff began to tell J.R. what had happened. Speaking in fits and starts, his eyes darting nervously around him, Jeff related to him the events of that afternoon—watching Mace, Nikki, and Bainbridge from the window of Dangerous Visions, watching Mace disappear down a manhole—and told him how they'd followed Mace's trail that evening. That was where Jeff lost him.

"Wait, wait just a second," J.R. said. "Who *is* this Mace guy?"

"I'm . . . not sure."

"How do you know who he is? Have you met him?"

"Once. Yesterday. In the Galleria." A shudder passed through Jeff, and he drew the robe together in front of his throat.

"What?" J.R. asked. "What aren't you telling me?"

Jeff slowly shook his head. "You'll think I'm crazy."

J.R. laughed. "You call me collect from six blocks away, I find you in front of a Chevron station covered with shit because, from what I understand, which isn't much so far, you spent the evening in a sewer. So don't worry, Jeff, if I were going to think you're crazy, I'd be thinking it by now."

Jeff turned away from him and looked out the window. J.R. knew that his attempt at humor had failed. He went on in a more serious tone.

"I can tell this guy scares you, Jeff. Why?"

"He . . . knows things about me. Things that he shouldn't know. Can't know."

"Like what?"

"My sister . . ."

"I knew you had a sister before I even met you. It was on my list. Just because—"

"No, no. He knew things . . . things I've never told anyone. Things I've only . . . only thought. Things . . ."

"Things about your sister."

Jeff turned fully away from him and looked out at the rainy darkness. He was fidgeting.

"How long before the clothes will be done?" he asked.

"Look, Jeff . . . if it's too personal, you don't have to—"

"It's not that it's personal, it's just . . ." His voice thickened, and he stopped to gulp loudly. "There's . . . something . . . wrong with me."

J.R. knew then that he'd been right about Jeff's feelings for Mallory, and he could see how deeply it disturbed the boy.

"I think I know what you're talking about Jeff," he said cautiously. "I'd have to be blind not to see it in your face when you talk about your sister, hear it in your voice. Believe me, there's nothing wrong with you. It's not uncommon. I used to spend a lot of time with my sister. We were very close. I was a late bloomer—I didn't start dating until college—so we were best friends. Lots of brothers and sisters develop crushes on each other. Cousins, too. No, there's nothing wrong with you."

Jeff said nothing.

"But . . . what makes you think Mace knows about this?"

"In the Galleria, he . . . he came up to me and started talking about girls, said he had just the girl for me. And he described her. Mallory, I mean. And he . . . he made a couple references to . . . well, I have these dreams about her, and . . . I think he knows."

"What? How . . . I don't understand."

"Neither do I. But I think he has my sister down there."

"Down where?"

Jeff went on to tell J.R. of the hole they'd found in the sewer and the room it had led to. He described it in detail, including the musical instruments he'd seen. Then he told him of Kevin's plans to meet with a man who'd promised to help the band.

"I think Mace is that man," Jeff said.

"So where is this room?"

"In the old health club at Ventura and Whitley. I followed them there one night." He chuckled coldly. "See? There is something wrong with me."

He told J.R. about the swimming pool, the reverend being there, the animals that were crawling around the room and that had chased him from the building once before.

And then he told him what they'd heard happen to Nikki.

"Jesus Christ!" J.R. blurted, standing up straight with a jolt of fear. "Jesus, we should call the police!" He suddenly felt frantic, started to leave the kitchen to go to the phone.

"Wait, J.R. It's not what you think. Nikki was pregnant. Bainbridge, the Calvary Youth guy, was the father. And Mace made him watch while . . . while he aborted the baby."

"For Christ's sake, Jeff, she could die, if she hasn't already! What did he use on her?"

Jeff seemed to pale a bit, and his hands trembled as he said, "I think he used his . . . tongue."

J.R. didn't think he heard right at first. "I'm sorry?"

"His tongue."

The conversation suddenly tilted, became something different altogether, a joke, maybe, or drugs, maybe they'd been taking drugs.

"Jeff, that's . . . what you're telling me is . . ."

Jeff began to cry. His face twisted, and his eyes welled with tears. "It came out of his mouth like . . . like a snake. He put it inside her and just . . . We ran out as fast as we could, but he caught up. Lily went on ahead of me. He . . . he was laughing at me, inside, he was laughing. As I left he said I'd need him, that he wanted to be my friend or something, and that I'd need him soon, and he . . . he called me . . . he said, 'You'll need a friend . . . big brother.'"

J.R. nearly cried out at the words.

Big brother.

You lose, big brother. . . .

J.R. said, "What . . . what does he look like, Jeff? This guy?"

"Tall, thin. Long platinum hair spiked on top. His eyes . . . he's got weird eyes. They're . . . I don't know, like a gold color."

J.R. sucked in a breath and pressed his lips together, remembering the woman who drove his sister away from him for the last time. Her eyes had been a pale gold . . . strange, so coldly confident and knowing. . . .

You're thinking crazy, J.R. told himself, shaking his head as if to rid it of his chilling thoughts.

"We have to call the police, Jeff," he said.

"No, no," Jeff replied, still trembling. "He's got three of them in there now, cops, friends of his. You didn't see what we saw, J.R. This guy . . . he's . . ." His whole body quaked. "He's not human, he's deadly, deadly as hell, and . . . and he's got my sister in there, I just know it. If he doesn't right now, he has in the past and he will again, and I'm afraid for her, J.R., I'm scared shitless."

"Okay, okay, just think a second, Jeff. Does your mom know about this? About Mace?"

He shook his head.

"Is she home now?"

"No. At work."

"All right. We're going to have to talk to her about this."

J.R. realized he was trembling, too, and he nearly shouted when he heard a sound to his left.

Lily stood in the doorway wrapped in a huge towel with a blanket over her shoulders. She looked upset but seemed much more composed than she'd been earlier.

"Can I use your phone?" she asked him.

"Sure."

"Who're you calling?" Jeff asked, following her into the living room.

"Nikki. Maybe . . . I don't know, I thought maybe I could talk to her mother. But she's probably drunk, passed out on the sofa." She punched the number out with an unsteady hand, glancing questioningly at Jeff.

"I told him," Jeff said, with a nod toward J.R.

The three of them were silent as Lily waited for someone to answer the phone.

"Nikki?" she gasped. "It's Lily, are you all right?" She began to cry but tried to hide it in her voice. "Asleep? How long have you been home? . . . Bullshit, I know you were out! Nikki, I was there! I saw you! With that—that . . . No, I wasn't spying, I just—no, no, wait a second."

J.R. released a quiet sigh of relief and exchanged a glance with Jeff.

"But what was he *doing* to you?" she asked impatiently. "Oh, that's bull—no, I just wanted to . . . Okay. Okay. I was just worried, Nikki, that's all." She looked confused, disoriented. "I'm coming over tomorrow. I want to talk to you. You're . . . you're sure you're okay? . . . Yeah, all right. 'Night." Her hand slowly lowered the receiver back to its cradle. She looked at them with a befuddled, open-mouthed expression. "She was asleep. She got home about half an hour ago. Says she's stoned and tired, but . . . but she's fine."

"What did he do to her?" Jeff snapped, sounding half-angry.

Lily shrugged. "She was pissed at me, accused me of spying on her, and . . . and said he was just a friend of hers. They were . . . fooling around. He was just . . ." She laughed humorlessly. "He was just going down on her."

"But what about the reverend and—"

"She wouldn't talk anymore. She's tired. We're supposed to talk tomorrow."

J.R. was immensely relieved. Jeff had had him going for a while, nearly speechless with dread. He smiled now.

"Look, you two," he said, "I hate to say this, but . . . well, did you do any drugs tonight?"

"No!" Jeff snapped. "We didn't! I told you what we saw."

"I'm not calling you a liar or anything, Jeff, but . . . what you say you saw is impossible. Absolutely impossible." Jeff started to reply, his eyes angry, but J.R. held up a hand. "Wait, I'm not dismissing what you've told me. This guy Mace sounds like trouble. I promise you, I'll do what I can about him. If your sister's hanging around with him, I'll have a talk with your mother, and we'll keep her away from him. But for now . . . well, when your clothes are done, I think you two should go home and get some sleep. Whatever you saw or thought you saw obviously scared the hell out of you. If you want, come back over here tomorrow, and we'll figure out who we can talk to about this Mace character. In fact, if you want, we'll go over there together, and I'll talk to the son of a bitch myself. Okay? But tonight . . . just get a good night's sleep. Everything sounds okay with Nikki. I'll talk to her. We'll take care of everything. There's nothing to worry about."

He was wrong. . . .

PART IV

Crucifax Concert

Twenty

October 15

It was still raining the next morning, and the sky was the color of dusk.

Lily picked up Jeff at ten o'clock, and they went to Tiny Naylor's. Neither of them spoke during the ride, but Lily seemed in much better shape than she had the night before.

They were led to a table by an enormous waitress with jowls and a cigarette-damaged voice. Their booth was by a window that looked out on Ventura Boulevard.

Once they'd ordered their breakfasts, Jeff said, "How did you sleep last night?"

"How do you think?"

"Yeah, me too."

"Jeff," she whispered urgently, "what did we see? What happened last night? Are we crazy?"

Jeff didn't know what to say. Last night, while they were in that strange dark room, he'd felt certain of what they were seeing; but since Lily had spoken with Nikki on the phone the night before, he was not quite so sure.

"I don't know, Lily," he said. "I really don't know."

She very casually reached across the table and took his hand, looking out the window.

"Did your sister come home last night?" she asked.

He shook his head. On the way home the night before, he'd explained to her why he suspected Mallory to be involved with Mace. He had not, however, told her as much as he'd revealed to J.R.

"Were your parents angry at you for being so late last night?" he asked.

"No. He was in bed when I got home. My dad. He doesn't worry too much about where I go. He trusts me."

"Your parents are divorced?"

"No. My mom died when I was a baby." She looked out the window again for a moment, thoughtful and distant, then back at Jeff again. "That's a lie. She left. I was fourteen months old. She decided she didn't want to be a wife and mother, so she took off."

Her hand was cool in his, and her fingers twitched nervously; he realized she hadn't smiled once all morning.

"Why did you tell me that?" he asked after a moment. "I mean, I don't mind, but . . . well, you didn't have to tell me."

She shrugged. "I don't like lies. My dad lied to me until about two years ago. He told me she'd died. Then my grandmother told me the truth."

"Does your dad know she told you?"

"Yeah. We talked about it. I don't like the fact that he lied to me all those years, but I understand why he did it. He didn't want me to, you know, develop a complex about it, like she'd left because of me or something. For a while, I didn't think I'd be able to trust him again, but . . . well, he trusts me so much. He's good to me."

"My dad left, too. I think he got tired of being a husband and father."

"Maybe they're living together somewhere." She laughed, and her smile made Jeff feel much better, almost as if nothing was wrong, as if they were together just for the sake of being together.

He squeezed her hand, and she returned the gesture warmly; then the moment was gone, along with her smile.

"We have to go see her after breakfast," Lily said. "Nikki, I mean. I don't care if she's still asleep or if her mother's having one of those morning fits she always has before her first drink of the day."

"What does her mother do?"

"Well, she gets a lot of money from her ex-husband. He's in the movies, like a producer or something. But she also . . . well, she's a hooker, too."

"You're kidding."

She shook her head. "Nikki pretends she doesn't know. Her mother is a licensed masseuse. Nikki seems to think that's all she's doing, giving massages. But I think she knows better."

Jeff silently hoped that Nikki did know what her mother was doing, because if she didn't, she would eventually find out somehow. He knew it would be a tremendous blow to learn such a thing about his own mother, and he felt a pang of sorrow for Nikki.

When Lily was finished eating, she dabbed her mouth with her napkin and pushed the plate away, folding her arms on the tabletop. Tilting her head slightly, she said, "Kinda weird, isn't it? I mean, the way we're getting to know each other. Most people, you know, have something in common, like classes or music. We've got this . . . Nikki and your sister. . . ."

"Yeah," he said, nodding. "But it could be worse. We could be on our own."

"Yeah, I guess so."

Nikki lived on Fair Avenue in North Hollywood. She and her mother had a small second-floor apartment. The stairs and walkway in front of the apartment were sheltered, but the wind blew rain in over them as they stood before the door.

When Lily pressed the hollow-sounding bell in the center of the door, there was no response.

"What time is it?" she asked, ringing again.

"Eleven-twenty."

She reached up and removed the top cover from the porch light. A key was taped to the underside. She took it off, put the cover back, and opened the door.

A small, pudgy woman with dark hair was sprawled on the sofa, eyes closed, mouth yawning open, wheezing steadily. On the coffee table there was a tall, empty glass and an empty vodka bottle; next to that was an ashtray overflowing with butts and ashes. An old western was playing on the television.

"Must've had an extra fifth last night," Lily said disdainfully, leading the way through the messy, cluttered living room and down the hall.

Nikki sat up in bed and squinted at them groggily when they entered her room.

"What . . . you guys . . ." She rubbed her eyes and yawned.

"Morning, Nik," Lily said. "Meet Jeff Carr."

Jeff smiled apologetically at her. "Hi."

"You met him yesterday, Nikki. Remember?"

"What're you guys doing here?"

"I told you I was coming over this morning," Lily said, sitting on the bed. "It's almost eleven-thirty."

"Oh. Well. It's Saturday."

"Wanna go to a movie with us today?"

Nikki shook her head. "Can't. I've got plans." The sheet and blanket fell away from her. She wore a low-cut tank top; resting in the cleavage of her breasts was the same odd cross Jeff had seen her wearing the night before. Beneath the leather cord around her neck there was a large purple hickey.

"What're you doing today?" Lily asked.

"Seeing some friends."

"Calvary Youth?"

"Oh, no," she said, wrinkling her nose. "Not them." She drew her knees up in front of her and hugged her legs.

"Anyone I know?"

"Well, you said you were there last night. I didn't see you, though. . . . You weren't really there, were you?"

Lily glanced up at Jeff, as if to say, *Here goes.*

"Yes, we were there, Nikki. I want to talk to you about that."

"'Bout what?"

"About what happened there."

"Mmm." Her brow wrinkled curiously. "Where were you? In the pool?"

"Nikki, why were you there?"

"Mace invited me. He's the guy who—"

"I know who he is. I want you to tell me what he did to you. You weren't just fooling around. There was blood and . . . and his tongue . . ." Her voice had become soft and a bit afraid. "What did he do?"

Nikki's eyes turned downward, and she picked absently at the blanket.

Lily whispered, "What about your baby?"

Her head jerked up with a gasp, and she looked, open-mouthed, at Lily, glancing twice at Jeff with embarrassment, humiliation.

"He knows, Nikki. He was there, too."

Nikki's mouth worked silently for a moment, and she finally said, "It's none of your business, you know, none of your goddamned business!"

Lily was obviously shocked at her language.

"I told you I couldn't keep it, Lily. I *couldn't!*"

"But why did you have him do it?" Lily asked, closing her eyes for a moment, as if hearing it all again. "Jesus Christ, Nikki, there's . . . there's something *wrong* with him, something very *wrong,* and you have to stay away from him!"

"No, no, Mace likes me, he wants me there. He won't lie to me like Reverend Bainbridge." She spat the name out bitterly.

Lily stood. "I'm going to talk to your mother about this, and—"

"Don't you *dare!* It's none of your business! You don't even know Mace. Why don't you come some night? He'd like to have—"

"I'm *not* going back in there."

Nikki smiled. "How come? He even has a band down there. They're gonna play Fantazm Wednesday night."

Jeff stepped forward and said, "Nikki, my sister's name is Mallory. Mallory Carr. Was she down there last night?"

"Yeah, Mallory, she was in the pool. I met her. But I didn't see you. . . ."

"What's that?" Lily asked, pointing to the cross.

Mallory looked down at it and her face changed; her smile softened, and her eyes seemed to be seeing something else, something far more beautiful than the plain, palm-sized object around her neck.

"It's a Crucifax," she whispered.

"A what?"

"Mace gave it to me." She stared at it awhile longer but said nothing more.

Lily said, "Nikki, why do you want to go there? Why do you want to *be* with someone like that?"

Still looking at the Crucifax, Nikki replied, "He's good to us. He likes us, likes having us around. And . . . and he's gonna take us out of here."

"Out of where?" Jeff asked.

"The valley. Away from all this. Our parents, school, things like the . . . the fucking Calvary Youth," she whispered.

Lily stared slack-jawed at her friend as if she were a rude stranger.

"Where's he taking you?" Jeff asked.

Still without looking at him, Nikki said, "To someplace better. That's all he'd say. But I trust him." She looked at him then, somewhat defiantly. "We *all* trust him."

"When is he taking you away?"

"He's not sure yet, but he says he'll know when the time is right."

Lily frowned. "Do you feel all right, Nikki? You sound . . . different. Weird."

"I feel fine." She swept the covers back, swung her bare legs off the bed, and stood, suddenly lively. "In fact," she said, slipping the tank top over her head, "I feel great." Naked except for panties, her breasts moving slightly as she crossed the room, she tossed the tank top onto her bed and smiled at them. "I'm gonna take a shower. I've gotta go soon."

Jeff felt himself blush, and he turned toward the door to leave, self-consciously clearing his throat.

"Jesus, Nikki," Lily snapped, "what's happened to you?"

"Nothing," she replied cheerfully.

Out in the hall, Jeff heard movement behind the closed bathroom door; Mrs. Astin was throwing up. He went out to the living room and listened to the muffled voices coming from Nikki's bedroom. A few minutes later Lily came out, walking fast.

"Let's go," she said, her voice tense.

As they left the apartment Nikki called, "See you guys later!"

She sounded very happy.

J.R.'s first thought that morning was of Sheila. He'd dreamed about her all night long. His dreams were muddled, confused; some of the things Jeff had told him the night before were intertwined with events that had surrounded Sheila's death.

In his dream, J.R. saw his sister off in the distance, standing before a dark building. It was the Old Red Barn that had burned down just outside of El Cerrito the week after Sheila died. She went inside, moving slowly. J.R. was suddenly frozen with dread because he knew what was beneath that building. He couldn't see it, but he *sensed* it: filthy, winding tunnels and huge, dark rooms, cold and drafty, thick with cobwebs and black, smelly slime that dribbled down walls and pillars, alive with things that crept in the dark in wait for someone to enter. He ran to the building, his feet heavy as lead, and burst through the door, only to see flames licking the walls and ceiling, his sister standing in the middle of it all with a tall, pale, silver-haired man who turned to J.R. and smiled. J.R. called Sheila, but she seemed deaf to his voice, oblivious to the growing fire around her. The man opened his mouth, still smiling at J.R., and a long, fat snake with smooth, shiny scales oozed from between his lips. The head was not that of a snake, however; it was the small head of a pale, bushy-black-haired woman with cold, calculating eyes. She opened her little mouth and said, "You lose, big brother. . . ."

There had been several variations of the dream, and he'd awakened suddenly after each one. None of them made much sense, but they all contained odd mixtures of familiar and unpleasant images.

J.R. knew very well that there were no tunnels or rooms

beneath the Old Red Barn; those were images borrowed from Jeff's story of the night before. What disturbed him the most was the snake with the very familiar human head. . . .

He got out of bed, fixed coffee and toast, and tried to read the *Times,* but he was preoccupied with Jeff and Lily.

Something had happened to so deeply upset them, but how could it have possibly been what they claimed? To satisfy its need for a logical explanation, his mind kept returning to drugs as an answer; surely they'd had some grass last night, maybe some mushrooms. Even if they had indeed seen everything they'd described, there was no explanation for the presence of Reverend Bainbridge. And if he did have a reason to be there, why didn't he try to stop what was happening? How could someone who professed to care so much about young people stand by and watch something so horrible?

The more he thought about it, the wilder it all seemed.

He couldn't finish his toast, and he quickly lost all interest in the paper. Listening to the rain against the window, he went to his briefcase and removed the Calvary Youth brochure Nikki Astin had given him. It gave the address of the Calvary Youth House, as well as the phone number and an invitation to the meetings and the Saturday brunch held every week. He decided to give Bainbridge a call and arrange to see him.

After dialing the number in the brochure, J.R. listened to the monotonous burring ring at the other end. It went on and on, and he was ready to hang up when he heard a thick, weary voice say, "Yes?"

"Hello, is this the Calvary Youth House?" he asked uncertainly.

"It is."

"My name is J.R. Haskell. I'm calling for Reverend Bainbridge?"

"That's me." He coughed, smacked his lips, and said, "What can I do for you?" His words slurred together, as if he'd been asleep.

"Hope I didn't wake you."

The reverend mumbled something, then coughed again.

"Uh, I'm a counselor at Valley High School, Reverend, and some of my students are members of your group. I'm pretty new in the area and unfamiliar with what you do. I thought maybe we could—"

"Exactly what would you like to know about the group, Mr. Haskell?"

"Well, nothing specific, I guess. I just wanted to meet you, mostly. See, um, see how you're getting along with the kids, that sort of thing. I've heard a lot about you since I got here."

"All good, I hope." There was no humor in his voice.

"Well, one of my students gave me your brochure. Sounds like you're working pretty hard with those kids."

"I give it my best. Which . . . which student might that have been?"

"Nikki Astin."

Silence.

When J.R. realized he was going to get no response, he went on. "She was very enthusiastic about the group. In fact, she invited me to drop by some time."

J.R. waited, but the reverend still said nothing.

"According to the brochure, you hold a brunch at the house on Saturdays. Would you, um, mind if I dropped by today and joined you?"

"Well," the reverend said, his voice hoarse. "We, uh, yes, we usually do, but this—this weekend we've postponed the brunch because I've been, I've been a little, uh, under the weather. I just thought it, uh, would be best to . . . to . . ."

His words trailed off absently.

Bainbridge was obviously very uncomfortable; J.R. had sensed a change in him at the mention of Nikki's name. In a perverse, shameful sort of way, J.R. was enjoying himself.

"Nikki says you two are very close," he went on. "That's good. I understand her mother drinks heavily. Nikki could probably use the good influence."

"Yes, well, I try, uh, to, to maintain a good relationship with all of my, my kids because . . . well, it's best if they feel I'm one of, of them."

Speaking as casually as he could, certain he was about to strike a major nerve, J.R. said, "By the way, Reverend, when was the last time you saw Nikki?"

"All *right!*" Bainbridge hissed. "What do you want with me? Why are you doing this?"

J.R. flinched, not expecting such an angry response. "I'm, I'm, I was just—"

"Are you a friend of his? Is that it?"

"Whose?"

"Don't play with me, Mr. Haskell."

"Hey, I'm not—"

"I don't appreciate being harassed, and if you feel I'm—"

"Reverend!" J.R. snapped firmly, losing patience with the man, "I am not harassing you. I'm not. I just . . . I'm . . . What do you know about a man named Mace, Reverend?"

Silence again.

"Something happened last night. I'm not sure what. Two of my students claim they saw Mace do something to Nikki Astin. They say . . . well, they say that you were there. Believe me, I'm *not* harassing you, I'm just concerned about—"

"I'm going to hang up now."

"No! No, please don't do that. I want your help, Reverend. You know, I didn't believe them at first, I figured they were on drugs or something. But you make it difficult *not* to believe them. If you can tell me what's—"

"I'm afraid . . . I can't . . . help you, Mr. Haskell."

J.R. sighed with frustration. "You know, Reverend, if what I've been told is true, you could be in a great deal of trouble. They said Mace . . . that he performed an abortion on Nikki last night. That you were the father. And that you stood and watched."

J.R. heard a breathy coughing sound and realized the reverend was crying.

"If that's true, Reverend, I'm going to find out, and there are a lot of people who won't be too thrilled about it. Especially Nikki's mother. Not to mention the parents of the others in your group."

The reverend took a deep breath and said, "You don't understand. You weren't there, you . . . don't know. . . ."

"Then *tell* me."

"I'm sorry, Mr. Haskell," he whispered.

"I'll go there myself," J.R. said quietly. "I'll go to the old health club myself and find out."

"No. Don't do that. Whatever you do, don't . . . go . . . there."

Reverend Bainbridge hung up.

Jeff and Lily came over a couple hours later, and J.R. made coffee for them. They told him about their brief visit with Nikki, and he recounted his conversation with Bainbridge.

As Jeff and Lily sat at the kitchen table J.R. paced around them, saying, "I have to admit, I thought . . . well, I thought at first that you two were seeing things, okay? I admit it. I mean, what you told me last night, that was pretty loopy, you know? But now . . . I know something's up. I just don't know what." He sat down at the table with them. "Jeff, how soon can I talk to your mother?"

"She's out all day and then goes to work until about two-thirty. In the morning, I mean."

"Mm. Maybe I'll catch her tomorrow. What are you doing today?"

"Lily and I were going to go to a movie. Get our minds off things, you know?"

"I don't want to be a party pooper, but I think it would be a good idea if you stayed home. If Mallory shows up, keep her there. Don't let her go back to Mace."

"Okay."

"And above all, don't worry yourselves into an ulcer. This may not be as bad as we think right now, so—"

"It is," Lily said quietly. "You didn't see what we saw. It is."

"Well, let's try to keep in mind that whatever's going on, we're doing the best we can to stop it. That's not much right now, but it's our best. Try not to worry too much." J.R. could not hide the emptiness in his words.

He was already worrying too much. . . .

Twenty-one

October 16

Kevin was awakened by a portly man in a white uniform who seemed unable to stop smiling.

"Rise and shine," the man chimed, patting Kevin's mattress with a beefy hand. He opened the curtains and let in the gray light of the morning. "This is your first full day here, and it'll be a busy one. I'm Phil."

Kevin rolled over and tried to cover his head with a blanket.

"Ah-ah-ah. Breakfast is served soon. You don't want to miss it because there's no eating between meals here."

"Jesus H. motherfucking Christ, Phil old buddy old pal!" Kevin suddenly bellowed, sitting up in bed. "How old do I look, man, six? Five, maybe?"

Phil's chubby smile disappeared, and his face became stern.

"You'll be treated like a child if you keep acting like one," Phil said. "Now get up and get ready for breakfast. That's the rule here. From now on you follow all the rules here." Slapping his big thigh as he left the room, Phil said, "Let's get to it, fellas."

Kevin moved stiffly. His left eye was still swollen from the fight; his lip had been cut, he had two stitches in his chin, and his ribs hurt. He was in better shape than he'd expected to be, but there was pain with every movement.

He looked at the other bed in the room. Sitting on the edge was his roommate Leif. He'd met him when he arrived the day before. Leif was bony and pale, and his head was completely shaved. He moved incredibly slowly, and when he was spoken to he took several seconds to reply.

He smiled groggily at Kevin. "Welcome to Laurel, man. If you're lucky, they'll give you medication. Elavil, dude. Elavil all the way."

The Laurel Teen Center was situated on a pleasant green hill just off of Laurel Canyon Boulevard. From the outside, it looked more like a school than an institution for troubled teenagers. His parents had brought him there the day before and registered him with the supervisor, a man who looked like he used to coach football. His name was Luke, and he assured Kevin that his stay at Laurel would not be easy.

"You're here to work, Kev," Luke said. "Work out your problems. And we're gonna help you. You're gonna work till you sweat, then work some more. When you go home, you'll be a new person. Together. Leakproof, I sometimes say. And you, Mr. and Mrs. Donahue, will be unable to believe the difference in your boy."

"I'd like to get one thing clear," Kevin's dad said firmly. "Our insurance will cover this . . ."

"Like a blanket. Health insurance. Because technically, Kevin here is ill. And we're going to make him better."

The center had three wards. Those who were simply depressed and just needed some therapy or counseling were put in Ward A. Ward B was for those who'd gotten into trouble with the law or had otherwise been a nuisance before their admittance. Ward C was the worst. There were a lot of locks on Ward C, restraints were used frequently, and, except for the receptionists, most of the staff was male and big, imposing, authoritative. That ward was for the violent ones, the suicidal ones.

Technically, Kevin was supposed to be on Ward B, but when he arrived, there were only two beds available. Both were on Ward C. They promised to give him the first available bed in Ward B, but they couldn't promise how long that would take.

Despite the fact that Ward C, which was located in the back of the large building that made up the center, was brightly lit, there was a darkness about it. Teenagers roamed the corridors, aimlessly shuffling in and out of the TV room and the recreation room. Some leaned against the corridor walls biting their nails, cracking their knuckles, or just staring. There was a girl who liked to sit on one of the vinyl-upholstered sofas in the corridor and watch people pass. Her eyes were deep-set, and patches of her auburn hair were missing. She had bruises on her legs—they were always visible because she wore the small nightshirt provided by the center with only a short robe over it—and her wrists were bandaged. Sometimes she would look up at passersby with big, watery brown eyes and say, "I hate daddies." She said it very quietly, so quietly that some never heard it. "I hate daddies. . . ."

Leif wandered the halls slowly, his slippered feet making shh-shh sounds, his eyelids drooping heavily, his jaw slack. Sometimes he would say hello to people who passed, but by the time he got the word out, they were gone.

Sometimes shouting broke out.

It seemed that someone was always crying somewhere on the ward.

Kevin didn't have to stay on Ward C. Since he was a B patient, he was allowed to walk down to B and use the TV room, but he didn't. It didn't seem right. He felt he should stay on C, *someone* should stay on C, someone who didn't *have* to be there. He wasn't sure why he felt that way, but he did. He went to the Ward C TV room and spent most of his time there.

In the middle of that Sunday afternoon, Luke came into the TV room looking for him.

"Just wanted to chat with you a little, buddy," Luke said with that big macho football coach smile, patting Kevin on the back.

Kevin hated being called "buddy."

"Now," Luke went on, "I gave you the schedule sheet

yesterday. You know that you're supposed to be in group at four. Remember, that is one of the most important parts of your stay here, so don't, under any circumstances, miss it. Dr. Morley will be in this evening to talk with you, examine you, determine whether or not you'll need medication."

Elavil, dude . . . Elavil all the way . . .

"There's a chance we may have a room for you in Ward B within the next three days."

"Three days?" Kevin asked. "How . . . how long am I gonna be here?"

Luke gave him that smile again. "As long as it takes, buddy, as long as it takes."

After he left, Kevin stared at the television without seeing the picture. Mace had promised the band they'd play Fantazm next Wednesday night. Kevin had no intention of missing that show.

He had no intention of staying at the Laurel Teen Center.

He touched the place on his chest where his Crucifax had been. He would get it back. He would get out. Mace would learn where he was and come for him. He prayed he would. . . .

When Jeff awoke, his mother was already showered and dressed and was in the kitchen making Belgian waffles. She gave him a big smile as she poured his coffee.

"Morning, handsome," she said.

"Hi. What're you so dressed up for?"

"I have to go shopping with Kyla. We're going to get some material, then we're going to her place to work on clothes for the puppets. But"—she raised a finger—"I'm coming back later this afternoon. And I don't have to work tonight. So let's do something, the three of us. Whatever you two want to do. Is Mallory up yet?"

"Mom," he said hesitantly, "a few days ago—last Thursday—something happened between you and Mallory. . . ."

Going into the kitchen to tend the waffles, she muttered, "We had a fight, that's all."

"It must've been bad."

"They're all bad," she sighed.

"Did you know . . . that she hasn't been home since then?"

"Wha . . . what?" She turned to him slowly, stunned. "Where is she?"

Don't tell her, Jeff thought. *Not yet.*

"I'm . . . not sure."

Walking toward him: "You knew all this time?" Leaning toward him at the table: "And you didn't tell me?"

"I . . ."

"Jeff, she could be hurt, she could be—be, well, we should call someone, the police. . . ." There was panic in her face.

"No, no—" He thought fast then, tried to come up with something that would keep her from calling the police. "—she's with Kevin, I know that much. She'll . . . she'll probably come back soon."

"Oh, Jesus, what have I done?" She seated herself and began chewing on a knuckle.

"Look, she's okay for now. But my counselor from school, J.R. Haskell, he wants to talk to you about it. He's—"

"He knows? You told him?"

"We talked about it, and—"

"But you didn't tell *me?*" she hissed. "Jesus Christ, Jeffrey, this is—well, it's my fault, and you could've at least—"

"Look, Mom, there's nothing you can do about it now. I'm gonna stick around here in case she comes home. When you get back, I'll call J.R. and—"

Kyla breezed in then, tall and thin with tossed blond hair and, as always, in a hurry.

"Sorry I'm late, but the traffic was terrible and—oh, hi, Jeffy—my phone kept ringing. You ready, Erin?"

Erin looked at Jeff for a long time, silently chewing her knuckle.

"I'll be back around five or so," she said. Then, to Kyla, "Yeah, I'm coming."

He spent most of the day watching television and doing homework, trying hard not to think too much. The bourbon his mother kept in the kitchen cupboard helped a bit, but he didn't have much; he didn't want to be drunk when she got back.

Lily came over around two, and they watched an old Jimmy Stewart movie, sitting close together on the sofa, their hands touching, fingers stroking fingers.

The phone rang halfway through the movie, and Jeff dived for it, hoping to hear Mallory's voice on the other end.

It was Brad Kreisler.

"Hey, Jeffy, how's it hangin'?"

"Fine, Brad."

"You don't sound so fine."

"Yeah, well . . ."

"I'm over at Nick's right now, and we're going out to eat. Wanna come?"

"Can't."

"Jesus, don't you *ever* go out and do *anything?* We're going to the Galleria, so you could stop by and see Lily what's-her-face."

"She's not working today."

"How do you know?"

"She's over here."

"Over *there?* You're shittin' me. Well, man, that's radical —Jesus, I better let you go. But first I gotta ask you something. You doing anything Wednesday night? 'Cause it's my birthday and, if you're not doing anything, my sister and her husband are kind of giving me a party, and I thought you'd like to come. My brother-in-law's pretty wild, so it oughtta be fun."

"Yeah, sure, I guess. I don't have any plans."

"Cool. I'll let you go"—he chuckled suggestively—"you slobbering humpbeast."

At ten minutes to five the front door opened, and Jeff looked over his shoulder expecting to see Erin.

It was Mallory.

Jeff was off the sofa and at her side in an instant.

She gave him a heavy-eyed smile and headed for her room, murmuring, "Hi."

"Mallory," he said, following her, but beyond that he

215

didn't know what to say. As Mallory went into her room Jeff turned to Lily and said, "Call J.R."

"Do you have his number?"

"Call Information. Hurry." He followed Mallory into her room. "Mallory, what are you doing here?"

"I thought you'd be glad to see me," she said wanly.

"I am, I *am*, but . . . Mallory, we have to talk."

She took a small suitcase from her closet, removed her coat, and opened a dresser drawer. "Have you seen my white jeans?"

"Mallory."

"What do we have to talk about?"

"Don't act dumb—you know. About where you've been, what you've been doing."

"You know. You were there. Friday night. Mace told me."

Hanging from her neck, Jeff saw one of the crosses—what did Nikki call it?—a Crucifax.

Jeff started to speak again, started to tell her to stop and talk with him, but there was movement in the living room. He heard the door open and close, heard footsteps and voices, Erin's voice, and then she was at the door of the bedroom, her eyes wide, her movements frantic.

"Mallory, where have you been, *where-have-you-been?*"

"With friends."

"Why didn't you tell us, why didn't you call or say something before you left?"

"Did Jeff tell you I was gone?"

Erin said nothing.

"You didn't even know I was gone, did you?"

No reply.

Mallory smiled. "See? What difference does it make?" She turned back to her dresser drawer and began removing clothes.

"What are you doing?"

"Getting some things together."

"Why? Where are you going?"

"To be with my friends."

"You're staying right here, we're going to talk, do you understand me?" She was raising her voice.

"I don't want to talk to you about anything."

They went on, but Jeff quickly began to tune them out. In seconds they were both shouting, and Jeff closed his eyes. Turning from them, he left the room and went to the living room, where Lily stood watching anxiously as he approached her.

"Did you get him?" Jeff asked softly.

She nodded. "He said he'll be over in a few minutes. Is everything . . . well, would you rather I went away?"

Jeff thought about it a moment and agreed that it might be a good idea. He walked her out to her car in the rain, stood beside her beneath the carport as she unlocked her door. She turned, gave him a brief kiss on the lips, got in, and drove away.

He didn't want to go back inside. It had been pretty quiet since school had started; now, though, even standing outside under the carport, he could hear their shouting voices, could see in his mind's eye their angry, twisted faces. . . .

Jeff returned slowly, letting the rain soak his clothes as he took long, deliberate steps across the grass in front of the apartment building. Before he went inside, J.R. pulled up in his car, parked illegally in front of the building, and got out, jogging over to Jeff.

"What's going on?" he asked.

"Mallory's home. So's my mom. They're fighting inside. Mom didn't know Mallory had been gone all this time, and now she's mad at me for not telling her."

"Jesus. How much have you told her?"

"Nothing, really."

"Okay. Let's go inside, and I'll try to talk with her."

They went into the apartment, and J.R. winced at the shouting that was coming from Mallory's room. Jeff felt as if he were shrinking; he wanted to disappear, or make everyone else disappear.

After a few moments, the voices were silent. Erin stormed out of Mallory's bedroom, pulling the door closed so hard the entire apartment shook.

"Mom," Jeff said as she stalked toward the kitchen, "this is J.R.—"

"Not now, Jeffrey." Cupboards slammed in the kitchen; the refrigerator door opened, then closed.

Hesitantly following her, J.R. said, "Mrs. Carr, I think it might be a good idea if we talked."

She returned with a glass of wine and looked coldly at Jeff, taking a gulp.

"This is your counselor?" she asked. "The one you've been telling our problems to?" To J.R.: "Jeff seems to be more comfortable talking to strangers than to—to his own mother. So I've been pretty much in the dark until today. What can I do for you?"

"Well, there are some things I think you should know about, Mrs. Carr."

"And my son can't tell me?"

"Well, not all of it has to do with your family."

Her face changed then, relaxed; she looked interested but afraid, and she moved to the sofa, slowly lowering herself, never taking her eyes from J.R.

"What's my daughter been doing?" she asked.

Taking a deep breath, J.R. turned to Jeff and said, "C'mon, let's sit down. . . ."

J.R. and Jeff took turns speaking, telling what they knew. As they talked, Erin seemed to sink deeper and deeper into the sofa. Several emotions crossed her face, but the strongest seemed, to J.R., to be guilt. Apparently, something more than just a simple mother-daughter argument had taken place between her and Mallory, something she seemed to feel had pushed Mallory away from her. He didn't feel he had the right to ask any personal questions just yet, but even if he did, J.R. wasn't sure he would.

Something about Erin Carr told him she was living behind a lot of walls. She seemed extremely guarded, as if she was protecting something.

She reacted to the story the same way J.R. had at first, with disbelief. But as they went on, her disbelief soon turned to puzzlement, and then fear. When the fear set in, she reached for Jeff's hand.

An hour after they began, once they'd told her everything they had to say, Erin sat silently on the sofa looking from Jeff to J.R. and back again. She said nothing, and after a few moments J.R. became uncomfortable with the silence.

"Look," he said, "I'm hungry. I haven't eaten since breakfast. Why don't I take you two to dinner?"

"No," Jeff said to his mother, "I'll stay with Mallory. You go." There was an encouraging tone in his voice, as if he wanted Erin to go out.

She seemed hesitant.

"I'd like to talk to you some more," J.R. said.

She nodded, agreeing, as if she knew it would be best if she got out of the apartment for a while.

In J.R.'s car, they both spoke casually for the first time since they'd met. They talked about the weather and about how fast the year had gone. Then there was a silence.

"I don't know what I've done wrong," Erin said.

"Pardon?"

"With Mallory. I . . . I feel like a failure."

"Jeff seems to think something happened between you two, you and Mallory, just before she left. Is that true?"

She hesitated a long time. "My husband left two years ago," she said, looking out the window. "He just took off, and I've been on my own since, trying to support the kids and myself. I've taken some jobs that aren't . . . well, that aren't exactly . . ."

"Yes?"

"I've been working for this phone sex agency. You know, guys call up, charge it to their credit cards, and some woman talks dirty to them for about twenty minutes. Last Thursday, Mallory came home while I was on the phone. Things weren't exactly peachy between us before that, but what she heard . . . well, that sent her over the edge. I guess she left that night and didn't come back until today."

"Does Jeff know about that, about your job?"

"No, and I want to keep it that way."

"Are you sure that's wise?"

She stared at him for a moment.

"Well," he went on, "after what happened with Mallory, maybe telling Jeff would be good. I mean, maybe it would avoid a repeat performance, know what I mean?"

"No. I don't want him to know. I'm going to quit both my jobs soon, as soon as I can find something else."

"Both your jobs?"

Another long silence, then: "Well, I . . . I also dance. In bars. I strip."

"And Jeff and Mallory don't know?"

She shook her head.

J.R. thought about that a moment, chewing his lip. "Mrs. Carr, it's—"

"Oh, God, please call me Erin," she laughed.

"Okay. Don't you think it would make things easier just to tell them? I mean, if you did, it wouldn't be such a big deal. But if you keep hiding it from them . . ."

She nodded. "I know what you mean. But they're temporary, these jobs. I don't want them to . . . well, to taint Jeff's and Mallory's opinions of me."

"But you're their mother! If you made them understand your situation—I mean, well, you're single, you've got to support them. . . ."

"Look, who's raising these kids, anyway?"

He nodded. "I'm sorry. I was just . . . well, I'm thinking of them, too. I mean . . . Jeff and I have become pretty good friends. He's a good kid. He thinks the world of you and Mallory. He's very sensitive, and if he found out . . ."

"I know, I know. But he won't. I'm looking for other work." She turned to him and gave him a half smile. "Really. He won't."

He smiled back at her as he drove.

"Now," she said. "Where are we going?"

"You like Chinese food?"

Jeff sat in the living room for some time after his mother and J.R. left. There were no sounds coming from Mallory's room, and he hesitated to go in to see her, although he wanted to very much. It seemed like she'd been gone much longer than three days, and he wanted to sit down and talk with her—not just about what had been going on, but the way they used to talk. . . .

He went to her bedroom door and knocked softly. "It's me."

"C'min."

Jeff opened the door and peered inside. Mallory was still

220

gathering things together and putting them into her suit-case.

"So," he said, going into the room, "how are you?"

"Well, until Mom got home, I was just fine," she laughed. Her eyes were tearstained and her voice was still a little sniffly, but she wasn't crying. "How are *you? I* haven't seen you in a few days."

"Yeah, I *know.* I've been okay, except . . . I've been worried about you."

"Oh, you shouldn't do that. I'm fine. I've been having a lot of fun, meeting lots of new people . . . you know, you should come."

He ignored that. "I wish you'd stop packing."

"I have to. I don't need much, really, but I need some-thing. I have to have a change of clothes and some—"

"You're not leaving, Mallory. I'm not going to let you."

She stopped packing and turned to him, smiling. Crossing the room, she put her hands on his shoulders and kissed his cheek. "You're sweet," she said. "You're always so worried about me." Mallory smiled at him, her face close to his. "You shouldn't be, you know. I'm fine. I can take care of myself."

"But I *do* worry. So does Mom."

"Yeah, I can tell," she laughed. "She didn't even know I was gone, Jeff! What does it take for you to see that she just . . . doesn't . . . give . . . a damn."

"But she does! And so do I."

She moved away and went back to her suitcase, adjusting its contents and closing it securely. "Anything to eat?" she asked.

"Well . . . I guess I could fix you a sandwich, maybe."

"Yeah. Do that. I'm gonna take a shower." She slipped her shirt off, tossed it aside, and left the room in her pants and bra, smiling.

Jeff turned away quickly, trying not to stare at the dark valley between her breasts, at the way they filled her bra and shifted slightly as she walked.

He went to the kitchen and made her a turkey sandwich while she showered. Several minutes later she came out in her robe and sat down at the table.

"It's delicious," she said as she ate.

Jeff sat down at the table with her and popped open a Coke.

"You know, I've missed you," Mallory said.

That was when he noticed it, a certain heaviness to her eyes, a slightly odd cadence to her speech. She was not the same; she'd changed during her absence. He remembered the smell of marijuana inside the health club Friday night and thought perhaps she'd been doing a lot of that. But it seemed more than a drug-induced change. She was more relaxed than usual, more at ease, more . . . herself.

"I wish you'd come back with me," Mallory went on, quickly finishing the sandwich. She took a sip of his Coke, smiled, and stood. "Want some grass?"

"Mallory . . ."

"C'mon, Mom won't be back for a while." She went to her room.

Jeff sat at the table and buried his face in his hands for a moment. When he got to her room, she was sitting on the edge of her bed sucking on a small pipe. Her room was filling with the sweet aroma of marijuana smoke, and she smiled up at him, tendrils of smoke curling from her nostrils.

"I wish you wouldn't do that," he said.

The room was dark except for a shaft of bluish gray from a light outside shining through the narrow opening between the curtains. When Jeff stepped inside, the bedroom door slowly closed on its own, as it sometimes did, leaving only a two-inch opening.

"Aw, c'mon." She offered the pipe to him.

Ignoring it, Jeff sat down beside her and said, "Mallory, don't go back. Please. Mace is . . . there's something wrong with him. He's dangerous. I saw what he did to Nikki Astin, and he's . . . Jesus, Mallory, he's deadly."

"Nikki Astin? Oh, he didn't hurt her, she was fine. He's my friend, Jeff," she said, her eyes taking on a slightly glazed look. She grinned. "I told you he talks about you, didn't I? He's always asking about you. He'd like you to come. . . ."

Jeff shook his head, started to speak, but she stopped him.

"He told me . . . he said you care about me a lot."

"I do, Mallory." He put a hand on her arm and squeezed. "That's why I don't want you to go back. Something's wrong, something bad is happening. I know that probably sounds stupid, but—"

She leaned on him, giggling, and took another drag from the pipe.

"If you'd just come," she said, "you'd see how much fun we have, how . . ." She stopped to smile at him. Despite her smile, she looked ten years older than her age. She put an arm around his shoulders, leaned slowly toward him, and gently touched her lips to his cheek.

A small shiver of pleasure went through him at the touch of her mouth.

"You know what else Mace told me?" she whispered. "Mace told me—he said, just last night—he said that you have a crush on me." Her face split into a grin.

Jeff chilled.

"Is that true, Jeff?" She touched his ear with a fingertip.

He fidgeted beside her.

"Is it?"

"Mallory . . ."

"Mace knows things, you know. I mean, he knows things most people don't." She ran her fingers through his hair, kissed his cheek again, leaving her lips against his skin for a long moment. "He's a good friend, Jeff, he really is." Her other arm moved across his chest and touched his neck on the other side.

"Don't, Mallory." Jeff began to feel dizzy, disoriented, as if caught in a dream. He tried to move away from her, but she pulled him closer.

"Is Mace right?" she whispered. "He usually is, you know." She ran a finger down the bridge of his nose, touching his lips.

Jeff felt her breath on his cheek, his throat, felt her lips brush over his chin, up his cheek to his ear, where her tongue flicked the fleshy lobe. . . .

"He said the reason you don't like me to see Kevin is that you're jealous," she giggled into his ear.

Although every ounce of strength seemed to have drained from his body, Jeff managed to pull away gently from Mallory.

"Stop," he whispered, his voice quavering. He stood and faced her as she took another drag on the pipe. "C'mon, let's put all this stuff back, Mallory," he said, gesturing toward her suitcase. "Okay?"

Mallory shook her head, slowly exhaling. "No, I'm gonna have to go soon." She put the pipe on the bed and stood before him, smiling. Her hair was still wet and had that familiar shampoo smell it had had that night she'd come to his bed two years ago. She untied the belt around her waist, and the robe fell open in front. The Crucifax rested between her breasts, glistening with moisture; she'd worn it in the shower. Mallory put her arms around his neck and moved close to him, her breasts pressing to his chest. "Why don't you come with me?" she whispered. "Please, Jeff? We can . . . do things. . . ."

"No, Mallory." He stepped back, but not soon enough to prevent the growing hardness in his jeans. "Look, Mallory, why—why don't you get dressed, and—and we'll go to a movie or something, huh? Sound good? How about it?"

"A friend is coming to get me," she whispered, stepping toward him again, stepping close. Through his clothes, he could feel the warmth of her skin, and he wanted to touch her—

There's something wrong with me.

—he wanted desperately to touch her, but instead he jerked away, clenched his fists, and said angrily, "You're not going anywhere, Mallory." He left her room, locked the front door, the sliding glass door, and seated himself on a chair facing the hallway, waiting for her to come out.

She laughed in her bedroom and said, "Mace was right."

Jeff's hands were trembling, and he realized how heavily he was breathing, so he relaxed—tried to, anyway—leaned his head back, and took deep, slow breaths. He wouldn't let her go, even if he had to tie her down until their mother and J.R. got back. He drummed his fingers on the chair's armrests until Mallory stuck her head out of the bedroom doorway.

224

"Jeff, could you come help me with this?"

"Not packing, I'm not gonna help you pack because you're not—"

"But my friend is coming any minute." She went into the bathroom, dressed now.

Jeff didn't move.

The doorbell rang.

"That's him," Mallory called.

Jeff stood and slowly went to the door. The bell rang again. He looked through the peephole in the door.

A uniformed police officer stood at the door. He looked sleepy; his hair was mussed.

The bell rang again.

"Mallory?" the policeman called.

"Jesus," Jeff muttered, his insides suddenly sinking. He quietly put the chain lock on the door. "Jesus, Jesus Christ," he breathed, hurrying through the living room into the bathroom, but Mallory was gone, so he went into her room and closed the door, hissing, "Mallory, you're not going, goddammit, just stay here for the night, okay? Just for tonight, and we'll talk, you, me, and Mom, we'll—"

It was still dark in the room, and Jeff didn't understand why she was shuffling around with no lights, but that wasn't important, so he didn't reach for the switch, just hurried toward Mallory—

—he stepped on something soft that squirmed beneath his foot and made a familiar hiss-squeal sound.

Jeff cried out and nearly fell trying to move away from it, but there was another and another.

He saw the eyes shimmering in the darkness around him, on the floor and the bed, on the dresser, even in the open closet.

He couldn't breathe.

He couldn't move.

"See, Jeff?" Mallory said softly. "I promised Mace I'd come back. He's waiting for me." She lifted her suitcase and moved toward the door, watching him. The pairs of eyes moved aside and out of her way. "These . . . these are . . . well, he calls them his eyes, Jeff. That's how he knows so much, sees so much." Sadness crept into her voice. "Won't

225

you come with me, Jeff? Mace doesn't push any rules onto us, he doesn't want us to change, he wants us the way we are. He takes care of us, pays . . . pays attention to us, *listens."*

"Ma . . . Mallory," Jeff whimpered, afraid to move an inch, "Mallory . . ." But he didn't know what to say.

The doorbell rang again.

"We can trust him," she went on, speaking faster. "Can you imagine that? Someone you can trust and respect? I know you trust Mom right now, but you shouldn't. There are things about her you don't know—I mean it, just like Dad—I loved him, trusted him, but he just left, just like that. Kevin's parents—you know what they did to him? They put him away, put him in some institution, some teen center. You can't trust them, Jeff, we're on our own. But we can trust Mace, really, so please, Jeff, come with me now!"

"Mallory," Jeff said, his mouth dry, "he's . . . I don't know what he's done to you, but you're wrong, you can't trust him"—he started toward her—"I saw what he did to Nikki, I watched him—"

The creatures closed in around him suddenly, squealing, and his entire body stiffened.

Mallory opened the bedroom door.

"He's taking us away, Jeff," she said. "Away to someplace better. He's . . . well, I don't understand him, he's not like us, maybe . . . maybe not even human. But he wants us to go with him. So I'm going." She stopped in the doorway and watched him a moment. "If you want to come, Jeff, you know where to find us." Mallory turned and went away.

Jeff remained still as they skittered out of the room behind her, long, tapering tails dragging behind them, claws catching noisily on the carpet.

Where did they come from? he wondered. *They weren't here a few minutes ago, they couldn't have—*

—unless they were here all along.

He heard the front door open, heard voices, dashed out of the bedroom and down the hall, but by the time he reached the living room the door was closed and Mallory was gone.

Cursing under his breath and trembling all over, Jeff went back to Mallory's bedroom, turned on the light, and looked around until he found it.

A hole had been chewed into the back wall of Mallory's closet. It was just big enough for one of those things to crawl through. They'd come from inside the wall.

He slammed the closet door, propped a straight-backed chair beneath the doorknob, then closed the bedroom door when he left.

He paced through the apartment for a while, trying not to cry, feeling angry, empty, helpless, and defeated.

After several minutes of pacing and fretting, he turned on the television, turned the volume up high so he couldn't hear the sound of the rain outside, sat down, and waited for Erin and J.R. . . .

Twenty-two

October 17–19

It had been raining off and on since the first week in October, but the rainfall had been heavy and constant since October thirteenth. The signs of winter settled in before autumn was half over. But the signs were different . . . odd. . . .

The sky remained a bone gray over the San Fernando Valley, crawling with fat, dark clouds, patches of which were the color of dirty smoke. Sometimes the wind blew so hard that street signs swayed back and forth and drivers had to keep a firm grip on their steering wheels to stay on the road. A section of Moorpark Avenue was closed in North Hollywood due to flooding, and a detour was set up.

A mudslide in the hills above Encino caused nearly one million dollars in damage to the home of a popular singer. The young black man who had broken records with his concerts and album sales had been reclusive for the last two years, and the story brought reporters out in flocks with microphones and cameras, each of them trying to be the first to have a word with the singer since his self-imposed exile from the public eye. The story made national news, bringing attention to the bizarre weather taking place in Southern California.

The death of Officer Bill Grady was all but forgotten. There were too many other stories making news.

At Washington Memorial High School in Van Nuys two students brutally attacked their biology teacher on October tenth. The story remained in the forefront because the teacher, three months pregnant, had miscarried after the attack, and the students, a boy and girl who had met with her after class to discuss their failing grades, had disappeared. Even their parents had no idea where they were.

A widower in Sylmar had been bludgeoned to death, and his fifteen-year-old daughter was the prime suspect; she'd disappeared, too. The police questioned many of her friends and acquaintances, but some of them were hard to find as well; some had not even been attending school.

High school teachers in the San Fernando Valley were noticing a difference in many of their students. Students who usually paid little attention to their classes were becoming more unattentive. The most striking difference, however, was in their best students, the ones who always came to class and usually got nothing less than As and Bs. The grades and attendance of a good many of them dropped considerably. Teachers' lounges in the Valley high schools were filled with talk of a peculiar lack of attention among the students, a restlessness similar to that in the springtime when the students couldn't wait to get out of the classroom. It was little more than a topic of casual conversation, and none of them thought it too strange. They attributed it to the odd weather. . . .

When J.R. went to the faculty lounge on Monday morning, however, the casual conversation struck him as something more. He hoped to catch Mr. Booth before the day began so they could discuss a student of J.R.'s who had refused to meet five appointments in a row. As he walked through the lounge to the coffee pot J.R. caught snatches of conversation:

". . . don't know what's wrong with them, but they all seem to be somewhere else, if you know what I mean. . . ."

". . . more hostile than usual . . ."

". . . thought the whole class was going to jump me last Thursday . . ."

Booth was late, so J.R. stood by the coffee pot, inconspicuously listening to the others, until Mr. MacDowal, the head of the music department, approached him and struck up a conversation. They talked about the strange weather, and MacDowal went on for a while about his plans to go to Europe for Christmas vacation. After a few moments of conversation, J.R. asked, "Mr. MacDowal, have you heard any of your students talk about a man named Mace?"

"Mace . . . oh, yes, as a matter of fact, I have," he said, scratching his cheek. He was a tall, thin man with a long face and steel-gray hair that came to a peak above his forehead. "I understand he's quite a musician. Has a band, from what I've heard. I've never met him myself, but the kids talk about him a lot."

"Pretty popular, huh?"

"Apparently. I understand his band is playing in some nightclub this week. Wednesday, I believe. Probably some bone-crunching rock band, but at least he's got the kids interested in something. That's more than I've been able to do lately."

J.R. chilled. If MacDowal had heard of Mace, J.R. figured a lot of students were aware of him. And if those students were speaking favorably of him . . .

After pouring himself another cup of coffee, J.R. went to his office, sighing wearily as he seated himself at his desk. He'd gotten very little sleep the night before and was tired.

His dinner with Erin Carr had gone well, but the circumstances of their meeting had cast a definite shadow over the evening. Although he was very uncomfortable with her dishonesty with Jeff and Mallory, she was a strong and admirable woman who had worked hard to rise above the difficulties of being a divorced and unskilled woman with two kids to support. Sitting across from her in the small Chinese restaurant where they'd eaten made J.R. realize how long it had been since he'd been out with a woman. It was easy to admit to himself that he found Erin Carr very attractive; but when she became upset again and began to fight back tears, he tried not to think about her proud and beautiful eyes and how good her hand felt in his.

Things got worse fast when they returned to the apartment and found Jeff alone and silently crying in front of the television. He explained what had happened while they were out, showed them the hole in Mallory's closet, told them everything she'd said. He spoke quietly, moved very slowly with his shoulders slumped; he looked defeated, beaten down, ashamed.

Erin was upset herself, frightened by Jeff's account of the creatures that had ushered Mallory out of the apartment.

"Mice," she'd breathed, putting a trembling hand on J.R.'s arm. "I've been hearing them in the walls, but I thought they were just mice. They sound like . . . Jesus, rats, we've got rats, do you know what kinds of diseases rats carry?"

Jeff started to protest, insisting that they weren't rats, but the phone rang. It was Lily saying she would be over soon. Erin had a couple drinks and calmed down, and later, as Jeff and Lily talked quietly at the table, J.R. assured her he would do all he could to get Mallory back home.

"Do you have any children?" She'd asked, her eyes heavy from the liquor.

"No, but I've . . . well, let's say I've got some idea of what you're going through."

Shaking her head, she'd muttered, half to herself, "I've blown it. Big. Soon as I saw things getting bad between us, I should have put a stop to it, should've sat down and had a long talk, straightened it out. But no, I was too . . . busy. Figured it would straighten itself out, I guess."

She was about to cry, and J.R. didn't want her to do that, didn't think he could bear her tears on top of everything else, so he gave her a big smile, squeezed her hand, and said, "You can do that as soon as she gets back."

On his desk, J.R. found a confidential memo informing him that one of his students, Kevin Donahue, was in the Laurel Teen Center for "extended counseling" and would be out of school indefinitely.

Just as Mallory had told Jeff the night before, Kevin's parents had "put him away."

J.R. looked through his schedule for the day. He had two appointments in the morning, some paperwork to take care of, an assembly to attend in the afternoon, and another appointment at the end of the day. He could get out of the assembly; that would give him enough time to go see Kevin. He called the Laurel Teen Center to arrange a visit. . . .

Jeff rode to school with Lily that morning. She picked him up at seven-thirty, and when he got into her car, she leaned over and cautiously kissed his cheek.

When Lily arrived at the apartment the previous night, they'd seated themselves at the table, and Jeff had recounted for her the events of the evening. When he was finished, she'd taken his hand and whispered, "Jeff, remember the last weekend before school started? That Saturday night? What were you doing? Do you remember?"

He remembered but only nodded in reply.

"Something weird happened, didn't it?" she'd asked. "Something you couldn't, like, put your finger on, right? *Right?*"

Another nod.

"Me, too. I mean, I was with some friends in the Galaxy Arcade on Lankershim, and all of a sudden—I don't know exactly what time it was—there was like a—I don't know, a power drain, or something. The pinball machines tilted, and all the video screens kind of, you know, went wonky. I looked around at my friends, and everybody looked like they'd just gotten the worst news of their lives. And—this is gonna sound stupid, but all of us, we all looked up at the same time, and the fluorescent lights—y'know, those tubes? —they were all dimming just a little, and we all hurried outside—I don't know why—and just stood on the sidewalk like everybody else, I mean *everybody else* was just standing there like they'd just been hit in the head or something. And we looked up, but . . . there was nothing there. Nothing to see, anyway. But . . . well, I *felt* like I'd seen something. I don't know *what*, because there was nothing there, but I had this feeling. . . . Then it was gone, and we were all walking along like nothing happened. We went out for ice cream and never talked about it. I'm not even sure they'd *remember*

232

it." She shook her head. "But ever since then—you're gonna think I'm so zoned, I swear, but ever since then, things haven't been quite . . . right. I haven't slept well since then, and my dad has been—this is really unlike him—he's been more worried about me than usual. He's, like, always asking me if everything's okay at school, stuff like that."

Lily sat there and looked at him for a long time, waiting for a reply, but Jeff said nothing. Not because he thought she was crazy, but because she was right. She was right, and he knew it, and it scared him.

"It isn't just you," she whispered. "I mean, your family, your sister—it's not just you, it's everybody. Nikki, Kevin . . . You know, I'd heard about this guy Mace before, I just had no idea who or what he was. I still don't, but I know enough to be scared of him. Last week I sat in the cafeteria and heard four different people talking about him like he was a goddamned circus clown and they were little kids or something. It's not just us, Jeff, it's just that he hasn't sucked us in yet. Not like he has everybody else."

"So what can we do?" he'd asked.

"Warn the others, the ones like us who haven't fallen for whatever Mace offers."

Nodding, he'd said, "Yeah, but that won't get my sister back."

As he lay awake in bed that night his insides felt cold and empty. His imagination took off with the speed of a runaway train, taking him into a future without his sister, a future in which he would have to live beneath a weight of guilt for having let her walk away again.

He thought about what Lily had said and wondered how many others thought Mace was their friend, how many would go to Fantazm on Wednesday night to hear Mace and his band play. . . .

Lily looked tired as she drove, and neither of them said much for a while. Traffic was backed up on Laurel Canyon Boulevard, and it only took them a few moments to realize they would be late for school. As they waited for traffic to move Jeff said, "What are you doing Wednesday night?"

"Nothing. Why?"

"Mace is playing with his band at Fantazm."

"You think we should go?"

"I don't know. I'm supposed to go to a birthday party that night. Maybe we should wait and see."

"Wait and see what?"

"See who else is going. Let's do some asking around at school the next couple days, try to find out exactly how popular this guy is."

"Why? I mean, what good will it do?"

"I don't know, but it's a start."

The wipers swept monotonously over the windshield, and the traffic clotted like blood in a corpse. . . .

The radio played loudly in the living room as Erin sipped her fourth cup of coffee. The traffic reporter was rambling on about a mudslide on Laurel Pass that had backed up traffic on Laurel Canyon Boulevard all the way to Burbank Boulevard; it was getting worse, and there was no sign of improvement for at least several hours. That meant surface street traffic would be chaotic for miles around Erin's apartment.

She had been sitting at the table for nearly two hours trying to make a list of possible jobs to look into. So far, she'd come up with WAITRESS and HOUSECLEANING. Neither would pay as much as dancing in strip bars, and she would have to get a smaller, less expensive apartment in what would probably be an undesirable neighborhood. If she waited tables during the day and got a job cleaning in a hotel or hospital at night, she might be able to swing it, but then she would have no life. Her time would be spent working and sleeping, and she would have none left to spend with the kids.

Erin pushed the list away, not wanting to look at it anymore. She reached for the crumpled pack of cigarettes on the table, removed one, and lit up. She'd stopped smoking a little over a year ago but awoke with a craving for a cigarette that morning. She'd found the pack buried in the back of her top nightstand drawer, and the cigarettes tasted as old and stale as she felt.

After J.R. had left the night before, she'd bid Jeff and his friend Lily goodnight and had gone to bed but didn't sleep. She tossed most of the night with an invisible steel band wrapping tighter and tighter around her chest; images of Mallory as a little girl, as a baby, as a lump in her belly went around and around in her head as she tried desperately to figure out where she'd gone wrong.

Erin was thankful for J.R.'s presence last night; it had helped a lot to have someone outside the family show so much concern. It didn't bring Mallory back, though.

Something he had said kept repeating itself over and over in her head: *If you keep hiding it from them . . . if you keep hiding it from them . . .*

She dreaded telling them, but she couldn't keep it from them any longer.

It's nothing to be ashamed of, she thought as she sipped her coffee. *It's just a job, nothing more; it keeps a roof over their heads, they'll understand that.*

But she wasn't so sure Mallory would understand that, especially after what she'd heard Thursday. Mallory and Jeff were very close, and if she wanted to, Mallory could strongly influence Jeff's way of accepting Erin's news. . . .

The steel band returned around her chest, tightening more and more.

The voice on the radio said, smilingly, "Well, kids, Mother Nature isn't being very nice to us, and according to our meteorologist, her mood isn't gonna change very soon, so I guess we're just gonna have to grin and bear it, huh?"

J.R. was made uncomfortable by the sterility of the Laurel Teen Center as he was led down a long corridor with cream-colored walls and fluorescent lighting. Other than a few bulletin boards and fire extinguishers on the walls, there was nothing to break up the monotony, just door after door.

He was led down the corridor by a beefy man with a smirklike smile and a name tag that read LUKE on the breast pocket of his thin white coat. He'd introduced himself as the supervisor, whatever that meant.

"We're usually careful about allowing visitors," Luke said pleasantly, leading J.R. into a well-furnished room with three shelves of paperback books against one wall and a big-screen television against another. "Mostly we just allow parents and siblings once a week. But we've never gotten a visitation request from a teacher or school counselor before. We'd like to get more. It's a show of concern. Lets us know we're not alone in this. Okay," he said, slapping J.R. on the back twice, "just have a seat right here, and I'll bring him in."

There were four others in the room, obviously patients (or inmates, whatever they called them at such a place): two boys and two girls.

Outside the room and some distance down the corridor shouting broke out. The voices were unintelligible at first, then one rose above the others, clearly crying, "I hate *daddies,* did you hear me, I said I hate *daddiiieees!*"

J.R. winced at the voice as he seated himself in a chair.

A few minutes later, Luke ushered Kevin into the room and seated him across a round table from J.R. There was an unfinished jigsaw puzzle spread over the table, and Kevin began toying with some of the pieces, his eyes avoiding J.R.

"There's a group meeting in here in about twenty minutes," Luke said, "so we'll have to clear the room out then." Slapping Kevin on the back, he left.

"We've never actually met, Kevin," J.R. said, "but I'm your counselor at school. My name's J.R. Haskell, but please call me J.R."

Kevin looked bored as he picked at the puzzle, still not looking up. He wore jeans and a plain white T-shirt.

"When I found out you were in here, I . . . well, I thought you might like to talk."

Kevin shook his head.

"Well, *I'd* like to talk."

Kevin looked up then, and J.R. realized his face was battered, bruised, one eye swollen. There were stitches in his chin.

"God, what happened to you?" J.R. asked.

"A fight. That's how I got here. A bunch of guys jumped me outside Mickey D.'s, the cops came, everybody ran away but me. My parents . . . they decided I should be here."

"That's crazy. For a fight?"

He shrugged and turned his attention back to the puzzle.

"Kevin, if you tell me who it was, those guys who did this to you, maybe I can help you. I'll talk to your parents—"

"Won't do any good. That wasn't the only reason. . . ."

"Oh?"

"I hadn't been home for a while. What difference does it make, man?" He suddenly began talking fast, scowling at J.R. "What difference does it make, huh? They've been looking for a reason to put me here for a long time. They searched my room, took my door off—you believe that? They took my fucking bedroom door off! They would've had me in here sooner or later anyway."

"Where have you been?"

"None of your fucking business, man."

"With Mace?"

Kevin looked at him, surprised, and, for a moment, seemed about to smile.

"You know Mace?"

"I know of him, Kevin, and what I know . . ." He leaned forward, moving closer to Kevin. "Who is Mace? Where is he from?"

Kevin glanced over J.R.'s shoulder at the window, and a hint of a smile crossed his lips.

"I . . . don't know," he said after a long pause. "But that doesn't matter."

"Why not?"

"Because he . . . when we met, I was suspicious of him, but not anymore. He offered to help me with my band—I've got this band, y'know—and he gave us a place to practice, music to play, good music—he's taught us a lot. And he's our friend."

"Why were you suspicious at first?"

"Well, I figured maybe he wanted to rip us off—the band, I mean. His offer sounded good, but . . . too good. Then I went home. My little brother . . . he started laughing at me because my mom had taken my bedroom door off, like I told you." His eyes darted around J.R., and his voice thickened slightly with emotion. "She'd gone through all my drawers,

237

my closet. She started yelling at me, telling me they were gonna put me away, teach me a lesson, shit like that."

"When was this?"

"Last month. I figured, like, what've I got to lose, y'know? So I went to see Mace, me and the band. And I'm glad we did. We're playing Fantazm Wednesday night."

"But you'll still be in here."

Kevin looked into J.R.'s eyes then and simply smiled.

"Your attendance has been good the last few weeks, Kevin. You didn't meet any of our appointments, but you went to nearly all of your classes. I checked my records before coming over here today, though, and all of a sudden, things stopped last week. You seemed to be trying hard for a while. Now you—what, you don't care? Why?"

He kept smiling.

"Kevin, I don't know if you're aware of this or not, but Mace is scaring a lot of people."

No reply.

"Something is wrong with what he's doing. Do you know Nikki Astin? Did you know a few nights ago he—"

Kevin stood.

"Wait, please, let me—"

He was still smiling, but his smile was cold as he headed for the door.

J.R. stood. "Kevin, please, you don't know what he's—"

Kevin was in the corridor, and J.R. followed him.

"*Kevin!*" he snapped, reaching for Kevin's arm but missing. J.R. was quickly approached by a round man in white whose name tag read PHIL.

"Excuse me, but we'd rather you not shout in here," Phil said.

"Look, I have to talk to him, he's—"

"We're very careful about visitation here, sir. Apparently he doesn't want to talk to you anymore."

J.R. watched Kevin walk slowly down the corridor and disappear through one of the many doors. . . .

A few minutes after J.R. was finished with his last appointment of the day, Jeff and Lily came to his office.

They both looked tired and scared. They made an attempt at small talk, but Lily and Jeff kept exchanging quick, cryptic glances, and J.R. knew something was up.

"Okay," he said seriously, sitting on the corner of his desk, "what's going on?"

Jeff leaned forward in his chair, elbows on knees, and said, "Remember that thing we told you Nikki was wearing? The weird cross she called a Crucifax?"

J.R. nodded.

"Mallory was wearing one, too. They got them from Mace."

"They're all over campus," Lily said softly.

"What, the crosses?" J.R. asked.

Jeff nodded. "Today I've seen—Jesus, I don't know, maybe twenty-five. More, probably."

"Those are just the ones you can see," Lily added. "Half the girls in my P.E. class were wearing them in the shower today. I went up to Sherry Cavanaugh and touched it, started to ask where she'd gotten it, and she freaked. She pushed my hand away like I'd hit her or something."

J.R. moved off the desk and into his chair, quickly thinking back over the day, trying to remember if he'd seen any students wearing the crosses; he didn't, but he hadn't been looking for them.

"My friend Nick was wearing one," Jeff said. "We usually don't hang around together much during school. Mostly in the summertime. We haven't talked in a while, but I met him today in the caf, and he was . . . different."

"Different how?" J.R. asked.

"I don't know, really. He's a pretty nice guy, usually quiet. He was moody during the last weeks of summer because his parents were getting a divorce. Now he's . . . he's still quiet, but he's got this weird smile on his face, like he knows something I don't, and he . . . he stares a lot. I asked him where he got that thing around his neck, and he said a friend gave it to him. I asked if it was anyone I know, and he didn't say anything for a few seconds, just gave me that creepy smile. Then he said, 'Yeah, you know him' and walked away."

"Everything around here is different," Lily said. There was frustration in her voice, and a frown wrinkled her brow. "Doesn't anyone else notice it? Is it just me?"

There was a burst of shouting down the hall, and J.R. listened a moment. He recognized Faye Beddoe's voice; she was arguing with a girl. He tried to ignore them.

"Different in what way, Lily?" he asked.

Glancing at Jeff as she spoke, Lily said, "Well, this weather, for one thing, and those damned crosses all over the place. . . . My friend Nikki, Miss Religion, starts acting like a slut . . . and I've got this other friend—she's bulimic —her mother's always telling her she's fat, so she throws up every time she eats, and for a while she was just wasting away."

She was one of J.R.'s students; it had been a few weeks since he'd seen her, and he couldn't remember her name, but he remembered that face, long and drawn with hollow cheeks and dark-circled eyes.

"She's gaining weight all of a sudden," Lily went on. "She's eating again, seems happy. . . ." She shrugged as the words trailed off.

J.R. remembered referring her to an eating disorder clinic—how long ago? Three weeks? A month? Longer?— he'd even made an appointment for her himself. He hadn't followed up on it to see if she'd gone, but J.R. could tell by the tone of Lily's voice that she didn't think the change in her friend had come from any clinic or professional counseling.

"Is she wearing a Crucifax?" Jeff asked.

"I don't know. She hasn't been to . . . school"—her eyes grew slowly with realization as she looked at Jeff—"in a while."

She's with him, J.R. thought. *That's what they're thinking, what they're afraid of, that she's with Mace.*

He tapped a pencil on his desktop, imagining what would happen if he went to Mr. Booth with everything he knew— which was really very little—and told him something needed to be done about these crosses that were being worn around campus, that they meant something, stood for something that might cause a lot of trouble soon. Booth would chuckle.

Haskell, he might say, *we've got kids here who put safety pins in their noses and razor blades in their ears and call them jewelry. You want me to make a fuss about some* crosses?

The shouting down the hall worsened; Jeff and Lily looked over their shoulders at the closed door.

"What do you think is happening?" J.R. asked them.

Before either of them could reply, Faye Beddoe screamed.

J.R. shot out of his chair, pulled the door open, and was in the hall in an instant, running toward Faye's office. There were hurried footsteps behind him and a scuffle coming from the office ahead. Faye's door opened, and a girl bolted out and started toward J.R., zigzagging from wall to wall as she ran. When he saw the blood, everything slowed down, way down, because he knew something bad had happened.

He'd seen the girl before: Hispanic, a little chunky, with black hair that used to fall to her waist but was now spiked. She wore a long tan coat that flapped behind her like a cape as she ran, and there was blood spattered on its lapels and on the front of her white sweater. Swinging back and forth over her chest like a pendulum was a cross with flared ends, dark red and heavy-looking, and with each swing it tossed more beads of blood over her coat and sweater, and he held out his arms to stop her, shouting, "Hey, *hey,* wait!" but she pushed by him, spinning him around and against the wall, and he almost ran after her even though there were others reaching for her, trying to hold her, but he heard Faye's voice rise in an agonized, guttural scream: "Gaawwwd! Gaawwwd!"

J.R. turned again, ran for her office, and pushed through the doorway, and his feet slid over the floor as he skidded to a clumsy halt, his arms flailing to hold his balance.

Faye's desk faced the door, and she was kneeling behind it, her arms sprawled over the desktop, her head lolling. There was a spray of blood on the wall behind her.

She was grinning.

"Faye . . ." J.R. breathed, moving toward her, feeling as

if his feet were plodding through quicksand because something was wrong with her face, with the grin that stretched all the way up her left cheek, then he realized that her black skin was glistening, wet, and he saw teeth, so many teeth. . . .

"Faye?" He was at the desk as she pulled herself up with a horrible gurgling sound, still grinning—

—but she *wasn't* grinning.

A flap of skin hung loosely from her cheek, jiggling as she tried to pull herself to her feet, dribbling blood over the papers on her desk. A smooth, clean cut swept up from the left corner of Faye's mouth to her mandible. She tried to speak but could only make wet sputtering noises, spraying more blood through the gash in her face. She swept her arms back and forth over the desk, knocking books and pens and papers and the telephone to the floor.

J.R. took her hand as he moved around the desk, saying, "Sit back, Faye, just sit back. *Somebody call an ambulance!*" he shouted, then: "C'mon, Faye, just sit back, now, c'mon. . . ."

She fell heavily into her chair and leaned her head back; the lower half of her cheek folded over, revealing her writhing tongue.

"Oh, God, dear God," J.R. gasped, moving behind her and pressing a hand over her cheek, holding the flap of skin in place. He could hear shouting and scuffling down the hall but heard no one coming.

"Goddammit!" he shouted, feeling lightheaded and queasy. "Let's get some help down here!"

Faye's blood, sticky and warm, ran between his fingers and over the back of his hand. . . .

Jeff stood in the office doorway as J.R. rushed down the hall.

"What's going on?" Lily asked behind him, her hand on his back.

"I don't—" He stopped when he saw the girl and the blood and the swinging Crucifax, stepped into the hall, muttering, "Jesus," and reached for her as she neared, snapping, "Hold it, *hold* it!" but she clenched a fist and swung her arm hard, hitting him in the chest and knocking him back into J.R.'s office, bumping him into Lily.

He rushed out the door again, gained on her quickly, and gripped her right arm firmly as she entered the front office. The girl spun around and, with an angry grunt, kicked Jeff hard in the shin. Pain shot up his leg as he loosened his grip on her just enough for her to pull away and dash across the office.

Mr. Plumley, the oldest and biggest counselor at Valley, was standing by the door that led to the main hall. He stepped in front of the girl, threw his arms around her, and hugged her tightly to his wide, round belly, saying, "Okay, okay, calm down, little lady, just hold the phone, let's—"

"No!" she shouted. "Let me go, let go! I'm going, I'm going away, going away!"

"You're not going anywhere just now, little lady, so let's—ah, Christ!" Plumley cried. "She's biting me!"

The girl had her mouth on his right wrist, and her head was jerking back and forth. Her words were garbled when she spoke: "Away . . . going . . . away . . ."

Plumley let out a high, quavering shriek and pulled his bitten hand protectively to his chest, stumbling backward, shouting, "Jesus Christ, she bit me!"

The girl pushed through the door and ran, her voice fading as she rushed down the hall: "Leave me alone, dammit, I'm going away. . . . going away . . ."

Miss Tucker, the receptionist, stood up behind her desk and shouted, "Stop her!" but Jeff was already through the door and running down the hall after her.

"Stop her!" Jeff called to no one in particular. "Help me stop her!"

Heads turned, but no one moved.

She rounded a corner, heading for the building's main entrance, and Jeff picked up his pace. Someone was running behind him, but he didn't take the time to look back.

As Jeff turned the corner, Dwayne Chalmers was wheeling a projection cart through a doorway into the hall, pushing it directly into Jeff's path. Dwayne always wore long-sleeved shirts buttoned to the neck, white socks with brown loafers, and his face was usually sprinkled with pimples. He was not an agile person or else he might have been able to pull the cart out of Jeff's way in time; he tried, but was not fast enough.

Jeff tried to backpedal when he saw the cart but slid into it feet-first. The cart toppled and the projector skidded down the hall, spinning like a top.

"Well, that's *fine!*" Dwayne barked. "That's *fine,* that's just *great!*"

The girl had already left the building, and the door was slowly swinging shut behind her. J.R. was running beside Jeff now, and they burst through the door together into the rain.

In the parking lot, students were climbing aboard idling buses and cars were leaving their parking spaces.

The sidewalk in front of the building looked deserted.

Jeff and J.R. stopped halfway down the steps and looked around.

"Where in the hell did she go?" J.R. exclaimed.

"Maybe somebody was waiting for her in a car," Jeff suggested, scanning the lot for a car that appeared to be leaving in a hurry.

"Not enough time."

Wind blew their clothes and hair as they stood on the steps, and rain cut through the air diagonally, slapping their faces. Jeff saw that J.R.'s shirt was covered with blood.

"Is it bad?" Jeff asked.

"Pretty bad, yeah."

"She was wearing a Crucifax."

J.R. nodded grimly. "I know."

They turned to go back up the steps and saw Lily coming through the door. She started to speak, but something splattered over her left arm and she lifted it with a start, looked at the dark fluid that was dribbling over her skin, washing away with the rain, then looked to her left over the handrail and into the shrubbery below.

Jeff's eyes followed her gaze to what looked, at first, like a miniature oil well spurting from the brush and splashing to the cement. The bushes were shifting, and as Jeff climbed the steps he heard a wet, sputtering gasp that was drowned by Lily's horrified scream as she stumbled away from the rail, covering her mouth with a palm. Jeff and J.R. rushed to the handrail, looked over the edge, and saw her.

The girl was sprawled in the bushes, her left arm stretched above her head, her right arm on her chest, fingers wrapped tightly around the Crucifax, her mouth opening and closing, opening and closing, eyes wide, and her throat—

Sweet Jesus, this isn't happening, Jeff thought, *please let this be a nightmare!*

—was yawning open like a second mouth, slashed from side to side and spurting blood orgasmically.

"Fuck!" J.R. cried, vaulting over the rail and landing with a grunt in the bushes. "Call an ambulance, get somebody over here *noowww!*"

Jeff followed him, feeling numb and disoriented, as if under the influence of a drug. As the girl's blood flowed, the rain washed it away almost as quickly, affording a clear view of the gash, of the sliced trachea and gushing veins and arteries.

J.R. began tearing off his shirt, pressing the tattered fabric to the girl's throat, but it was obviously too late.

Her eyes were glazing, her motions ceasing, and the flow of blood was coming to a halt.

"Jesus, Jesus Christ, what is going on here?" J.R. rasped as he continued to press his torn shirt to her open throat. "Just what in the holy fuck is going on here?"

Jeff sat back, taking his eyes from the dead girl's face, trying to catch his breath, trying to keep from throwing up.

Lily had gone inside; Jeff could hear her screams echoing through the halls.

He covered his face with his hands and imagined the Crucifax around Mallory's neck, around Nikki's, and he prayed that they were safe.

That they were still alive . . .

Twenty-three

When J.R. returned to the counseling office that evening, the lights were out and everyone was gone. Without the hushed buzz of fluorescent lights and the constant drone of voices and activity, the only sounds were his footsteps and the whisper of rainfall.

He went to Faye's office, flicked on the light, and immediately diverted his eyes from the opposite wall. The blood had been cleaned away, but he knew that if he looked, he would see it as clearly as if her face had just been slashed.

J.R. had followed Faye's ambulance to the hospital and had gone into the emergency room with her. She'd been propped into a sitting position on the gurney to keep the blood from running down her throat, and a temporary bandage had been put over the cut. As the paramedic wheeled her into ER, he'd said again and again, "Don't try to speak, Faye. . . . Hold your head still. . . . Don't try to speak. . . ."

When J.R. went to her side, Faye took his hand in a firm grip, ignored the paramedic, and sputtered, "J-Junior, is . . . sh-she dead?"

As he silently nodded his head she closed her eyes and released a raspy sigh, as if she'd expected and dreaded his reply.

He'd called Mr. Booth from the hospital; the girl's name, Booth said, was Sherry Pacheco, and her parents were on their way to the hospital, although they did not yet know their daughter was dead.

After Faye was taken into surgery, J.R. headed back to the school, still disturbed by the knowing look of defeat on her face once she'd learned of Sherry's death, by the expectant way she'd asked, "Is . . . sh-she dead?"

In Faye's office, J.R. opened the metal filing cabinet in the corner and pulled Sherry Pacheco's file.

Faye had been her counselor two years in a row. According to the record, the girl had been a straight-A student with a nearly perfect attendance record and had never been in any trouble—

—until six weeks ago.

Her attendance dropped by half, and teachers had been complaining that Sherry was turning in incomplete assignments, or not turning them in at all. Two weeks ago, she'd started a fight in the shower room, injuring another student.

J.R. opened Sherry's personal history folder and was surprised to see how much it contained. Apparently, Faye kept extensive records.

He thought, *And Faye told me not to get involved* . . .

Sherry's father was an RTD bus driver; her mother was a babysitter three afternoons a week and worked in a day care center the other two days. They were devout Catholics, Sherry was their only child, and, from Faye's sketchy notes, J.R. gathered that they had hoped to send her to a Catholic high school but had been unable to afford the steep tuition. *Wanted her to be nun,* she'd written in a margin, and, next to that, underlined twice: *Disappointed.*

Sherry was disappointed? He wondered. *Or they were disappointed in Sherry?*

The Pachecos either came into some money or had decided to cut back on expenses, because shortly after Sherry began her junior year at Valley High School, they decided to send her to Our Lady of the Valley High School in Encino. Sherry had resisted strongly; *threatens to leave home,* Faye had written.

When J.R. compared her personal history to her academic records, he found that it was at that time that Sherry's grades dropped.

Near the bottom of the third page of Sherry Pacheco's personal history, J.R. found something written in the margin and circled in red: *Haircut—attitude change—"crucifax"—like Steve Paulson.*

J.R. put Sherry's file on top of the cabinet, opened the drawer again, and searched through the Ps until he found Paulson.

Steve Paulson was a senior. His parents were divorced, and his younger brother and sister lived with his mother; Steve lived with his father, a plumber in North Hollywood. *Mother refused to take him,* Faye had written.

Steve had been trouble all through high school and had apparently made no effort to change. His father had met with Faye once the year before; *uninterested* was written beside the record of the meeting. Faye had tried to contact Steve's mother, who now lived in Santa Monica, but none of her calls or letters had been answered.

On the back of the first page in Steve's personal history file, Faye had written in very precise, careful print, *Restless and rebellious to angry and violent in three weeks.*

At the bottom of the page: *Oct. 8 wears crucifax. Got it from "friend." Won't explain—same as others.*

"Same as others," he muttered. In the silence, his voice sounded too loud. *"What* others?" he asked, paging through the other files in the drawer.

Within fifteen minutes, J.R. had found four other references to Crucifaxes. Feeling a sudden surge of energy, as if he were close to something important, he cleared a space on Faye's desk, stacked several of the files before him, and settled into her chair.

He was at her desk for nearly three hours going through her files—severely unethical, he realized, but under the circumstances, he was willing to bend the rules—and taking notes on a small pad. Occasionally, he ran his fingers through his hair and muttered, "Christ, what is going on here?" or "What do you know that you're not telling, Faye?"

When he was done, he had a list of names of students who were apparently involved with Mace; their behavior had changed, their grades had dropped—even the ones whose grades had not been good in the first place had fallen noticeably—and some of them were not only getting into trouble but appeared to be looking for it.

He sat at the desk for a long time, staring at the notes he'd made, feeling smaller and smaller, as if he were sitting in the shadow of something enormous that was looming over him threateningly, a shadow that was growing bigger and bigger. . . .

"God," he breathed as he looked through the notes a second time, seeing something, vague at first, but clearer the third time through—clearer and undeniable, impossible to ignore, as outrageous as it seemed. . . .

There was a pattern. There seemed to be a definite pattern among the students who had connections with Mace.

But only in Faye's files, he thought.

He looked at his watch; it was eight-nineteen.

He knew all this information would mean nothing unless he could see the same pattern among other students, students who were not under Faye's counsel.

There were five counselors in the department. Five different files of student records.

He pushed away from the desk and sighed to himself, "You've got all night, Haskell. . . ."

After leaving the school, Jeff and Lily went to Jeff's apartment, drained by what they had seen. Erin had already gone to work but had left a note promising to call home later in the evening.

Although each of them had homework assignments that were due the next day, neither felt like working. They turned on the radio, and Jeff called out for pizza while Lily rolled a joint with a little marijuana she'd gotten from a friend over the weekend. Neither said much. Lily walked by Jeff while he was on the phone and briefly touched the back of his neck; after Jeff hung up the phone, he went to the kitchen for a Coke and gently stroked her hair as he passed her. He cracked a window when she lit up the joint, and the sound of rainfall mixed with the music on the radio as they each took a drag in turn.

They sat side by side for a while, finished the grass, leaned on one another as they listened to the music and waited for their pizza.

The pizza never came.

"Stay off those roads, people," the disc jockey said, a sultry-voiced woman named Regina. "It's bad out there. If you're in Northridge right now, you probably can't hear me unless you're runnin' on batteries. Seems there's been a power outage in that area. . . ."

Lily put her head in Jeff's lap and stretched her legs on the sofa; he began to stroke her hair.

". . . somebody drove into a telephone pole, and there are reports of live power lines squirming around in the road on Jarette, so stay away from there. . . ."

He lightly touched her forehead with his fingertips, her cheek; she turned her head and kissed his hand.

". . . Laurel Canyon Boulevard is still backed up, and I mean *waaay* up, because of a slide on the pass. It's the second slide in the last twenty-four hours. The first one was cleaned up by four-thirty this afternoon but was followed by another. And there's been some pretty heavy flooding on Ventura near Whitset. If it gets any worse, there may be a detour . . ."

Lily pressed her head back against Jeff's erection as his hand slid over her throat. He slipped his other hand beneath her neck and lifted her head, kissing her as his hand moved between her breasts, over her belly, then back up again, cupping a breast gently.

". . . I'm tellin' you, people, it looks like the Valley is just falling apart at the seams. If you're in the middle of it, just stick with me, and I'll keep playing the hits for you until midnight. . . ."

Lily wrapped an arm around his neck and pressed herself closer to him, and they both sighed as they tangled together on the sofa. She put a hand between his legs and squeezed the firm bulge in his jeans—

—and Jeff thought of Mallory.

He wanted to push her away, hoping it would remove the thought from his mind, take away the image of his naked, sweating sister from behind his eyes, but before he could move, before he could separate his mouth from Lily's, there was a sound in the wall of the living room, a brief but distinct scuttling sound that seemed to come from behind the bookshelf, and Jeff lifted his head, turning his eyes toward the sound as Lily sat up with a gasp, hissing, "Jesus, what was that?"

Jeff was on his feet, moving down the hall to his sister's room, where he found the door open a crack, and he reached out his hands before he was even close to the door, grabbed the knob, and pulled it shut hard, imagining the hole in the closet on the other side as Lily began to cry in the living room.

"It's okay, it's okay," he assured her, "the door's shut, they may be in the walls, but they're not getting out; it's okay." He went to the living room, moved toward her, but the light dimmed, and Lily spun around with a gasp, stared at the lamp by the sofa, and they waited for it to go out, waited for the darkness.

The light stayed on.

She turned on the television; it clashed with the sound of the radio, but it buried any other sounds in the apartment. They sat close on the sofa, watching MTV as the disc jockey said, "Hell, people, it's hell out there, and I mean hell. . . ."

The power was restored in Northridge by the next morning, but the slide on Laurel Pass was still backing up traffic. Several traffic lights had gone out in Van Nuys shortly after dawn, creating a jam on Sepulveda, and a section of Woodman was blocked off due to flooding, only adding to the backup.

J.R. hadn't gone to bed until shortly after three A.M., and even then his sleep had been restless. He'd come home with a stack of notes gathered from the files of his fellow counselors. He'd gone over them one last time before getting into bed as Faye's words repeated themselves over and over in his head:

Then one day the piper comes. And he seldom leaves empty-handed.

When he arrived at work that morning after an interminable wait in bumper-to-bumper traffic, J.R. postponed his morning appointment and went to the hospital to see Faye.

She was asleep when he entered her room. The left side and lower half of her face were bandaged, and there was an I.V. in her left arm.

He stood at her bedside for a moment and watched her sleep, listened to her slow, regular breathing, remembered the troubled look in her eyes last Friday, and wondered what she knew that would drive her to keep such tedious records on all of her students, particularly those involved with Mace. The other counselors had obviously not noticed the things Faye had, and their records were not nearly as detailed; but having gone through Faye's files, J.R. knew what to look for—and he found it.

When he touched her hand, Faye's eyes opened suddenly, and she made a hoarse noise in her throat.

"Hi, Faye."

She moved her head slightly and gestured with her hand.

J.R. looked around until he found a pad and pen on her nightstand. When he handed them to her, she began writing, her hand moving slowly, then handed the pad to J.R.

The note was shakily written but readable:

How did Sherry die? No one will tell me.

"She killed herself," he said quietly.

How?

"With the Crucifax. She cut her throat."

Her heavy eyes widened for a moment.

You know about them? About the Crucifaxes?

He nodded.

How?

J.R. pulled a chair close to the bed, sat down, and leaned toward her, propping an elbow on the railing.

"I found out from a student of mine. But that was just a few days ago. You've known for quite a while, haven't you?"

She cocked a brow curiously.

"Look, Faye, I know it's unethical, but . . . well, last night I went through your files. After what happened, when you asked about Sherry, I got the feeling you knew something. I wanted to find out what."

She made a noise that sounded like, *Well?*

"You know more than I do. And you're scared. Tell you the truth, I'm scared, too, but I'm not quite sure why."

Faye closed her eyes and sighed through her nose; J.R. couldn't tell if it was a sigh of relief or unrest. She lay still for a long time, and he thought she'd fallen back to sleep, but she reached for the pad again.

What do you want to know?

"Who is Mace?"

I don't know.

"What *do* you know?"

She closed her eyes again, thought a moment.

He's got something the kids want. Need.

"But only certain kids, right?"

A slight nod.

"Look, Faye . . . this is just between us, right?"

Another nod.

"I went through all the files in the office. Every one of them. We're the only ones who know something's going on, but even though the others don't see it, it's in the records. Changes in some of the kids, in their behavior and grades. Most of the kids, it seems. But there's a thread, a pattern among the ones who change. Something bad has happened recently in their lives, a divorce or a problem with a sibling or . . . here." He reached into his coat pocket and took out the notes he'd made. They were bound together by a rubber band, which he quickly pulled off, flipping through the pages. "This was in your file. Sherry Pacheco. Her parents wanted her to be a nun, is that right?"

She nodded.

"They were going to send her to a Catholic school. She changed then, went straight downhill. Then she started wearing a Crucifax. Like Steve Paulson and Brandon Ott and Holly Porter and many others, Faye, many others. It's beginning to look like—"

He stopped when he saw that she was writing again.

There's nothing you can do.

"What do you mean, there's nothing . . . ? Listen, Faye, these kids seem to think this guy Mace is gonna take them away soon. They don't seem to know where he's taking them, but they want to go. When Sherry was running out of the office, she was shouting something about going away. 'I'm going away, I'm going away,' she kept saying, then she went outside and—" He realized he was speaking faster and his voice was rising; he leaned closer to her and spoke softly. "—and she cut her throat open with that *thing.* Do you see the connection, Faye? They're all wearing those things, and Mace tells them they're all going away. Do you see why I'm so worried?"

There is nothing you can do.

"Why *not?* I don't understand. Can't we tell someone? Warn someone?"

The only people who can do something haven't done it.

"The only . . . who?" He slowly nodded when the answer came to him. "The parents. But they don't know. I can tell them."

She closed her eyes again.

"Can't I?"

You can try.

"Faye, I have the feeling you're . . . well, familiar with all of this. How?"

From watching. For many years. It happens again and again.

"You've come across this guy before? Mace?"

She shook her head and scribbled some more, writing slowly.

If it wasn't Mace, it would be someone else. Something else.

"Something?"

With a long sigh through her nose, she began writing again, filling two pages with her big, wavy script.

4 years ago—Newark, N.J.—7 kids killed themselves in a garage—carbon monoxide. Left notes saying they "had to leave."

6 years ago in Wisconsin 12 teens slashed their wrists in a field. No notes, but in previous weeks two other teens in area did same.

The pages quivered in J.R.'s trembling hand, and he almost stopped reading, almost asked Faye how she knew those things, why she kept records of them, but the next sentence stopped his words in his throat.

13 years ago in El Cerrito, CA, 22 kids hanged themselves in an abandoned restaurant. In weeks before that 7 individual kids did same. Some left notes saying they were—

"—going someplace better," J.R. finished aloud. There was more, but he put the notes on the bed and leaned on the chrome railing. "One of those kids was my little sister," he whispered.

Faye reached for his hand and held it for a moment, then took the pad and began writing again.

Did you meet John and Dara?

"John and . . . how did you know about them?"

In each case there are accounts of a stranger or strangers in town weeks or months before deaths, hanging around kids, throwing parties, sometimes handing out drugs. Always gets little more than two paragraphs in papers. Strangers are never seen again, and their connection to deaths is always ignored.

"How long have you been doing this? Gathering all this information?"

Many years. And it goes on. I go to the library, watch the papers, the news.

"Who are all these people? Where do they come from? Why are they so powerful?"

Don't know who or what they are—what it is. They're different each time—a man or a woman or a couple—but always the same.

"You talk about them like they're not human."

You don't clean your house, it gets dirty, dusty, windows get grimy. Where does it all come from? Don't know. It comes while you're not watching, not looking for it. They're like that. They come while no one's watching. They're not very powerful—only as powerful as their victims are weak.

She closed her eyes a moment, breathed deeply, then wrote:

Sorry. Medication makes me rummy. We'll talk later. Don't let it eat you, J.R. They can't be stopped, only held off. And the only people who can hold them off usually don't notice them until it's too late. There's nothing you can do.

She patted his hand and drifted to sleep, leaving him to stare at the last five words of her note.

He didn't agree. . . .

"I've been calling her all day," Lily said as she tried to maneuver her car through the soup-thick traffic on 101. "There was no answer until about fifteen minutes ago."

Lily had come to the gymnasium during Jeff's P.E. class and frantically asked him to go with her to Nikki's. He'd cut the class before his teacher arrived and changed back into his clothes.

"Nikki finally answered," Lily said, taking the Cahuenga exit. "*I* said I wanted to see her today, but *she* said she was leaving. Wouldn't tell me where she was going, though. 'I'm leaving, that's all,' she said. I told her to wait a few minutes, that I'd be right over there, because I wanna get to her before she goes again, you know? If I have to tie her *up*, I will. Anyway, then she said, 'I'm leaving now,' and she hung up." She stopped at a red light and nervously rapped a knuckle on the steering wheel as she waited for it to change. "There was something about the way she said 'I'm leaving now' . . . something that just didn't sound right."

When they got to Nikki's apartment building, they hurried through the rain and up the stairs, where Lily pounded on the door.

There was no answer.

"Damn," Lily hissed, knocking again. When there was still no answer, she removed the key from the porch light and opened the door. "Nikki?" she called.

Jeff followed her through the living room reluctantly. The apartment was dark, all the curtains were drawn over the windows, and the only light came from the hall; somewhere in the apartment a clock ticked loudly and the refrigerator hummed.

"Wait!" Jeff snapped.

She stopped at the entrance to the hallway and turned to him. "What?"

Jeff remembered Sherry Pacheco's last words: *I'm going away, going away. . . .*

"I'm leaving now," Nikki had said.

Jeff felt a chill and stepped forward, saying, "Let me go first."

The light was coming from Nikki's bedroom, spilling through the half-open door and onto the tan carpet. The door creaked slightly as Jeff pushed it.

Nikki was lying on top of her neatly made bed, her back to the door. There was a sheet of notebook paper on the pillow behind her head, and Jeff sucked in an involuntary gasp. He stood in the doorway for a moment, waving his hand behind him at Lily, trying to speak but finding no voice for several seconds, until finally he said in a dry and hoarse voice, "Wait, just . . . wait a second."

He entered the room, slowly walked around the bed, his knees feeling weak, saw Nikki's arm hanging over the edge of the bed, saw the Crucifax on the floor inches below her hand—

—and the blood.

It had soaked into the white bedspread and run onto the floor where it darkened the carpet; streams of it glistened on Nikki's forearm and ran to her fingertips.

"What?" Lily called from the hall. "What's wrong, dammit, what's happened?"

"Call . . . an ambulance."

"What's wrong?"

"Just call an ambulance now, Lily, now!"

He heard Lily's frantic voice fade down the hall and into the living room.

Jeff turned away from the blood and swallowed again and again, trying to hold down the thick lump he felt rising from his stomach. He went to the other side of the bed and picked up the note. After staring at Nikki's still body for a moment, he read it once, twice, three times. . . .

I'm going away to someplace better.

* * *

Jeff's phone call stunned J.R. into silence.

He'd been on his way out of the office for the day. Except for the two he'd postponed that morning, J.R. had met all of his appointments, but not without difficulty. As he talked with his students he'd had to fight the urge to warn them about Mace, but he wasn't sure that would be wise, considering what had happened to Faye. Instead, he watched their necks for leather cords concealed by shirts and jackets.

Of the eight students who had entered his office that day, five of them were wearing Crucifaxes.

By the end of the day, J.R. had worked himself into quite an unsettled state.

"Paranoid," he'd mumbled to himself as he put his things into the briefcase. "Something's going on, but you're taking it too far, you're too damned paranoid." He'd planned to go home, take a hot shower, pop a frozen lasagna dinner into the microwave, read the paper, watch "Moonlighting," and think of nothing but relaxing.

Then Jeff called.

It wasn't Nikki's death that so disturbed him, although that was horrible enough. What made him clutch the telephone receiver in a white-knuckled grip was the note Nikki had left.

Licking his suddenly dry lips, J.R. asked, "What . . . did that . . . note say again, Jeff?"

"'I'm going away to someplace better,'" Jeff replied.

J.R. lowered the receiver from his ear, put his face in his hand, and muttered, "Oh, God." He felt a rush of emotions, a sickly, dizzy feeling of emptiness, helplessness, that he had not experienced in years. Not since Sheila had died.

Killed herself, a silent voice reminded him.

"Hello?" Jeff said.

It happens again and again. . . .

"J.R., you still there?"

. . . again and again . . .

J.R.'s mother had kept Sheila's note near her for days after the funeral, reading it over and over, staring at that single, neatly written line as if it might change. But no matter how many times she read it, the note remained the same: *I'm going someplace better.*

"You there, J.R.?"

"Yeah. Where are you now?"

"Nikki's. They took the—uh . . . took her away. We're waiting for Nikki's mother to get home."

"Is there anything I can do?"

"No, I just thought you'd want to know."

"Yeah, thanks for calling. I'm going home soon, so if anything comes up, call me there."

"J.R.?" Jeff suddenly sounded years younger. "Do you know anything about this? Because Lily and I are—" There was a nervous fluttering sound in his throat, a sort of chuckle that came out sounding like a whimper. "—we're pretty scared. Nikki's note, Sherry's words just before she killed herself . . . what's he doing to them, J.R.? My sister's with him!"

"I know, Jeff, and we're gonna get her away from him. Call me tonight. We'll get together and talk, okay?"

"Yeah. Okay."

After he hung up, J.R. ran his fingers through his hair and wished he was already home.

"Nope, not yet," he sighed, picking up his phone and dialing.

"Principal's office."

"Hello, Mrs. Lehman, this is J.R. Haskell in counseling. Is Mr. Booth still in?"

"Well, he's on his way out. Is it important?"

"Yes. Very important, I'm afraid. . . ."

259

Twenty-four

The TV room in Ward C of the Laurel Teen Center was closed at ten o'clock every night, and everyone was in bed by eleven. The early bedtime was Kevin's least favorite rule. Before being admitted to the center, he'd seldom gone to bed before two A.M. Now he went to bed but did not sleep.

Instead, he lay in bed listening to the rain or the sounds coming from the desk just down the corridor or the occasional outburst of shouting or crying from other rooms on the ward. Sometimes he closed his eyes and listened for the whisper of Leif's breathing, tried to separate it from the other sounds.

And sometimes he listened for Mace's eyes.

He'd heard them during his second night at the center. He'd been lying in bed staring into the darkness, thinking about what he would do to Larry Caine once he got out, when he heard the first movements in the wall behind his head. He'd sat up and turned to the small poster over his bed that read YOUR LIFE IS IN YOUR HANDS—DON'T SIT ON THEM. He'd pressed his hand to the poster and tilted his head to listen.

He'd heard them again—felt them, too, scurrying within

the wall—and he'd smiled, suddenly much more at ease in that strange and unwelcoming place knowing they were there, knowing that Mace was watching over him.

He'd heard them each night after that.

Except for tonight.

He lay back on the bed with a sigh and clasped his hands behind his head. Maybe he'd been wrong; he'd heard nothing from Mace since he'd been admitted. Maybe he'd been wrong to put so much faith in Mace and wouldn't hear from him.

Mr. Haskell had been his only visitor so far. Kevin had enjoyed the man's nervousness and had flopped onto his bed laughing after walking out on the conversation. Haskell was worried about Mace; that meant others were worried, too. Kevin liked that. If they were worried, that meant they thought Mace was important in some way, and their concern gave him power.

Kevin's parents called but never talked to him. Luke came in each afternoon and said, "Well, Kev, your parents just called to ask about you. They're very concerned, so I hope you'll cooperate with us and make them proud."

One day, Kevin had said, "I can't make 'em proud when I'm at home; what makes you think I can do it here?"

"Now, Kevin, buddy," Luke had said, slapping him on the back, "that's not the attitude we're after here."

A psychiatrist named Dr. Blanchette had visited him that day. He was a soft-spoken black man with speckles of gray in his hair and thick-lensed glasses. He asked Kevin a few questions about his problem and examined him briefly, then told Kevin that he would be put on medication starting tomorrow.

"Your problem seems to stem from depression, Kevin," Dr. Blanchette had said. "With the help of your group sessions and private counseling, we'll eventually get to the root of that depression, but in the meantime, the medication will lift your mood and, at the same time, calm you down."

"What medication?"

"Elavil."

Elavil, dude . . . Elavil all the way . . .

Kevin looked across the room at the long sleeping shape beneath the blankets in the other bed and thought of the way Leif shuffled around with his eyes half-closed, the way his jaw hung open, the long pauses between words as he spoke . . .

I won't be like him, he thought. *I won't.*

The door opened, and light spilled in from the corridor, but only briefly. Someone stepped inside and quickly closed the door.

Kevin sat up on the bed and squinted through the darkness.

"Who's there?"

Footsteps crossed the room.

"Hello, Kevin," Mace said quietly, sitting on the edge of the bed.

"Mace!" Kevin whispered. "What are you doing here?"

"I came for you," Mace laughed. "We've missed you. And we can't perform without you tomorrow night, can we?"

Kevin swung his legs over the bed and stood. He was so excited, it was difficult to keep his voice down.

"Jesus, I didn't think I'd see you again, I didn't think . . . well, I thought maybe you . . ."

"You said you trusted me, Kevin."

"Well, I did, but . . . but I was scared."

"Don't blame you. This is a scary place. But I've been watching you. You knew that, didn't you?"

Kevin nodded. "How did you get in here? They don't allow visitors at night."

"I'm fast and quiet," he whispered mischievously.

"So how're we gettin' outta here?"

"Trust me. Just wait a few minutes."

Mace patted the mattress, and Kevin sat down again.

"How's your roomie?"

"Quiet. A zombie. I think it's the medication they give him. They were gonna start giving it to me tomorrow."

"Mm, I'm just in time. We'll wake him before we go. Maybe he'd like to come with us."

"Come with us? But he's—"

"Trust me." Mace turned fully toward Kevin and said,

"So. You've probably been thinking about Larry Caine a lot. You must be eager to see old Larry again, huh? I know I would be if I were you."

Kevin made a bitter snorting sound.

"Yeah, thought so. Well, I've got a plan, my friend. You can see him tonight, if you want. Give Larry and his friends a surprise, sound good?"

"Where? How?"

"Don't worry about that, let me take care of it. All you have to do is promise me something."

"Sure."

"We're all going away soon. All of us—you, me, Mallory, all the others. Some have already left. Others will go before me. I can't leave until everyone has gone. The others look up to you, Kevin. They respect you." He gently placed a hand on Kevin's cheek; his large palm and long fingers covered half of Kevin's face. "Will you go with them? Ahead of me?"

"Go where?"

Mace leaned closer to him, so close that Kevin could feel his breath on his face.

"A place where no one will ever let you down again. Where no one can disapprove of your achievements, a place where everyone is equal and there are no lies. You'll know it when you find it, but you can't find it without this. This is your key."

He held a Crucifax up to Kevin's face.

Someone screamed in the corridor.

"I lost my other one," Kevin said, "when I was—"

"I know. This one is yours. If we have a deal. Will you go?" Mace breathed.

"My parents will just . . . they'll have me put back in here."

"Your parents will never find you. You have my word."

Maybe it's someplace out of the country, Kevin thought, *someplace safe and away from here, away from them.*

"Yeah. I'll go."

Mace leaned back, lifted his arms, and put the Crucifax around Kevin's neck as another scream tore through the corridor, followed by running footsteps and a male voice shouting, "Holy Jesus, what the fuck is—grab her arms! Get 'em off, get 'em—Christ!—get 'em off her!"

"Get dressed," Mace whispered. "Hurry."

Kevin stood and felt around in the dark for his clothes as Mace went to Leif's bedside. As he dressed Kevin heard Mace whisper something. Leif stirred and mumbled, "Wha-*huh?*" More whispering. "Oh. Yuh . . . yeah. Yeah." Leif got out of bed and began to dress, too.

"Stay close to me when we leave the room," Mace said. "The power will go off soon, and it'll be dark."

A woman screamed, "It's—God, it's biting me, biting me, Jesus, somebody—"

Glass shattered.

A door slammed.

A peal of bitter, hateful laughter—Kevin recognized the voice of the jittery, chain-smoking boy two rooms down—rose above the noise, and someone shouted, "Look at her run!"

"Ready?" Mace said calmly once the boys were dressed.

They said they were, and Mace went to the door.

There was more running just outside the room, and the shouting voices were becoming more and more frantic.

"Call somebody!"

"Who, who?"

"Anybody, the front—oh, shit, *ow!*—the front office!"

"Where'd they come from?"

"I-I don't know, th-they—ah, *Jesus,* pull it *off!*"

Reaching for the door, Mace said, "Remember, stay close," and then he pulled it open.

The corridor was flowing with Mace's dirty-gray creatures; they scurried in every direction, crawling over one another, wriggling madly, snapping their teeth and snarling at the white-clothed employees who were dashing through the corridor trying to jump over clusters of the things to avoid being bitten.

Barry, the night janitor, a stocky, stubble-faced man in jeans and a dirty blue work shirt, was swinging a push-broom back and forth over the floor, trying to knock the creatures aside so he could move forward. One of them scurried up the handle, and Barry stepped back, tripped, and fell. He began to scream shrilly, waving his big arms through the air and kicking his legs like a swimmer.

Doors were opening, and curious heads were peering out of dark rooms; some of the teenagers pulled the doors all the way open to watch, seeming more entertained than frightened by what they were seeing.

Kevin could not even guess how many of the creatures were in the corridor. They seemed to be coming from both directions. In the light, Kevin got his first clear look at the wet, flat-nosed snouts and glistening black lips that curled beneath yellowed tusks and the slanted, deep-set eyes that burned gold beneath small pointed ears that lay back flat as sharp black claws clicked over the floor.

"The goddamned phone's dead!" a woman shouted from the desk.

Willie, an attendant with a quarterback build and smears of blood on his white coat, came around a corner kicking at the creatures, spotted Mace, and shouted, "Who the fuck are you?"

Mace smiled at him and the lights went out.

The woman at the desk screamed.

The teenagers began to sound fearful then. . . .

". . . the hell is going on . . ."

". . . Jesus, somethin's really wrong. . . ."

". . . can't see a fuckin' thing . . ."

The auxiliary power came on, not as bright as the regular lights, casting long, dancing shadows through the corridor.

"Call the police, Allen!" Willie shouted. "Sound the alarm, maybe the—" His voice was swallowed by a scream as he fell to the floor and began thrashing while the creatures covered him in a rush.

Mace's eyes scanned the faces in the doorways and said, "We're leaving. Anybody wanna come?"

Laughter broke out among the teenagers then, and someone shouted, "Fuckin' A!" as Allen, another attendant, stepped away from the desk a few yards from Mace and snapped, "Hold it right there, buddy. I don't know who the fuck you think you are, but you're not gonna—"

Several of Mace's pets pressed in around Allen's feet, and

he backed up clumsily, grabbed the edge of the desk, and lifted himself on top of it, grabbing a three-ring notebook and holding it before himself protectively as one of the things sprang through the air, its mouth open, lips pulled back in a snarl. It clamped its jaws shut on Allen's crotch and began to jerk its body from right to left in a frenzy. Allen screamed and hit the creature once with the notebook, twice, a third time, but it would not let go, and he fell backward off the desk, his scream breaking off into a ragged, pained gasp.

Mace walked calmly down the corridor, and the creatures moved aside to let him pass as he said, with a wave, "Let's go."

The others followed him, some in their underwear with clothes bundled in their arms, dressing as they walked, others already dressed, watching the creatures on the floor with a mixture of repulsion and fascination.

As they rounded a corner, Mace removed a small flashlight from his coat pocket and flicked it on as the auxiliary lights blacked out. The flashlight beam passed over the floor and was reflected in golden eyes that were darting in every direction, then upward to the doors that were opening along the corridor to reveal curious teenagers in robes and pajamas and underwear. The beam stopped in an open doorway, cutting into the room and falling on the pale, narrow face of the girl Kevin had come to know as the Daddy-Hater. Her long, stringy dirty-blond hair fell down over her naked, gaunt body, reaching nearly to her waist, covering her tiny breasts. Her eyes were wide, her mouth open and sucking on the side of her hand. Mace stepped toward her, she took a step back.

"I . . . I . . ." she whispered.

"Hmm?" Mace said, his tone pleasant. "You what, honey?"

"I . . . hate . . . daddies."

"That's okay," he said smilingly, taking another step toward her. "I'm not your daddy. I'm your friend. Why don't you put your clothes on and come with us?"

She watched him for a long moment, sucking silently on her hand, then turned, disappeared into the room for a minute, then returned, still timid but clothed, and joined them.

Kevin walked at Mace's side; the others behind them invited those standing in their doorways to come along.

"Hey, man, we're haulin' ass outta here!"

"C'mon, we're blowin'!"

There seemed no end to the creatures as Mace lead the teenagers through the corridors, around corners, through swinging double doors, from one ward to the next, toward the front of the building. It was so dark, Kevin was tempted to grasp a fold of Mace's long coat, but he didn't want to show his fear; the others behind him were following gladly, laughing and chatting as if they were at a party, and Kevin did not want Mace to think he had less trust in him than a bunch of total strangers.

If they're strangers, he thought. Most of them acted as if they were already quite familiar with Mace.

As they neared the main entrance they passed more attendants running blindly through the darkness, some of them shouting—

"Call the police, goddammit, call—oh, Jesus, Jesus—call somebody, goddammit!"

"Get the lights on, for Christ's sake—the lights!"

—some of them screaming wordlessly, trying to stagger over the animals that were snapping at their feet and clinging to their legs.

The flashlight beam passed over a gray-haired woman on the floor, her back against the wall, whimpering as her hands pulled weakly at the creature that was clutching her chest, blood running down her cheeks like black tears.

They passed into the main lobby. There was no one at the desk, and one of the two glass doors in front was wide open. Rain was blowing in and soaking the carpet.

As they neared the open door Mace put an arm around Kevin and said, "Say goodbye to this shithole, Kevin. Larry Caine is waiting. . . ."

At exactly ten-thirty, just as Mace had instructed her, Mallory pushed through the entrance of Mickey D.'s NY Pizza, followed by three other girls, Paula, Dena, and Lynn.

She spotted Larry and his friends almost immediately. They were on the dance floor with four girls, dancing to something by Journey.

Mallory led the other girls to a table at the edge of the dance floor; they ordered soft drinks and waited for the song to end.

Earlier that evening, Mallory had been sitting at the edge of the pool with Mace, his legs straddling her, his arms around her waist and his hands on her stomach.

"Do me a favor?" he'd whispered into her ear.

"What?"

"Tonight, take three of the girls with you to Mickey D.'s. Go in at ten-thirty. Larry Caine and three of his friends will be there. Get their attention, flirt with them awhile, but not for long. Get them out of there by ten forty-five. Take them to the alley behind the restaurant. Then just step aside and watch."

"What are you going to do to them?"

"I'm not going to do anything. But I think Kevin has a little score to settle with them."

"Is Kevin coming?" she'd asked excitedly, turning around to face him.

"I'm going to get him. And maybe a few of his friends."

"What if Kevin hurts them?"

"What if he does?"

"I thought you wanted to take as many people with you as you could."

"I do, but Larry and his friends don't want to come. They're too happy here. We have no use for them."

The song ended, and another video began on the big-screen television, but Larry and his friends started off the dance floor, leaving the four girls behind them, still dancing.

Larry spotted her.

Mallory smiled and tilted her head back slightly, then turned away.

They were at the table in seconds.

"Hey, Mal," Larry said, pressing both palms to the table and leaning close to her, "haven't seen you in a while. Thought you'd disappeared. You give up on school, or what?"

"Something like that," she said with a smirk, looking over his shoulder at the dance floor, feigning disinterest.

"Mind if we sit with you?" Larry asked, already pulling a chair from the next table and seating himself across from Mallory. His friends did the same, smiling at the girls.

"I don't care," Mallory said with a shrug. The waitress brought their soft drinks, and when Mallory opened her change purse, Larry quickly pulled out his wallet.

"On me," he said with a wink, paying the waitress. She made change, and Larry handed her three one-dollar bills. "This is for you."

"We're not staying long," Dena said with a secretive glance at Mallory.

"Oh? Where you going?"

"A party."

Mallory could tell the other girls were enjoying themselves; they seemed to be having trouble keeping straight faces.

"Yeah?" Larry said, turning to Mallory. "So, is this a private party, or can anybody come?"

"You going to school tomorrow?" Mallory asked.

"Yeah."

"Then you don't want to come. The party hasn't started yet. Doesn't quit till dawn. If then."

"Fuck," Larry laughed, looking at his friends. "Screw school, then. Where's the party?"

The girls laughed, but not at Larry's remark. They were laughing at the ease with which he and his friends were snagged.

"Unless your little boyfriend is gonna be there," Larry said to Mallory.

"Kevin? Who said he was my boyfriend?"

"I figured. Jesus, you spend so much time with him."

"So? That doesn't mean anything. Besides, Kevin's gone."

"Oh, yeah, that's right. I heard. Got into a little trouble." Larry let out a deep laugh, glancing knowingly at his buddies. "Well, since leather boy's gone, you don't wanna go to your party alone, do you? And look at this, the numbers are right, huh? Four girls, four guys."

Mallory looked at Paula, Dena, and Lynn, and the four of them stifled laughs.

Larry rose from his chair and leaned over the table toward Mallory, saying, "Y'know, you look like you've been doing some partying already. Those're pretty red eyes."

"We had a few tokes," Paula said quietly, her voice nearly buried by the music.

"Yeah? You got any on you?"

"A little," Mallory said.

Larry sat in his chair again and shrugged, saying, "Well, didn't your momma teach you to share?" His friends guffawed.

"Not here," Mallory said with a shake of her head. "Wait till we get outside."

"Who's driving?" Larry asked.

"We can walk. It's really close. Just behind this place, really. A couple houses over."

"Walk? In this rain?"

"Haven't you ever walked in the rain?" Lynn asked. "It's romantic."

"It's stupid," the guy with the earring said.

Dena sighed. "Fine. Don't come."

"Whoa, hold on," Larry blurted. "I guess a good party's worth getting wet for. Let's go."

"Not yet." Mallory glanced at her watch; they needed another five minutes. "Let us finish our drinks."

Five minutes later, they were on their way out of Mickey D.'s. Once outside, the guy with the earring groaned, "Jesus Christ, we're gonna walk through this?"

"Shut up, Gregg," Larry snapped, putting his arm around Mallory as they turned left on the sidewalk and hurried through the rain. He put his mouth to her ear and said, "Lead the way, babe."

Mallory smiled as Larry slipped his hand beneath her arm and pressed it to the side of her breast, not minding that he was getting a good feel through her heavy coat. She almost laughed as they neared the alley, anticipation fluttering in her chest. She knew she was going to enjoy this.

"What're we going down here for?" Larry shouted, trying

to be heard above the wind and rain as she steered them into the alley.

"Back way," she replied.

A gutter ran down the center of the alley and was gushing with dirty water. The tall lamps that lined the alley cast reflective pools of light in the water. Mallory heard the others splashing behind them.

"How far is this party?" Larry asked.

Two yards ahead of them, the flowing water gurgled into the holes in a manhole cover.

"Not far."

A voice cut through the noise, clear and powerful; Mallory recognized it immediately.

"Now!" Mace shouted from below.

The manhole cover shot upward, then fell to the ground with a splash and a clang. Two hands rose from the hole and gripped the edges, and Kevin pulled himself up. One of Mace's pets was perched on his left shoulder and he held a heavy chain in his right hand. He was on his feet in an instant, raised his left hand, flicked his wrist, and a switchblade clicked open, glinting in the hazy light as raindrops spattered loudly onto his black leather jacket. He smiled, and his laugh sounded like thick ice being cut.

Larry's arm dropped away from Mallory, and he stuttered, "Who the—I thought—what the fuck's going on?"

Kevin moved toward him and asked, "Hey, Larry, how's it hangin'?"

Two more hands reached out of the manhole behind Kevin, and another figure rose up through the rain.

Another manhole cover clattered off behind them, and Larry's three friends spun around, stepping away from the girls, who were moving to the side of the alley, laughing.

Larry turned to Mallory, his smile gone, his eyes narrow with sudden realization as he growled, "You cunt."

The creature on Kevin's shoulder dove with a piercing shriek toward Larry, but he threw himself to the left, out of its way, moving straight into the chain as Kevin swung it through the air like a whip. It caught Larry on the shoulder, and he splashed to the ground with a cry of surprise.

Footsteps splattered over the wet pavement; chains whistled through the air, and switchblades clicked; fists met flesh, and skulls cracked. In the dim light, Mallory could make out little more than shuffling forms and glistening metal, but the sounds were vivid enough.

A bone broke with a thick, moist smack, and Mace's laugh rose from below as the water in the gutter darkened with blood. . .

When Kevin returned to the dark basement of the old health club, there was still blood in his hair, and his hands were cold and numb. The others were laughing, smoking grass, drinking. He'd never seen the basement so crowded and noisy. He peeled off his wet jacket and settled onto one of the cushions in a corner. Mallory hurried over to him, leaned down, and kissed his forehead.

"Welcome back," she said, curling up on his lap. She was still out of breath and laughed with each exhalation. "Hey, c'mon, cheer up," she said, giving him a big kiss, slipping her tongue into his mouth, sloppily nibbling on his lower lip.

Kevin felt nothing but a pounding in his skull and a gnawing ache in his stomach.

The events of the last two hours were already beginning to fade, as if he'd dreamed them; he began to feel uncertain if the fight had actually happened, if he'd felt the crack of Larry Caine's skull through the chain he'd held, if he'd actually heard bones breaking around him and the final raspy breaths of four boys his own age. . . .

"I didn't want to kill them," he whispered as Mallory pulled away from him. "I just . . . just wanted to . . . beat the shit out of 'em. But we . . . we killed 'em."

"You don't know that. Did you check? No. They were just . . . beat up. Like you wanted." She laughed as she wriggled out of her coat.

"They're all dead. I know it."

"They'll be okay. We won't be here much longer, anyway. Excited about the concert?"

A girl with dark circles under her eyes wearing a bathrobe

came over and handed Mallory a joint. She took a long drag and offered it to Kevin; he shook his head.

"C'mon, Kev," she said. "You've been stuck in that place for—"

"No," he snapped. "Get up."

"But I wanted to—"

He pushed her crumpled coat away, took her arm, and started to move her aside, but he stopped when he saw the bruise.

It looked like a bruise in the flickering lantern light, but when he lifted her arm closer to his eyes, he saw the tiny marks on her inner elbow—three of them, each surrounded by discolored flesh.

"The fuck is this?"

"What? Oh, those. Needle marks."

"Needle . . . What the hell have you been doing here?"

"I just did a little. A few times is all. I wanted to try it. One of the girls—Geneva, I think—her mother is a diabetic, and Geneva steals her syringes." She took another drag, held it, blew it out slowly. "Just wanted to try it, that's all."

"Jesus Christ! What're you, stupid? I mean, that's major fuckin' stupid!" He backed away from her, suddenly not wanting to touch her anymore, and pressed himself against the wall. "You think you just do that stuff a few times, then no more? That stuff'll fuck you *up,* Mallory, I *mean* it!"

Her eyes widened, and she stared at him openmouthed. "Well, listen to *you.* Mr. Cleancut Goodboy!"

"Hey, I don't do *that* shit!"

"Glad to be back, Kevin?"

He looked up to see Mace towering over them, smiling, his hands behind his back, his narrow frame backlit by the lanterns, his face dark.

"Something wrong?" Mace asked when Kevin said nothing.

"Mace," Kevin said, getting to his feet. "What's this?" He pulled Mallory up beside him and held out her arm.

"Needle marks."

"I know, but . . ." Kevin stared at the marks, then looked up at Mace again, confused. He'd thought Mace cared, thought he'd wanted to watch out for them, protect them from those who didn't care. That no longer seemed the case. "How could you do this?"

"I didn't do it. She wanted to try it."

"But you . . . I thought . . ."

"There are no rules here, Kevin. You know that. You can do whatever you want."

"But this is dangerous!"

Mace shrugged one shoulder, said, "Everything's dangerous," and went back to the pool.

Mallory offered the joint again. "Sure you don't want some?"

Sitting on the cushion again, hugging his knees, Kevin shook his head.

"Fine." Mallory joined the others.

Kevin put his head in his hands and groaned. At least he'd felt safe in the center, as much as he'd hated it. Somehow, he didn't feel safe now that he was out.

He'd been so excited to see Mace, so relieved, so eager to get back to Mallory and the others, the band. Now it all seemed different. Wrong. He'd been gone only a few days, but it seemed like a year. Everyone, everything, seemed different, especially Mace.

Kevin had wanted to make Larry Caine and his friends hurt, that was all, blacken an eye, loosen a few teeth. Mace had thought that was a fine idea and had given him and Trevor and Mark some chains from the sub-basement.

It was just going to be a fight, that was all.

But Kevin had not counted on getting so carried away. He'd not counted on his parents' faces flashing so vividly in his head as he swung the chain, or on the rush of hatred that had been building up in him during those days in the center.

He looked at the crowd in the basement and wondered how many others had needle marks in their arms.

Kevin stayed in the corner for hours, watching them come and go, familiar faces from school, from his neighborhood, and from the center. A few police officers came in wearing their rain slickers; they used the door upstairs instead of the sewer and seemed to enjoy making a lot of noise when they entered, stomping their feet, laughing loudly, then coming down to the pool and choosing companions for the next few hours. That was how Mace kept them happy and quiet.

As he watched the others Kevin kept an eye on Mallory. She stayed close to Mace, followed him around the room, in and out of the pool. Mace paid no more attention to her than he did to any of the others, but she did not stray far from his side. She touched him frequently—an arm, his hair, his ass—and sometimes tilted her face up when she had his attention, offering her lips.

I could leave, Kevin thought, turning away from her as she pressed herself against Mace's side, *get out of here and away from Mace, away from all of them.*

Then: *And go where?*

Everyone he knew and was closest to was here, and after what had happened at the Laurel Teen Center there were going to be a lot of people looking for him and everyone else who'd left the center that night.

And I made him a promise, he thought with a tremor of dread. He was still not sure what that promise meant, but thinking about it brought a tense, smothering feeling to his chest. *This is your key. . . .*

The music stopped, and Mace clapped his hands once and called, "Kevin! Let's make some music."

Kevin slowly got to his feet; he felt weak, tired, and wanted to sleep. Instead, he made his way to the instruments along with the others in the band.

Mace gently placed a hand on Kevin's shoulder and said, "We're gonna make this valley eat metal, Kevin. Just like you wanted."

Kevin wasn't sure he wanted to anymore. . . .

Twenty-five

Dawn came slowly on the day of the concert, spreading over the San Fernando Valley like a dark gray blanket. There had been no break in the rain the night before, and dirty water flowed into the streets from clogged gutters.

The top story on every local radio and television news broadcast was the inexplicable escape of nearly every teenager at the Laurel Teen Center. Seven of the thirty-nine teenagers staying at the center remained; four of them had been injured, and all seven had been moved to a hospital in Burbank. Two attendants were dead, eight were seriously injured, and four had received minor physical injuries but had been taken to the hospital in gibbering states of hysteria. There was still no explanation for what had happened, and none of the escaped teenagers had yet been found, but authorities assured the public that at least some of them would be recovered within twenty-four hours.

When J.R. awoke on his sofa, where he'd spent the night dozing, fully clothed, in front of the television set, a local morning news show was in progress. A perky Asian woman and an authoritative middle-aged man with an immaculately trimmed beard—some kind of psychiatrist, from what J.R. could tell—were discussing the attack on Faye Beddoe and the disturbing similarities between Sherry Pacheco's and Nikki Astin's subsequent suicides.

"I think one of the chief reasons teenage suicide is on the upswing," the man was saying, gesticulating dramatically with his right hand, "is the glorification of death and violence on television, in the movies, and particularly in the lyrics of so many of today's popular songs. You'll find the prevailing message is one of hopelessness and discouragement, which, *I* feel, brings about a great deal of negativity and can encourage these confused and highly impressionable teens to turn to suicide, sometimes individually, sometimes in groups, which is precisely what I think we're seeing now in the case of—"

"Fuck yourself," J.R. grunted, taking the remote control from the floor and turning to a Porky Pig cartoon.

The day before, J.R. had spoken with Mr. Booth before going home. Choosing his words carefully, trying not to sound too upset, he'd told him about Mace, about the Crucifaxes, about everything but Mace's pets and Nikki's abortion; he still wasn't too sure of the validity of those particular details. He'd informed Booth of Nikki's suicide and told him about the similarities between Sherry's last words and Nikki's note.

Booth had heard him out, flicking his right earlobe with his index finger as he listened. When J.R. was finished, Booth had said, "So what you're saying here is that this group, this club, whatever, could be some kind of—oh, a suicide cult? Is that right?"

"I think it's a very good possibility."

Leaning forward, folding his hands on his desk, Booth said, "Well, now, I certainly don't want to appear unfeeling, J.R., because I do understand your concern, but I think you'll realize, as you spend more and more time in the field of education, that it's often necessary to develop a few calluses. While it's sometimes very easy to become involved with the problems and lives of our students, we must draw a distinct line between educating and parenting." He'd leaned back in his chair then, his face firm, as if he'd just made a statement of great import.

"I'm sorry, but I'm not . . . I'm not sure I understand."

"Well, if you honestly believe that this fellow—Mace?—is a danger to the students, you should inform the police."

"But I told you, I'm afraid there's some involvement with—"

"Now that, I must admit, is a bit too farfetched for me to swallow. I mean, the police? Involved with this man? This—this self-proclaimed rock-and-roll messiah, or whatever he is? I really don't think so, J.R. As I said, you should go to the police. Tell them what you know. But don't expect miracles. Remember, those streets are filled with pushers and pimps and all manner of undesirables who prey on young people. Your man Mace is certainly not a new problem. There's really nothing more you can do, though. Anything beyond that is up to the parents."

"But what if the parents don't know? Don't care?"

Booth shrugged and held up his hands in a gesture of helplessness. "It's simply not our problem." He started to get up but looked at J.R. again with a cocked brow and said firmly, "And J.R., I hope you don't plan to spread this around and start some kind of panic among the kids. Or among the parents—that would be even worse. Lord knows, they've got enough to worry about, don't you think?"

J.R. had left the principal's office angry but quiet, thinking, *I should have known.*

The notes he'd made after going through the files in the counseling offices were stacked on the end table by the sofa. J.R. sat up and looked through them.

Mace's group was performing that night, and J.R. was willing to bet each of the students in his notes, as well as many more, would attend the concert. He wondered how many of their parents knew or cared.

Maybe if they knew, he thought, *they would care. If they knew the danger their sons and daughters were in . . .*

If he tried to tell them, most would probably think he was crazy. He would have to pad the story to avoid giving them any of the more farfetched details. Of course, he would have to deal with Mr. Booth later; he realized he might be suspended or even fired.

"Unless I'm right," he grunted as he got off the sofa. His back and neck ached, and he felt like pulling out the bed, undressing, and crawling between the sheets. Instead, he stretched his arms, yawned, and headed for the bathroom.

As J.R. showered and dressed for work Jeff lay asleep in his bed, where he'd been tossing and twisting beneath the blankets since three-thirty A.M.

Erin silently opened his bedroom door, watched him a moment, then backed out. She had been looking in on him every half hour or so since he'd gone to bed.

When she got home from work, Erin had found him standing at the glass door staring out at the rainy darkness; all the lights were on, and the radio was playing loudly. His arms were folded over his chest, and he was shaking. When he heard her come in, Jeff spun around, and words began to spill from his mouth in a rush.

She embraced him, tried to comfort him, and listened as he told her about Nikki. Erin considered taking him to see a doctor soon; he was so upset, she even thought of taking him to a hospital then. He hadn't taken Mallory's behavior well; he'd been a bundle of nerves lately, not sleeping, easily startled. She'd been especially worried by his description of the rats in the apartment on Sunday night. He seemed to think the rats had actually led Mallory out. That, of course, was ridiculous, but that did not mean Jeff didn't actually believe he'd seen it happen. Witnessing two deaths within twenty-four hours didn't help his state of mind, and that concerned her even more.

She'd spent most of the night looking through the classifieds of several local papers. By dawn, Erin had circled countless help-wanteds.

When she left Jeff's room, Erin returned to the table, where a cigarette still burned in an ashtray already filled with crumpled butts. Taking a drag, she decided to let Jeff sleep; it wouldn't hurt him to miss a day or two of school, and he needed the sleep.

She looked over the job openings she'd circled and began copying addresses and phone numbers onto a piece of notebook paper. She'd already quit her job with Fantasy Phone Lines but planned to hang onto her four dancing jobs until she'd landed something else.

Jeff woke up at eight-thirty and, despite Erin's protests, insisted on going to school.

"Can't you miss a day?" she asked. "You need to sleep, hon."

"It's not just school. I've gotta see J.R. I was supposed to talk to him last night, but . . . well, I couldn't. I need to see him today."

"Listen, Jeff, I don't want to sound—well . . . like a mother, but I'm worried about you. Are you sure you're well?"

He slumped onto the sofa and ran his fingers through his hair wearily, sighing, "I'm okay, Mom. It's not me I'm worried about."

"That's what I mean." She sat down beside him and put her arm around his shoulders. "I know some pretty awful things have been happening, and I know you're worried about Mallory. I am, too. But maybe you're getting a little too worried about all this, you think? You can't take the weight of the world on your shoulders, Jeff."

She was surprised at the anger she saw in his eyes when he turned to her. "Didn't you hear anything I told you Sunday night? Weren't you listening? Didn't you hear me last night when I told you about Nikki?"

"Yes, sweetheart, but you can't—"

"Mom, something's going on here, and if some-body doesn't do something, Mallory may end up dead, too!"

"Oh, Jeffy," she whispered, holding him to her, "Mal-lory's not going to do anything like *that*, not Mallory, she's—"

"You didn't think she'd *leave* either, did you? You didn't even know she'd left until I told you."

Erin didn't argue; she couldn't bear the thought of Jeff harboring any bitterness toward her.

After showering and dressing, Erin drove Jeff to school;

then, with her list of addresses on the seat beside her, she set out to look for a new job.

The sidewalks in front of the school were uneven and in need of repair and had flooded in places; Jeff had to hurry around large puddles to get into the administration building. Third period was about to start, and he hurried through the busy halls, hoping no one would stop him to talk. He was tired and didn't feel like explaining his tardiness to anyone.

Mrs. Astin had not arrived until a few minutes after midnight the night before. She'd staggered into the apartment smelling of booze and had looked at them blankly for a moment before asking, "What're you two doing here? Where's Nikki?"

Jeff had let Lily do the talking; he'd watched Mrs. Astin's sagging and heavily made-up face wither as Lily told her what had happened.

"That's not true," she'd muttered, sinking into a chair and letting her purse drop to the floor. She began to shout and pound her thighs with her fists. "That's not true! She was here today, she's fine, Nikki's *fine!*"

Lily had driven him home afterward, both of them silent; before he got out of the car, she'd held him for a long time.

When Jeff got to J.R.'s office, he found J.R. at his desk sorting through a stack of crumpled papers covered with sloppy scribbles. They exchanged small talk for a while, and Jeff explained in detail what had happened at Nikki's.

"You should go home and get some sleep," J.R. said. "You look tired."

"So do you."

J.R. shrugged.

Jeff looked out the small window at the parking lot where deep puddles forced cars to slow down as they drove through. The traffic on Chandler was heavy and moved slowly, cautiously, through the pouring rain. The wind made tree branches wave madly through the air and kicked up water from the puddles.

"He said there would be a storm," Jeff muttered.

"Hm?"

"Mace. In the Galleria. He said, 'Big storm comin'.'" He turned to J.R. and said, "Crucifax is performing tonight. At Fantazm."

"I know."

"I'm scared of what's going to happen."

"Me, too, Jeff. But"—J.R. handed him the stack of papers—"I have an idea. . . ."

Before noon that day, conditions on the freeways became disastrous.

Part of a hillside near the Sepulveda Pass, weakened by the constant rainfall, collapsed and slid onto the northbound side of the San Diego Freeway; within thirty minutes, that side of the freeway resembled a parking lot for miles southward.

J.R. was unaware of the traffic problems outside. After Jeff left, he went through his records, jotting down the phone numbers of students he suspected were involved with Mace. It was a long shot, but he planned to call their parents and urge them to keep their children away from Fantazm that night. He realized that many of them would be at work and planned, if necessary, to keep calling all day until he reached as many as possible. . . .

Jeff planned to go to the rest of his classes but only attended two before deciding he had to get away from the school; there were too many empty seats. He called Lily from a pay phone in the cafeteria and asked if he could come over. When she said yes, he caught an RTD bus.

She greeted him at the door with a long, warm hug. She looked weary and saddened, even a little angry as she told him that Nikki's funeral would be on Friday. Nikki's father was taking care of the arrangements; Mrs. Astin was too devastated to deal with anything but bed and a bottle.

Jeff met Lily's father for the first time, a barrel of a man with short-cropped brown hair and a kind face. He was a night watchman at one of the studios in Burbank and was on his way back to bed when Jeff arrived, but he visited with them for a few moments, dressed in a black bathrobe. He was soft-spoken with a ready smile, and Jeff liked him immediately; he realized where Lily got her open friendliness.

After he went to bed, Lily drove them to Tiny Naylor's for burgers, but neither of them could eat. Tired and low on conversation, Lily dropped Jeff off at his apartment, saying she wanted to get some sleep. They agreed to meet at eight that night at Fantazm. . . .

J.R. got stuck in traffic on the way to Reverend Bainbridge's and turned on his radio. A man was speaking rapidly, trying to be heard above the sounds of traffic in the background.

"—where they came from, but they were big as babies, and they had tusks, long, sharp tusks."

The efficient voice of a female newscaster took over: "Mr. Connery, who worked at the Laurel Teen Center for three years, escaped the confusion with minor injuries and was released from the hospital this afternoon. His story has been confirmed by two other employees of the center who are still hospitalized, although no sign of the alleged rats has been found. As yet, none of the escaped teenagers has been—"

Rats? J.R. thought. He remembered the confident look in Kevin's eyes as he'd walked away from J.R. at the center on Monday. Rats . . . Then he muttered, "Jesus Christ, Jeff wasn't imagining it. . . ."

Once he got to the Calvary Youth House, he moved with an urgency he had not felt before hearing the report on the radio. J.R. rang the doorbell; then, receiving no response, he knocked on the door. Not only was the door unlocked, it was not completely closed; it opened a few inches under the impact of his knock. There was no one in the living room, but it was not empty. Looking in, he saw a chair tipped over and four empty Jim Beam bottles lined up on the floor before the sofa. There was a pile of clothes on the floor at the entrance to the hall. J.R.'s nose wrinkled at the smell of liquor, body odor, and vomit as he took off his coat and tossed it on a chair.

"Hello?" he called.

There was a clatter from the kitchen, and glass broke. J.R.

found Reverend Bainbridge lying on the floor in his bathrobe beside a shattered fifth of whiskey. He wore only one slipper, and his fair hair was dark from grease and stuck up in unkempt spikes.

"Oh, God," J.R. breathed, going to his side and hunkering down. "Reverend? Are you all right?"

"Who . . . what . . . who is it?"

"J.R. Haskell."

"J.R. Has . . . I'm sorry, I . . ."

"From Valley High School. We spoke last week."

"Last week," the reverend muttered, rolling onto his side and squinting up at J.R. "Last week was a hundred years ago." His eyes were red and watery; his face glowed with a sheen of perspiration and was puffy around his eyes and mouth.

"I need to talk to you, Reverend."

"Talk . . . oh, yes," he said, nodding with vague recognition. His breath reeked of whiskey. "Yes, I remember you. Talk? About what?"

"Mace."

"Mace, Mace . . . oh-ho, yes, Mace, you want to talk about Mace." He tried to sit up but couldn't, so J.R. lifted him into a chair at the kitchen table. "What about him?"

J.R. looked around the kitchen. Empty Jim Beam bottles were everywhere; there was a lumpy yellowish puddle on the floor by the sink where the reverend had apparently vomited. "My God, what's happened?" he asked Bainbridge softly.

"Happened?" The reverend looked around and smirked, then scrubbed his face. "Yes. Well. You haven't caught me at, um, my best, I'm afraid. It's been . . . a bad week."

"Where's the coffee?"

"Fridge. Help yourself."

"It's for you," J.R. said, opening the refrigerator.

"Oh, no-no-no, I don't want any, thank you."

"I need you sober." He hurried around the kitchen, looking for coffee filters, rinsing out the pot, trying to avoid the mess on the floor.

"Oh? Now, what could you possibly need me for?"

"I need your help. Mace and his group are performing at Fantazm tonight."

"And?"

Once J.R. was finished and the coffee was brewing, he sat across from Bainbridge.

"How long have you been like this, Reverend?"

"Uuhhh, I'm not sure. What day is it?"

He doesn't know, J.R. thought. He was about to tell him of Nikki's suicide gently, ease into it, but he thought the shock might be good for him. "Nikki Astin killed herself yesterday."

Bainbridge ran a hand slowly through his unwashed hair, staring at J.R. as if he'd spoken in an unfamiliar tongue. He lowered his hand and was still for a moment, then began to tremble, clutched the table, and groaned as he slipped out of the chair. "Dear God, wh-what have I *done . . . ?*" He sounded heavier than he looked when he hit the floor.

J.R. knelt beside him and said, "Another girl killed herself, too, Reverend, and there may be others. And all of them have been spending time with him."

Bainbridge seemed unconscious for a moment, and J.R. shook him, saying, "Reverend, can you hear me?"

His head began to move back and forth. ". . . my fault . . . my fault . . . Mace . . . was right. . . ."

"Right about what?"

"Doesn't matter. Go . . . away. Leave me alone."

"Look, a lot of these kids know you, Reverend, respect you. I think you can help me. Before any more die."

He propped himself up and looked into J.R.'s eyes. "Respect?" he asked as tears rolled down his face. "No. No, I let them down. Failed them."

"But you can still help them."

Bainbridge rubbed a temple with his thumb as he smacked his dry lips. "The . . . the parents . . . what about the parents?"

"I've been calling parents all day. Most of them—nearly all of them—are at work, and a lot of them won't be coming home very soon. The freeways are a mess. Of those I talked to, some are concerned and said they would try to keep their kids away from Fantazm tonight; others resented being told how to raise their kids. Two of them hung up on me. I'm going to keep calling, but I don't know how much good it'll do. That's why I want your help. I need it."

"What could I do?"

"Come with me tonight to the concert. Talk to them, to the ones you know. Convince them they're making a mistake. I think that's what they need, Reverend—someone they know and trust, or once trusted, to show that he cares, to let the kids know they have an option, that Mace is dangerous and whatever he's telling them is a lie." He helped Bainbridge into a sitting position and leaned him against the wall. "Please."

The reverend scrubbed his face hard with both hands, groaning into his palms.

"I've failed them," he said, his voice raspy. "I thought I was doing the right thing—I—I meant well, I did, but . . . Mace was right. I was changing them, fitting them into—into little boxes, trying to—to make them into something they weren't. That was wrong. It . . . I think it nearly destroyed some of those kids. It seemed to work for some, but . . . but I wonder. . . ." He slowly shook his unsteady head. ". . . I wonder what kind of effect it had on some of them as they grew older, as—as they realized they couldn't fit into those boxes I made for them forever. Because no . . . nobody can, you know." He turned his bleary eyes to J.R. and whispered, "I couldn't." He coughed and held his stomach, as if suddenly nauseated. "Just—just leave me alone, I can't help you, I can't expect those kids to—to listen to me ever again, not after the way I let them down, let . . . let Nikki down." His lips pulled back over his teeth as if he were in pain; his eyes clenched, and J.R. could hear his teeth grinding. "Nikki," the reverend hissed, "I'm . . . so sorry."

J.R. went to the coffee maker and poured a cup, put it on the table, then helped the reverend back into his chair.

"Here," he said, handing the cup to Bainbridge, making sure it was firmly held between his trembling hands, "drink this."

"I'll drink," he said, putting the cup down, "but not this."

"Reverend, I'm not a religious man, but isn't a person in your position supposed to have faith, supposed to believe that God forgives and—"

"Believed, Mr. Haskell, I *believed* those things, past tense. If there is a God, He has no reason to forgive me, but I'm not so sure there is a God. I'm not sure what I believe anymore, because everything I've lived for, the work I've done, seems to have been a . . . a mistake!"

"It wasn't a mistake if it worked, if it did some good. And you can make it work again if you'll just sober up. I don't necessarily approve of some of your methods, but I—"

The reverend stood cautiously and looked around the kitchen at the bottles, slowly rubbing his eyes one at a time; then he tightened the buckle of his bathrobe, mumbling. Moving slowly, he reached for the cupboard above the sink, opened it, and removed one of his last two Jim Beams.

"What're you doing?" J.R. asked.

He took another coffee cup from its hook over the counter and sat down, saying, "I am trying to prevent myself from sobering up."

"Reverend . . ."

Bainbridge smiled up at him as he slowly removed the cap from the Jim Beam and said, "Mr. Haskell, I took my first drink of alcohol when I was nine years old and for the next nine years was seldom sober. When I found the Lord and took up the ministry, I believed that God ended my craving for alcohol, took the bottle out of my hand. But I've been doing a lot of thinking lately. Thinking and drinking," he laughed, pouring some whiskey into the coffee cup. "That craving never went away. I stopped drinking. I put the bottle down. I stopped. Ah, but to a preacher, everything comes from God. All this"—he waved his arm toward the ceiling—"the house, the low rent, the furniture. All provided by the Lord for . . . the work. But you know what? I worked *hard* for this. *I* did. I've put my whole *life* into this, into those kids." His hand shook as he lifted the cup, and a shudder passed through him as he drank the whiskey. His voice was wet and throaty as he continued. "I told them that everything they'd learned, everything they were, was wrong, and they had to become what He—what I—wanted them to be. I did it for *Him,* because I thought that's what He wanted. But last week, Mr. Haskell, I saw something." He poured again. "Something . . . hellish. I saw Mace kill—did you hear me?—kill my unborn baby." Another pour, another swallow. "I don't know what Mace is, or where he's from, but the God I worshipped, the God I thought I was serving, would never . . . ever . . . let that happen. Especially to a soul as kind and caring . . . as simple . . . as Nikki Astin. But I *saw* it." He drank again. "If there *is* a God, it's not the God I thought I was serving. If . . . there is a God. And *that,* Mr. Haskell, means that my whole life has been a waste. It means that at the age of eighteen I changed my way of thinking, living, my personality—*me,* I changed me—for nothing, because some other ignorant, misguided man of God told me to. Because I saw in that man someone who cared for me, respected me as my parents never did. I could never seem to please my parents. No matter what I did. But Mortimer Bigley *wanted* me . . . as long as I became what *he* wanted. So I did. Oh, I liked him, he was a dear man, and I had all the signs, all the religious fire and fervor. But I wanted it. Because I wanted so very much to be wanted."

J.R. sat down across from the reverend, listening attentively, but frowning; the pain in Bainbridge's eyes and voice made it difficult, but he seemed to be working his way to a point and not just rambling drunkenly.

"I've thought about all that a lot these last few days, Mr. Haskell"—another drink—"and I've realized that I have been doing the same thing to them. The kids. Changing them. Because they're not good enough for a God who's going to let them suffer anyway. And they allow me to do this because they want . . . to be wanted. They have parents who don't care or don't notice, who are too drunk or too caught up in their marriages, their divorces, their affairs, their jobs . . . too caught up in their lives to be parents. They have children, but they just don't . . . they don't . . ."

J.R. cleared his throat and said quietly, "Pay the piper?"

"Yes, yes, you could say that. So. These kids turn to me. Or, God help us"—another drink, this time followed by a ragged cough that turned his face red—"to Mace. Or drugs. Maybe sex. Even suicide. Whatever's there to fill the holes or numb the pain. Like this." He giggled drunkenly as he held up his drink, then finished it off.

"And you're not gonna *do* anything about it?" J.R. asked. "You're just gonna sit here and drink? You're scared, right? What, you think I'm *enjoying* this? I'm scared shitless, I feel helpless. And I'm putting my fucking job on the line here. I'm trying to stop something I don't understand, and I haven't the slightest idea how I'm gonna do it, and you're just gonna sit here, you and Jim Beam, and not do a goddamned thing to help?"

Bainbridge smiled at J.R. again, but tears rolled down his puffy cheeks and his lips trembled.

"I can't help *myself* right now," he whispered. "I'm not sure I want to. I'm mourning a death, Mr. Haskell. The death of my faith. My belief. Everything I've worked for. So." He stood with his bottle in one hand and his cup in the other. "If you don't mind, I'd like to be left alone in my sorrow." He began to shuffle out of the kitchen, scattering bits of glass with his feet. "I'd show you the door, but—hah, I'm not sure I could find it myself." He went into the living room and fell onto the sofa, nearly dropping the bottle.

J.R. decided to give up; he knew he was going to get no help out of James Bainbridge. As he slipped into his coat on his way to the door he heard the reverend mutter, "Good luck, Mr. Haskell." Then, with a chuckle, Bainbridge added, "I'll pray for you. . . ."

An hour after J.R. Haskell left, the reverend awoke to an ominous stirring in his gut. He gulped as he clambered off the sofa and staggered down the hall, careening from wall to wall, trying to hold down the contents of his stomach. Two doors from the bathroom, the stirring became a rush, and he fell to his knees vomiting.

It covered the front of his robe and slopped to the carpet, spattering his arms and hands, dribbling down his chin. Kneeling on the floor, he waited for some of his strength to return, then limped into the bathroom, hugging the wall for support. He removed his robe, threw it in the tub, and washed up.

Reverend Bainbridge stared at the filthy, trembling, unshaven stranger in the mirror. Naked except for a pair of stiff, soiled briefs—*When did I change them last?* he wondered—his body looked bony and frail. There was a massive dark purple bruise on his right thigh; he had no idea how he'd gotten it.

Splashing more cold water on his face, he sputtered in a weak voice, "What'm I *doing?*"

He cautiously took a hot shower, and as he stood beneath the hot spray he went over his conversation with J.R. Haskell, remembering what he'd said about giving up the bottle and working hard to build Calvary Youth. He lifted his face to the water and grumbled to himself, "If I can do that, I can do this."

After he dried, he walked naked to his bedroom and began sorting through his closet for some clean clothes. He was putting on a shirt when he heard the familiar scraping sound in the wall over his bed. He spun around and stared at the wall for a moment, afraid for only an instant, then hot with anger as he growled, "Keeping an eye on me, huh? Like what you see?"

The scuttling continued as he dressed, then he went to his bed, sat down, and picked up the phone. He dialed directory assistance and asked for J.R. Haskell's number. As he dialed the number, it seemed appropriate to pray for strength, for guidance. Instead, he muttered, "Never thought I'd say it, but if You're out there"—he lifted his eyes to the ceiling—"I don't need You anymore."

"Hello?"

"Yes, um, Mr. Haskell? This is Reverend Bainbridge. I'm calling because I . . ."

"Yes?"

"Well, I don't know if I'm worth much. In this condition, I mean. But I want to help you. . . ."

Twenty-six

Brad's sister Becky and her husband Neil lived in a small apartment with a leaky roof on Cartwright Avenue in North Hollywood. Becky was twenty, a slightly overweight brunette with crooked teeth and a bleeding heart tattoo on her left shoulder.

When Brad and Jeff entered the apartment, Becky hurried out of the kitchen grinning, arms open, ample breasts bouncing freely beneath her loose-fitting spaghetti-strap top, and hugged Brad warmly. "Happy seventeen, little brother," she said, kissing his cheek. "Who's your friend?"

Brad introduced Jeff, then Becky put an arm around each of them and quickly led them into the kitchen.

"Who else is coming?" she asked.

"Nick, Keith, Jason, and maybe Rob from Santa Monica, but probably not."

"Well, I hope they hurry," Becky said. The kitchen was dark except for the candles on Brad's birthday cake and the ember of a smoldering joint in an ashtray on the counter. The apartment smelled of marijuana and kitty litter. Becky opened the refrigerator and said, "Beers?"

Both boys nodded, and she handed each of them one.

The beer was ice-cold, and Jeff sighed quietly with pleasure as he took a swallow.

Jeff considered backing out of Brad's party that night, but after his mother left and he was alone in the apartment, he began to notice sounds he hadn't noticed during the day. His mind turned to thoughts of Mallory—

There's something wrong with me.

—and it became impossible to concentrate on his homework. When Brad arrived, Jeff went with him gladly.

"Plans have changed," Becky said. "Neil was gonna join us for a couple beers and some grass, then take you guys over to the bar, but he can't make it."

"What bar?" Jeff muttered.

"Radical!" Brad shouted simultaneously.

"C'mon, guys, let's go ogle the T and A."

"What? Where are we going?" Jeff asked.

"To watch women take their clothes off. At the Playpen . . .

Erin put her drink tray on the bar and shouted above the music, "Hey, Neil!"

He was mixing a drink and spun around to say, "Yo!" He was a big man with a round face and long black hair gathered in a ponytail.

"Am I up next?"

"Yep." He went back to his drink.

The Playpen was loud, smoky, and crowded. Pool balls clacked together and Robert Palmer pounded from the jukebox as Chaunte, the bustiest girl working that night, licked both index fingers and wet her nipples, grinding her hips at one end of the stage while Lori worked the other.

Erin gathered her tips from the tray and walked between two pool tables and down the dark, narrow corridor to the dressing room. It was really just a large bathroom with lockers against one wall and a couple bare lightbulbs hanging from the ceiling.

She'd danced one set already and had been serving drinks for the last hour. The dancing would be a relief from the lewd remarks, suggestions, and propositions sneered at her as she went from table to table taking orders. At least on the stage she had some distance from them and didn't have to concentrate on getting the right drink to the right customer. As long as she kept smiling and moving to the music, showing her tits and shaking her ass, she could let her mind wander.

Chaunte burst through the door dabbing her face with a hand towel and said, "The guy in the fishing cap sitting at runway two's a big tipper. He likes it when you shake your tits."

"Thanks."

Debbie hurried in, adjusting an earring. "I'm up with you next. I'll be right out."

Dressed in a black teddy with silver handprints over her breasts, Erin left the dressing room, crossed the bar, put a quarter in the jukebox, and punched in two selections.

A Tina Turner song began, and Erin hurried through the mirrored door by the jukebox, passed through the small room off the stage, and picked up the beat by slapping one black-stockinged thigh. She put on a big smile and strutted out to a chorus of whistles, catcalls, and stomping feet.

The stage had two runways with men seated around each one, a mirror along the back, and a copper-colored firepole at each end. When Debbie joined her, the shouting and clapping grew louder. Erin kicked up a leg, swung her hips as she went to the firepole, straddled it, and slid herself up and down suggestively, smiling over her shoulder, licking her lips.

At the other end of the stage, Debbie, a young woman with a svelte dancer's figure, turned her back to the audience, bent over, and smiled between her legs as she playfully wriggled two fingers under the elastic of her panties.

Erin spotted the man in the fishing cap sitting at the runway. He was fiftyish, with eyebrows that sprouted from his forehead like little gray bushes. He beckoned her with callused hands, flashing a silver-capped tooth when he grinned and called, "C'mon over here, babe, come to Poppa!"

She danced her way over, lowering part of her teddy just enough to reveal one breast, then covering it again.

"Yeah! That's what I like!" He slapped a five-dollar bill on the edge of the runway and tilted back the bill of his cap.

Erin flashed the other breast as she danced closer to him.

"Keep it comin'!" he bellowed, putting down another five.

You keep it comin', too, she thought.

There were four other men with him, laughing, cheering her on, tossing singles onto the runway.

Erin pulled the top half of the teddy down to her waist, baring both breasts, and turned her back to the man, bending down until she could see him between her legs. She reached both arms through her legs and stroked the cheeks of her ass slowly, then lifted her arms at her sides and expertly shook her shoulders, making her upside-down breasts swing in a circular motion.

His lumpy hand smacked a ten onto the runway.

There was a flurry of movement behind him, and Erin stood and turned in time to see someone stand so quickly that a chair fell over and clattered across the floor. It was a young man who did not look at all familiar at first as she squinted against the bright lights shining on the stage, still moving to the music, running her fingers over her breasts, but he seemed to recognize her as he stood a yard away from the runway, arms at his sides, jaw slack.

When she recognized Jeff, all the noise in the bar seemed to fade away, as if someone had turned down the volume on a radio; hands clapped together silently, mouths moved without words.

Jeff began to walk backward clumsily, his mouth opening and closing. *Mom . . . Mom . . .*

Erin felt her knees weaken as she stood frozen in place, gaping at her son. Peripherally, she saw Brad and three other boys sitting at a table near Jeff, saw Brad lean toward them, his eyes staring at her in disbelief, and vaguely heard him say, from a great distance, "Jesus, it's his fuckin' *mother!*"

"Jeff," she said, but it was only a whisper. Her hands fumbled with the teddy until her breasts were covered.

As he backed away Jeff bumped a table and spilled drinks

on two men who began to shout silently at him, and he turned, dodged another table, and hurried toward the rear exit.

The big tipper was pounding a fist on the runway shouting, "Hey, honey, what's yer problem?"

The music was pulsing again, and she could hear the whistling and hooting from the men who were waiting impatiently for her to go on dancing. She stepped off the runway onto an empty stool and hit the floor as Brad and his friends hurried away from their table to follow Jeff, who had tripped through the door and was gone.

The boys reached the exit before Erin because tears were filling her eyes, making everything around her run together in a sparkling blur of light and color. She wiped her eyes with numb hands, ignoring Neil as he called, "Hey, whattaya doing? Where you going?"

She thrust her arms out before her, locked her elbows, and slammed the door open, hurrying into the rain. A furious gust of wind made her stop and hug herself protectively as the rain soaked her teddy and made it cling to her body like a second skin.

Erin watched Jeff hurry across the rear parking lot, water splashing around his feet; Brad and his friends were close behind, their shoulders hunched against the rain. Jeff stopped and leaned heavily against the post of the single streetlight that glowed over the lot; he leaned forward, held his stomach, and vomited as the others gathered around him.

She called his name, but he did not respond. Brad patted him on the back and, when he was finished and standing straight again, put an arm around his shoulders and led him away from the light post.

"Wait, Jeff!" Erin shouted, running across the parking lot.

The boys went to an old white Mustang and began to get inside.

"Jeff, please wait!" Her voice had risen to a desperate shriek, and she waved an arm above her head to get his attention. The heel of her right shoe snapped off, and she tumbled to the pavement. A shattering pain ripped through her leg, and she cried out as she fell forward, scraping her palms on the wet pavement. "Please wait!" she shouted, but her words were lost in her sobs. *"Please!"*

Her view of the Mustang was blocked by two other cars, but she heard the doors slam, the engine roar, and the tires whoosh through a puddle as the car drove away.

A jagged streak of lightning lit the sky for a heartbeat as Erin remained on her hands and knees, sobbing. She slowly stood, taking off her right shoe, and staggered back into the bar.

Inside it was just as loud and busy as it had been when she rushed out, as if nothing had happened and everything was the same. But Erin felt fifty years older, and the bar somehow felt different to her—ugly, filthy, darker than before.

Neil caught up with Erin as she headed for the dressing room.

"Jesus, look at you!" he blurted. "What happened?"

Clutching her shoe in a white-knuckled fist, Erin snapped, "Since when did you start letting minors in here?"

"What? Oh, them. That was my brother-in-law and his friends. It's his birthday, and I—"

"Well, one of those friends was my son!"

"Oh, Jeez," he sighed as she stalked down the corridor, still limping. "Hey, you wanna go after 'em?" he called.

Erin stopped.

"They're goin' to Fantazm tonight. Some band's playin'. You can take a couple hours off, if you want."

"A couple hours?" she replied over her shoulder. "I won't be back, Neil. I quit."

In the dressing room, she threw her shoe into the sink. She was soaked all over, her mascara was running, and her stocking was torn.

But if you keep hiding it from them . . . J.R. had said.

Erin laughed bitterly through her tears, hating herself for not heeding J.R.'s advice, for taking a stripping job in the first place, for not finishing her education so she could get some decent work. . . .

"You okay in there, honey?" Chaunte asked.

She thought of her mother's weekly phone calls and of how good it had always felt to assure her mother that she and the kids were okay. It would probably be a while before she could honestly say that again.

"No," Erin muttered. "No, I'm not okay. . . ."

An hour before Crucifax was to play, Fantazm was so crowded that the teenagers on the dance floor could do little more than stand in place and move their shoulders to the music. J.R. and Reverend Bainbridge entered the club uncertainly, and J.R. winced at the noise level, guessing he would have a headache in thirty minutes, maybe less.

A burly young man with a crewcut and sunglasses stood behind a small window in the wall to the right of the entrance.

"Six dollar cover," he said, his mouth hardly moving.

"You're kidding," J.R. said.

The man pointed upward. A sign over the window read $6.00 COVER CHARGE—2-DRINK MIN.

"Six bucks for a headache," J.R. muttered as he took a twenty from his wallet. He waited for the change, then led the reverend past the window to the steps that led downward into the throng.

Bainbridge wore a wrinkled tan corduroy suit under his raincoat. He looked better than he had earlier but still appeared haggard. Despite the two showers he'd taken before leaving the house, he seemed in need of another. He looked around with wide, bewildered eyes, absently scratching his cheek with a trembling hand, glancing at J.R. and trying to smile.

"Loud," he said.

"Would you like a table?" asked a petite blond girl with a streak of magenta in her hair.

"We'd like to see the manager," J.R. said. "Or whoever's in charge this evening."

"Is Mr. Bascombe expecting you?" she asked.

"No. My name's J.R. Haskell. He doesn't know me, but please, tell him it's very important."

"Wait right here." The girl disappeared into the crowd.

The ceiling of the club was high, and strings hung from the bottoms of red and blue lights shaped like balloons that had floated up to the rafters.

"Look at them," the reverend said, leaning close to J.R.'s ear.

They crowded the dance floor, bunched together around tables, shouldered through the crowd laughing and shouting above the music, restless, energetic. Couples stood between tables kissing and fondling, and groups of girls moved to and from the ladies' room.

"Do you see?" Bainbridge asked.

On every third teenager—maybe more—J.R. spotted a Crucifax. The dark crosses caught the light in brief glimmers of black-red.

"Yes," J.R. said. "I see."

The stage was at the other end of the club, black except for an occasional glint of reflected light on the band's instruments. And something else . . .

Almond-shaped spots of gold sparkled in the darkness behind the instruments. . . .

"They're here," Bainbridge said fearfully. "Watching us . . ."

Jeff sat in the back seat of Brad's Mustang with the burning taste of bile in his mouth. Nick and Keith were in the back with him; Jason sat in front, handing back cans of Budweiser. When Jason offered one to him, Jeff shook his head and turned his eyes to the window at his left and absently watched the watery blur of lights go by slowly as they waited for the traffic on Ventura to get moving again.

"C'mon, Jeffy," Brad said, "you need it."

He considered it, took the can, and popped the tab, hoping he'd be able to hold it down. He gulped the beer quickly, deciding to have another as soon as he finished it. Maybe beer would help rid him of the images of his mother reaching between her legs and clutching her ass, swinging her bare breasts, of the leering men throwing down their money and howling like animals each time his mother cocked a hip or jutted her pelvis.

I know you trust Mom right now, Mallory had said, *but you shouldn't.*

Jeff wondered if she'd known, and if so, for how long.

He wondered how long their mother had been stripping . . . and what else she'd been keeping from them.

Was that why their father had left?

Was that why Mallory had left?

There are things about her you don't know. . . .

A storm of questions swirled in his mind, but—and this surprised him—he felt nothing, didn't know what to feel, as if he were totally detached from what had happened, as if he'd watched some other guy find his mother dancing in a strip bar.

"Okay," Brad said, "so the Playpen was a bad idea. How about we go back to my sister's place and get some grass, then to Fantazm?"

Everyone agreed but Jeff. He'd heard Brad but was busy finishing his beer and trying not to think.

"Hey, Jeff?" Brad said. "You okay?"

Jeff leaned forward, handed his empty can to Jason, took another beer, and said, "Yeah, I'm okay." It was a lie, but he would be drunk in a while, and he was sure he'd be seeing Mallory at Fantazm; he would be okay soon. . . .

A bullet-shaped man with a goatee and frizzy hair the color of straw approached J.R. and the reverend. He wore an oversized white shirt with several zippers over the chest and sleeves. His left arm was in a cast, and there was a small blood-spotted bandage above his left eye. The blond girl was at his side.

"Marty Bascombe," he said to J.R., glancing around the club as he spoke, preoccupied. "I'm kinda busy, but, uh, what can I do for you?"

J.R. introduced himself and said, "I'd like to talk with you about the band that's playing here tonight."

"Yeah, Crucifax?" He nudged his way up to the bar, and they followed him. "Gimme a Coke, Perry," he said to the bartender. "Okay, what about the band?"

"Well, I was wondering . . ." J.R. suddenly realized he

didn't know what to say to this man. He hadn't given it any thought. He decided shortly before arriving at the club that it might be a good idea to have a word with the manager about Mace. He found himself stammering and at a loss.

"We have reason to believe," the reverend spoke up, "that the band you've scheduled for tonight is a serious danger to the young people who—"

"Hey, I know you," Bascombe said. The bartender brought his Coke, and he swirled the ice for a moment as he eyed the reverend suspiciously. "You're that little Bible-beater who stands out in the parking lot preachin' to everybody. So what's the deal here, you think they're gonna poison the kids' minds? They got Satanic messages in their music?"

"I'm certainly not going to say I approve of that music, Mr. Bascombe," the reverend replied. "But it's nothing like that at all."

J.R. said, "The bandleader—Mace—we think he might—"

"Hey," Bascombe gulped, putting down his drink and looking around him as he took J.R.'s arm. "C'mere, c'mere, c'mon with me." He led them quickly down a short carpeted hall and into an office cluttered with stacks of magazines, papers, loose files, and empty beer cans. Rock music posters were tacked haphazardly to the walls. Bascombe closed the door and turned to them. "Okay, what's this about the band?"

J.R.'s ears rang in the silence of the office. He coughed nervously into a fist and said, "I'm assuming you know Mace."

"Met him."

"He's been connected to some recent suicides. High school kids."

Bascombe rolled his eyes. "Jesus, what're you, some PMRC nut? You think rock music's making kids kill themselves? Is that what you—"

"It has nothing to do with the music, Mr. Bascombe, it's Mace. He's dangerous. I'm telling you, he's—"

"Get to the point, okay? I don't have all night. Whatta you want from *me?*"

"You have to cancel the concert tonight."

Bascombe laughed, sitting on the edge of his messy desk. "We've got, what, about an hour before the show, a little less? And you want me to tell these guys to, what, go home? Look, these are just local kids getting their first shot at—"

"They're local kids," J.R. said emphatically, "who've been living in the basement of an abandoned building with this guy for weeks. Their parents don't know where they are or what—"

"So what'm I now, a *babysitter?*"

The reverend stepped forward and said, "Don't you feel some responsibility toward these young people?"

Bascombe's irritated smile disappeared. "Hey, c'mon, guys, I'm trying to run a nightclub here, okay? You paid the cover, right? Tell you what, I'll refund your cover, and drinks're on the house, okay? No booze at the bar—this is a teen club, y'know—but I got some here." He went behind his desk, opened a drawer, and held up a bottle of Tanqueray gin. "What about it, huh? Just don't make any trouble for me, okay?"

He's scared, J.R. thought.

"Mr. Bascombe," he said, "we didn't come here for free drinks."

Bascombe put the bottle down and came around the desk, scowling. "Okay, *you* wanna deal with that guy? Go right ahead. *You* wanna tell him he can't play tonight? Be my guest. But as far as I'm concerned, Crucifax is playing here tonight, and for the rest of the fucking week if they want to, and I don't care if they stand on the stage, whip out their cocks, and piss on the audience!" He stepped between them and opened the door. "Now I've got some calls to make, so if you don't mind . . ."

J.R. noticed beads of sweat glistening on Bascombe's forehead, saw his lips tremble slightly. The spot of blood on his bandage had spread a bit; it was a recent injury. The cast was clean and white; no one had written on it.

"How did you hurt yourself?" J.R. asked.

Bascombe rolled his eyes again. "I ran into a big door, okay? Now get outta here."

They left the office, and the door closed firmly behind them.

"He's scared," the reverend said, sounding a bit ill at ease himself.

J.R. nodded as they headed back into the club. "I know. And probably with good reason. He didn't run into any goddamned door. . . ."

Erin tried to keep her eyes clear as she drove through the storm, but each time she thought she'd stopped crying, more tears came. She spotted Fantazm a block away. The marquee above the entrance read:

WEDNESDAY
NEW BAND NITE
WED OCT 19
—CRUCIFAX—

The word *Crucifax* sent a spear of ice through her chest, and she muttered, "Mallory . . ." She suddenly felt twice as weary knowing she would have to face both of them.

The parking lot behind Fantazm was full, so she had to park half a block away and hurry through the rain.

Inside the club, she paid the cover charge and surveyed the crowd with a dismal groan. It was a smoky lake of bobbing heads and shoulders with not a familiar face in sight. Erin regretted the fact that she knew only a couple of Jeff's and Mallory's friends. She knew a lot of names, but few, if any, faces. The only reason she knew Brad was that he'd spent more time at the apartment than any of the others.

What kind of mother are you? she asked herself bitterly. *You don't even know who your kids are growing up with, let alone what kind of people they might be.*

She walked into the crowd looking from face to face, stopping to turn and look behind her. She bumped chairs and tables, was pressed against sweaty, smoky teenagers, even walked onto the dance floor without realizing it.

Erin did not notice the crosses until after she'd been wandering through the club for several minutes. When she did, she stopped in the crowd, saw another . . . and another. . . .

They looked like small sculptures cut from chunks of dried blood, just as Jeff had described them.

And they were everywhere she looked.

"Mrs. Carr? Erin?"

The voice was a faint mutter at first but became louder, and when she saw J.R. Haskell, she smiled with relief at the sight of a familiar face.

"What are you doing here?" he asked.

"Looking for my kids. Have you seen them?"

"Not yet, but Jeff should be here soon, if he isn't already." J.R. introduced her to Reverend Bainbridge, then said, "You look upset. And you're limping. What's wrong?"

She tried to tell him, thinking she could get it out with perhaps a casual chuckle and a toss of her head so he couldn't say "I told you so," but when she started to speak, tears sprang to her eyes again, and she covered her trembling lips. J.R. stepped forward, muttering, "What? What?" and she let him put his arms around her, rested her head on his shoulder. With her mouth close to his ear, she told him what happened.

"I tried to stop him," she said, "but he ignored me and left with his friends. He was . . . God, he was shaken. When I think of how he must have felt, looking up on that stage and seeing . . . his mother . . ."

J.R. pulled back and faced her, hands on her shoulders, his face dark with sudden worry. "How long ago did this happen?"

"Thirty or forty minutes."

He turned away from her suddenly with the look of someone just realizing his keys were locked in the car. He turned to the reverend and said something she couldn't hear, then took her arm and said, "Let's go." There was an urgency in his voice that disturbed her. He quickly led her through the crowd and to the entrance, where it was a bit quieter.

"Could he have gone somewhere else?" he asked, clutching her arms.

He was more than concerned now; he was scared. He

waited intently for her reply, his eyes locked onto hers, but as she tried to think of somewhere else Jeff might have gone her thoughts jumbled together with the throbbing noise and her sudden fear.

"I-I don't know, J.R., he might have, but . . . what's wrong? What's going on?"

"Did he say anything to you?"

"No, he just left. Now, what's happening?"

"I can't give you the details right now, but something very scary is going on. Everything Jeff told us—those things in your apartment?—it all happened just as he said. These kids Mace has rounded up—God knows how many—they've all been hurt, let down recently by someone close to them, someone they trusted. A friend, a sibling, a preacher, maybe. A *parent.* He hooks them by their weak spots and reels them in like fish."

"J.R., that's—what are you—how can that be, it's all—"

"Listen to me!" he growled, shaking her. "You may not believe it, but it's happening, and if you want to save your kids, you're just gonna have to live with it for a while, because it's happening to them! I've been on the phone calling parents all day. Some of them are coming down here tonight to get their kids. At least they *said* they were." He glanced around. "I don't see any of them yet." He turned to her again, and his face was a hard mask of anger and fear. "Some of these kids here, they're scared because they know what's happening. They've seen it happening around them. I met a girl who's looking for her brother, a guy who's trying to find his girlfriend—they're trying to get them away from Mace. Kids are *killing* themselves, Erin. Mace is promising to take them all away to a better place, a place where they're wanted, not ignored, not judged, like Mallory said, but that place is in a box six feet underground. He's poison, but they think he's their friend. They want to think that, need to. Mallory's decided to go with him, and now, after what happened tonight, I'm afraid Jeff might decide he wants to go, too. Unless we can get him—*both* of them—out of here and away from Mace tonight. Because it's gonna happen soon. Don't ask me why, but I can feel it, the reverend feels it, too; something's brewing. And if we don't wake up, we're

gonna lose a lot of kids. If not tonight, then soon. Very soon."

Erin didn't want to believe what he was saying, didn't even want to think that he believed it, but his grip on her arms was beginning to hurt, and his eyes burned with such intense conviction and determination that all she could say was "What do I do?"

He released his grip on her arms and, for a moment, looked embarrassed, as if he hadn't realized he was holding her so tightly. "I'm tired of shouting," he said, taking her outside. The music diminished to a hum when the door closed. They stood beneath the marquee, where the rain and traffic noise completely drowned out the rock and roll inside.

J.R. asked, "What kind of car was Jeff in?"

"Mustang. White. Seventy-one or -two."

"I'm going out to the parking lot to look for it. You keep an eye out for Jeff and Mallory. If you find them . . ." He hesitated, flinched at a flash of lightning overhead. "Well, I can't tell you what to do, but I can suggest. I know you and Mallory haven't gotten along well for a while, and now Jeff . . . When we find them . . . well, swallow your pride. Apologize for any mistakes you've made, forget about any they've made, and . . . I guess I'm suggesting that you start over. And make sure they know that's what you want. A clean slate. Don't get angry, don't snap back at them, because at this point I think the best you can do is to say very little. Just make sure they know you love them."

"Of course they know I love them!" she shouted angrily. "I've busted my—"

J.R. held up a palm. *"That,"* he said, "is exactly what you shouldn't say."

Erin turned away from him and paced in front of the door for a moment, exhausted and angry and scared, wishing her tears would stop.

"Go back inside, Erin," he said gently. "Stay by the door so I can find you. And if you see Mallory and Jeff, hold *onto* them." He placed a hand on her cheek and gave her a halfhearted smile. "I'll be right back."

* * *

Brad's car was stuffy with the smell of marijuana smoke and spilled beer. They'd gone back to Becky's after leaving the Playpen. Jeff sat in the corner quietly drinking a beer while the others all talked at once. Becky sat down beside him on the squeaky, worn sofa and handed him a joint the size of his index finger, saying, "A consolation prize, sport." She held up a light for the joint. "Neil called earlier and told me what happened. You okay?"

"Yeah, I'm . . ." He'd dragged on the joint without finishing his sentence.

"Well, don't let it get to you. I mean, think about it. She's not dying, she's not going to jail, and she's making a buck."

Jeff remained unsociable for the rest of their stay at Becky's, trying to get as stoned as he could because his feeling was coming back. The safe and comfortable numbness was fading away, and the images of his mother were flashing in his mind at a staccato pace like slides being projected on the backs of his eyes.

Brad parked a block away, and they jogged through the downpour. A bone-white flash of lightning brightened the sky, and thunder purred in the distance as they went into Fantazm.

Big storm comin' . . .

In the club, Jeff was the first to step forward and pay his six dollars. When he moved aside to wait for the others, he saw her with J.R. She stood with her back to him, but he recognized her. He nudged Brad and said, "My mom's here," pointing her out.

"You want to see her?"

He shook his head.

Brad grinned and said, "No prob." Without walking by Erin, he led them down a side corridor past the restrooms, a cigarette machine, and a bank of pay phones, and into the crowd of mingling teenagers beyond the door at the other end.

Jeff ordered a Coke and looked around for Lily. He spotted several others from school. Paula McGillis sneaked up behind him and pinched his ass; she wore a Crucifax. Noella Coleman and Shawn Cruise tripped over to him, laughing drunkenly, and Shawn tipped a small flask over Jeff's Coke; black-red crosses glinted on their chests.

As Jeff looked at the countless Crucifaxes around him he felt nothing. The deep, clammy fear they had stirred in him previously was little more than a discomforting memory. He had other more personal things on his mind, like what he might do or say if his mother found him. Besides, he was feeling pretty good, feeling the beer and the pot and—

—the arms wrapping around his waist from behind and hot breath against his ear.

"I'm so glad you came, Jeff!" Mallory said, pressing herself against his back.

When he turned around, Jeff faced an older Mallory. Her face was pale and drawn, cheeks hollow, and half-moons of puffy skin hung below her eyes. Her smile was still bright but seemed weary. He caught a vague but unpleasant whiff of the sewer mixed with Windsong perfume.

Mallory's hands moved like those of a blind person, touching his chest, his arms and shoulders, his face and hair, as if she hadn't seen him in years. She hugged him quickly, then pulled away to look at him some more, ebullient despite her apparent exhaustion.

"Are you alone?" she asked.

"I'm with Brad. And a few of the guys. And I'm waiting for a friend."

"Oh? A girl?" She grinned mischievously.

"Um, yeah."

Mallory reached behind him and under his jacket and slipped her fingers into the back pockets of his jeans. "What are you doing later?"

"How much later?"

"After the first song?"

"Well, I don't know, I was going to, um . . . I don't know." He finished off his Coke with a few big gulps.

"What's wrong, Jeff?"

"Wrong?" *I'm losing you,* he thought. *Mom's screwed up, and there's something—*

Mallory's hands slid up his sides to his neck—

—*wrong*—

—over his ears and into his hair—

—*with me.* . . .

—to his face, where her fingertips gently caressed the line of his jaw, his lower lip, sending featherlike tingles over his skin.

"C'mon," she said, "something's wrong. Tell me." Her breath was slightly sour, but not offensive.

"I don't want to talk about it."

"Is it her? Mom, I mean?"

"Really, Mallory, I don't want—"

The music stopped abruptly, and the voices lowered, silenced. The lights over the dance floor began to dim, and a deep, practiced male voice spoke over the PA system.

"It's Wednesday . . . new-band night here at Fantazm!"

Cheers and applause rose from the floor as the voice continued.

"Tonight we're happy to present a local band that's been generating a lot of talk around the Valley."

Mallory put an arm around Jeff's waist and squeezed close to him as they faced the stage.

"Here they come," she said excitedly.

"This is their first live performance, so make 'em feel at home."

The cheers grew to a small roar and blended into one voice as the stage lights slowly came up.

"Please welcome . . . *Crucifax!*"

Twenty-seven

An odd sound filled Fantazm, a sound alien to a nightclub for teenagers, a sound that was every bit as startling and spectacular as any music ever played within its walls: reverent silence.

Soft light oozed over the stage, illuminating the band and the tall, thin figure standing at the front. His head was bowed; his silver hair cascaded over his chest and gathered on the shiny black guitar that hung across his stomach. A pale red spotlight spread over him like thin blood, and as the spotlight grew he slowly lifted his head and raised his long arms until they were open wide, as if he were about to embrace the crowd before him. A small, distant sound began, the sound of a gnat flying close to the ear, growing slowly, becoming larger, richer, like a jet in the distance drawing closer.

The teenagers watching attentively began to stir, and the stirring became excited shouts as the sound grew louder and the light brighter.

As the sound crescendoed Mace's arms slowly fell until he gripped the guitar and ripped his right hand over the strings. An explosion of music shook the club, and the teenagers went wild. Drinks were spilled as they waved their arms and jumped and danced.

Mace leaned toward the microphone, opened his mouth, and released a skin-shredding scream that seemed to last much longer than a normal breath would allow, and the scream became a word, and then he was singing. The heavy beat was throbbing through the walls and floor, was felt deep in the bones of the dancing, cheering teenagers, and made the air hum with a hot, crackling energy. . . .

J.R. stood beside Erin at the top of the steps. Unable to find the white Mustang or any other sign of Jeff, J.R. had come back inside shortly before the band began to play. Erin was scanning the crowd, her eyes narrowed to slits as she looked for her children.

J.R.'s eyes were on Mace.

When J.R. was a little boy, he'd seen a nature film that had remained vivid in his memory. The film included footage of a rattlesnake stalking a field mouse. The snake had followed the terrified mouse through tall grass until it was cornered between two rocks. It tried to dig beneath one of the rocks for a moment, then stopped, faced the snake, and waited for its death, its tiny body trembling helplessly. But the snake had been in no hurry and took its time positioning itself before the doomed mouse, slowly, gracefully coiling up, its black tongue flicking in and out. That was what J.R. remembered so clearly: the hypnotic way the snake had curled itself up, the deadly choreography of its movements as its small black eyes remained locked on its victim, and the way the mouse made no further attempts to save itself, as if it was convinced it had no other option but to die, to give in; it could have fought, kept digging, or even hopped over the snake, and maybe—just maybe—it would have lived to see another day. Instead, it had huddled against the rock until the snake's dreamlike movements ended in a blurred strike and the mouse's hind legs and tail hung twitching from its mouth.

As he watched Mace on the stage, playing his guitar, moving with fluid grace, leaning toward the edge of the stage and spreading his arms over the crowd, smiling, his gaze moving over the teenagers as if he were looking into the eyes of each and every one, J.R. thought of that snake. . . .

Lily arrived, wet from the rain, and, shouting to be heard, asked J.R. if he'd seen Jeff.

"We're looking for him," J.R. replied.

She stood with them, looking tired and upset, haggard— far more so, J.R. thought, than a girl her age should look.

On the edges of the crowd, J.R. spotted some other adults scattered around the room. They looked painfully out of place as they stepped here and there, craning their necks to peer through the lake of teenagers, frowning as they searched. He assumed they were some of the parents he'd called earlier. It really didn't matter, though, as long as they'd come to take their children home.

He thought, *Before the snake strikes . . .*

"There he is!" Erin shouted, grabbing J.R.'s arm and pointing toward the stage. "He's with Mallory!"

J.R. followed the direction of her finger. They were on the dance floor near the stage. Unlike the others around him, Jeff was standing still, looking back and forth between the stage and Mallory, who was standing close to him, first with one arm around him, then both. She was holding his hand, stroking his hair; they looked like lovers.

With a shiver of dread, J.R. realized that if seeing his mother strip in a bar wasn't enough to send Jeff away with Mace and his friends, perhaps the temptation of being with Mallory would be the extra needed incentive.

Glass shattered somewhere within the mob of teenagers, and a shriek rose above the music, then diminished and became a shrill laugh.

Erin started down the steps, and J.R. imagined her going down there, being swallowed up by that writhing throng; he held her back.

"Wait a while," he shouted. "Till this set is finished."

Frowning, Erin came back up the steps, watching Jeff and Mallory closely.

J.R. searched for the reverend. Something told him it was

not safe to be down there on the floor. Bainbridge was nowhere in sight, but he could still see Jeff and Mallory. She was tugging on his arm persuasively, as if to pull him away from the crowd, but he shook his head. Mallory said something to him, gesturing toward the entrance, then glancing in that direction. She did a double take, then turned to look straight at J.R. and Erin. She turned to Jeff angrily, said something, then stalked away. Jeff followed her, waving a hand, his mouth moving frantically.

"Jesus, they're *leaving!*" Erin snapped.

"They have to come through here," J.R. tried to assure her.

"We didn't see them come in, what makes you think we'll see them go out?" She hurried down the steps, and Lily followed her.

J.R. paced at the top of the steps as he watched them weave through the swarm of teenagers. The headache he'd expected had arrived with a vengeance. . . .

Erin pushed boldly through the audience, not bothering to be polite. Lily was beside her, but she paid no attention to her.

"Mrs. Carr! Please—Mrs. *Carr!*"

Reverend Bainbridge was hurrying toward her; she tried to avoid him, but he stepped in front of her, his face shining with sweat. He lifted a palm to stop her; his hand was trembling.

"Mrs. Carr, I think you should come with me," he said.

"What? Where?"

"Back up there." He pointed to the steps. He turned to Lily and gave her a nervous smile, touching her shoulder. "You, too, dear."

Lily jerked away from his hand, muttering, "Don't touch me."

"Please. It's not safe down here." With a sudden jolt, he let out a frightened cry and quickly stepped aside, looking down at the floor.

Erin looked down, too, and swallowed a scream.

Something dark with matted fur was winding between

their legs, around their feet, scurrying through the crowd. There was another right behind. The creature stopped, lifted its head, and looked at Erin with its golden eyes, its lips twitching slightly around its yellowed tusks.

Erin stumbled backward, swung her arm out, and held onto Lily to keep from falling. The creature continued to gaze up at her, and Erin envisioned the thing crawling up her leg, clinging to her coat with its small black claws as it made its way to her throat.

"No, no," the reverend said, taking her arm, touching Lily's back as she turned around, "let's just walk back, okay? We'll just walk back slowly."

The crowd moved around them like a single entity, pathways opening and closing before them, and Erin clutched the reverend's hand tightly in her own, wondering how many of the creatures were in the building, scuttling over the crowded floor.

The reverend squeezed her hand and kept up a soothing patter: "We won't hurry, we won't make any sudden moves—"

Something brushed against Erin's right shin . . .

"—we'll just wander over to those steps there, okay?"

She felt a tug on the hem of her coat . . .

"Okay? We'll just keep walking . . ."

The steps seemed miles away; she wanted to break into a run, wanted to knock everyone out of the way and get to the entrance, get outside and away from the building, except—

—Mallory and Jeff. They were still somewhere in the horde of dancing, shouting teenagers.

"My children," Erin said.

"No, no, we'll worry about them later," Reverend Bainbridge assured her as he led them up the steps to J.R.'s side. "They're everywhere," he said to J.R., his soothing tone gone, "all over the floor."

J.R. looked out over the floor, his eyes narrowed and searching.

The reverend said, "He's using them to hold us off, us and the other parents."

"Don't the kids notice them?" J.R. asked.

"Some. Some of them are scared, but the others, *his* kids, the ones with Crucifaxes, are calming them down, telling them those things are harmless."

Erin felt dizzy with fear and looked for Mallory and Jeff, searched the crowd from wall to wall, but couldn't see them. The band was still on the same song. Mace was walking back and forth along the edge of the stage, his right arm stretched out, his hand flat, passing through the air from right to left, as if blessing his audience. Erin listened to him, tried to make out the words he was singing, but her mind was too full—

It's too late, you've waited too long and now it's too late, you've lost them both. . . .

"What are we going to do?" she asked J.R.

"I don't know," he replied, still watching the teenagers, his face lined with worry. "Just wait, I guess. Other than that, I don't know. . . ."

Jeff followed Mallory out the stage door and into the dark alley that ran along the northern side of the building. Water poured from the clogged rain gutters, and the alley smelled of wet garbage. He ducked his head and ran after her, shouting, "I didn't bring her, Mallory!"

"Then what's she doing here?"

"She's looking for me."

Mallory stopped at a manhole in the middle of the alley; water gurgled through its cover and fell below with echoing splashes.

"Why?" she asked, facing him.

He could feel the rain soaking through his clothes and pulled his jacket together in front. "Can we go inside?"

"Not while *she's* in there." Mallory seemed oblivious of the rain, although her hair was slick against her head and the usually loose dark red sweater she wore was clinging to her. She looked angry at first, standing with her arms folded and one foot forward, her hip cocked, but her arms slowly went to her sides, her face softened, and she said, "Come with me, Jeff."

"Where?"

She bent down and pulled the cover off the manhole. "Down here."

Jeff stared silently at the manhole, remembering his last trip into the sewer. Logically, he knew he should not go back down there. But he didn't feel any fear, only the pleasant buzz of beer and marijuana.

"C'mon, we're getting soaked. And she won't find you."

"We don't have a light."

She pulled up her sweater and took a small black flashlight from beneath the top of her jeans. Walking toward him, she flicked it on, and Jeff winced at the surprisingly bright beam. She stopped an inch in front of him, shining the light upward between them. She was smiling, but the shadows cast by the beam made her face look like a death mask. Only her eyes remained warm and familiar, although they were heavy, distant.

"Come with me," she whispered. "We can talk. We need to talk."

He hadn't told Brad or the others where he was going and they might worry—if they noticed he was gone—but he didn't want to face his mother. Mace was occupied with the band, so he wouldn't have to deal with him. And he would be with Mallory . . .

There's something wrong with me . . .

Jeff went to the manhole and gestured for her to go first, then followed her down, replacing the cover with a resounding clang. When he reached the bottom and, once again, smelled the familiar odor of filth, his mouth became cottony, and for a moment he was afraid to move.

Mallory took his hand and said, "C'mon, it's okay."

"It wasn't okay the last time I was down here."

"You weren't with *me.*"

She led him by the hand along the wall, ducking pipes and valves. Rats squeaked and darted out of their path. She kept flashing the light over the wall to their left until it disappeared into a narrow black passageway. She turned to go through it, saying, "Shortcut," but a sharp blade of fear cut through Jeff's otherwise relaxed state, and he stopped, let go of her hand, and said, "Uh-uh, I'm not going in there."

315

He backed up a step, remembering the hand that had reached through a similar opening last week, and prepared to run if it happened again.

"It's *okay*," Mallory said impatiently.

"What's in there?"

"Just a bunch of pipes and gas lines, stuff like that. Maybe a few bums, but they won't hurt us. Mace feeds them, brings them all kinds of food. They leave us alone now. Even talk to us sometimes."

He still didn't move.

"Look, if I'm not scared, there's no reason for you to be."

Jeff followed her cautiously, watching for any sign of movement in the darkness beyond the flashlight beam. He saw nothing but thick sheets of cobwebs stretched between pipes and cables, a glimpse of filthy walls now and then, a scurrying rat. But he heard things.

Crunching footsteps . . .

A harsh, phlegmy cough . . .

Whispers . . .

His legs felt wobbly, and his heart was pounding so hard, he wondered if Mallory could hear it. He followed her across one of the metal footbridges and through another passageway.

The light passed over faces in the dark, long, bony, hollow faces with shadows for eyes . . .

By the time they reached the jagged hole that led into Mace's building, Jeff was winded from holding his breath in fear each time they passed through one of the cavelike rooms with its gutlike pipes and ghostly faces.

There was an empty, crumpled Doritos bag and an empty English muffin box outside the hole.

"See?" Mallory said, stepping through the hole. "He feeds 'em."

Upstairs, the lanterns glowed, but the room was nearly empty. A few shuffling figures lurked in the shadows, and the coals of cigarettes and marijuana joints glowed like red eyes.

"Over here," Mallory said, leading him to the pool.

Jeff stared for a moment at the spot where he'd seen Nikki lying the week before, but he could not find in himself the fear he knew he should feel. He was too tired, too stoned, and still too numb.

Taking his hand again, Mallory led him into the pool, flicking the flashlight off as they carefully went down the stepladder.

"Careful," she whispered, stepping over body-shaped lumps curled beneath blankets on the way to the deep end. She went to a corner and sat Indian-style on a cushion, patting the space beside her. "This is my spot."

"Your spot?" He hunkered down beside her, nervously eyeing the shapes in the pool. Then he saw Mallory's smile in the glow of a nearby lantern; she was perfectly comfortable, so he tried to relax.

"Yeah, we all have our own spots. Well . . . not so much anymore." She fumbled with a blanket heaped at her side and pulled out a small oblong box. "New people come every day. Now it's so crowded when everybody's here—most of 'em are at the club now—that some of them have moved upstairs." She opened the box and removed a plastic Ziplock bag, opened that, and took out two joints, handing one to Jeff. "One for each of us. Pretty rad, huh? Mace is real generous."

He decided he'd already had so much grass that evening that a little more wouldn't matter. She lit the joint for him, and he inhaled.

"Okay, tell me what happened," she said.

Jeff spat and wiped his mouth after his second drag; the marijuana tasted harsh, sort of . . . greasy. As he recounted his evening at the Playpen, taking another drag now and then, his speech began to slow down, his eyes grew heavy, and in a few minutes he heard his own words as if someone else were speaking them.

"I *told* you, Jeff. You can't trust her. I came home last Thursday, and she was on the phone talking filth with some guy. 'Wanna rub our nylons together, Lou?' " she mimicked in a breathy voice. " 'Grind our crotches?' Jesus. She was, like, fucking him over the phone. Now, Jeff, now do you see why Dad left?"

He'd heard everything she'd said but didn't answer because he felt very strange.

"What . . . what kind of pot is this?" he asked.

"Good shit, huh?"

"But . . . it's . . ."

Her hand was cool on the back of his neck; she lifted him away from the wall of the pool and put a pillow behind him.

"Lie back," she said, putting her other hand on his chest. "Here, lift your arms. . . ." She helped him take off his jacket.

Jeff was starting to feel afraid. He knew the grass shouldn't have such an effect on him; his limbs felt leaden, his head cool and empty; his eyes seemed to float in their sockets. But none of the strange sensations was unpleasant.

"What's . . . happening, Mal? What was . . . that stuff?"

"Just some grass. With, oh, maybe a few goodies mixed in. Nothing much." She plucked the joint from his hand. "Thirsty?"

His tongue felt like a piece of beef jerky, and he nodded.

Mallory hurried away, leaving him to stare up at the yellow-tinted darkness above him. It seemed to swirl and shift, pull away, then press in on him, and he watched it with curiosity and amusement, smiling when he realized he was tempted to reach out and try to touch it. Something was peering down at him from the edge of the pool with golden eyes and black claws that *scritched* on the cement as it backed away.

When Mallory returned, she held two bottles of Miller in one hand and a lantern in the other. Her sweater was gone, and she wore a dry white T-shirt that clung to her still-wet breasts; her Crucifax rested between them. In the lantern light, Jeff could see the dark circles of her hard, wet nipples through the thin material. She put down the lantern, took the cap off a beer, and handed it to him.

After they'd each taken a good long drink, Mallory lay down beside him, smoking her joint again. She put her hand on his chest and began fingering a button on his shirt.

"It's just us now, Jeffy," she whispered. "Dad knew enough to cut out two years ago." She unfastened a button and ran her finger over his chest beneath the shirt. "Now that we know why . . ." Loosening another button, she slipped her hand under the shirt and stroked him in soft, slow circles. ". . . are we gonna stick around?"

Jeff closed his eyes and sighed as another button went and another, and her hand moved over his stomach, tugging his shirt out of his pants a bit at a time, nudging her fingers beneath his belt.

"You want to stay with her?"

Mallory's lips touched his ear, and he shuddered, feeling the touch through his whole body.

"Knowing what she does? How she lies?"

Jeff opened his eyes when she touched the joint to his lips; he shook his head.

"C'mon," she breathed. "A little more."

Jeff inhaled.

Her fingers slid through the hairs beneath his pants.

"What else has she lied to us about, Jeff?"

He shook his head, started to say, "She didn't really lie," but he couldn't say that because he didn't believe it, and because he couldn't quite catch his breath. . . .

"How much do you think she cares," she went on, her voice velvety soft against his neck, "when her whole life—*everything*—has been a lie?"

He arched his back slightly when her fingers reached his erection; he tried to think, tried to put words together in his head. . . .

Maybe . . . maybe she was . . . doing her . . . best . . .

But the thought came with no conviction, only with effort.

Mallory crooked one leg over his, pulled her hand out, and slid it over the top of the bulge in his jeans.

"Mace was right," she giggled, squeezing. "Wasn't he?" She playfully straddled his thighs and put her hands on his shoulders, leaning close to his face. The Crucifax swung above him like a pendulum. "Wasn't he?"

"How . . . could he know?"

With a throaty laugh, she reached for the joint, took a drag, put her mouth over his, and gently pried his lips apart with her tongue, then blew the smoke into his mouth.

"He isn't human," she whispered secretly. "I don't know

what he is, but he's not one of us. He's . . . *better*. Something bigger and more powerful. He knows things . . . he can do things . . . and he's come for us, Jeff."

Even as he inhaled the smoke, a small, distant voice told him he shouldn't. As Mallory leaned forward her pelvis pressed against his, her breasts lightly brushed his chest, and the Crucifax fell, cool and heavy, against his throat.

"You don't want to stay with her, do you?" she whispered.

"I sure don't. I'm going with him. You can come, Jeff. Come with me."

His head was a jumble of disconnected thoughts, and he could not remember exactly why that was a bad idea, why he shouldn't agree to go with her—

. . . someplace better . . . going someplace better . . .

—but it wouldn't come together. It had something to do with J.R. and Lily—

Where's Lily?

—and the Crucifax, but his thoughts were clouded with pleasure as Mallory unfastened his belt, unbuttoned his pants, and slowly pulled down the zipper, saying, "Please, Jeffy. We can be together as much as we want. . . ."

She hooked a finger under the elastic band of his briefs and slowly moved it back and forth.

"Do whatever we want . . ."

Mallory put her other hand over his taut undershorts and gently cupped his erection; Jeff shivered, clenched his fists, and released a long, trembling moan as she pulled down his briefs, took his stiff penis in her hand, and stroked it lovingly.

Jeff sucked in a sharp breath and touched her hand, stroked her flesh for a moment, but—

There's something wrong with me . . .

—then pushed her arm aside, gasping, "No, we . . . we shouldn't, Mal, it's . . . it's not . . ."

"Not what?" she laughed. "It's not right? Not normal? Well, you know what, Jeffy?"

He felt her breath against his cock as her hand kept moving.

"Where Mace is taking us? There is no right, no wrong. There are no rules. No normal or abnormal."

She licked the underside of his cock, holding it at the base like a Popsicle.

"So it's okay," she said with a smack of her lips. "This, I mean. When we leave with Mace, we'll be free, Jeffy, we can do anything we want."

She plunged her mouth over him, and Jeff's back stiffened.

"Will you come?" she mumbled, lifting her head for a moment. "I'm not sure, but I think we're leaving tonight. Will you come?"

He was gasping for breath, eyes closed, hot tendrils of sensation shooting through his body from the spot where she touched him.

"We can be together like this, Jeff," she said, sliding her lips along the side of his cock. "Together like this all the time, and no one will find us or stop us or . . ."

Her voice faded away because now she was sitting up, removing the T-shirt, taking Jeff's hands and putting them on her breasts, pressing them over the mounds of flesh that he had wanted to touch for so long, and far away he could hear himself laugh, hear his voice say, "Yes, yes, yes," feel his head nod, smell her musky odor, and as he slipped inside of her he knew that wherever she was going, he would go with her. . . .

The crowd in Fantazm continued to grow more and more restless. More than once, J.R. saw a chair lifted above the bobbing heads and tossed through the air. Screams and laughter mingled until it became impossible to distinguish the two.

More parents arrived, and some had gone into the mass of teenagers, searching, some of them shouting. One man, an executive type with black hair and gray tufts above his ears and wearing a dark suit, shouldered into the crowd, towering above the others. He cupped his hand to his mouth and shouted, waved a hand, trying to get someone's attention. Apparently he'd found who he was looking for.

The music never stopped. One song blended into another as Mace strutted and sneaked across the stage, passing his arms back and forth before him as if casting a spell over the audience. As far as J.R. could tell, a new song had just begun, and for the first time since the band had begun playing, he listened for the lyrics as he scanned the horde of teenagers below.

> *Take me deep inside you*
> *Squeeze tight and don't let go*

"They're gone," Erin said. "I don't see them, do you see them?"

Standing on tiptoe, shading her eyes from the stage lights, Lily shook her head.

J.R. watched the man in the suit reach for a girl in a shiny red jumpsuit a few feet ahead of him. She was backing through the crowd to get away from him, screaming something at him, her face twisted into the expression of a cornered animal. . . .

> *We'll leave this mess together*
> *And no one will ever know*

The stage lights and the dim lights in the entryway flickered for a moment, and J.R. thought they would go out, but the flickering stopped.

The man stopped, too, stopped reaching for the girl and looked down at his feet; his head began bobbing as he hopped this way and that, as if he were doing an odd sort of dance. He almost fell once—

They're holding him off, J.R. thought.

—but he grabbed someone's shoulder, regained his balance; and when he saw the girl getting away, being led toward the stage by a boy with long blond hair, he pushed two others aside and headed after her.

> *Say goodbye to Mom and Dad*
> *Say goodbye to Sis*
> *I'm goin' while I got the chance*
> *I've had enough of this*

The words made the skin on the back of J.R.'s neck shrivel; when his eyes met Lily's and saw the cold gray look of dread on her face, he knew she felt the same.

The man in the suit pushed a girl aside roughly, knocking her to the floor—

> *A slice of skin*
> *A spurt of blood*

—and leapt forward, grabbing the collar of the jumpsuit.

> *A scream, a cry*
> *A hisssss*

The girl jerked backward, her arms flailed before her, and she spun around to face the man.

> *A crack of bone*
> *An open skull*

He clutched her shoulders and began shaking her violently as he shouted at her. The girl spat in his face.

> *Gonna say goodbye*
> *To all of this*

For a heartbeat, the club was plunged into darkness as the lights flickered again. More glass shattered in the crowd, and a boy stood on a table and dived into the mass with a loud scream. The thought of the power going off, leaving the club in total darkness, made J.R. shudder, and he put his arm around Erin, turning her toward the doors and saying, "I think you and Lily should get out of here."

"Are you kidding?" she shouted, pulling away. "I'm not leaving here until I find Jeff and Mallory."

Frustrated, J.R. turned to the stage again, and the bottom of his stomach fell away.

Mace was staring directly into J.R.'s eyes and smiling as

he sang, his voice powerful, solid, a trumpet of flesh and blood making a sound that entered J.R.'s brain like a chilled icepick. . . .

> *No more deaf ears, no more blind eyes*
> *No spittin' in my face*
> *No more hands that pull away*
> *Goin' to a better place*

His smile spread, oozed over his face as he made his guitar scream like an angry demon, still watching J.R.

He can't see me, J.R. thought, *not with those lights shining in his eyes, he can't.*

There was another tremble in the lights; it lasted longer this time.

J.R. held Erin's arm, just in case; if the lights did go out, he didn't want to stick around in the dark.

Through the music, J.R. heard a scream so shrill and so filled with hate that it hovered in the air long after it had stopped, and he turned his eyes to the man in the suit again.

He held his daughter's left arm, pulling her through the mob as he might pull on the leash of a stubborn dog, angrily shouting at her over his shoulder. She was slapping at him with her free hand, spitting and screaming as she snapped her head back and forth.

Mace screamed into the microphone. His voice rose clear and distinct above the band. *"That's where we're goin', a better place!"*

The girl in the red jumpsuit was still screaming and fighting, but the man was near the edge of the crowd, pulling her toward J.R. and the double doors.

> *A scream, a cry*
> *A hisssss*

J.R. spotted other parents in the group waving and shouting at their kids, arguing, cajoling, but none of the other teenagers was reacting as violently as the girl in the red jumpsuit.

A crack of bone
An open skull

He saw it coming seconds before it happened. He pulled Erin to him as the girl reached under her collar, her fingers fumbling for something just below her throat, pulling out a cord, pulling until something flipped onto her chest, hanging from the cord, swinging back and forth over her breasts.

Gonna say goodbye

She clutched it in her fist and lifted it from her chest.
"No!" J.R. shouted.
Erin sputtered, "What? What?"
Lily saw it, too, and screamed, lifting a trembling hand to her face.
The man's back was to the girl, and he didn't seem to notice that she was no longer resisting him, didn't see her raise the Crucifax to her throat—

To all of this
Yeah, I'm gonna say goodbye

—press the edge to her flesh . . .
The lights dimmed.
Blinked.
Went out.
The music stopped and a brief, startled hush passed through the darkness, punctuated by a long, gurgling wail.
"*Jesus God!*" J.R. blurted, pushing Erin back toward the doors, reaching for Lily's hand to pull her with them.
An instant later, the auxiliary lights clicked on, bathing the club in a harsh, antiseptic white light as a grown man screamed like a young girl.
J.R. saw the man in the suit throw up his arms and fall out of sight as a gout of blood spurted from his daughter's open throat. She dropped, twitching, to the floor with her father, buried by the crowd, which was coming back to life with a few cheers and some applause. The man went on screaming, but Mace raised his arms and spoke; even without a

microphone, his voice cut through the club like a sharp knife through tender flesh as he said, "What are we waiting for?" and the crowd roared as one, drowning out the man's shrieks.

Mace put down his guitar, lifted his arms, gestured to the band, and jumped off the stage; a path opened in the crowd, allowing him to pass through. The path closed behind him as the teenagers followed, and Mace looked up at J.R. with a happy, confident smile, heading straight for him.

Something at the bottom of the steps below caught J.R.'s eye.

Three of the creatures were hurrying across the floor, loping up the steps toward them.

J.R. pulled Erin and Lily toward the door, calling, "Reverend, come on now!"

"But—Jeff!" Lily cried. "Where's Jeff?"

"Just come on, we're getting the hell out of here now!"

Erin began to protest, too, but J.R. opened the doors and pushed her through. He followed them outside to the parking lot and into darkness.

There were no streetlights, no traffic lights, no lit windows; only the headlights of cars on the boulevard lit the night, reflected on the wet pavement of the parking lot in shifting, glowing patterns.

"Jesus, a blackout," J.R. muttered.

The wind threw the rain into his face, and the drops stung like pebbles; a jagged tentacle of lightning cut the sky to the south, and the thunder that followed sounded like the crack of an enormous tree trunk.

Behind them, beyond Fantazm's double-door entrance, J.R. heard another kind of thunder, the thunder of voices and rushing feet, laughter and screams.

"Where are you parked?" J.R. shouted at Erin.

"A block away."

"I'm closer." He waved at Lily and the reverend. "Come on, let's—"

The doors burst open and hit the walls with the sound of two gunshots, and Mace came out, arms held up, elbows locked, smiling. His arms dropped, and the wind blew his hair around his head as the teenagers followed him into the parking lot, gushing out of the club like blood from an open wound.

Mace led them between two rows of parked cars, passing less than ten feet in front of J.R. and the others as if they weren't there. The teenagers following him were just as loud as they had been in the club and their laughter and shouting was whipped away by the wind, echoing across the parking lot.

J.R. watched with sickening horror as they continued to pour out of the club. He saw, with some relief, that not all of them were following Mace. Some remained apart from the group, keeping pace, shouting as they hurried along.

"—do you think you're *going,* Matty, what's he gonna—"

"—ease come back, *please,* something bad is gonna—"

"—this is *it* with us if you go, do you under—"

There were parents following the crowd, too, staying to the side, keeping a good distance, some arguing among themselves, others calling their sons and daughters.

A heavyset woman wearing a tan raincoat over a nurse's uniform: "Dammit, Rhonda, come back here right now, do you hear—"

A small black woman held her purse over her head to protect her hair from the rain and paced agitatedly as the parade of teenagers passed by. "You be back by eleven-thirty, Beth," she shouted, "or you're grounded for a *week!*"

There were about fifteen others—not very many, considering how many J.R. had called—looking for their children, shouting disciplinary threats. J.R. recognized a few of them as parents he'd spoken with that day, but one in particular caught his attention. He didn't recognize the face, but the voice was unmistakable. It was Mr. Brubaker, Wayne Brubaker's father. J.R. had had a very unpleasant telephone conversation with him earlier, and the man looked exactly as he'd sounded on the phone: short dark hair and a bushy beard and mustache, thick neck, a red plaid shirt under a camouflage down jacket. Brubaker had become irate when J.R. explained why he was calling, accusing J.R. of trying to tell him how to raise his son.

"I'm not doing that at all," J.R. had said patiently, "I'm just trying to keep him out of trouble."

"Well, that's my job, okay?" the man had barked. "The trouble stuff is *my* job, and you stay out of it."

J.R. assumed the timid-looking woman with him was Mrs. Brubaker. Her hands fluttered nervously at the buttons of her long brown coat, and she looked as if she might blow away with the wind.

"I *knew* we shouldn't've come!" Brubaker shouted. "I wish I hadn't told you about that goddamned phone call."

Mrs. Brubaker craned her neck, searching the passing horde for her son.

"I don't *see* him!" she cried. "Do you? Do you see him?"

"Oh, Christ, Barbara, he'll come back, he always *does.*"

"But I just saw him a second ago, he was right in front of me. Something's wrong here. Wayne! Waaayyyne!"

"Oh, God, don't go wailin' for him now!"

Mace led the teenagers around the corner of the building and down the sidewalk on Lankershim. There were still some more coming out of the club, hurrying to catch up. J.R. wondered how many there were. A hundred and fifty? Two hundred? More?

"Jeff isn't with them," Erin said, moving closer to him. She sounded weak, sick with fear. "Jeff and Mallory must still be in the club."

"I don't think so," J.R. said. "I think they left earlier."

"We have to go back in and see if—"

"*No.* We don't know how many of those things are in there."

"I think I know where he's taking them," the reverend said, watching the last of the teenagers disappear around the corner.

Lily spoke up: "The health club." She was crying quietly.

The reverend nodded and turned to J.R. "The basement."

It sounded ludicrous at first; surely the basement of that abandoned building was not big enough to accommodate that many people. But he knew Mace wasn't taking them there for a social gathering. An unexpected thought sent a physical jolt through his body:

You can stack dead bodies . . .

J.R. looked around the parking lot; the parents and

remaining teenagers were quickly breaking up, hurrying through the rain to their cars.

"Wait!" J.R. called, stepping away from Erin. "Please, wait a second!"

In a flash of lightning, he saw them turning to him one by one. There were about thirty of them, their skin corpse-white for an instant. After the thunder shot through the sky, J.R. said, "We have an idea where they're going. If we can—"

Mr. Brubaker stepped forward and barked, "Hey! You the guy who called me today?"

"Yes, I called because—"

"Look, who the hell do you think you are, scarin' people like this, makin' 'em think their kids are in trouble when they're just hangin' out at a goddamned nightclub, for Christ's sake? C'mon, Barb, let's get outta here."

J.R.'s jaws burned as he angrily ground his teeth together. Brubaker was probably the type who loudly sucked his teeth after meals, belched his beer, and spent weekends shouting orders from his easy chair in front of the television. He didn't know the man but suddenly hated him as if they'd been enemies for a lifetime.

"Listen, mister!" J.R. shouted. "A girl just *killed* herself in there, and the man who walked off with those kids is responsible. Maybe for a lot of other suicides, too. And I can promise you, he's not taking those kids to see a movie! I've got a pretty good idea that a lot more are gonna die tonight." He took a few steps toward Brubaker as he went on. "Now, if I'm wrong, and I hope to God I am, then I'm sorry for inconveniencing you. But if I'm right, and you go back home, you might be getting a call later tonight from someone who wants you to come down to the morgue and identify your son's corpse. And if that happens, Mr. Brubaker"—he was inches from the man now and poked his chest with a stiff index finger—"if that happens, I'm gonna look you up, get in your face, and say I fuckin' told you so!"

Brubaker slapped J.R.'s hand away, growled an obscenity, took his wife's arm, and turned toward the car again.

Mrs. Brubaker pulled away and snapped, *"No!* If you

want to go home, you can, but I'm not going until our son is with me!"

Brubaker was clearly shocked at his wife's tone of voice and stared at her openmouthed.

The others in the parking lot slowly gathered closer, looking on like an attentive theater audience.

With quiet threat, Brubaker said, "You're gonna get in that car and—"

"No. No, I am not! I don't think you've noticed in the last sixteen years, but we have a son! And if there's a chance something might happen to him tonight, I'm going to find him, and if you want to go home, then go. Just get in the truck and go. I don't care. I'll find a—"

Mr. Brubaker rushed toward her as if he was going to hit her; instead, he hunched forward and said, "Okay, all *right,* goddammit, we'll—" His voice dropped to a confidential hiss that was drowned by the wind.

J.R. turned to the others and said, "I think he's taken them to the abandoned health club on the corner of Ventura and Whitley. There are a few things you should know. . . ." He wasn't sure how to go on without sounding like a nut; he needed to warn them about Mace's animals, but he didn't want to destroy any credibility he might have with them. When he turned uncertainly to the reverend, Bainbridge stepped forward.

"This fellow Mace," he said, "he has . . . animals. Small, vicious animals. Maybe you saw some of them here tonight. They're well trained."

"So we're going to have to protect ourselves," J.R. said. "If anyone has any weapons . . ."

There was no response at first. They stood in the dark parking lot, soaked and shivering, looking confused and scared. A Hispanic man spoke up.

"Why don't we just call the police?"

"It looks like Mace has some friends in the police department," J.R. replied. "I don't think that would be a good idea."

"Who is this man?" asked the woman in the nurse's uniform. "What does he want with our children?"

"We aren't sure who he is, but whatever he wants, it's not good. Now. Weapons?"

No reply for a moment, then Brubaker nodded and said hesitantly, "Yeah, I've . . . I've, um, got some guns at home."

Relieved, J.R. said, "Okay. We'd better get moving. We may not have much time. . . ."

PART V

Crucifax
Exodus

Twenty-eight

Kevin had not followed Mace and the others out of the club; he'd gone out the stage door, furiously slamming it behind him, and down the manhole in the alley. He had no light but felt his way along the walls and flicked his butane lighter as he hurried through the black, cobwebbed passages where he could hear the raspy breathing of bums curled in the corners.

Kevin was angry and hurt; he felt betrayed by Mace. The band had performed only two songs, and neither had been songs Kevin had written. Once the crowd in Fantazm began to get out of hand, it didn't take Kevin long to realize that he and his band were being used. He wasn't sure exactly how or why, but it was obvious that Mace's intentions went beyond merely giving a performance. Kevin had heard of working a crowd, but Mace had done much more than that; the moment he'd stepped onto the stage, he'd *owned* that crowd. Kevin realized that a lot of the kids in the audience already knew Mace, but even those who didn't acted as if they'd been waiting for him, needed him. It was a little scary. Kevin was already kicking himself for putting his trust in Mace, but after the concert at Fantazm, it seemed more than just a betrayal; he felt he'd been deceived on a deeper level, in a way that he was just now beginning to see and might never truly understand.

He'd taken no drugs since returning from the center. Perhaps, he'd considered, his gullibility had been due to his perpetually altered state of consciousness; maybe he was seeing his mistakes now because his head was finally clear. Mace *had* been very persistent in his offer of drugs during their first meeting. . . .

As if it weren't enough that the band's first performance had been a huge disappointment, Mallory had left shortly after they'd begun playing the first song.

Like she all of a sudden didn't give a damn, he thought as he ducked through the hole and into the sub-basement of the health club. Mallory had been so supportive, so excited about the concert, that Kevin had nearly stopped playing when he saw her rushing out of the nightclub followed by her brother.

But the worst thing of all was the girl who had dragged the edge of her Crucifax across her throat and collapsed in a convulsing, bleeding heap onto the floor. The blackout had helped to cover it. In fact, it made him wonder if that was really what he'd seen or if, in all the noise and smoke, he'd been mistaken. But the more he thought about it, the more certain he became that he had not imagined the girl's suicide. And with her Crucifax . . .

Kevin felt his own Crucifax shifting beneath his shirt and thought of the sharp edges, the first time he'd touched one and cut his finger. . . .

This will be your escape from all that you hate, from all the people who don't understand you. . . .

Mace had also said something about the Crucifax being a key. A key to what?

A place where no one will ever let you down again . . .

The girl in Fantazm had not hesitated for an instant when she lifted the Crucifax to her throat. . . .

. . . a place where everyone is equal and there are no lies.

. . . as if she was not only willing to cut her throat open, but eager.

336

Mace had been talking about going to someplace better, someplace perfect, ever since they'd met—

. . . a place where everyone is equal and there are no lies.

—but that place no longer sounded so perfect after all.

Lantern light glowed from the deep end of the pool, and Kevin went to the edge. Mallory was sitting naked against the side of the pool, a blanket gathered around her. There was a lantern at her side, the cover off, the reflected light of the flame glimmering in a spoon that rested on a fold of the blanket. Jeff lay across Mallory's lap, his body limp, eyes only half open, naked but for the blanket that covered his legs. A belt was wrapped tightly around his upper arm. Mallory was lovingly stroking his hair.

Kevin took a breath to call her name, to ask her what she was doing, but stopped when he saw the syringe in her right hand.

"Mallory!"

She looked up slowly, her eyes heavy, and stared at him as if he were a stranger.

"Mallory, what the hell . . ."

Recognition dawned in her dulled eyes, and her mouth worked silently, then smiled.

"Hi," she said.

"What . . . what're you . . . Jesus, Mallory, he's your *brother.*"

She giggled, then looked down at Jeff again, lowering the needle to his arm.

"No!" Kevin shouted, running along the edge of the pool to the stepladder. He stumbled into the pool and dodged the stirring figures on the floor as he hurried to Mallory. He grabbed her wrist and squeezed hard. "Drop it."

"Nooo," she whined, trying to pull away, but he held on, using his other hand to pry her fingers off the syringe.

When he had it away from her, she turned from him, pouting, stroking her brother's hair again. Kevin hunkered down and lifted Jeff's arms, looking carefully at the elbows for needle marks. None.

"Mallory." He lifted her face. "What's he on?"

"Just some of Mace's grass."

"How much of this shit have you had?"

337

"Just . . . a little. I told you I don't like it much."

"Then why the *fuck*—"

"Hey, what's the problem?" a groggy male voice asked from another corner of the pool.

"Get up," Kevin said, ignoring the voice.

"No. And gimme that."

Mallory reached for the syringe, but Kevin dropped it to the floor and crunched it beneath his foot. "Get up and put your clothes on."

"You don't own me, Kevin!"

Jeff opened his eyes and wearily lifted his head, confused.

"Mace is gonna be here any minute," Kevin said.

"So?"

"We've made a mistake, Mallory. Getting involved with him was a mistake. He's lied to us, he used the band. And there was a girl in the club tonight—she slashed her throat with her Crucifax. She *killed* herself, Mallory, and I think that's what Mace wanted. I think . . . I think maybe that's what he wants all of us to do."

"I don't want to go. You leave if you want."

A month ago, Kevin would not have hesitated to leave without her. But seeing her there with Jeff, hearing the chill in her voice as she so casually dismissed him, made Kevin's chest feel hollow, empty, as if it had been scraped clean.

"Mallory, I thought . . . I thought you cared about me."

"I thought you cared about me. If you did, you wouldn't want me to leave here, go home to my mother"—she spat the word with disgust—"instead of staying here where I'm happy."

"You're not happy, you're stoned."

She turned away from him again, as if he weren't there. Frustrated, Kevin gripped Jeff's arm and pulled him into a sitting position.

"Leave him alone!" Mallory cried, trying to push Kevin away.

Kevin roughly pulled the belt off Jeff's arm, tossed it aside, then shook him by the shoulders, trying to rouse him.

Jeff blinked, looked around, and muttered, "What? What's-matter?"

338

"We've gotta go, Jeff," Kevin said. "C'mon, get dressed, we've gotta get outta here."

"Stop it!" Mallory hissed, standing. "Leave him alone! He wants to stay with me!" She slapped at Kevin's hands until he let go of Jeff, who modestly pulled the blanket around himself and stood, bracing himself against the wall.

There was a loud clamor from upstairs; voices echoed down the spiral staircase—laughter and rowdy catcalls and howls—and footsteps sounded on the stairs.

Kevin said, "C'mon, hurry, get dressed!"

"Why?" Jeff asked as Mallory pressed close to him, slipping an arm beneath the blanket and around his waist. "What's wrong?"

Kevin looked at Mallory and was shocked at the look of defiance in her eyes, as if she knew Jeff would never go against her wishes. She was not the Mallory he'd known a week ago.

"Mace is coming!" he whispered.

"Well . . . Mallory says she wants to stay, so . . ." Jeff shrugged a shoulder.

"So you come. Jesus, if you can't save her, at least save your—"

"Hello, Kevin."

Kevin turned and looked up. Mace stood between two of the creatures; they each stared at Kevin, neither moving so much as a whisker. Kevin looked up, followed Mace's body from his black boots at the edge of the pool to his head, which seemed to be a hundred feet above him. His arms were folded over his chest, and the lantern in the pool cast deep shadows over his face.

Kevin's mouth became dry, and he could feel his heart beating in his throat.

"Something wrong, Kevin?"

"N-no, I was—I was just—"

"Kevin!" Trevor came to Mace's side and grinned down at Kevin. "Was that rad or what? Did you see that crowd? They went crazy! Jesus, they loved us—loved us!"

Mark was standing behind Trevor; both of them were nearly dancing with excitement.

The room was suddenly booming with movement and voices, webbed with slinking shadows.

"I thought it went pretty well, didn't you, Kevin?" Mace asked. Even through the shadows that crept over his face, Mace's sparkling golden eyes remained clearly visible, daring Kevin to disagree.

Kevin said nothing but tried to stare Mace down, tried to keep his eyes locked with Mace's, unblinking and unaverted, hoping to show him that he was no longer willing to bend to Mace's every wish.

He couldn't do it; his eyes closed for a moment, and he turned away.

Someone called Mace, and he moved away from the pool, out of sight.

"Get out of here, Jeff," Kevin whispered harshly, "before he notices you. Take Mallory with you! I'm not fuckin' *kiddin'* you, man, this is trouble. Now get your clothes on and go!" He turned to get out of the pool; the two creatures at the pool's edge had not moved. They stared at him with narrowed eyes, and one of them flicked its tongue over its black lips.

Kevin tried to act as if he hadn't noticed them and climbed up the stepladder at the other end.

It was standing room only in the pool room. Kevin had to push people out of the way to get through, and he was suddenly overcome with a panicky, trapped feeling.

Mace's head stood above the others; his back was to Kevin.

The spiral staircase was blocked by teenagers going up and down the steps, sitting, standing against the rail. If he was going to get out, Kevin would have to go down to the sub-basement and through the sewer.

Mace was watching him now, moving toward him.

Kevin tried to push through faster, but the crowd was too thick to hurry through, and a moment later Mace's hand rested on his shoulder.

"What's on your mind, buddy?"

Kevin turned slowly to face him.

"Something's wrong. What is it? The concert? You were disappointed."

"Well, we . . . we didn't play any of my songs," Kevin said haltingly.

"Didn't have time."

"Why didn't we have time?"

"Because of this." He smiled, gestured at the roomful of teenagers.

"What do you mean?"

"I stopped so we could bring them here. They were ready. Besides, the power went out anyway."

"Ready for what?"

"To come here. To leave with us."

"Leave?"

"I told you we were going away. And we made a deal, remember? You promised you'd go ahead of me to be with the ones who've already gone."

Kevin was bumped and jostled as he stood before Mace, anger and fear stirring together inside him, confidence building slowly but surely.

"Who?" he asked with a slight tremble. *"Who's* already gone? That girl in the club, maybe? The one who cut her throat?"

Mace silently stared at him with a shadow of a smile playing at his lips; he looked as if he was about to wink.

"Where is this place?"

"I told you," Mace said. "A place where there are no—"

"But *where?* I mean, is it in California? Back east? Out of the country?" He was suddenly out of breath as he took a step back and bumped into someone. "Or does it exist at all? Huh? Does it?"

Again, Mace didn't reply. Instead, he bent down, held out an arm, and let one of his pets scurry up to his shoulder, then stood again. The creature's eyes were level with Kevin's, and an almost inaudible growl came from deep in its throat.

"You're not taking us anywhere, are you?" Kevin said, but his voice was a whisper, as weak and thin as he felt, lost in all the noise. Still, he was certain Mace had heard him clearly. Kevin spun away from him and fought his way toward the back of the room and the sub-basement door. With a backward glance, he saw that Mace was following him, moving with ease through the open path Kevin was leaving behind.

"We have a deal, Kevin!" he called.

"*Fuck* your deal!" He made it to the doorway and started down the stairs, trying not to slip on the wet metal steps.

"We're leaving tonight!"

"I'm not going." Mace's boots clanged on the stairs behind him.

"You don't have a choice, Kevin. You don't have anyplace else to go."

Kevin reached the bottom of the stairs, crunching over rubble, hunched down, and put a leg through the hole, his foot crinkling the Doritos bag on the other side. When he was out of the sub-basement, he looked back through the hole.

Mace was off the stairs and striding toward him.

"It's too late now," Mace said. "You have nowhere to go. You need me now more than ever."

Kevin made a soft humming sound, hoping to drown Mace's voice from his ears as he felt his way along the wall of the sewer.

"Don't you take their food!" Mace shouted, his voice resounding through the dark. "They deserve to eat too, you know!" Then he laughed.

Take their food? Kevin thought, stopping a moment, puzzled. It made no sense.

Over the rushing sewage and the sounds of dripping water, Kevin heard distant sirens and bleating car horns through the grates above him.

He moved on again, groping for the metal rungs on which he would climb out of the sewer. His hand slid along the coarse, slimy wall—

—until the wall disappeared, and his arm passed through dark, cool emptiness, and his hand fell on a clammy face that moved as it said in a phlegmy voice, "You gonna take our foooood?"

A greasy hand slapped onto his wrist, and bony fingers closed in an iron grip, pulling as Kevin cried out. He held the edge of the opening and tried to pull himself back.

Shuffling footsteps came toward him in the dark, and another hand clutched the sleeve of his jacket.

"Our food?" a voice rasped. "Take our food?"

"No, *no!*" Kevin shouted.

Once again, Mace's laughter echoed musically through the sewer.

Kevin's sleeve tore as he wrenched his arm away, nearly falling backward and into the waste. His hand slapped over the wall as he hurried on.

He was followed by unsteady footsteps and heavy breathing, and he expected at any moment to feel that hand grab his shoulder. . . .

"Just who you think you are, comin' to take our food?" the voice growled behind him.

Kevin skidded to a clumsy halt when he felt one of the rungs and he pulled himself up off the floor. The rungs were wet, and his palms were sweaty. Each time he closed his hand around one of the bars, he felt his grip rapidly slipping, so he quickly reached for the next and the next, concentrating on the manhole above him and not the raspy breathing just below.

"Nowhere to go, Kevin!" Mace called. "Nowhere except with us!"

As he reached the top and pushed hard on the underside of the manhole cover a hand closed on his right foot.

The cover clattered on the pavement above, and rain fell on Kevin's face, blinding him for a moment as he began kicking his foot, chanting under his breath, "No, no, no, no, no . . ." He put his left foot on the next rung, reached a hand through the hole, gripped the edge, and bounded upward. His foot tore away from the clutching hand, and he lifted himself out of the hole and into the fresh, rainy air above.

Kevin rolled away from the hole and onto his knees, then stood over the open hole and began to kick the cover back in place.

Lightning illuminated the long white face, the yawning mouth, and the deep-set shadow-black eyes framed by the manhole. The thunder that followed was loud enough to bury the heavy clang of the cover being kicked back into place.

Gasping for air, he took a moment to look around and get his bearings. He was in the alley behind the health club.

Mace was right; he had nowhere to go, no one to turn to. . . .

Except his family.

He headed west down the alley toward Woodman, walking at first, then jogging, then running as if pursued. He had no idea where he would go yet; it was movement he wanted, free and fast movement to shake away the feeling of being trapped and the thought that ate at him relentlessly:

He's right, he's right, Mace is right, nowhere, I've got nowhere to go, nowhere, nowhere. . . .

Except home.

"C'mon," Mallory whispered, tugging on Jeff's arm, "down here." She pulled him back down on the cushion with her and cuddled up to him, kissing his neck. "Want some more grass?"

Jeff relaxed against the side of the pool. He had never been so stoned.

"Don't think so," he muttered.

"Sure?"

The effect of the drugs enhanced his senses, making the warmth of Mallory's body next to him so overwhelming, he feared that if he had any more, their skin would melt together.

"Yeah, I'm sure."

The crowd gathered in the room sounded like a machine clattering and rattling away above them. Faces floated overhead like ghosts, and more people came into the pool. Jeff had to pull his legs in so they weren't stepped on, and as he moved them his foot brushed something sharp. He leaned over and squinted to bring the small object into focus.

A smashed syringe.

"Jeff," said a voice from above. Mace stood at the edge of the pool and smiled down at them. "I'm glad you decided to come. I knew you would. Are you going to leave with us?"

344

Before he could reply, Mallory said, "Yes, he's coming."

"Good," Mace nodded, holding out a hand. Something dangled from his fingers. "Put this on. You'll need it later. Catch." He tossed it into the pool, and the Crucifax fell into Jeff's cupped hands. He stared at it uncertainly for a moment, and Mace said, "Go ahead. Put it on."

Jeff put the cord around his neck and let the Crucifax rest just below his throat.

Mace gave him a broad, friendly grin, then turned and walked away.

Behind him, Mallory brushed her hands over Jeff's back, moved them down to his lap and licked his shoulder.

"C'mere," she breathed.

Glancing at the syringe again, Jeff said, "Mallory, what—" But her hands were lightly stroking his genitals, and as he turned to her his eyes fell on her outstretched arm and he saw the bruises. . . .

"Hey, Mal, what . . . what did you . . ."

"Never mind that. Come here, babe."

An alarm sounded somewhere in Jeff's murky brain. He looked at the needle again, then at Mallory's bruised arm, and he knew what he'd been seeing in his sister's eyes that did not belong, knew what was wrong. He wanted to take her out of that building immediately, but her hands were on him, and his head was full of cotton candy, and she felt so good in his arms, her skin was so smooth beneath his hands. . . .

"How about a little attention?" Mace bellowed. "Come on, quiet down."

The buzz of voices softened, died.

Jeff looked up and saw Mace standing on the diving board holding a lantern. The light shone on his face, giving it an ethereal glow.

"Can you all hear me?" he asked.

The response came as a roar, not only in the pool room but from upstairs as well.

"The storm outside," Mace said, "will be dead by tomorrow night. The sun will come out, and a lot of people will start telling you that you can't spend any more time with me. There are already some who've decided you're not

345

going to leave with me. They'll be here soon. They'll try to take you home. Away from me. I want to take you away from them, away from all that. And if you want to come, we have to leave tonight. Now."

The parking lot behind the abandoned health club was flooded with an inch of water, deeper in places, and J.R.'s feet sloshed through it as he walked away from his car, flashlight in hand. With him were Reverend Bainbridge, Erin, Lily, and twenty-six others. Three of the parents had gone home from Fantazm.

"My daughter is *not* a stupid girl!" a woman had said indignantly. "She's here with her friends. I just came to pick her up, that's all, and if she doesn't leave with me, you can bet her father's going to lay down some law tonight!"

The girl had not gone home with her mother, but the woman had refused to go after her with a bunch of "paranoid *nuts!*"

An Asian man, accompanied by his silent wife, had insisted that their two sons would be home by their curfew, eleven o'clock. The only reason he and his wife had come to the club, he claimed, was that they'd received an alarming and apparently misleading phone call from one of their sons' friends warning them of the danger their sons would be in if they went to the concert.

Before leaving, J.R. had abandoned caution and, with the reverend's support, told them everything he knew about Mace. They had stared silently at him, and J.R. couldn't tell if they were frightened by what he'd said or convinced that he and the reverend were insane.

"I've got a .357 in my truck," Brubaker had said, sounding a bit more interested once he knew Mace and his pets might be dangerous. "A knife and a tire iron, too. If he gives us any trouble . . ."

They avoided the traffic problems on Ventura and the other boulevards by taking side streets and alleys to the health club, traveling as a small caravan of five cars and Will Brubaker's black Dodge Ram.

When they arrived, Brubaker ignored J.R.'s warning that any shooting might hurt some of the kids and got the gun from his truck. He handed his tire iron to the reverend and a large bone-handled hunting knife to J.R.

When J.R. tried the door, it wouldn't open.

"Locked on the inside," he said, giving the handle another strong pull.

"We could use the sewer," Lily suggested.

Brubaker turned to her and barked, *"What?"*

"The sewer. That's how he usually comes and goes. There's a hole in the wall of the sub-basement."

Brubaker stepped forward, laughing coldly. "I'm not going down no goddamned sewer." Stuffing the gun beneath his belt, he gripped the door handle with both of his large, meaty hands and pulled with a powerful heave; the door made a resounding crack and wobbled open with a rusty squall.

The corridor beyond the door glowed with a smoky yellowish light that danced over the walls playfully, almost invitingly. At the end of the corridor, shadows spilled over the floor and walls, human-shaped shadows that shifted and melted together into a shapeless mass.

The silence inside the building surprised J.R. Like the hush that had fallen over the nightclub earlier, it had an attentive reverence to it, a churchlike silence interrupted only by throat-clearing coughs and a few sniffs, and finally a voice, full and clear, that broke the brief silence like a pick through ice.

". . . a place where there is no immorality . . . no morality, either . . ." the voice boomed, speaking in a lulling tone, with a rhythmic cadence that bobbed up and down like a boat on gentle waters.

"Mace," Lily whispered.

". . . where you are accepted as you are, with no changes required . . ."

"Okay, what the hell we waiting for?" Brubaker growled quietly.

J.R. started through the door, but Brubaker pushed ahead of him.

"There are people who don't want you to go with me," Mace went on.

Halfway down the corridor, J.R. glanced over his shoulder to make sure the others were following, then rounded a corner to the right with Brubaker, coming to a stop.

"They want to keep you here, under their hands. . . ."

They faced the backs of a dozen teenagers gathered at the top of a staircase that spiraled downward, blocked by many more, all silent and listening. In spite of the loud noise Brubaker had made opening the door, none of the teenagers seemed to know anyone had come in. Their attention was pinned to the voice below.

J.R. wondered if this was how his sister's friends and classmates had spent their last moments of life in the Old Red Barn in El Cerrito; if they had stood in such dead silence, listening to the last words they would ever hear, spoken by the man and woman who had led them to their deaths.

". . . they want you to think that they care about you so much that they don't want you to go away, when they really don't care about you at all . . ."

He took a step forward and looked over a few shoulders and into the room below. From where he stood, he had a profile view of Mace from the chest up; his smile seemed to cover his whole face and glowed with warmth.

". . . and those people," Mace continued, slowly turning toward him, gazing up through the crowd and into J.R.'s eyes, "have arrived. . . ."

Kevin had never seen his neighborhood so black.

He'd run until he could run no more, leaving the alley for side streets, zigzagging through Studio City and North Hollywood, finally coming to a gasping stop against a darkened lamppost. When he spotted the police helicopter coming his way, spotlight cutting the rain, he'd limped between two houses and hunkered down in the shelter of a carport to catch his breath. Once his heart had slowed its machine-gun pace, he realized his shoulder was pressed against the front wheel of a bicycle. Quiet as a whisper, he walked the bike out of the carport, hopped on, and sped down the street.

During his wet and miserably uncomfortable ride to Encino, the past weeks replayed themselves in his mind:

meeting Mace . . . his excitement over the possibility of getting the band on a stage . . . convincing Mallory to join him . . . giving more trust and admiration to Mace than he'd ever given anyone in his life . . .

Twice he had to double back to avoid streets and sidewalks that had been flooded, and the sirens howled in the distance like lonely wolves. In a platinum instant of lightning, he saw a dead cat floating down a flooded gutter. Everything around him seemed to be splitting open and spilling its insides like cattle being butchered. He had to slow his speed on the bike because hot tears were filling his eyes and blurring his vision. He felt angry at himself not only because he'd allowed Mace to deceive and use him, but most of all because he'd gotten Mallory involved.

As he passed through his neighborhood in Encino he saw candlelight glowing in windows, secretive shadows flitting over curtains. His parents' house showed no signs of life.

Legs aching, side burning, Kevin staggered around the garage and went in the side door. Inside, the garage was black, but Kevin was familiar enough with its layout to feel his way around the two cars and his motorcycle. At the door that led into the kitchen, he stopped.

He had come only because he had nowhere else to go. Now that he was there, he didn't know what he was going to say or do. Surely they wouldn't turn him away. Surely once they heard what was about to happen to Mallory and the guys in the band, they would help them. Especially if he promised to cooperate with them, to go along with any rules or punishments they wanted to administer. Anything was better than letting Mace do what Kevin was certain he had planned. . . .

As he lifted his arm to knock, leaning heavily against the doorjamb, he felt his Crucifax move against his chest, cold and wet.

"Who's there?" his mother called when he knocked. Her voice was distant, from another room.

"Mom?" Kevin called timidly, his voice hoarse and mangled from crying. "Dad? It's me. Kevin."

Silence.

"Unlock the door?"

"What are you doing here?" his father snapped, obviously standing at the door. "What have you done?"

"Done? I, I, I—"

Speaking quickly and with growing anger, he said, "Do you know the police are looking for you, do you know that people are dead because of what happened at the teen center, *dead?* What did you do to them?"

"I didn't, I didn't—"

"And you have the nerve to come back here?"

"Just let me in and I'll—"

"You're not coming back into this house, not now, not ever!"

Kevin slid down the doorjamb and thumped onto the step below, crying. "I need—I need help, Dad. My, my girlfriend—Mallory?—she's in—in trouble."

"In trouble, huh? You want money, is that why you're here? Well, that's over. We've given to you, given and given, and all you do is—"

"No, she's gonna—gonna *die,* Dad, she's—"

"What are you on, Kevin? I can't believe you've come here on drugs after what you've done—"

"They're all gonna die!" he screamed.

"Get out. Get out of the garage and away from this house. Now!"

"Please, Daddy, please, you gotta help me, they're all gonna—"

"That's it. Renee, call the police."

"Nooo!" Kevin cried.

"Just call them now, goddammit."

"Dad, they're gonna kill themselves, all of them, and he's—"

"Your mother's calling the police, and if you think I'm going to protect you when they get here, you're wrong. I hope they put you behind bars! We've tried, Kevin, we have tried so hard to work with you, give to you, make you happy, but nothing we do ever seems to . . ."

His father's voice faded beneath the pounding in Kevin's head as he tried to crawl away from the door—

It's too late now. . . .

—choking on his sobs—

. . . you have nowhere to go. . . .

—leaning against the back wall of the garage beneath the large shelf Kevin had helped his dad make when he was a little boy.

. . . you need me now more than ever.

As his father's voice rambled on and on, Kevin became acutely aware of the leather cord around his neck and the Crucifax hanging beneath his soaked shirt. He leaned his head back against the wall, and when he closed his eyes he saw it, black-red and smooth, edges sharp as steel blades. . . .

. . . nowhere to go . . .

". . . that we have done all we can, Kevin, we're finished!" his father continued. "You are on your own from now on, do you understand?"

Mace was right. He had nothing, no one. The police would arrive soon and take him away, question him endlessly, lock him up, and question him some more. By tomorrow, Mallory would be gone, if her brother didn't get her away from Mace, and Kevin doubted he would. Kevin would be alone, even more alone than he felt at that moment in the dark, damp garage.

Nowhere to go, Kevin!

And he knew he would be unable to bear that.

Nowhere except with us!

Kevin pulled the Crucifax out of his shirt, held it tightly in a fist—

"You've lied to us, defied us, ignored us, and all we do is give, give, give!"

—turned his head to the right and tilted it back, pulling the skin of his throat taut—

"Well, we've *stopped* giving, Kevin, we've—we've—we've given up! You're hopeless, worthless, you've proven that to us!"

—and slowly lifted his hand until the deadly edge of the Crucifax was pressed just beneath his jaw.

351

Lightning flashed through the small windows, and for an instant the garage was brightly lit. Peripherally, Kevin saw his motorcycle, unridden for over a week, saw his parents' cars, the lawnmower, and he realized in a small corner of his mind that they might be the last things he would ever see.

But he saw something else in that fraction of time, something directly in front of his eyes, hanging on the wall beside him, beneath the shelf: his father's double-bladed axe.

The end of the handle was inches from his left eye, and hanging above him on two nails was the rusted head, with a flaring blade on each side.

Kevin let go of the Crucifax, reached through the dark, and touched the smooth wooden handle.

"Until you grow up, until you learn a little responsibility and decency and gratitude," his father continued, "well, as far as I'm concerned, I have only one son!"

Struggling to his feet, Kevin took the axe from its nails and hefted it in his hands. It felt good, heavy and solid, and it seemed to suck his grief and sadness, the unbearable loss he was feeling, from him and put in its place a fiery, boiling hate. A hate he'd never felt for anyone, not even his parents in their worst moments. A hate so powerful, it constricted his throat and forced him to take in a sudden gasp of breath. This time it was for those golden eyes, that disarming, heart-winning smile, and that cool, clear, soothing voice: Mace.

. . . *you need me now more than ever.* . . .

"Wrong," Kevin rasped.

He took the keys to his motorcycle from the hook beside the kitchen door, went to the other end of the garage, and pulled open the long rectangular door with a loud clatter.

"Kevin?" his father shouted. "Kevin, what're you doing?"

He took his helmet from the seat of his motorcycle, put it on, and climbed aboard the bike, placing the axe across the handlebars.

The lock on the kitchen door rattled, and his father pulled the door open as Kevin started his bike.

"Kevin, you can't—"

His voice was drowned by the engine's roar.

Kevin eased the bike between his parents' cars, then shot down the driveway in an explosion of light from the sky. . . .

Twenty-nine

Standing beside Will Brubaker, Erin could see nothing beyond J.R.'s shoulders. The others behind her pressed forward to look for their children or their friends, and Erin began to feel claustrophobic, trapped.

Touching J.R.'s back, Erin whispered, "Can you see them? Are Jeff and Mallory down there?"

J.R. reached back for her hand and gently pulled her forward to his side.

All eyes were turned to the top of the staircase, human eyes as well as slanted eyes that glittered from the darkest corners below.

"Jeff? Mallory?" Erin called, and, as if on cue, several other names were called behind her—

"Wayne?"

"Janet?"

"Brenda?"

"Mark!"

"Davey?"

"Linda!"

—a chorus that rose sharply and then died.

Mace stepped off the diving board and walked around the pool, smiling up at them all the while.

"Mallory," he said, "your mother's here."

A figure rose slowly out of the pool, climbing the stepladder, and went to Mace's side.

Mallory was draped in a blanket, which she held together at her throat. She leaned on Mace, her eyes turned upward but focusing on nothing in particular.

Erin relaxed against J.R., relieved to see her daughter again; something was obviously not right with the girl, but at least she was alive.

Mace called Jeff, and he, too, came out of the pool and joined Mallory. He wore only his jeans, unbuttoned in front; a Crucifax glistened against his chest. With a graceful flourish, Mace put his arm around Mallory's shoulders and said, "She wants to take you home, Mallory," gently stroking her hair and still smiling at Erin and J.R.

Erin was sickened by the sight of him touching her daughter; she gripped the cold metal railing of the staircase and shouted, "Leave them alone, let them *go!*"

"But I'm not holding them," Mace replied amiably. "They're all free to go whenever they want. They just don't *want* to. Why do you suppose that is, Mrs. Carr?"

Erin closed her eyes a moment, knowing precisely why they didn't want to come home and hating herself for it.

J.R. took her hand again and led her down the crowded, dizzying stairs.

"Jeff," he said softly, "Mallory, you know this is wrong. It's a mistake, you know it. Don't you? Jeff? What are you doing here?"

Erin watched her son frown, confused, and look from J.R. to Mallory, then to her, his face bathed in the glow from the pool, his eyes filled with hurt.

"I . . . I'm not . . . sure," he whispered.

"I know what you saw," J.R. said, slowly leading Erin through the crowd toward them. "I know what happened this evening, and I know you're hurt, disappointed . . . but *this?* This isn't going to help anything."

He kept looking at Erin, and it took all of her strength not to turn away from his pain.

"Jeff, remember when I told you I had a younger sister?" J.R. asked. "Remember? Can you hear me, Jeff?"

Jeff looked slowly from Erin to J.R. and moved his head in a slight, almost imperceptible nod.

"She died, Jeff," he went on, his voice growing unsteady. "Killed herself. Hanged herself in a closet. Do you know why? Because two people, John and Dara, convinced her they would take her to a better place. *A better place*, Jeff. You hear me, Mallory? John and Dara told my sister the same thing Mace has been telling you, and because of them, my sister and twenty-nine others killed themselves." His voice sounded clogged with tears now, and he took a deep breath to hold them back.

When Erin realized what he was saying, she felt a deep, profound chill. Whatever was happening was much bigger than she'd thought.

"They didn't go to a better place," J.R. said. "They just died and got buried. My parents weren't willing to work with my sister, accept her, be honest with her, so she felt she had no other choice. But your mother isn't that way." He reached back and squeezed her arm, as if telling her to take over.

"I'm sorry, Jeff," she said, her voice a quavering murmur. They stopped three yards away from Jeff and Mallory. "Mallory? I'm *sorry*. I was doing everything I could to support you, both of you. I didn't mean to lie to you or be deceptive. I just didn't tell you, that's all. You're my life, you're all I have. We just haven't . . . I haven't tried hard enough to stay close. And I'm so . . . very . . . sorry."

Jeff's face softened for a moment.

"Mom . . ." he muttered.

Mallory turned to him and calmly, coldly said, "She's a whore."

The words pierced Erin's gut like a barbed spike.

"Okay," Will Brubaker boomed from above, his feet clanking heavily down the stairs. "Fuck *this* noise." He pushed by Erin, gun in hand. J.R. tried to stop him, but Brubaker pulled away.

"Oh, Wayne?" Mace called, amused. "Your dad brought a gun!"

There was a small stirring in the crowd behind Mace, and a slump-shouldered boy with gold-streaked black hair wearing a white T-shirt came to his side.

"Wayne!" Mrs. Brubaker called from the stairs. "Wayne, you come up here right now!" Her voice was ragged from crying, and she seemed to be straining to keep it under control.

As she was calling her son Will Brubaker was plowing through the crowd toward Mace, growling, "You're goddamned right I brought a gun, and I'm gonna use it on your ugly long-haired head if you don't let these kids go." He stopped and leveled the gun with Mace's head less than two feet away.

"Brubaker . . ." J.R. warned.

Mace said, "You don't need that, Mr. Brubaker. Anyone here who wants to go can leave now. No problem!" He grinned and opened his arms a moment, looking around, then let them slap to his sides.

Silence pulsed through the building for a moment. A long, dreamlike moment. Erin watched her children, sweat seeping between her fingers as she clenched her fists.

All at once, as if they had rehearsed it, the parents on the staircase rushed down to the pool room calling their sons and daughters, some pleading, some shouting disciplinary threats.

The teenagers behind them pleaded with their friends and siblings to leave, to get away from Mace, and their voices mixed with those of the parents around them until they were all indistinguishable.

Lifting his hands above his head, Mace shouted, "Please, people! This is not a white sale at Macy's. Let them decide."

A silence thick as mud oozed through the room until only the whisper of the sewer below and the shuffling of feet on the floor could be heard. . . .

As Jeff watched his mother he felt something change in him, felt some of the fog clear behind his eyes.

"Mom," he said softly, but in the silence, his voice seemed louder than it actually was.

Erin took another step toward him, her eyes moving from Jeff to Mallory and back again.

"Did you hear me?" Mallory whispered. "She's a *whore*, Jeff, and a liar."

Erin sobbed as she moved a bit closer, and Jeff watched a tear roll down her cheek.

"Please don't say that, Mallory," she said. "I didn't know you would be so—so hurt, or I never would have—"

"How do you know she's not lying again, Jeff?" Mallory hissed.

Around them, voices rose from the crowd, timidly calling out to parents and friends, sounding weak and confused. One of the teenagers, a boy with short, spiky blond hair, stepped forward, reaching out a trembling hand.

Others came forward, shouldering their way to waiting parents who sighed their children's names with relief, taking their hands, hugging them, leading them to the stairs with cautious whispers.

". . . yes, let's go now, let's just go. . . ."

". . . go home and talk, your sister will be so happy. . . ."

". . . everything's going to be fine, now, honey, just . . ."

But not many decided to leave.

"Any more?" Mace called finally. "Anyone else want to go? It's up to you. You know what you're in for better than I."

His gun still raised, Brubaker said, "Okay, enough of this bullshit. None of these kids're staying here, got it?"

"You want to take them, Mr. Brubaker?"

"Damn right, and I'm starting with you, Wayne. Get your ass over there to your mother."

"Fine," Mace said. "You take them. But I . . . am leaving." Raising his voice to a booming shout, he said, "Anyone who wants to come with me will have to come now."

"And just where the fuck're you going?" Brubaker demanded.

Mace ignored him and began speaking in the same lulling manner he had minutes ago.

"There will be no pain," he said, "only a sudden relief, an immediate escape from the life you know now, the life you've tried so hard to leave behind. . . ."

"No!" the reverend shouted from the staircase, hurrying down to the floor. "Don't listen to him, he's *lying*. Think about what he's saying, what he's asking you to do!"

". . . you'll be free of the demands made upon you, the love denied you . . ."

Jeff felt dizzy because suddenly too many people were speaking at once.

The reverend was shouting, pleading. . . .

Mr. Brubaker was cursing Mace, moving the gun closer to his head, insisting that he shut up. . . .

J.R. snapped at Jeff as he tried to move closer, Erin at his side. . . .

An unexpected voice called from the staircase.

"Jeff!" Lily screamed. "Don't! Remember Nikki! You think she's happy now? Get up here, get Mallory and get up here!" Even in the poor light, the white of her knuckles was visible as she clutched the rail.

Others were shouting unfamiliar names from the staircase, some pleadingly, some angrily.

Jeff turned to his mother again.

Her eyes were open to their limit, her mouth gaping in horror as she tried to push toward them unsuccessfully, helplessly slapping J.R.'s shoulder and pointing at Mallory, screaming.

Jeff felt a small, soft hand on his bare arm, and he turned to Mallory as the blanket fell away from her naked body. She put her other hand between her breasts and closed her fingers over the Crucifax, slowly lifting it—

—and he suddenly became deaf to all the other sounds and voices in the room, could only hear his lungs filling with air as he sucked in a breath to shout at her, make her stop.

Jeff reached for her wrist as she spoke, but no matter how fast he tried to move, he couldn't move fast enough. Her soft voice seemed piercing in the blanket of silence that engulfed him:

"Please come with me, Jeff."

He thought he heard the tearing of her flesh as she pulled the Crucifax across her throat, the liquidy gush of blood that spurted from the gash and cascaded over her breasts and gathered in thick black-red droplets on her erect nipples.

The Crucifax dropped from her hand and splatted onto her bloody chest as she tried to gurgle his name, her hand clawing the air. Her grip on his arm tightened a moment, then eased up as her body began to sway.

When Jeff finally screamed—it was a long, ragged scream that seemed to tear the inside of his throat—the noise around him returned with a vengeance. Jeff heard his mother's wail and J.R.'s strained curses, but could not take his eyes off Mallory. Her blood spattered his face and chest as it continued to shoot from her throat in dark, wet strings. Jeff became dizzy and grabbed her shoulders, both to keep her from falling and to hold himself up. But he was still weak from the drugs, and his hands slipped through all the blood. Mallory fell forward, and she tried once again to say his name, but only more blood poured from her mouth.

She toppled into the deep end of the pool, landing with a muffled thump on the blankets and cushions. As she kicked and writhed in her last moments of life Mallory hit the uncovered kerosene lantern with a blood-streaked arm, knocking it on its side and spilling flames over the blankets.

By the time Mallory's hair began to burn, she was dead. . . .

Reverend Bainbridge saw Mallory Carr slash her throat seconds after he reached the floor of the pool room. An instant later, Wayne Brubaker did the same, spraying his father with his blood. Mr. Brubaker came apart; he dropped his gun, held his head in his hands as he stepped back, and began shrieking like a child as he watched his son die.

"We're leaving *now!*" Mace shouted, lifting his arms as if about to embrace the teenagers around him. "Don't let us be separated! Go now! *Now!*"

"Noooo!" the reverend screamed, his eyes filling with tears.

Smoke began to rise from the pool as Bainbridge pushed through the crowd, desperately looking for familiar faces, hoping to stop them, but knowing, as blood showered him from every direction, that he was too late.

He screamed the names of those he knew, pleading with them to stop, but their throats were already open, and their blood mingled with his tears, dribbled onto his lips and into his mouth. He tripped over the legs of a girl twisting on the floor and fell on top of her, trying to cough away the slick, coppery taste in his mouth, retching as more blood rained down on him.

Mustering his last ounces of faith, the reverend closed his eyes and prayed, hoping against hope that if there was a God—and there had to be some presence, some power, something, even if it was not the God he'd thought he was serving for so many years—He would have some feeling, some sympathy, for the kids.

As he began to pray—

Dear God, if You're there, if You have any feelings for us at all—

—one voice rose above the others and cut through the reverend's thoughts—

—*please, please make this stop now before we lose any more of them—*

—a voice that first made a flame of anger flare reflexively in the back of his mind, then brought a shadow of guilt—

—*if You would just give me the strength to help them, to help just one of them, just one—*

—Jim's voice. Jim, who had loved so much to write and whose work Bainbridge had torn up and thrown away. His voice—

—*Jim, let me help Jim, Lord, let me redeem myself, please. . . .*

—was growing louder, closer . . .

Bainbridge opened his eyes and sat up on his knees, saying Jim's name aloud as the boy's voice became even louder, and the reverend looked up into a screaming face of fire. The smell of sizzling flesh filled Bainbridge's nostrils as the flames fell on him, engulfed him, sucked the breath from his lungs.

The reverend's final thought as Jim's fiery arms embraced him was a silent plea for forgiveness, but it was not directed at God. . . .

* * *

J.R. gripped Erin's shoulders and shook her hard as she screamed again and again, her body trembling violently as she tried to push him aside.

"Erin, *stop* it, Erin!" he shouted. "You've gotta get out of here! Do you hear me? Listen to me!"

She pummeled him with half-clenched fists, screaming "Malloreeee! Malloreeee!"

"You can't help her, Erin, you've got to go now while you still can, before the fire—"

"Juh-Juh-Jeff, my God, where's Jeff?" Erin suddenly clutched his chest, her eyes darting around the room.

The stench of blood was beginning to cling to J.R., curdling his stomach; he thought he could feel it as well as smell it, like grease in the air, and he curled his nose against it, narrowed his eyes, and tried to swallow down the rebellious contents of his stomach.

The room was becoming bright with fire, glowing a bright pumpkin-orange, the light shimmering, writhing, as if in its death throes. Over Erin's shoulder, J.R. saw a squat, overweight boy hacking at his throat with a Crucifax, blood spraying from the opening like warm, foamy beer from a shaken can. J.R. tried to keep his eyes fixed on Erin's face. He felt his mind beginning to numb, felt parts of it shutting down like overworked machinery, unable to function in the face of all the violence around him, and he tried to keep his attention off the bloody, convulsing, and burning bodies, tried to shut out the wet, sputtery screams of the dying and the mournful wails of their survivors.

Everyone was running madly around the pool; those who were not dying were confused by the blood and the fire, dashing blindly in fear, crying out for their children or friends.

"I'll find Jeff!" J.R. shouted at Erin. "I promise I'll bring him out with me if you'll go now!"

"And Mallory? You'll bring—"

"Mallory's gone, Erin, she's—"

"You'll bring Mallory?"

Reason had left her eyes, and they shone only with tears now; her face had lost decades and was now that of a child begging for promises and reassurances.

"I'll bring Mallory, I promise," he said. "Just go."

As he turned her toward the stairs a rusty-haired freckle face fell between them, and J.R. reflexively caught him in his arms only to be showered with warm, sticky blood that shot from the boy's mouth and throat.

Erin clutched handfuls of her hair as she stepped back, screaming, and J.R. lowered the dying boy to the floor as a ball of flames screeched by inches from his body. J.R. watched it as it scurried between feet, catching pant legs afire, burning shoes, spreading the flames like a disease from person to person, and J.R. realized it was one of those creatures trying to run from its pain. Through the legs that stood around him like small trees in a miniature forest, he saw others, some burning, some madly chewing on the bloody bodies that littered the floor.

J.R. stood quickly, reaching for Erin, but her back was to him now, and she was moving away from him, arms outstretched and reaching for Jeff, who stood only a few feet in front of her.

"Jeff-reeeee!" she called. "Jeff-reeeee! It's time to go home now, Jeff-reeeee! Come on, it's time to go home!"

Behind Jeff, flames roared from the pool like a giant bonfire, and smoke was beginning to blacken the air, but J.R. could still make him out, could still see his dazed, blood-splashed face, and he could see the Crucifax in Jeff's hand, poised at his throat. . . .

"Please, Jeffrey," Erin coughed, staggering toward him, "let's go now."

J.R. grabbed her, held her to him to keep her away from the fire, and tried to get Jeff's attention as the smoke thickened. But the boy seemed oblivious to everything but the Crucifax, which kept slipping from his bloody hand.

As if from nowhere, Lily was suddenly at Jeff's side, pulling at the leather cord around his neck, sobbing and coughing at once. She lifted it over his head and threw it into the smoke.

"Jeff?" she shouted into his face. "We're getting out now. Just walk with me."

"I . . . I've gotta—gotta find Mal-Mallory," he babbled, shaking his head.

Lily's shoulders sagged with an invisible weight, and she bowed her head a moment, crying, then stood up straight, filled her lungs, and screamed, "She's dead, Mallory's dead. Now, goddammit, we're getting out of here!"

She began pulling on him frantically, pulling his arms, his neck, the belt loops of his jeans, until finally he began to walk with her.

J.R. put his mouth to Erin's ear and tried to sound comforting as he told her to go with Jeff.

"You'll bring Mallory?" she whimpered.

"Yes." The word felt like a rock in his stomach.

The stairs were packed with people hurrying out and littered with the bodies of those who had taken their lives on the steps. A heavy woman leaned over the rail, screaming, "Michael! Where are you?"

A man behind her wrapped his arms around her waist and pulled her back, shouting, "There's nothing we can do now; we *have* to *go!*"

Pressing his wet, blood-spotted coat sleeves to his mouth and nose for protection from the thickening smoke, J.R. turned away from the staircase to find Reverend Bainbridge.

The crowd had thinned out some, but the floor was strewn with corpses, some in flames that sent up plumes of smoke that reeked of spoiled meat and burning rubber. Smaller fires were bursting out around the room as flames were spread to piles of cushions and blankets and wooden crates stacked in corners against the wall.

Mr. Brubaker was kneeling beside his dead son, hacking at the smoke and wailing tearfully as his wife pulled on Wayne's legs, trying to drag him over the floor, saying, "We've got to get him to a doctor, to a hospital!"

J.R. stepped over bodies and hunkered down between them, putting an arm around Mrs. Brubaker.

"Look, Wayne's dead," he shouted. "You'd better get out of here. The smoke's getting—"

"This is your fuckin' fault!" Brubaker shrieked in a mad, shrill voice, shooting to his feet and pointing a thick finger at J.R. "I don't know what you done, but you fucked up, mister, and I'm gonna have your ass for it, understand? I'm gonna—"

J.R. hurried away, knowing he had no time for Brubaker's hysterics, but the big man came after him, his words slurring together in a senseless babble. J.R. heard Mrs. Brubaker call her husband and was relieved by the hint of sanity and order left in her grieving voice. Brubaker's screams crumbled into pathetic sobs.

J.R.'s flashlight beam shone in the haze of smoke like a glowing sword as he searched for the reverend, calling his name repeatedly. He had to step around three bodies that had fallen one atop the other. The top one, a naked girl, bony and pale with stringy blood-tangled hair, reached out and clutched his pant leg, trying to turn herself on her side. Startled, J.R. turned the beam on her as her eyes rolled back in her head. She tried to speak and blood bubbled out of the long black opening in her throat, then her arm fell limp away from him, her head dropped forward and she was silent.

He wasn't sure, but J.R. thought she'd said, "Daddy . . ."

The flashlight beam fell on a dilapidated wall, slid along its length—

—and caught a glimpse of long platinum hair disappearing around its crumbled edge.

"Mace," J.R. growled, hurrying after him. Remembering the reverend, he stopped again, turned, and shouted for him.

The others in the room were no more than darting shadows in the smoky orange glow. He wiped his watery eyes with the heel of his hand, calling one more time. When he did not hear the reverend's voice reply amid the remaining screams and cries, he hoped he'd already gotten out but feared he was hurt or dead in the fire.

J.R. rushed around the end of the wall, shining the light ahead of him. He spotted the back of Mace's head bobbing rapidly as he clanked down some metal stairs.

There were more bodies beyond the wall, and he had to slow down to avoid tripping. His light passed over a black, charred corpse sprawled in a corner, and he immediately looked away and hurried down the stairs.

The dreadful, threatening sounds at the bottom of the stairs made him stop halfway down.

Two dozen golden eyes sparkled up at him from the foot of the stairs, and his light glistened on sharp yellowed tusks. He moved the beam through the room and saw more of them all over the floor and crouching among the pipes that twisted from the low ceiling. Across from the stairs he saw the hole in the wall Lily had spoken of, and peering through it with a satisfied grin was Mace.

Their eyes met and held for a long moment. J.R. felt his testicles pull up inside him, saw Dara again, her eyes so confident and cold as she drove away with his sister.

Mace laughed a dry, bone-clacking laugh and said, "You lose, big brother."

Then he was gone, his laughter washed away by the rushing hiss of the sewer.

Smoke curled through the beam of light as the creatures, two and three at a time, hopped over the edge of the hole and followed Mace into the sewer. He felt the knife's hard, smooth handle in his palm as he slid it from beneath his belt. Holding the blade outward and screaming like an attacking animal, J.R. charged down the stairs, ducking his head low to avoid the pipes.

Like monkeys from trees, three of the creatures dropped on his back as he passed beneath them, tearing their teeth and claws into his coat, releasing long, guttural squalls, their breath warm and moist on his neck. As he ran down the stairs J.R. slammed himself against the rail and felt one of the creatures drop off. Two more pounced from above to replace it, and a few steps farther down he turned and threw himself back hard against the wall, felt bones crunch against his back. Two of them let go, and J.R. went on, swinging his shoulders until another dropped off. The remaining creature clung to his left shoulder, and he paused a moment to swing his right arm back, felt the blade of the knife pierce thick flesh, and heard the creature's wounded squeal as it fell away.

When he reached the floor he screamed again, this time with fear as well as rage because they were scurrying up his legs, teeth snapping. Like a helpless drunk, he staggered in circles as he kicked his legs, knocked them away with his flashlight, and swept the knife downward again and again, cutting his own thighs as well as stabbing his attackers. Others continued to clamber through the hole to follow Mace.

The flashlight beam danced madly through the dark sewer until J.R. regained his bearings. Several yards down the walkway to J.R.'s right, the light fell on Mace's back. He was walking at a leisurely pace, his stride confident and unhurried, long arms swinging at his sides, followed by a scurrying column of his pets. More were coming through the hole behind J.R., and he started after Mace at a slow jog, hoping to stay away from them.

Mace disappeared around a corner, and J.R. picked up a little speed, not wanting to lose him. His lungs were on fire, and his mouth was so dry, his throat so thick, that each breath threatened to make him gag. His legs and back were stinging from the cuts he'd received, and he felt the warm, slow trickle of blood mixing with the sweat that drenched him beneath his clothes.

When he rounded the corner, J.R. slowed to a walk, then stopped six feet from Mace, who was leaning against the wall, arms folded over his chest, ankles crossed, smiling. His pets were at his feet facing J.R., eyes bright in the sewer's darkness.

"Looking for me, are you?" Mace asked.

J.R.'s chest heaved as he gasped for air, swaying with dizziness. He tried to lean against the wall, but there was no wall, just a rectangular passageway that led into cold, drafty darkness. J.R. wanted to shine his light through it to see what lay beyond, but he was afraid to take it off of Mace.

"You look exhausted, Mr. Haskell," Mace said.

The genuine concern in his voice confused J.R. for a moment, threw him off, made him feel unprotected, vulnerable.

"You should go home. Take a hot shower and go to bed. Get a good night's sleep. Don't worry about any of this. It's not your problem."

It took J.R. a few moments to catch enough breath to speak.

"You . . . you're not . . . gonna . . . get away with it . . . this time," he wheezed.

"*This* time? Sorry, guy. You must have me confused with someone else. I don't know what you're talking about." His smile dripped with smug sarcasm.

"I don't . . . don't know what you are, but . . . I know what you're doing."

Mace threw back his head and laughed. "And what's *that?*" He took a step forward.

J.R. wiped his sweaty brow with the back of his hand. "You know what I'm talking about, Mace."

"No. No, I don't think I do. Why don't you explain it to me?" Another step forward.

J.R. moved back but heard a low, ominous growl behind him and glanced over his shoulder.

Countless eyes glared up at him from the walkway.

"The kids," he said unsteadily. "These kids . . . others . . . my sister . . . what you do to them . . ." His thoughts were not holding together; his growing fear was getting in the way of his words.

"Mmm," Mace purred thoughtfully. "And I'm not going to get away with it? What, exactly, are you going to do?" Another step.

"I know about you. Others do, too. It'll be harder for you the next time."

"You think you're the first one to figure things out? *Hah!* It never changes, big brother. They never learn. There's always room for me somewhere else." His next footstep slapped softly into a puddle.

"Not if word spreads."

"What will you tell them? You just said you don't know what I am." Step. "They'll think you're crazy." Step. "They'll think—"

"Stay back." J.R. held up the knife warily.

"—you're just another nut with an imaginary cause. Especially if you don't know what I am. So what are you going to tell them?"

"I'm serious. Don't come any closer."

"Do you want to know what I am, big brother?" Step.

"Goddammit, I mean it, don't—" He swung at him with

the knife, and there was a dark rush at his feet as the creatures pressed in around him.

Without flinching, Mace held up a hand, and the animals were still. "Do you?"

J.R. swung the knife again, but moving like lightning, Mace's hand struck his wrist, and pain shattered through his forearm like splinters of glass. His fingers stiffened and dropped the knife; it clattered to the cement and splashed into the black stream to J.R.'s right.

"Do you want to know, big brother?" There was laughter in his golden eyes; he was enjoying himself.

J.R. wanted to move away from him but could feel the creatures at his heels, brushing against the hem of his pants. He shone the beam directly into Mace's eyes, but he seemed not to notice.

Mace reached for his hand, and J.R. threw himself to the left, into the darkness beyond the passageway, screaming when his light illuminated half a dozen long, pale faces, and cold, bony hands clutched at him, grabbing his clothes and scratching his face. Thin arms embraced him, and the powerful stench of body odor and decay reduced his scream to a sickened cough.

"Don't you hurt him!" a phlegmy voice exclaimed.

". . . gives us food . . ."

". . . our friend . . ."

"Don't hurt him," Mace ordered. "Hold him, but don't hurt him."

Suddenly weak with fear, J.R. clutched the flashlight as if for life as the hands turned him around until he was facing Mace. The arms encircled him like tentacles.

Mace moved forward until he stood no more than a couple inches from J.R. He crooked a finger beneath J.R.'s chin and lifted his face until their eyes met.

"Do you want to know what I am?" he whispered.

J.R. could not speak or move, could not take his gaze from those caramel-flecked eyes, although he tried.

Mace's hand cupped J.R.'s chin, almost lovingly.

"I am the weeds in your garden," he breathed, placing his other hand on J.R.'s cheek.

J.R. felt as if his insides were turning to ice.

"I am the moldy bowl of *goo*"—he chuckled—"on the bottom shelf of your refrigerator." He moved closer until his body was pressed against J.R.'s.

A memory came back to J.R., a memory of something Jeff had said, something that made him fear his life was over.

"I am . . ."

His tongue . . .

". . . what happens . . ."

. . . it came out of his mouth like . . .

". . . when no one . . ."

. . . like a snake.

". . . is paying any attention."

A snake . . .

Mace opened his mouth slowly, opened it wide, as if he were yawning, and J.R. saw his tongue move forward, saw sparkling reflections of light on the wet, pink lump of flesh, and he wanted to scream but had no breath, wanted to struggle but had no strength, and the moment that J.R. was certain would be his last seemed to go on forever until—

—the creatures outside the passageway began to squeal as if in pain, and there were footsteps on the walkway, hurrying closer, punctuated by panting breaths, and Mace's eyes rolled around in their sockets as if he were watching a fly buzz around his head, and he let go of J.R.'s face to turn around slowly as—

—the creatures were kicked aside, and someone came through the passageway, stepped forward into the light—

—"Kevin!" J.R. gasped—

—and lifted an axe over his head, eyes wide with rage—

—Mace said, "You don't want to do—"

—his scream filled with madness as he brought the axe down.

The heavy blade landed in Mace's forehead with the sound of a large melon being dropped.

Mace's arms flew outward at his sides, and he staggered backward with a guttural grunt, bumping J.R., and Kevin jerked the axe from his skull and lifted it again.

The arms released J.R. and reached for Mace; the pale faces screamed, and frail, filthy bodies pushed by J.R. to

370

Mace's rescue, backing away again as Kevin swung the axe a second time, burying it in Mace's left shoulder.

J.R. shouted Kevin's name and stepped around Mace, who was falling backward, arms flailing to keep his balance.

"Okay, Kevin!" J.R. cried. "That's enough!"

"Noooo!" Kevin screamed, jerking the axe out of the huge gash in Mace's shoulder. "You were wrong, Mace! *Wrong!* I don't need you! I don't fucking need you!"

Mace slammed against the wall and slumped down to a sitting position as several of his pets dived, shrieking, through the air and latched onto Kevin, biting and clawing. He seemed not to notice and lifted the axe again.

J.R. backed away as Kevin screamed again, bringing down the axe and taking away a chunk of Mace's skull just above his left temple. He pulled back the axe, and the blade dragged noisily over the cement as he backed away from Mace, preparing to lift it again.

J.R. turned the light on Mace and thought he could feel the last threads of his own sanity unraveling.

Mace was lifting his sagging head; his forehead was caved in and opened down the middle, part of his skull was gone, and the gaping openings glistened blackly, but there was no blood. His golden eyes were bulging like a toad's, and he was smiling as he looked at Kevin, pulling himself to his feet, but—

There's no fucking blood! J.R. thought.

"Kevin, Kevin, Kevin," Mace said admonishingly.

"Kevin, get out of here!" J.R. shouted as Kevin swayed back and forth, axe lifted over his head, creatures hanging from his clothes, others still leaping at him from the floor.

The thin figures in the shadows seemed to sense a moment of weakness in the boy and rushed forward, arms outstretched to seize the axe, but Kevin began to swing it wildly, blindly, and J.R. lifted his arms protectively, stumbled back, and fell as fearful, agonizing screams echoed through the darkness. Eyes closed, J.R. heard the axe fall again and again, meeting flesh and bone, heard the scrambling, limping footsteps of the people who had held him earlier, and then—

—just the sound of Kevin's manic cries and the heavy clank of the axe against the floor, the wall, the grimy pipes.

J.R. opened his eyes slowly and lifted the flashlight.

He was alone with Kevin, who was still wildly swinging the axe. A clump of rags was heaped at Kevin's feet, and what appeared to be a dirty sheet was attached to the axe head, fluttering with each swing. The animals that had been hanging from him a moment before were gone, leaving behind only torn clothing.

J.R. called Kevin's name, stumbling to his feet, pleading with the boy to stop.

"He's gone, Kevin, he's gone now. . . ."

Kevin suddenly dropped the axe and moved away from it as if it were a deadly snake, tripping, falling back onto the floor, crawling backward, and finally collapsing in a weak, sobbing heap.

"Where did he go?" he blubbered. "He's just—just—just *gone!* Where the fuck did he *go?*"

J.R. knelt beside the boy, flashing his light over the rags on the floor.

Mace's clothes. No blood, no sign of Mace, just clothes.

Kevin leaned on J.R. and cried.

Somewhere deep in the sewer, low, throaty groans and babbling voices mingled with the flowing rush of waste.

J.R. held the boy for a long time, finally realizing that he was crying, too.

"Come on, Kevin," he whispered after a while. "Let's get out of here. . . ."

PART VI

Crucifax
Aftermath

Thirty

October 20

By Thursday afternoon, the storm was reduced to a damp gray shadow that covered the Valley. The rain became a light drizzle, and the wind died to a whisper until it was gone entirely.

The power had come back on sometime during the early morning hours; traffic was once again flowing at a relatively normal pace, although the streets were a mess. Ventura Boulevard was littered with debris; boxes were scattered over sidewalks, and gutters were strewn with soggy clumps of newspaper, splintered wooden slats, wind-tossed banners and posters, and unidentifiable clots of garbage. Toppled trash cans rolled about on sidewalks. Storefront windows were dappled with filth.

All day long, the attention of the entire country had been focused on the burned building at the corner of Ventura and Whitley. Local news teams as well as network crews had flocked to the building in their vans and station wagons not long after midnight, set up their cameras as close as the police would let them, and clamored to get footage of the corpses being carried out of the smoking building, one after another.

By seven-thirty that morning, eighty-seven bodies had been taken out, with many more left inside. Local television stations preempted their regular morning programming to cover the story; it wasn't until later that morning however, that they began to make any sense of it all.

By the time fire trucks had arrived late the night before, some people had already left with the teenagers they'd managed to coax out of the building. Those remaining were too hysterical to explain anything to the authorities, and most of them were taken away in ambulances to be treated for what at first appeared to be serious injuries. The ambulance attendants soon realized, however, that the blood that covered these people was not their own.

By eight A.M., word of what had actually happened began to reach the media. The first person to talk was Will Brubaker. He and his wife were rushed by reporters outside the hospital after being released; Brubaker had received eight stitches on his left hand where he'd cut himself on the stair railing on his way out of the building. His wife had been treated for smoke inhalation. The police had already asked them countless questions, but the police were not yet talking to the press, so the Brubakers' answers had not been passed on. Brubaker took advantage of the opportunity, and, with one arm around his wife, holding her close, both of them looking haggard and bereaved, he explained slowly and emotionally that the corpses in the abandoned health club were those of teenagers and that they had been coerced into committing suicide by a man named Mace. When asked why he and his wife had been there, Brubaker replied, "We got a phone call from a man named Haskell. Said he was a counselor at my son's high school. I don't know how, but he *knew* what was going to happen. He knew about it but waited until the very last minute to tell anyone. And I hope, for his sake, that he's got some damned good reasons."

Within the hour, the tragedy was being compared to the Jonestown mass suicide in Guyana; the press dubbed it the Valley Massacre and immediately began to call on "experts" to speculate on the possible reasons why so many teenagers would take their lives all at once.

Throughout the valley, parents who did not know where their teenagers were waited fearfully for a phone call, agonizing over the possible fates of their sons and daughters.

The final death toll was one hundred and sixty-three.

It would be days before all the bodies were positively identified.

Over a week before the last funeral was held.

Months before the story faded from the public eye.

But the scars left behind would never heal. . . .

Mr. Booth paced the length of his office, walking fast, as if late for an appointment. He'd smoked two cigarettes down to the filter in the few minutes J.R. had been seated before his desk.

"You've avoided the press so far?" he asked, his voice breathy, tense.

"Yes."

"Said nothing?"

"Nothing." J.R. looked at his watch; it was a few minutes to ten. His shoulders and neck burned with pain, his head throbbed, and he was buzzing from all the coffee he'd been drinking for the past several hours.

"Any idea what you will say once they catch up to you?" Booth asked, blowing smoke.

J.R. sighed and slumped down in the chair. The previous night had been the longest J.R. had spent since Sheila died. After climbing out of the sewer with Kevin, they found themselves in an alley off Ventura. They spent a few moments collecting themselves; J.R. lifted his face to the rain and drank in the fresh, cold air. With his arm around Kevin, J.R. led him to the edge of the boulevard and, to their right, saw the orange glow of the fire through the narrow gaps between the boards over the health club's windows. He knew immediately what would happen within the next hour; first the fire trucks would come, then ambulances, the police, and, worst of all, the reporters. It would be spread over the news like butter on toast; they would tack some catchy name on the whole thing, hound the families of the dead teenagers, and go through half a dozen versions of

377

what had happened before getting to the truth. If they ever got to it at all.

He led Kevin through the motionless line of cars on Ventura and behind the building to the parking lot. People were stumbling out of the building, clutching their chests, crying, racked with coughs. Smoke was billowing out of the door behind them. Cars were starting, doors were slamming.

Jeff, Lily, and Erin were not in the parking lot. They were on the other side of the bushes that ran along Whitley. When Lily called J.R. over, he found Jeff and Erin sitting on the curb, their feet in a flooded gutter, embracing and crying. He got them to his car and drove them to Erin's apartment. After lighting some candles, he was relieved to find that no one was badly hurt; he was the worst, with cuts and scratches on his back and legs, but they were easily taken care of.

He put Erin to bed; Jeff sat with her awhile, wanting to be left alone. Kevin plopped onto the sofa when he arrived and remained there for a long time, silent and dazed. He found a pack of Erin's cigarettes on the end table and lit up.

"So, what do we do now?" Lily asked J.R. in the kitchen as he poured himself some vodka.

"I don't know. Wait, I guess."

"Shouldn't we have, like, stayed there awhile?"

"Why? If the police want to, they can talk to us later. That place is probably a carnival sideshow by now."

He found a portable radio, and sure enough, the story had already broken.

He spent the night in the apartment, sitting up with Lily and Kevin, comforting Erin and Jeff through frequent attacks of tears and quaking sobs. After a few drinks, they calmed down and eventually slept.

J.R. could not sleep. Neither could the others. They talked their way through the nightmare again and again, trying to understand exactly what had happened and why.

"He was just . . . gone all of a sudden," Kevin whispered. "One second there, the next . . ."

After the lights came on at two-thirty, J.R. switched from

vodka to coffee. He didn't want to sleep; he was afraid he would dream.

He sat in front of the television from two-thirty on while the others slept and the rain clawed at the windows. The story unfolded slowly; the all-night movies were interrupted again and again, and there weren't as many used car commercials as usual. At a little after eight, he saw Will Brubaker on the screen, arm around his wife, talking about him, about J.R.

"Holy Christ," J.R. growled, sitting up on the sofa. He leaned over and woke Kevin, who was asleep at the other end. "Do me a favor and wake Lily. Keep an eye on the others, and don't answer the phone or the door. I've gotta leave for a while."

He drove to his apartment to shower and change his clothes. As he briskly dried himself in his steamy bathroom the phone rang, and he almost didn't answer it, certain it would be a reporter. But it occured to him that something might be wrong over at the Carrs'; it might be Lily or Kevin.

"Mr. Haskell?" an officious-sounding woman asked. "I'm calling for Faye Beddoe."

"Faye? What's wrong?"

"Nothing. She just wanted me to give you a message. She's fine. A little stubborn this morning, but fine. She's been insisting that I call you. I told her—"

"What message?" he snapped.

The woman sniffed. "The note reads, 'Say as little as possible. Talking isn't worth it.' She said you'd know what it means."

He nodded silently to himself. "What's she doing?"

"She's been watching the television all morning. There was a big fire over at—"

"Tell her I'll be in to see her later. And thank her for me." He hung up, dressed, and drove to the school, sneaking by the horde of reporters out in the hall.

"Well?" Booth asked again. "Any ideas?"

"I'm going to say as little as possible," J.R. replied.

"And what will that include?"

"It depends on what they ask me."

Booth started pacing again. "You saw Brubaker on television this morning?"

"That's why I'm here."

"You will not bring the school into this." It wasn't a question or request, but an order. "As of today . . ." He went to the window behind his desk and stared out at the murky day. "As of today, you are no longer employed here."

J.R. took a deep breath and sighed. "I expected that."

"Please don't think I enjoy this. But I did warn you." He turned. "Remember?"

"I remember."

"I wish you would've listened to me."

"Well," J.R. said sarcastically, raising his voice a bit, "you'll have to forgive me for not putting the school's image above the lives of—"

"I wasn't talking about the school's image, Haskell, I was talking about the limitations of your job."

"Limitations of my . . ." J.R. shot to his feet and leaned over the desk, palms flat on its top. "You didn't see what I saw last night. If you had, you'd—"

"I didn't because it did not happen on this campus. Our jobs end, Mr. Haskell, at the borders of this campus. They go no further."

J.R. studied the man's face, looking for some sign that he did not mean what he'd just said. Booth's eyes were surrounded by tiny, deep wrinkles. His fleshy cheeks sagged and would be jowls before long. His mouth drew downward at the ends, and speckles of perspiration glistened on his upper lip. His stern gaze did not waver; he meant what he said. J.R. slowly lowered himself into the chair again.

"How can you be that cold?" he asked quietly.

Booth stabbed his cigarette into the ashtray on his desk, lit another, then turned to the window again, silent for a while.

"Don't damn me for my walls, Haskell," he finally said. "You'll have them, too, one day. You know, I started out like you. I used to teach math in a little junior high in Arizona. I was like a born-again Christian, on fire for education, eager to teach all those young minds." His last words were bitter, dark with disillusionment. "I made a point to get to know each of my students, find out about their interests, their problems, and I tried so hard—*so hard*—to help them, protect them, keep them happy. I got married, had a son, and we moved to California. As my boy grew up, I lost some of my enthusiasm for my work. Everyone seemed so ungrateful—the parents, the kids. . . . It seemed that every time one of them stubbed a toe, I was blamed or the school was blamed. It got worse when I became a principal. Then, when he was fifteen, my son developed a drinking problem. Well, I *noticed* it when he was fifteen; he *developed* it before that. He'd been filling his thermos with bourbon every morning, taking it to school with him. We didn't even notice until he dropped the bottle one day. Well. I was shocked. My son—my fifteen-year-old son—an *alcoholic!* It was his school's fault; they weren't watching him closely enough. It was Madison Avenue's fault; they were glorifying booze. Later, it was the fault of the treatment centers and therapists I sent him to, because they didn't help him. They all seemed so cold and uncaring, like they didn't give a damn. And still later—nearly two years after he got a license, drove his brand-new car into an abutment, and opened his skull on the windshield—later I realized the blame belonged on no one's doorstep but mine. Those people weren't cold and uncaring; they were just doing their jobs, protecting themselves from people like me who wanted to blame them for my failures. A little too late to realize all that then, of course. And to this day, I still don't know where we went wrong, but . . ." He shrugged.

J.R.'s mouth was dry, and he swallowed, wiping his lips with his thumb. Anything he might say seemed inappropriate, so he said nothing.

Facing J.R. again, he said, "We're fair game when it comes to handing out blame, Haskell. Extending ourselves beyond the limitations of our jobs is like standing up in the middle of a gunfight. So please. Don't think of me as cold. Just practical."

J.R. stood, nodding. As he turned to the door he said, "Sorry about your son, Mr. Booth."

"And I'm sorry about what happened last night. Sorry that you had to go through it. And . . . your job. I'm sorry about that, too."

"I'll clear my things out later today," J.R. said as he left the office.

Faye's eyes widened when J.R. walked into her room, and she held a hand out to him. He sat down beside her bed and tried to speak but couldn't. He wasn't sure if it was the warm touch of her hand, the pained sympathy in her eyes, or just his exhaustion, but something cut him open. It was as if he'd been wearing blinders since the night before and they suddenly fell off. In the space of a few seconds, he experienced it all again and felt what he had not allowed himself to feel the first time. At first, he coughed; the coughs became sobs, and he leaned forward, placing his head on Faye's stomach, and cried like a child for a long time as Faye stroked his hair. . . .

After Wednesday night, a haze seemed to settle over Jeff. It was heavy and oppressive and seeped through his pores, into his body, short-circuiting his emotions.

He felt nothing.

He tried to cry the second night. He lay in bed on his back and willed the tears to flow, tried to squeeze the sobs from his lungs, but nothing would come.

He stayed in the apartment and did little more than watch television, aimlessly switching around the dial, staying on no one station for more than a few minutes.

J.R. spent a lot of time with them. It was good to have him there, even though Jeff said little to him.

Late Thursday morning, a doctor came and examined Jeff and his mother, who stayed in bed. The doctor gave her a shot, left some pills with J.R., then went out after mumbling secret instructions. Jeff didn't know where he'd come from or who had sent him, and he didn't care.

By Thursday afternoon, Jeff's grandmother arrived, wailing and sobbing and smelling of Ben-Gay. She sat with her daughter for a while, then came from the bedroom, composure regained, and said confidently, "After everything is taken care of here, you're coming home with me."

Jeff didn't care where they went or with whom. All he knew was that they would be going without Mallory.

He dreamed of her every time he slept, dreamed that she was touching him, gently waking him; and when he awoke he could smell her, as if she'd been beside him but had hurried away before he could open his eyes.

Lily stayed close to him, a quiet and affectionate comfort. She was the only friend from school he'd seen since Wednesday. He thought it odd that no one had called or dropped by to give their condolences. Then it occurred to him that most of his friends were probably dead. He hadn't heard anything and didn't know who had survived or perished; he wasn't sure he cared yet.

Paying no attention to the time, Jeff was surprised each time the sun rose and set.

He had no idea what day it was or how many had passed. He didn't care. . . .

J.R. played hide-and-seek with reporters for days. Knowing his parents had probably heard about everything, he phoned them, assured them he was okay, and told them he would be home sometime next week.

"What about your job?" his father asked.

"Well, I'm currently unemployed, Dad." J.R. didn't know if his father's silence was reproachful or sympathetic. "I'll find some work up there. I prefer to live up there, anyway."

When he returned from seeing Faye, J.R. had found Kevin still sitting on the sofa, silent and unresponsive.

Jeff was lethargic and distant, but at least he spoke now and then. Kevin seemed to have left his body on the sofa, still functioning but void of any real life. His eyes had lost their rebellious fire and now seemed to be windows looking into an empty room. J.R. repeated the boy's name several times, and finally Kevin turned to him, looked into his eyes, but seemed not to see him.

J.R. called the Donahues and told them where their son was; they agreed to come get him.

"I've called your parents, Kevin," he said after hanging up the phone. "They'll be here soon. Is there anything you want to tell me . . . anything you want me to do before they come?"

Kevin's lips twitched and writhed like two agitated earthworms attached at the ends, and he frowned but said nothing.

J.R. hoped the boy would come out of it with a little time, but he feared that Kevin would be taken back to that place, that institution, or one like it. His parents couldn't deal with him when he was coherent; they certainly wouldn't be able to handle this.

Mr. Donahue came alone, looking dapper and uncomfortable. J.R. left Kevin on the sofa and greeted Donahue at the door.

Shaking J.R.'s hand, Donahue said, "I'm terribly sorry for the inconvenience, Mr. Haskell."

"Incon . . . On whose behalf are you apologizing?"

"Well, my son's, I suppose." He shrugged halfheartedly.

"Don't, Mr. Donahue. Don't apologize for your son."

Donahue cleared his throat nervously and called, "Kevin? You ready to go?"

"Look, I think he should see a doctor right away. He hasn't spoken since last night."

Donahue nodded, then shook his head sternly. "I just . . . don't understand how such a thing could—could happen. If we'd known, my wife and I, we would've tried to do something. Anything . . ."

"I'm sure you would have," J.R. said, hoping his sarcasm showed through.

Memorial services for Mallory Carr were held at one P.M. on Saturday at the United Methodist Church in North Hollywood. Erin's mother had made the arrangements. Mallory's remains were to be buried in Stockton.

It was a small service. Kyla stayed close to Erin and Jeff. Several relatives had flown in at the request of Erin's mother. Some of Jeff's classmates came to mutter their condolences, but they all seemed preoccupied; their minds were on other losses.

J.R. arrived late and pushed silently through the photographers and reporters waiting on the steps of the church. They babbled countless questions, but J.R. held up his hands and pressed his lips together until he was inside.

He'd been held up by a phone call from a police lieutenant who wanted to have a word with him. J.R. agreed to go down to the police station at four that afternoon, although he did not yet know what he would tell them.

He stayed in the back of the church during the service, then stepped aside as people slowly filed out afterward. He spotted Jeff walking down the center aisle a step ahead of his mother, hand in hand with Lily.

Jeff's face was a blank, but his cheeks were red and wet from tears, so J.R. knew he'd opened up a little. When Jeff saw J.R., his mouth quivered into a tense and painful parody of a smile, and he led Lily behind the column of pews to J.R.'s side.

"My grandma's reserved a couple seats on a plane to Stockton tomorrow," Jeff said quietly. "We're going up there with her for a while. Moving up there, I guess."

J.R. nodded. "That will probably be good for you."

Lily moved closer to Jeff, and he put an arm around her waist.

"I'd like to keep in touch," he said.

"We'll do that, Jeff. I'll be coming north soon. Maybe we can get together."

"Sure. I . . ." Jeff looked around at the people slowly passing by, heads bowed, as organ music played softly. "I wanted to thank you for . . . for everything you did."

"I'm sorry I couldn't do more."

"You did everything you could."

"So did you, Jeff. Never forget that."

Jeff's eyes clouded, and he frowned, fidgeting; he didn't look convinced.

"You were closer to her than anyone, Jeff," J.R. whispered, stepping closer to him. "If *you* couldn't help her . . . no one could. She was just out of reach."

Jeff pursed his lips and nodded stiffly.

"Well, thanks again," he said, his voice unsteady. "Take care."

As Jeff led her away, Lily turned to J.R. and said, "'Bye."

J.R. stayed for a few minutes, listening to the organ music, thinking about how much Mallory probably would have hated it.

"Should've played Twisted Sister," he muttered, heading for the side exit. . . .

"The police want to talk to me this afternoon," J.R. said, pulling up a chair beside Faye's bed.

What will you tell them? she wrote.

"I don't know. They're going to ask why I was there, how I knew about what was going to happen. Brubaker caused quite a stir with his little remark. They probably would have gotten to me sooner, but I've been making myself pretty scarce."

You didn't know, you suspected. You were there because you were afraid for the kids. Tell them only what you absolutely have to.

"And if I tell them everything?"

I'll visit you on weekends between group therapy and basket weaving.

He chuckled.

What will you do after all of this?

"Move back up north. Look for work. I don't know what *kind* of work, but . . . What will you do?"

Get better and go back to work.

"At Valley?"

Where else? Surely you don't intend to change careers now.

"I've thought about it more than once these last few days."

Why? Too much for you? You're going to go sit at a computer terminal in some office and pretend it didn't happen and isn't happening still?

J.R. put the pad down and scrubbed his face with his palms. His body ached with weariness, and he was uncomfortable in the suit he'd worn to the church.

"I don't know," he sighed. "What's the difference?"

Jeff Carr, for one. And the others who left that building. If you hadn't done what you did, they would've been lost.

He stood and went to the window that overlooked the

parking lot three stories below. He cracked open the window, and a soft breeze whispered against his cheek.

A long line of cars was slowly rounding the corner in front of the hospital, headlights dim in the afternoon overcast, led by a shiny black hearse.

Four little children playing on the sidewalk stopped to stare curiously as the cars passed.

A tall figure wearing black pants and a blousy powder blue shirt approached the children. The figure had long platinum hair.

A razor-sharp icicle shot upward through the center of J.R.'s body and he pressed his hands to the cool pane, breathing, "No, Jesus Christ, *no!*" His words appeared as a foggy blotch on the glass before his face, then slowly faded.

The children turned, smiled, and nodded as the figure spoke to them.

A cold sweat suddenly made J.R.'s suit feel like Saran Wrap clinging to his skin and he wanted to scream, wanted to shatter the glass, lean out and scream at the children to run as fast as they could, but the figure turned so he could see it in profile and he noticed the curve of breasts, the glint of a badge . . .

A meter maid.

J.R. leaned his forehead on the windowpane and closed his eyes, suddenly weak with relief.

"Why do you do it, Faye?" J.R. asked, going to her bedside again. "Year after year, why do you do it?"

I like to keep my summers open.

He laughed as he read her words, and above her bandages, a smiling fudge brown eye winked at him.

Traveling on the breeze, the sparkling clear laughter of children drifted through the window.